W9-BHX-200

"A deeply passionate love story, tender and touching, in the heat and danger of the brutal arena that was Ancient Rome...a remarkable new talent."
—Kate Furnivall, author of *The Russian Concubine* and *The White Pearl*

"[Quinn] skillfully intertwines the private lives of her characters with huge and shocking events. A deeply passionate love story, tender and touching, in the heat and danger of the brutal arena that was Ancient Rome . . . Quinn is a remarkable new talent."

—Kate Furnivall, author of
The Girl from Junchow and *The Red Scarf*

"Quinn's command of first-century Rome is matched only by her involvement with her characters; all of them, historical and invented, are compelling and realistic . . . This should make a splash among devotees of ancient Rome."

—*Publishers Weekly*

"Equal parts intrigue and drama, action and good old-fashioned storytelling. Featuring a cast of characters as diverse as the champions of the Colosseum, *Mistress of Rome* is destined to please."

—John Shors, bestselling author of
Beneath a Marble Sky and *Dragon House*

"Stunning . . . a masterful storyteller. . . . It is no mean feat to write a novel that is both literary and a page-turner."

—Margaret George, author of *Helen of Troy*

"Full of great characters . . . So gripping your hands are glued to the book, and so vivid it burns itself into your mind's eye and stays with you long after you turn the final page."

—Diana Gabaldon, #1 *New York Times* bestselling author of
the Outlander series

Books by Kate Quinn

MISTRESS OF ROME
DAUGHTERS OF ROME
EMPRESS OF THE SEVEN HILLS

MISTRESS
of
ROME

KATE QUINN

B
BERKLEY BOOKS, NEW YORK

BERKLEY BOOKS
Published by the Penguin Group
Penguin Group (USA) Inc.
375 Hudson Street, New York, New York 10014, USA

Penguin Group (Canada), 90 Eglinton Avenue East, Suite 700, Toronto, Ontario M4P 2Y3, Canada
(a division of Pearson Penguin Canada Inc.) • Penguin Books Ltd., 80 Strand, London WC2R 0RL,
England • Penguin Group Ireland, 25 St. Stephen's Green, Dublin 2, Ireland (a division of Penguin
Books Ltd.) • Penguin Group (Australia), 250 Camberwell Road, Camberwell, Victoria 3124, Australia
(a division of Pearson Australia Group Pty. Ltd.) • Penguin Books India Pvt. Ltd., 11 Community
Centre, Panchsheel Park, New Delhi—110 017, India • Penguin Group (NZ), 67 Apollo Drive,
Rosedale, Auckland 0632, New Zealand (a division of Pearson New Zealand Ltd.) • Penguin Books
(South Africa) (Pty.) Ltd., 24 Sturdee Avenue, Rosebank, Johannesburg 2196, South Africa

Penguin Books Ltd., Registered Offices: 80 Strand, London WC2R 0RL, England

This is a work of fiction. Names, characters, places, and incidents either are the product of the author's
imagination or are used fictitiously, and any resemblance to actual persons, living or dead, business
establishments, events, or locales is entirely coincidental. The publisher does not have any control
over and does not assume any responsibility for author or third-party websites or their content.

MISTRESS OF ROME

A Berkley Book / published by arrangement with the author

PRINTING HISTORY
Berkley trade paperback edition / April 2010
Berkley mass-market edition / October 2012

Copyright © 2010 by Kate Quinn.
Cover and stepback design by George Long.
Cover and stepback art by Alan Ayers.
Book design by Kristin del Rosario.

All rights reserved.
No part of this book may be reproduced, scanned, or distributed in any printed or
electronic form without permission. Please do not participate in or encourage piracy of
copyrighted materials in violation of the author's rights. Purchase only authorized editions.
For information, address: The Berkley Publishing Group,
a division of Penguin Group (USA) Inc.,
375 Hudson Street, New York, New York 10014.

ISBN: 978-0-425-26362-4

BERKLEY®
Berkley Books are published by The Berkley Publishing Group,
a division of Penguin Group (USA) Inc.,
375 Hudson Street, New York, New York 10014.
BERKLEY® is a registered trademark of Penguin Group (USA) Inc.
The "B" design is a trademark belonging to Penguin Group (USA) Inc.

PRINTED IN THE UNITED STATES OF AMERICA

10 9 8 7 6 5 4 3 2 1

If you purchased this book without a cover, you should be aware that this book is
stolen property. It was reported as "unsold and destroyed" to the publisher, and neither the
author nor the publisher has received any payment for this "stripped book."

ALWAYS LEARNING   PEARSON

*To my grandparents
Glenn and Marylou Reed-Quinn,
who are no longer here to read this book,
but who would undoubtedly have cracked a bottle of
champagne and bought a dozen copies.*

Acknowledgments

Additional acknowledgments to my mother, Kelly, this book's first reader; my husband, Stephen, who never lost faith it would be published; my agent, Pam Strickler, who shopped this massive manuscript all over New York until she found someone who believed in it as much as she did; and my editor, Jackie Cantor, whose careful editing and unbridled enthusiasm proved a lifeline. Many thanks to you all.

I undertake to be burnt by fire, to be bound in chains, to be beaten by rods, and to die by the sword.

—Gladiator oath

Prologue

⟨꙳⟩

THEA

I opened my wrist with one firm stroke of the knife, watching with interest as the blood leaped out of the vein. My wrists were latticed with knife scars, but I still found the sight of my own blood fascinating. There was always the element of danger: After so many years, would I finally get careless and cut too deep? Would this be the day I watched my young life stream away into the blue pottery bowl with the nice frieze of nymphs on the side? The thought much brightened a life of minimum excitement.

But this time it was not to be. The first leap of blood slowed to a trickle, and I settled back against the mosaic pillar in the atrium, blue bowl in my lap. Soon a pleasant haze would descend over my eyes and the world would take on an agreeably distant hue. I needed that haze today. I would be accompanying my new mistress to the Colosseum, to see the gladiatorial games for the accession of the new Emperor. And from what I'd heard about the games . . .

"Thea!"

My mistress's voice. I muttered something rude in a combination of Greek, Hebrew, and gutter Latin, none of which she understood.

The blue bowl held a shallow cup of my blood. I wrapped my

wrist in a strip of linen, tying off the knot with my teeth, then emptied the bowl into the atrium fountain. I took care not to drip on my brown wool tunic. My mistress's eagle eyes would spot a bloodstain in half a second, and I would not care to explain to her exactly why, once or twice a month, I took a blue bowl with a nice frieze of nymphs on the side and filled it with my own blood. However, fairly speaking, there was very little that I would care to tell my mistress at all. She hadn't owned me long, but I already knew *that*.

"Thea!"

I turned too quickly, and had to lean against the pillars of the atrium. Maybe I'd overdone it. Drain too much blood, and nausea set in. Surely not good on a day when I would have to watch thousands of animals and men get slaughtered.

"Thea, quit dawdling." My mistress poked her pretty head out the bedroom door, her annoyed features agreeably hazy to my eyes. "Father's waiting, and you still have to dress me."

I drifted obediently after her, my feet seeming to float several inches above the floor. A tasteless floor with a mosaic scene of gladiators fighting it out with tridents, blood splashing copiously in square red tiles. Tasteless but appropriate: My mistress's father, Quintus Pollio, was one of several organizers of the Imperial gladiatorial games.

"The blue gown, Thea. With the pearl pins at the shoulders."

"Yes, my lady."

Lady Lepida Pollia. I had been purchased for her several months ago when she turned fourteen: a maid of her own age to do her hair and carry her fan now that she was so nearly a woman. As a gift I didn't rank as high as the pearl necklace and the silver bangles and the half-dozen silk gowns she'd also received from her doting father, but she certainly liked having her own personal shadow.

"Cut yourself at dinner again, Thea?" She caught sight of my bandaged wrist at once. "You really are a fumble-fingers. Just don't drop my jewel box, or I'll be very cross. Now, I want the gold bands in my hair, in the Greek style. I'll be a Greek for the day . . . just like you, Thea."

She knew I was no Greek, despite the name bestowed on me by the Athenian merchant who was my first owner. "Yes, my lady," I murmured in my purest Greek. A frown flickered between her fine black brows. I was better educated than my mistress, and it annoyed her no end. I tried to remind her at least once a week.

"Don't go giving yourself airs, Thea. You're just another little Jew slave. Remember that."

"Yes, my lady." Meekly I coiled and pinned her curls. She was already chattering on.

". . . Father says that Belleraphon will fight this afternoon. Really, I know he's our best gladiator, but that flat face! He may dress like a dandy, but all the perfume in the world won't turn him into an Apollo. Of course he is wonderfully graceful, even when he's sticking someone right through the throat—ouch! You pricked me!"

"Sorry, my lady."

"You certainly look green. There's no reason to get sick over the games, you know. Gladiators and slaves and prisoners—they'd all die anyway. At least this way we get some fun out of it."

"Maybe it's my Jewish blood," I suggested. "We don't usually find death amusing."

"Maybe that's it." Lepida examined her varnished nails. "At least the games are bound to be thrilling today. What with the Emperor getting sick and dying in the middle of the season, we haven't had a good show for months."

"Inconsiderate of him," I agreed.

"At least the new Emperor is supposed to love the games. Emperor Domitian. Titus Flavius Domitianus . . . I wonder what he'll be like? Father went to no end of trouble arranging the best bouts for him. Pearl earrings, Thea."

"Yes, my lady."

"And the musk perfume. There." Lepida surveyed herself in the polished steel mirror. She was very young—fourteen, same as me—and too young, really, for the rich silk gown, the pearls, the rouge. But she had no mother and Quintus Pollio, so shrewd in dealing with slave merchants and *lanistae*, was clay in the hands of his only child. Besides, there was no doubt that she cut a dash. Her beauty was not in the peacock-blue eyes or even the yard of silky black hair that was her pride and joy. It was in her Olympian poise. On the basis of that poise, Lady Lepida Pollia aimed to catch a distinguished husband, a patrician who would raise the family Pollii at last into the highest ranks of Roman society.

She beckoned me closer, peacock fan languidly stirring her

sculpted curls. In the mirror behind her I was a dark-brown shadow: lanky where she was luscious, sunburned where she was white-skinned, drab where she was brilliant. Very flattering, at least for her.

"Most effective," she announced, mirroring my thoughts. "But you really do need a new dress, Thea. You look like a tall dead tree. Come along, Father's waiting."

Father was indeed waiting. But his impatience softened as Lepida dimpled at him and pirouetted girlishly. "Yes, you look very pretty. Be sure to smile at Aemilius Graccus today; that's a very important family, and he's got an eye for pretty girls."

I could have told him that it wasn't pretty *girls* Aemilius Graccus had an eye for, but he didn't ask me. Maybe he should have. Slaves heard everything.

Most Romans had to get up at daybreak to get a good seat in the Colosseum. But the Pollio seats were reserved, so we tripped out just fashionably late enough to nod at all the great families. Lepida sparkled at Aemilius Graccus, at a party of patrician officers lounging on the street corner, at anyone with a purple-bordered toga and an old name. Her father importantly exchanged gossip with any patrician who favored him with an obligatory smile.

". . . I heard Emperor Domitian's planning a campaign in Germania next season! Wants to pick up where his brother left off, eh? No doubting Emperor Titus cut those barbarians down to size, we'll see if Domitian can do any better . . ."

"Quintus Pollio," I overheard a patrician voice drawl. "Really, his perfume alone—!"

"But he does his job so well. What's a smile now and then if it keeps him working hard?"

So Quintus Pollio went on bowing and smirking. He would have sold thirty years of his life for the honor of carrying the family name of the Julii, the Gracchi, or the Sulpicii. So would my mistress, for that matter.

I amused myself by peering into the vendors' stalls that crowded the streets. Souvenirs of dead gladiators, the blood of this or that great fighter preserved in sand, little wooden medallions painted with the face of the famous Belleraphon. These last weren't selling very well, since not even the artists could give Belleraphon a pretty face. Portraits of a handsome Thracian trident fighter did much better.

"He's so beautiful!" Out of the corner of my eye I saw a cluster of girls mooning over a medallion. "I sleep with his picture under my pillow every night—"

I smiled. We Jewish girls, we liked our men to be fighters, too—but we liked them real and we liked them long-lived. The kind who take the head off a legionnaire in the morning and come home at night to preside over the Sabbath table. Only Roman girls mooned over crude garish portraits of men they'd never met, men who would probably be dead before the year was out. On the other hand, perhaps a short-lived man was better for daydreaming about. He'd never be old, he'd never lose his looks, and if you tired of him he'd soon be gone.

The crowds grew thicker around the Colosseum. I'd walked often enough in its vast marble shadow as I ran errands for my mistress, but this was my first time inside and I struggled not to gape. So huge, so many marble arches, so many statues staring arrogantly from their plinths, so many seats. Fifty thousand eager spectators could cram inside, so they said. An arena fit for the gods, begun by the late Emperor Vespasian, finished by his son the late Emperor Titus, opened today in celebration for Titus's younger brother who had just donned the Imperial purple as Emperor Domitian.

So much marble for a charnel house. I'd have preferred a theatre, but then I would rather hear music than watch men die. I imagined singing for a crowd as large as this one, a real audience, instead of the frogs in the conservatorium when I scrubbed the tiles . . .

"Keep that fan moving, Thea." Lepida settled into her velvet cushions, waving like an Empress at the crowds who had a small cheer for her father. Men and women usually sat separately to watch the games, but Quintus Pollio as organizer of the games could sit with his daughter if he liked. "Faster than that, Thea. It's going to be gruesomely hot. Really, why won't it cool down? It's supposed to be *fall*."

Obediently I waved the fan back and forth. The games would last all day, which meant that I had a good six hours of feather-waving in front of me. Oh, my arms were going to ache.

Trumpets blared brassily. Even my heart skipped a beat at that thrilling fanfare. The new Emperor stepped out into the Imperial box, raising his hand to the crowd, and I stretched on my toes for a look at him. Domitian, third Emperor of the Flavian dynasty: tall, ruddy-cheeked, dazzling the eye in his purple cloak and golden circlet.

"Father." Lepida tugged on her father's sleeve. "Is the Emperor *really* a man of secret vices? At the bathhouse yesterday, I heard—"

I could have told her that all Emperors were rumored to be men of secret vices. Emperor Tiberius and his little slave boys, Emperor Caligula who slept with his sisters, Emperor Titus and his mistresses—what was the point of having an Emperor if you couldn't cook up spicy rumors about him?

Domitian's Empress, now, was less gossipworthy. Tall, statuesque, lovely as she stepped forward beside her Imperial husband to wave at the roaring crowds—but disappointed reports had it that the Empress was an impeccable wife. Still, her green silk *stola* and emeralds caused a certain buzz of feminine admiration. Green, no doubt, would become *the* color of the season.

"Father." Lepida tugged at her father's arm again. "You know I'm always so admired in green. An emerald necklace like the Empress's—"

Various other Imperial cousins filed after the Emperor— there was a niece, Emperor Titus's younger daughter Lady Julia, who had supposedly petitioned to join the Vestal Virgins but had been refused. Otherwise, a dull lot. I was disappointed. My first sight of the Imperial family, and they looked like any other clutch of languid patricians.

The Emperor came forward, raising his arm, and shouted the introduction of the games. Secret vices or not, he had a fine reverberating voice.

The other slaves had explained the games to me many times, incredulous at my ignorance. Duels between wild beasts always opened the morning festivities; first on the list today was a battle between an elephant and a rhinoceros. The rhinoceros put out the elephant's eye with its tusk. I could have happily lived my entire life without knowing what an elephant's scream sounded like.

"Marvelous!" Pollio threw a few coins into the arena. Lepida picked through a plate of honeyed dates. I concentrated on the peacock fan. *Swish, swish, swish.*

A bull and a bear battled next, then a lion and a leopard. Tidbits to whet the appetite, as it were. The bear was sullen, and three handlers with sharp rods had to goad its flanks bloody before it attacked the bull, but the lion and the leopard screamed and flew at each other the moment the chains were released. The crowd cheered and chattered, sighed and settled back. Pomp and spectacle came next, dazzling the eye after the crowd's attention was honed: tame cheetahs in silver harnesses padding round the arena, white bulls with little golden boys capering on their backs, jeweled and tasseled elephants lumbering in stately dance steps accompanied by Nubian flute players . . .

"Father, can't I have a Nubian slave?" Lepida plucked at her father's arm. "Two, even. A matched pair to carry my packages when I go shopping—"

Comic acts next. A tame tiger was released into the arena after a dozen sprinting hares, bounding in a flash of stripes to collect them one by one in his jaws and return them unharmed to the trainer. Rather nice, really. I enjoyed it, but there were scattered boos through the stands. Fans of the Colosseum didn't come for games; they came for blood.

"The Emperor," Quintus Pollio was droning, "is especially fond of the goddess Minerva. He has built a new shrine to her in his palace. Perhaps we should make a few large public offerings—"

The tame tiger and his handler padded out, replaced by a hundred white deer and a hundred long-necked ostriches who were released galloping into the arena and shot down one by one by archers on high. Lepida saw some acquaintance in a neighboring box and cooed greetings through most of the blood.

More animal fights. Spearmen against lions, against buffaloes, against bulls. The buffaloes went down bewildered and mooing, the bulls ran maddened onto the spears that gouged their chests open, but the lions snarled and stalked and took a spearman with them before they were chased down and gutted. Such wonderful fun. *Swish, swish, swish.*

"Oh, the gladiators." Lepida cast the plate of dates aside and sat up. "Fine specimens, Father."

"Nothing but the best for the Emperor." He chucked his daughter's chin. "And for my little one who loves the games! The Emperor wanted a battle today, not just the usual duels. Something big and special before the midday executions—"

In purple cloaks the gladiators filed out of the gates, making a slow circle of the arena as the fans cheered. Some strutted proudly; some stalked ahead without looking right or left. The handsome Thracian trident fighter blew kisses to the crowd and was showered with roses by adoring women. Fifty gladiators, paired off to fight to the death. Twenty-five would exit in triumph through the arena's Gate of Life. Twenty-five would be dragged out through the Gate of Death on iron hooks.

"Hail, Emperor!" As one they roared out toward the Imperial box. *"We salute you from death's shadow!"*

The clank of sharpened weapons. The scrape of plated armor. The crunch of many feet on sand as they spread out in their pairs. A few mock combats first with wooden weapons, and then the Emperor dropped his hand.

The blades crashed. The audience surged forward, straining against the marble barriers, shouting encouragement to the favorites, cursing the clumsy. Waving, wagering, shrieking.

Don't look. Swish, *swish*, went the fan. *Don't look.*

"Thea," Lepida said sweetly. "What do you think of that German?"

I looked. "Unlucky," I said as the man died howling on his opponent's trident. In the next box, a senator threw down a handful of coins in disgust.

The arena was a raging sea of fighters. Already the sand was patched with blood.

"The Gaul over there wants mercy." Pollio peered out, sipping at his wine cup. "Poor show, he dropped his shield. *Iugula!*"

Iugula—"Kill him." There was also *Mitte*—"spare him"— but you didn't hear that nearly so often. As I was to find out, it took an extraordinary show of courage to move the Colosseum to mercy. They wanted heroism, they wanted blood, they wanted death. Not scared men. Not mercy.

It was over quite quickly. The victors strutted before the Imperial box, where the Emperor tossed coins to those who had fought well. The losers lay crumpled and silent on the sand, waiting to be raked away by the arena attendants. One or two men still writhed in their death throes, shrieking as they tried to stuff the guts back into their own bellies. Laughing tribunes and giggling girls laid bets on how long it would take them to die.

Swish, swish, swish. My arms ached.

"Fruit, Dominus?" A slave came to Pollio's elbow with a tray of grapes and figs. Lepida gestured for more wine, and all through the patrician boxes I saw people sitting back to chatter. In the tiers above, plebs fanned themselves and looked for the hawkers who darted with bread and beer for sale. In his Imperial box the Emperor leaned back on one elbow, rolling dice with his guards. The morning had flown. For some, dragged.

For the midday break, business was attended to inside the arena. The dead gladiators had all been carted away, the patches of blood raked over, and now the arena guards led out a shuffling line of shackled figures. Slaves, criminals, prisoners; all sentenced for execution.

"Father, can't I have more wine? It's a special occasion!"

Down in the arena, the man at the head of the shackled line blinked as a blunt sword was shoved into his hands. He stared at it, dull-eyed and bent-backed, and the arena guard prodded him. He turned wearily and hacked at the chained man behind him. A dull blade, because it took a great deal of hacking. I could hardly hear the man's screams over the chatter in the stands. No one seemed to be paying attention to the arena at all.

The arena guards disarmed the first slave roughly, passing the sword to the next in line. A woman. She killed the man, roughly cutting his throat; was disarmed, killed in turn by the next who tried vainly to stab her through the heart. It took a dozen strokes of the dull sword.

I looked down the chained line. Perhaps twenty prisoners. Old and young, men and women, identical in their bent shoulders and shuffling feet. Only one stood straight, a big man gazing around him with blank eyes. Even from the stands I could see the whip marks latticing his bare back.

"Father, when does Belleraphon's bout come up? I'm dying to see what he can do against that Thracian—"

The guards gave the blunt sword to the man with the scars. He hefted it a moment in his shackled hands, gave it a swing. No hacking for him; he killed the man who had gone before him in one efficient thrust. I winced.

The arena guard reached for the sword and the big scarred man fell a step back, holding the blade up between them. The guard gestured, holding out an impatient hand, and then it all went to hell.

HAND it over," the guard said.

He stood spraddle-legged on the hot sand, heaving air into his parched lungs. The sun scorched down on his naked shoulders and he could feel every separate grain beneath his bare, hardened feet. Sweat stung his wrists and ankles under the rusty cuffs of his chains. His hands had welded around the sword hilt.

"Hand over that sword," the guard ordered. "You're holding up the show."

He stared back glassy-eyed.

"Hand—over—that—sword." Extending an imperious hand.

He cut it off.

The guard screamed. The slick of blood gleamed bright in the midday sun. The other guards rushed.

He had not held a sword in over ten years. Much too long, he would have said, to remember anything. But it came back. Fueled by rage it came back fast—the sweet weight of the hilt in his hand, the bite of blade into bone, the black demon's fury that filmed the eyes and whispered in the ear.

Kill them, it said. *Kill them all.*

He met the first guard in a savage joyful rush, swords meeting with a dull screech. He bore down with every muscle, feeling his body arch like a good bow, and saw the sudden leap of fear in the guard's eyes as he felt the strength on the other end of the blade. These Romans with their plumes and pride and shiny breastplates, they didn't think a slave could be strong. In two more thrusts he reduced the guard to a heap of twitching meat on the sand.

More Romans, bright blurs in their feathered crests. A guard fell writhing as dull iron chewed through his hamstrings. A liquid scream.

He savored it. Lunged for another bronze breastplate. The blade slid neatly through the armhole. Another shield falling, another scream.

Not enough, the demon voice whispered. *Not enough.*

He felt distant pain along his back as a blade cut deep, and smiled, turning to chop down savagely. A slave's toughest flesh was on his back, but they didn't know that—these men whose vineyards were tended by captive warriors from Gaul and their beds warmed by sullen Thracian slave girls. They didn't know anything. He cut the guard down, tasting blood in his rough beard.

Not enough.

The sky whirled and turned white as something struck the back of his head. He staggered, turned, raised his blade, felt his entire arm go numb as a guard smashed an iron shield boss against his elbow. Distantly he watched the sword drop from his fingers, falling to hands and knees as a sword hilt crashed against his skull. Sweat trickled into his eyes. Acid, bitter. He sighed as the armored boots buffeted his sides, as the black demon in his head turned back in on itself like a snake devouring its own tail. A familiar road. One he had trodden all his years under whips and chains. With a sword in his hand, everything had been so simple.

Not enough. Never enough.

Over the sound of his own cracking bones, he heard a roar. A vast, impersonal roar like the crashing of the sea. For the first time he turned his eyes outward and saw them: spectators, packed tier upon tier in their thousands. Senators in purple-bordered togas. Matrons in bright silk *stolas*. Priests in white robes. So many . . . did the world hold so many people? He saw a boy's face leap out at him from the front tier, crazily distinct, a boy in a fine toga shouting through a mouthful of figs—and clapping.

They were all clapping. The great arena resounded with applause.

Through dimming eyes, he made out the Imperial balcony. He was close enough to see a fair-haired girl with a white appalled face, one of the Imperial nieces . . . close enough to see the Emperor, his ruddy cheeks, his purple cloak, his amused gaze . . . close enough to see the Imperial hand rise carelessly.

Holding out a hand in the sign of mercy.

Why? he thought. *Why?*

Then the world disappeared.

L EPIDA chattered on as I undressed her for bed that night— not about the games, of course; all that death and blood was old news. Her father had mentioned a certain senator, a man who might be a possible husband for her, and that was all she could talk about. "Senator Marcus Norbanus, his name is, and he's *terribly* old—" I hardly heard a word.

The slave with the scarred back. A Briton, a Gaul? He had fought so savagely, swinging his sword like Goliath, ignoring his own wounds. He'd been snarling even when they brought him down, not caring if he lived or died as long as he took a few with him.

"Thea, be careful with those pearls. They're worth three of you."

I'd seen a hundred slaves like him, served beside them and avoided them. They drank too much, they scowled at their masters and were flogged for troublemakers and did as little work as they could get away with. Men to avoid in quiet corners of the house, if no one was near enough to hear you struggling. Thugs.

So why did I weep suddenly when they brought him down in the arena? I hadn't wept when I was sold to Lepida. I hadn't even wept when I watched the gladiators and the poor bewildered animals slaughtered before my eyes. Why had I wept for a thug?

I didn't even know his name.

"Well, I don't think Emperor Domitian is terribly handsome, but it's hard to tell from a distance, isn't it?" Lepida frowned at a chipped nail. "I do wish we could have some handsome dashing Emperor instead of these stolid middle-aged men."

The Emperor. Why had he bothered to save a half-dead slave? The crowd had clapped for his death as much as for the show he put on. Why save him?

"Go away, Thea. I don't want you anymore. You're quite stupid tonight."

"As you wish," I said in Greek, blowing out her lamp. "You cheap, snide little shrew."

I weaved my way down the hall, leaning against the shadowed pillars for balance, trying not to think of my blue bowl. Not good to bleed myself twice in one day, but oh, I wanted to.

"Ah, Thea. Just what I need."

I stared blurrily at the two Quintus Pollios who beckoned me into the bedchamber and onto the silver sleeping couch. I closed my eyes, stifling a yawn and hoping I wouldn't fall asleep in the middle of his huffing and puffing. Slave girls aren't expected to be enthusiastic, but they are expected to be cheerful. I patted his shoulder as he labored over me. His lips peeled back from his teeth like a mule's during the act of . . . well, whatever you want to call it.

"What a good girl you are, Thea." Sleepily patting my flank. "Run along, now."

I shook down my tunic and slipped out the door. Likely tomorrow he'd slip me a copper.

PART ONE

JULIA

In the Temple of Vesta

Yesterday, Titus Flavius Domitianus was just my brusque and rather strange uncle. Today he is Lord and God, Pontifex Maximus, Emperor of Rome. Like my father and grandfather before him, he is master of the world. And I am afraid.

But he has been kind to me. He says I will marry my cousin Gaius soon, and he promised me splendid games for the celebration. I couldn't tell him that I hate the games. He means to be kind. He says his Empress will fit me for my wedding gown. She is very beautiful in her green silk and emeralds, and they whisper that he's mad with love for her. They also whisper that she hates him—but people like to whisper.

I stare at the flame until there are two flames.

I'm afraid. I'm always afraid. Shadows under the bed, shapes in the dark, voices in the air.

My uncle watched a thousand men die in the arena today—and he saved just one. He hates the rest of the family—but is kind to me.

What does my uncle want? Does anyone know?

Vesta, goddess of hearth and home, watch over me. I need you, now.

One

❧❧

THE atmosphere at the Mars Street gladiator school was contented, convivial, and masculine as the tired fighters trooped in through the gates. Twenty fighters had sallied out to join the main battle of the Cerealia games, and fourteen had come back alive. A good enough average to make the victors swagger as they filed through the narrow torch-lit hall, dumping their armor into the waiting baskets.

". . . hooked that Greek right through the stomach! Prettiest piece of work I . . ."

". . . see that bastard Lapicus get it in the back from that Gaul? Won't be looking down his long nose at us anymore . . ."

". . . hard luck on Theseus. Saw him trip in the sand . . ."

Arius tossed his plumed helmet into the waiting basket, ignoring the slave who gave him cheery congratulations. The weapons had already been collected, of course—those got snatched the moment the fighting was done.

"First fight?" A chatty Thracian tossed his own helmet into the basket atop Arius's. "Mine, too. Not bad, huh?"

Arius bent to unlace the greaves about his shins.

"Nice work you did on that African today. Had me one of those scrawny Oriental Greeks; no trouble there. Hey, maybe next time I'll get Belleraphon and then I'll really make my fortune."

Arius unlaced the protective mail sleeve from his sword arm, shaking it off into the basket. The other fighters were already trooping into the long hall where they were all fed, whooping as they filed along the trestle tables and grabbed for the wine jugs.

"Quiet, aren't you?" The Thracian jogged his elbow. "So where you from? I came over from Greece last year—"

"Shut up," said Arius in his flat grating Latin.

"What?"

Brushing past the Thracian into the hall, he ignored the trestle tables and the platters of bread and meat. He leaned over and grabbed the first wine jug he saw, then headed off down another small ill-lit hallway. "Don't mind him," he heard another fighter growl to the Thracian. "He's a sour bastard."

Arius's room in the gladiator barracks was a tiny bare cell. Stone walls, a chair, a straw pallet, a guttering tallow candle. He sank down on the floor, setting his back against the wall and draining half the jug in a few methodical gulps. The cheap grapes left a sour taste in his mouth. No matter. Roman wine was quick, and all he wanted was quick.

"Knock knock!" a voice trilled at the door. "I hope you aren't asleep yet, dear boy."

"Piss off, Gallus."

"Tut, tut. Is that any way to treat your *lanista*? Not to mention your friend?" Gallus swept in, vast and pink-fleshed in his immaculate toga, gold gleaming on every finger, magnolia oil shining on every curled hair, a little silk-decked slave boy at his side. Owner of the Mars Street gladiator school.

Arius spat out a toneless obscenity. Gallus laughed. "Now, now, none of that. I came to congratulate you. Such a splendid debut. When you sent the head flying clean off that African . . . so dramatic! I was a little surprised, of course. Such dedication, such savagery, from one who swore not an hour before that he wouldn't fight at all . . ."

Arius took another deep swallow of wine.

"Well, how nice it is to be right. The first time I saw you, I knew you had potential. A little old for the arena, of course— how old are you, anyway? Twenty-five, thirty? No youngster, but you've certainly got *something*." Gallus waved his silver pomander languidly.

Arius looked at him.

"You'll get another fight in the next games, of course. Something a little bigger and grander, if I can persuade Quintus Pollio. A solo bout, perhaps. And this time"—a glass-sharp glance—"I won't have to worry that you'll deliver, will I."

Arius aligned the wine jug against the wall. "What's a *rudius*?" The words surprised him, and he kept his eyes on the jug.

"A *rudius*?" Gallus blinked. "Dear boy, wherever did you hear about that?"

Arius shrugged. They had all been waiting in the dark under the Colosseum before their bout, nervous and excited, fingering their weapons. *Here's to a* rudius *for all of us*, one of the others had muttered. A man who had died five minutes later under a trident before Arius could ask him what it meant.

"A *rudius* is a myth," Gallus said airily. "A wooden sword given from the Emperor to a gladiator, signaling his freedom. I suppose it's happened once or twice for the stars of the arena, but that hardly includes you, does it? One bout, and not even a solo bout—you've got a long way to go before you can call yourself a success, much less a star."

Arius shrugged.

"Such a dear boy." Gallus reached out and stroked Arius's arm. His plump fingers pinched hard, and his black peppercorn eyes locked onto Arius's with bright curiosity.

Arius reached out, picked up the tallow candle beside him, and calmly poured a stream of hot wax onto the soft manicured hand.

Gallus snatched his burned fingers away. "We really will have to do something about your manners," he sighed. "Good night, then. Dear boy."

As soon as the door thudded shut, Arius picked up the wine jug and drank off every drop. Letting the jug fall, he dropped his head back against the stones. The room wasn't spinning anymore. Not enough wine. He closed his eyes.

He hadn't meant to fight. He'd meant what he'd told Gallus, standing in the dim passage underneath the arena, hearing the roars of the crowd and the screams of the wounded men and the whimpers of the dying animals. But the sword had been placed in his hand, and he'd gone out with the others in the brisk group battle that served to whet the crowd's appetite for the solo

bouts, and he'd seen the African he'd been paired to fight . . .
and the black demon had uncoiled from its self-devouring circles in his brain and roared joyously down the straight and simple path of murder.

Then suddenly he had been standing blinking in the sunlight
with another man's blood on his face and cheers pouring down
on his head like a swarm of bees. Just thinking about those
cheers brought an icy sweat. The arena. That hellish arena. It
spoiled his luck every time. Even slaughtering its guards had
failed to get him killed.

After that savage beating seven months ago, he had awak-
ened in bed. Not a soft bed; Gallus didn't waste luxuries on
half-dead slaves. Dragging himself painfully into the light, he
heard for the first time Gallus's voice: high, modulated, reeking
of the slums.

"Can you hear me, boy? Nod if you understand. Good.
What's your name?"

Hoarsely he croaked it out.

Gallus tittered. "Oh, that's absurd. A Briton, aren't you? You
barbarians always have impossible names. Well, it won't do.
We'll call you Arius. A bit like Aries, the god of war. Quite
catchy, yes, we can do something with that.

"Now. I've bought you, and paid a pretty price, too, for a
half-dead troublemaker. Yes, I know exactly why you were sentenced to the arena. You were part of a chain gang making repairs
on the Colosseum, until you strangled a guard with his own whip.
Very foolish, dear boy. Whatever were you thinking?" Gallus
snapped for his little slave boy with the tray of sweetmeats. "Well,
then"—eating busily—"you can tell me for starts how you ended
up working a chain gang in the Colosseum."

"Salt mines," Arius forced out through swollen lips. "In Trinovantia. Then Gaul."

"Dear me. And how long have you been working in those
sinkholes?"

Arius shrugged. Twelve years? He wasn't sure.

"A long time, clearly. That explains the strength of the arms
and chest." A plump finger traced over Arius's shoulders. "Hauling rocks of salt up and down mountains for years; oh yes, it
builds fine men." A last lingering stroke. "One doesn't learn to
use a sword in the mines, however. Where did you learn that, eh?"

Arius turned his face toward the wall.

"Well, no matter. Time to listen. You'll do your fighting for me from now on, when and where I say. I am a *lanista*. Know what that is? No? I thought your Latin was a little rough. Everything about you is a little rough, isn't it? A *lanista* is a trainer, dear boy, of gladiators. You're going to be a gladiator. It's a good life as they go—women, riches, fame. You'll take the oath now, and begin training as soon as those bones patch up. Repeat after me: *'I undertake to be burnt by fire, to be bound in chains, to be beaten by rods, and to die by the sword.'* That's the gladiator's oath, dear boy."

Arius told him hoarsely what he could do with his oath, and collapsed back into blackness.

It had been days before he could get out of bed, weeks before his bones were whole, and nearly five months before his training in the gladiators' courtyard was complete. His fellow fighters were petty criminals and bewildered slaves scummed off the bottom of the market: a cheap cut-rate bunch. Arius slid indifferently into the school's routine: just one more thug with Gallus's crude crossed-swords tattoo on his arm. Better than the mines.

Rudius. The word came back to him. Sounded like a snake, not a wooden sword. He didn't see how getting a wooden sword from the Emperor made you free, but the mist-shrouded mountains of home rose up before his eyes, impossibly fresh and green and lovely.

A wooden sword. He used wooden swords every day when he trained. He always broke them, hitting too hard. An omen? He thought back to the white-robed Druids of his childhood, dimly remembered, smelling of mistletoe and old bones, reading the gods in every leaf's fall. They'd call it a bad omen, breaking a wooden sword. But he'd never had many good omens in his life.

He shook off the thought of home. The Mars Street school wasn't bad. No women and riches as Gallus had promised, but at least no merciless sun, no chains eating the flesh off his ankles, no uneasy sleep on bare mountainsides. Here there were blankets and bread for the days, wine to drown the nights, a quick death around the corner. Better than the mines. Nothing could be worse than the mines.

The applause of the games fans flickered uneasily through his mind.

THEA

FROM the moment I saw Senator Marcus Vibius Augustus Norbanus, I longed to fix him up: give him a proper haircut, get the ink stains off his fingers, take his slaves to task for pressing his toga so badly. He had been divorced for more than ten years, and slaves take advantage when there's no mistress of the house. I would have bet five coppers that Marcus Norbanus, who had been consul four times and was the natural grandson of the God-Emperor Augustus, poured his own wine and put away his own books just like any pleb widower.

"Your name, girl?" he asked, as I offered a tray of little sweet marchpane pastries.

"Thea, sir."

"A Greek name." He had deep-set eyes; friendly, penetrating, aloof. "But not, I think, a Greek. Something too long about the vowels, and the shape of the eyes is wrong. Antiochene, perhaps, but I would guess Hebrew."

I smiled in assent, backing away and examining him covertly. He had a crooked shoulder that pulled him off-balance and made him limp, but it was hardly visible unless he was standing. Seated he was still a fine figure of a man, with a noble patrician profile and thick gray hair.

Poor Marcus Norbanus. Your bride will eat you alive.

"Senator!" Lepida danced in, fresh and lovely in carnelian silk with strands of coral about her neck and wrists. Fifteen now, as I was; prettier and more poised than ever. "You're here early. Eager to see the games?"

"The spectacle always provides a certain interest." He rose and kissed her hand. "Though I usually prefer my library."

"Well, you must change your opinion. For I am quite mad for the games."

"Her father's daughter, I see." Marcus made a courtly nod to Pollio.

Lepida's father swept his eyes with just a hint of contempt over Marcus's uncurled hair, the carelessly pressed toga, the mended sandal strap. He himself was immaculate: snowy linen pleated razor-sharp and perfume heavy enough to tingle the nostrils. Still, no one would ever mistake him for a patrician. Or Marcus Norbanus for anything else.

"So, you really *know* the Emperor's niece?" Lepida asked her betrothed as we left the Pollio house and sallied out into the April sunshine. Her blue eyes were wide with admiration. "Lady Julia?"

"Yes, since she was small." Marcus smiled. "She and her half-sister were playmates of my son's when they were very young. They haven't met since they were children—Paulinus is with the Praetorians now—but I still visit Lady Julia now and then. She's been very downcast since her father died."

The wedding morning of Lady Julia and her cousin Gaius Titus Flavius burst clear and blue as we went to watch them join hands at the public shrine—on foot, since the litters would never get through the crowds. I was jostled from side to side by shoving apprentices, avid housewives, beggars trying to slip their hands into my purse. A baker in a flour-sprinkled apron trod heavily on my foot, and I tripped.

Marcus Norbanus caught my arm with surprising agility, setting me on my feet before I could fall. "Careful, girl."

"Thank you, sir." I fell behind, chagrined. He really was far too kind to be Lepida's husband. I'd been praying devotedly for an ogre.

"Oh, look!" Abandoning Marcus's arm, Lepida elbowed her way to the front of the crowd. "Look, there they are!"

I peered over Pollio's shoulder. The shrine of Juno, goddess of marriage—and the tall ruddy-cheeked young man beside the priest must be the bridegroom. He was in high spirits, jostling and joking with his attendants. "He's handsome," Lepida announced. "Fat, though. Don't you think?"

Marcus looked amused. "The Flavians tend toward heaviness," he said mildly. "A family trait."

"Oh. Well, he's not really fat, is he? Just *imposing.*"

The blast of Imperial trumpets brazened in our ears. Servants in Imperial livery began to wind past. The Praetorian Guard lined the road in their ceremonial breastplates and red plumes, making way for the bride. "Is that Lady Julia?" Lepida craned her neck.

I studied the Emperor's niece curiously—the one who supposedly wanted to be a Vestal Virgin. She was very small, her hair straw-pale, her figure straight and childlike in the white robe. The flaming bridal veil drew all the color out of her face. Her pale lips were smiling, but she didn't really look—well, bridal.

"She doesn't have the complexion for red," my mistress said, too softly for her betrothed to hear. "Her skin's like an unripe cheese. I'll look much better at *my* wedding."

The bridal pair joined hands at the shrine, speaking the ritual words: *Quando tu Gaius, ego Gaia.* They exchanged the ritual cake, the rings. The marriage contracts were signed. The priest intoned prayers, and a bellowing white bull gave its blood in a gout over the marble steps as a sacrifice to Juno. Usually Imperial weddings were conducted more privately, but Emperor Domitian was a lover of public pomp. So was the public.

"She should smile," Lepida criticized. "No one wants to see a bride looking like a corpse on her own wedding day."

Before the procession, the groom had to wrest his bride from her mother's arms in symbolic theft. Lady Julia's mother was dead; her uncle stood in for her. She folded the red veil back over her pale hair and walked meekly into his arms. As the bridegroom used both hands to jerk her away, my gaze shifted to the Emperor.

He was a tall man, vigorous and well made, a little more than twice my age, reflecting back the sun in his gold-embroidered purple cloak and golden circlet. Thickset Flavian shoulders that would run to fat in his old age. Ruddy cheeks and broad, friendly features.

My eyes shifted back to his niece, huddled in the arm of her new husband. I felt sorry for her. A slave feeling sorry for a princess—I don't know why. Then her eyes shifted, falling for a moment on mine, and in the instant before I dropped my gaze to the ground I saw that on the day of her own wedding—a bright and beautiful spring day when the whole world stretched before her—Lady Julia Flavia felt lost and terrified and alone.

"Well, that's that!" Pollio clapped his hands, and I jumped. "We'd better go on to the arena. The first show is very splendid, I assure you. I found a dozen of the strangest striped horses from an African trader; he called them zebras—"

On Senator Norbanus's suggestion, we took a hired litter on a shortcut through Mars Street. I trotted behind on foot while Lepida squeezed in beside her betrothed, hanging on his every word, looking up at him through long black lashes. A spider reeling in the fly.

Pollio was still droning on about how clever he had been to buy twenty tigers at a bargain price from India when the litter was forced to pull up short. A huge cart blocked the road, ironbound and padlocked, and a litter borne by six golden-haired Greeks. As we watched, a gate barred like a prison swung open and a team of men marched out. Armor gleamed beneath their purple cloaks as they climbed into the wagon, and their faces were somber under their helmets. Gladiators, on their way to the Colosseum.

"Gallus's fighters." Pollio twitched back the curtains for a better look, frowning. "Third-raters, all of them. Still, they make good bait for the lions. So would Gallus himself, if you ask me. That's him in the litter."

A fat man with a fringe of oiled curls around his forehead leaned out through the orange silk curtains to shout through the gates. "You're holding us up, dear boy."

Out through the gates of Gallus's school strode a big man, russet-haired, a Gaul or a Briton. He wore heavy iron plates over his shins, a green kilt, an absurd helmet with green plumes. A mail sleeve protected his fighting arm, the leather straps passing over his unprotected chest and scarred back. His face was granite-still—and I knew him.

The slave. The one who had fought back in the games of the Emperor's accession months ago. I remembered weeping a little for him, the same way I wept when the lions fell in the arena with spears through their great chests. I'd thought he was dead. Even after the Emperor decreed mercy, they'd had to drag him out on a hook like they did the dead lions. But he wasn't dead. He was back: a gladiator.

"Hurry up, Arius," the *lanista* called impatiently from the litter. "We're blocking the road."

He caught the side of the wagon and vaulted up. Arius. So that was his name.

For once, I was longing to see the games.

T HE underground levels of the Colosseum hummed like the pipes of an aqueduct. Slaves rushed through the torch-lit passages, some with whetstones to sharpen the weapons, some with sharp sticks to prod the animals into a fury before they were released up into the arena, some with great rakes to scrape up the dead. Somewhere a lion screamed, or maybe a dying man.

"The main battle's in two hours," a steward barked at Gallus in greeting, eyes raking over the gladiators. "Keep them out of the way till then. Which one's the Briton? He goes after the tigers finish off those prisoners."

A few hissed words from Gallus, and Arius found himself shunted down a dark passage. Spring warmth never penetrated the bowels of the Colosseum; the passages were dank and cold. Fine clay dust filtered down, shaken loose by the vibrations of the cheers.

A pulley carried Arius to the upper levels; a slave led him to a gate and hastily shoved a sword and heavy shield at him. "Luck to you, gladiator." Arius waited, rasping a mailed finger up and down the edge of the blade. Against the darkness he saw a wooden sword.

The applause died down. Dimly he heard the voice of the games announcer: "And now . . . wilds of Britannia . . . we bring you . . . Arius the Barbarian . . . playing the part of . . ."

With a clank of machinery the heavy gate cranked up. Blinding sunlight flooded the passage.

"ACHILLES, THE GREATEST WARRIOR IN THE WORLD!"

The cheering hit him like a wall as he strode out into the sunlight. Fifty thousand voices shouting his name. A blur of bright silks and white togas, pale circles of faces and black circles of open mouths, backed by a roof of dazzling blue sky. He'd never seen so many people in his life.

He caught himself staring, and slammed down his visor. No need to know who Achilles was, or what kind of part he was playing. Killing was killing.

The demon uncoiled joyfully in his gut.

The announcer's voice again, hushing the cheers. "And now, from the wilds of Amazonia, we bring you fitting opponents to the mighty hero Achilles—"

The gate at the other end of the arena rumbled. Arius shrugged his cloak off and his sword up, shifting into a crouch.

"THE QUEEN OF THE AMAZONS AND HER CHAMPIONS!"

Arius's blade faltered.

Women. Five women. In plumed golden helmets and crescent-moon shields and gold anklets. Breasts bare for the audience to leer at. Slim bright swords raised high. Lips clamped into hard lines.

The demon rage drained away. Left him cold and shaking. His sword point dropped, brushed against the sand.

The red-plumed leader let out a kestrel shriek as she swooped down toward him.

"Oh, damn it," he snarled, and brought up his sword.

He picked them off one at a time. The smallest first. No older than fourteen. She stabbed at him with more desperation than skill. He killed her quickly. Then the dark-haired one with the birthmark on her shoulder. He clipped the sword out of her hand, turning his eyes away as he hewed her down. Every stroke lasted a century.

In extreme slow motion he saw the leader cry out, trying to pull them together. She knew what she was doing. Charging together, they might have brought him down. But they panicked and scattered. And, to the raucous enjoyment of the crowd, he chased them down one at a time and slew them.

He just tried to do it fast.

The leader in her brave scarlet plumes, she was the last. She put up a good fight, catching his sword again and again on her slim shield. Her blade landed twig-light against his own. Her eyes showed huge and wild through the visor.

He knocked her sword aside and drove his shield boss against her unprotected breast. Her neck arced in agony. She crumpled to the sand like a broken clay figurine.

Not dead. Not yet. Just strangling on her own blood, crushed ribs trying to expand. He took a tired step forward to cut her throat.

"Mitte! Mitte!"

The cry assailed his ears, and he looked up dumbly. All across the tiers of spectators, the thumbs called for mercy. The cheers were good-natured, the opinion unanimous: mercy for the last of the Amazons.

His eyes burned. Sweat. He flung the blade away and dropped to one knee to slide an arm under her shoulders. She was bleeding everywhere—

Her eyes swept him feebly. A swaying hand reached up to tilt back his visor. And then he was jolted all the way down to his bones as she spoke to him in a language he had not heard for more than a dozen years. His own language.

"Please," she rasped.

He stared at her.

She choked again on her own blood. "Please."

He looked down into those great, desperate eyes.

"Please."

He slid his hand up into her hair, turning her head back to expose the long throat. She closed her eyes with a rattling sigh. He eased his blade into the soft pulse behind her jaw.

When her crushed body was cold in his arms, he looked up. His audience had gone silent. He rose, stained all over with her blood and weighed down by unbelieving eyes.

The demon's fury roared up, and with all his strength he hewed his sword sideways against the marble wall. He struck again and again, feeling the muscles tear across his back, and at last the blade snapped in two with a dissonant crack. He flung the pieces away, spat on them, then ripped the helmet from his head and flung that after. Rage surged up in his throat and he shouted—no curses, just a long wordless roar.

They applauded him.

Applauded.

They cheered, they shouted, they screamed praise down on his head like a stinging rain. They threw coins, they threw flowers, they surged upright and shrieked his name. They stamped their feet and rocked the marble tiers.

It was only then that he wept, standing alone in the great arena surrounded by the bodies of five women and a thousand downward-drifting rose petals.

Two

꩜

THEA

H E'S magnificent." Lepida's voice was lazy. "Don't you
think, Thea?"

I murmured something, reaching for the vial of rose oil. My
mistress lay facedown on the green marble massage slab in the
Pollio bathhouse, a beautiful black-haired mermaid among the
tasteless fish mosaics and the gaudy clutter of perfume bottles.

"Really, I've never seen anything like him before. Much
more interesting than Belleraphon. Belleraphon's too civilized.
This Arius, he's a real barbarian." She shifted an arm so I could
massage the rose oil into her side. "There's something untamed
about him, don't you think? I mean, no civilized man would kill
women. But this Arius, he just mowed them down without a
thought."

I kneaded my fingers along her spine, and she arched her
back. "He even looks like a savage! Covered in gore, and you
could tell he didn't even notice. A real man shouldn't care about
getting his hands dirty, don't you think? Belleraphon, now, he
never really closes in with his enemies. Too afraid of getting
blood in that pretty beard of his. And really, what kind of show
is that? I don't go to the games to see someone being careful; I
go to see something thrilling. Some*one* thrilling."

In my mind's eye I saw Arius cradling the poor crushed
Amazon.

"—and when he just stalked out afterward like he didn't even hear the cheering! He doesn't care about the applause; he does it because he *likes* it." Lepida stretched her arms languorously over her head. "Do you think he's handsome, Thea?"

"I don't know, my lady. Do you want the pumice stone for your feet?"

"Yes, the pumice stone, and put your back into it. You do too think he's handsome, Thea. I saw your face when he was fighting." She turned with a little laugh. "Well, these rough types appeal to those with *lower* instincts."

"Mmm," I murmured. "And how does my lady's betrothed appeal to her?"

"Marcus?" She snorted. "Do you know he's forty-six? His *son* is two years older than me! Really, I don't know why I can't marry the son instead. What's the use of being young and beautiful if it's all going to some boring old man with a crooked shoulder? He kept telling me about his books. As if I cared about his stupid library." Lepida reached for the wine cup. "If that's the best Father can do for me, well, he'll just have to look harder. I want someone young, someone exciting. I want a real man."

She twined a curl of hair around her fingers. "What do you suppose this Arius is like in person?"

I didn't like his name in her mouth.

"CONGRATULATIONS, Barbarian!"

"Good show!"

"Not a bad—hey, where are you going?"

Arius brushed straight through the Mars Street dining hall, not looking to either side. Dropping his cloak in an unceremonious heap, he leaned over the long table and grabbed the wine jug.

"Hey, that's for all of us!"

He drank straight from the jug, gulping without thirst. The other fighters, piling in with their congratulations and their envy, gradually fell silent.

He rocked back on his heels and dragged a hand across his mouth as a single drop of sour wine fell from the lip of the jug to the floor. For a moment he contemplated the jug, swinging by its handle from one finger, then he drew back and hurled it against the wall. Everyone swore and jumped back as clay shards crashed to the floor.

"Bloody sour barbarian," a Gaul muttered.

Arius turned and kicked out in one lightning-smooth motion. The Gaul yelled as his stool collapsed underneath him. Then he yelled in earnest as a table knife clipped a chunk from his ear. He charged like a bull, and they thrashed across the floor in a vicious tangle. Gladiators piled in, shouting.

"Nail him! Nail him!"

"Get the bastard!"

"THAT'S ENOUGH!" Gallus shouted from the doorway.

The gladiators fell back. The Gaul, streaming blood from the side of his head, tore loose and staggered to his feet, swearing in his native tongue. Arius rose in silence, brushing his hands off and regarding his *lanista* coldly.

"Well, well," said Gallus. "Congratulations, dear boy. You're living up to your name, I see. In the streets they're already calling you 'the Barbarian.'"

The Gaul glared. "He cut my *ear* off—"

"Oh, stop whining. Get along to the infirmary." Gallus's eyes never left Arius. "Stay out of trouble, and I'll get you a bigger fight next time. Something really grand to round off the spring season. Then there's summer training—"

Arius picked up another wine jug. His eyes never shifting from his *lanista*'s, he drank a deliberate mouthful and spat it accurately out between Gallus's well-shod feet. Then he turned and stalked back into his bare cell. Everyone braced for a resounding crash, but the door clicked quietly shut.

THEA

JUNE. A pretty month in some places—blue skies, gentle warmth, blooming flowers. Not so pretty in Rome, where the sun beat down like a brass coin and the streets shimmered like water. Hateful, molten June. The nights gave me dreams to frighten ghosts in their tombs.

The city spilled over with a last round of frantic gaieties as the wealthy citizens prepared to set out for their cool summer villas. The games of Matralia were breathlessly anticipated, an extravaganza of blood and excitement that would close out the season, and patricians, politicians, charioteers, courtesans, and plebs alike buzzed with the news: At the pinnacle of the festivities, the great Belleraphon was to be matched against a rising newcomer. A certain Briton named Arius, already nicknamed "Barbarian" by the mob.

"It's all my doing," Lepida crowed. "I persuaded Father to pair them up. They're starting Arius at five-to-one odds."

"Optimistic," I ventured.

"I know," my mistress agreed. "Won't it be fun, watching the Barbarian die bravely? I wonder if Father might consider hosting a dinner party for all the gladiators the night before . . ."

Father would indeed consider it. Especially when his daughter pointed out that any party with Arius and Belleraphon as star attractions would be sure to attract guests of the highest rank.

"And I'll go, too," Lepida concluded, tossing her blue-black ringlets. "Right next to you, Father, so you can protect me if things get, well, *rowdy*." Dimpling. "I know it'll be a wild crowd, but Aemilius Graccus might be there, and Julius Sulpicianus— very important families! Who knows? Maybe one of them will ask for me, and then I wouldn't have to marry boring old Marcus Norbanus, and we'd both be happy. *Please?*"

The entire household was thrown into frenzy. The cook was up till the small hours designing a menu fit to be served to the expected patrician guests as well as to the gladiators who might well be eating their last meal. The silver-inlaid dining couches were sumptuously draped and the tables garlanded with visibly out-of-season flowers so that every guest from the most noble of patricians to the most menial of the gladiators should see the Pollio wealth. Too much wealth, I could have told them; too many flowers and ornaments and slaves on display for good taste, but who asked me? When the night finally arrived, my feet were sore and my cheeks stinging from slaps before Lepida pronounced herself tolerably satisfied with her appearance.

"Not bad." She pirouetted, angling her head before the polished steel mirror. "No, not bad at all." Sapphire-blue silk molded artfully against her rounded body, the sway of her hips causing the golden bells around her ankles to chime, pearls glimmering at her ears and throat, mouth painted a luscious red. I smoothed the front of my rough brown wool tunic.

"I shan't need you again tonight, Thea," she declared, adjusting a gold filigree bracelet. "Can't have a drab thing like you hanging around all those glittering people; you'll put them off their supper. Clean up this mess first!"

"Yes, my lady." But I left her gowns where they lay, thinking of my blue bowl and a quiet room somewhere away from the clatter of voices already rising from the triclinium. And despite Lepida's warning, I did steal a peek around the edge of the inlaid satinwood door.

A much better crowd than usually attended Pollio's parties: one or two senators, Emperor Domitian's personal chamberlain, Lady Lollia Cornelia, who hosted Rome's most famous dinner parties and was cousin to the Empress. They lounged among the flowers and cushions in their bright silks, picking at the roast elephant ears and ostrich wings and flamingo tongues on their golden plates, and never ceasing to gossip in that elegant patrician drawl that Pollio had never quite managed to acquire. The only jarring chord in that gracious company was the presence of the scarred and muscle-bound gladiators—dark wool among the silks, common accents among the refined, vultures among the peacocks. And the peacocks liked it that way. Tomorrow those powerful men would curl their lips at the sight of the gladiators; tonight they would wax expansive and clap the scarred shoulders with their ringed hands. Tomorrow those elegant ladies would draw their skirts aside from any fighter they encountered on the streets; tonight they would fawn and even flirt. Why not? By tomorrow, these men would likely be dead.

On the couch of honor where all could see them sat Arius and Belleraphon. "Ah, yes, the Barbarian," Belleraphon had said languidly as they were introduced, and extended a manicured hand. Arius just stared at it until it was withdrawn. "How quaint," whispered Belleraphon to a tittering patrician lady at his other side. "One presumes he does know how to speak?" Side-by-side on the dining couch, the two of them proceeded to ignore each other utterly.

No one could help but compare them. Belleraphon smiling and joking, Arius sour and uncomfortable. Belleraphon nibbling daintily from every dish, Arius fueling himself from whatever plate was put before him. Belleraphon lounging on the silk cushions as if born to it, Arius sitting as stiffly upright as a statue. Belleraphon the civilized and Arius the barbaric.

I drew a fold of my cloak up around my face and slipped quietly away.

ARIUS was tired of the overheated chamber, tired of the too-soft cushions, tired of the constant babble, but most of all he was tired of the girl at his side.

"You're frightfully brave, risking your life in the arena day after day." She shifted on her couch, and one varnished nail brushed against his arm. "Are you ever afraid? I'd be terrified."

He imagined her clamped between the jaws of a lion. "Yes," he agreed.

"A whole word!" She tossed her head back and laughed. "What progress."

He reached for the wine decanter.

"Don't be cross with me." She pouted, sliding over onto her back so he could admire the curve of her breasts under the blue silk. Beautiful breasts. Beautiful hair, too. Beautiful face. Eyes like a ferret. A burst of music from the flute players drowned him out before he could tell her to leave him the hell alone. The guests were slipping off their couches and wandering toward the gardens. Senators took the arms of women who were not their wives and made discreetly for the moonlit paths of the conservatorium, while gladiators openly grabbed slave girls and pulled them into the privacy of the night. The great Belleraphon disappeared behind a statue of Neptune with a distinguished matron of the Sulpicii.

A hot little hand descended on his. "Would you care for a stroll in the gardens?" said the girl with the ferret eyes. "Don't worry about my father. He's busy cutting deals with your *lanista*." Her tongue flickered over her painted lips.

He let her drag him off the absurd couch, stopping only to seize up a flagon of wine. The soft hand with its lacquered nails tucked into his elbow, propelling him down a gravel path that curved away from the house. The smell of jasmine and roses cloyed his nose.

"So," she smiled up at him. "Wherever did you come from? I'm mad with curiosity."

"Nowhere, Lady."

"Everyone's from somewhere—"

"Isn't that your father, Lady?" He pointed over her shoulder.

When she turned to look, he twisted his arm out of her hand and ducked into the bushes.

"Arius!"

He came up against the atrium wall and veered around the corner to the rest of the Pollio house. The lamps were unlit, the rooms dark. Glancing over his shoulder, he saw his host's daughter still standing on the garden path, craning her neck. He ducked inside the first available doorway before she spotted him.

The bathhouse. He could see the faint glimmer of the pool. The marble felt wonderfully cool against his back as he slid down by the wall and uncorked the flagon. Now here was a place a man could get drunk in peace. Who cared if his head ached the next morning? He was going to die, anyway. He took a long swallow of wine.

A soft scrape from the far corner froze him sober. He rose noiselessly, stealing along the edge of the pool.

Another soft sound. He lunged into the dark and caught hold of a wrist. "Don't move. Or I'll kill you." The demon snapped on its leash. "Who are you?"

"I'm Thea," said a polite female voice. "Do you always start conversations this way?"

Her wrist was narrow and smooth, easily circled by his hand. He dropped it, stepped back—and realized his fingers were sticky. "You're bleeding."

"Yes," the voice agreed. "Quite a lot. The blue bowl's got a good inch on the bottom. I think I cut too deep this time."

He wondered if she was drunk. "Who are you?"

"Thea," she repeated. "You can't see my hand, but it's extended for a proper shake. The unbloodied hand, that is."

Her narrow hand was callused across the palm: a slave's hand. "Cut yourself?" he asked.

"Yes, I cut myself," she returned agreeably. "I do that, rather often. My wrists look like your back."

He started.

"It's Arius, isn't it? A Roman name on a Briton. 'Thea,' though—that's a Greek name on a Jew. Sorry, I'll be quiet now. I imagine you just want to sit in some dark corner and get drunk."

He sat, propping his back against the wall, and drank off the rest of the wine in a few swallows. His eyes were used to the darkness now. He could make out a dim profile, a straight nose, a shadowy cable of hair, a wrist flexed over the bowl. She was singing something softly in an odd tongue.

"*She'ma Yisroel, Adonai Aloujanou, Adonai echod.*" Her voice slid around the marble walls of the bathhouse; a warm, melodious alto. He closed his eyes as the strange music trailed off into silence.

"Arius?"

"What?"

"Are you going to lose tomorrow?"

"Yes."

"Pity. I'll have to watch. I get dragged to all the games," she added, "and I hate them. Hate them, hate them, hate them."

He imagined he could hear her blood sliding down the side of that blue bowl. "Yes."

"You, too? I thought so. You're no Belleraphon, drinking up the applause."

So dark. It could have been the beginning of the world. "What am I, then?"

"Barbarian," she sang softly. "Barbarian, barbarian, barbarian. Where did you come from, Barbarian?"

"Brigantia." With fumbled amazement he heard the wine-slowed words uncoil. "In Britannia, but we call it Albion. Far to the north. Mountains by the sea." He could still see the mountains, pressed up against the night like a dark wild song.

"Family?"

"Two brothers. My mother died young. My father . . ."

"He was a great chieftain?" she prompted.

"A smith. He believed in iron and bronze, not fighting. My brothers taught me to fight. Brought me up on stories of Vercingetorix."

"Who?"

"Vercingetorix. A Gallic chieftain—nearly defeated Julius Caesar. Hero of my childhood."

"How did he die?"

Arius smiled without amusement. "In the arena."

"Oh." There was a little silence. "What else?"

"There was—there was a Roman fort. Nearby. We paid tribute—cattle, grain, iron. My brothers, they liked to raid the Romans. They got cocky, killed a few sentries. The Romans killed them."

The arrows, the advancing shields, the screaming men and

screaming horses . . . Madoc falling beneath a circle of stabbing spears, Tarcox trampled by a tribune on a tall horse.

"And you?"

"I was thirteen. Stupid. Made a stand over my brothers' bodies instead of running to warn my father. Thought I was Vercingetorix the Invincible. Romans captured me, of course. My father, killed. The village, burned. The rest of us . . . sold."

The smoke, the blood, the screams of the women. A thirteen-year-old boy grabbing up a sword too heavy for him and running at his enemies.

Stupid boy. Arius turned his eyes away from the memory.

"And then?"

He had almost forgotten Thea. "The salt mines. I was big for my age; went to haul rocks in Trinovantia. Then in Gaul. Kept making trouble, kept getting sold. Rock-carrier. That's the Barbarian's glorious history."

His head was full of mist. He wanted more wine. She said nothing, and he was grateful. Hearing the quiet whisper of her breath, he glanced over. The bowl in her lap tilted, a shining disc in the dark. "Why?" he asked simply.

For a long time he thought she wouldn't answer. Then: "Have you ever heard of Masada?"

"No."

"It's a fortress carved out of a cliff top in Judaea. It's hot, dry country, baking under the sun like an iron plate. I was born there. Fifteen years ago."

Fifteen. She sounded older.

"Masada was full of Jewish rebels. The Romans decided to smoke us out, but they couldn't. Not until they built a ramp up to the top of the cliff, and used Jewish slaves to build it so we couldn't hurl down our rocks and pitch. Six months' worth of Jews built that ramp, and then they brought up the battering ram to break down the gates."

"You remember?"

"Not much. I was too young. I remember peering over dusty stone walls to watch the little armored men swarming around like ants . . . I remember being happy. I pieced out the facts later, from rumors."

"What happened?"

"This part—this part I remember. I remember it perfectly. A hot night. Such a hot night. Like tonight. I've hated hot nights ever since. My father was talking with the other men in low voices. My mother looked grave. Even my sister Judith was worried—she was fourteen, old enough to worry. I was only six. I was still playing with dolls."

Her profile was perfectly still. "It was night when Father came back. He talked to my mother for a long time, in the bedroom with the door shut. He came out alone, and drew Judith aside. I wandered into the bedroom. I saw my mother on the floor, with her throat cut. I ran out screaming. Just in time to see Judith stab herself while my father covered his eyes. Then he turned and looked at me, and told me to be a good girl and come give him a hug, and when I saw he had a knife in his hand I ran.

"I ran to the next house, where my friend Hadassah lived, and it was the same there. Everyone stabbed. The same everywhere, in every house in Masada. So when the Romans battered their way in the next day, they found a fortress full of dead Jews—and one six-year-old girl sitting in a room full of bodies, waiting for her family to wake up."

"You—you were the only one?"

"A few others lived. I don't remember."

His throat felt thick. "Why?"

"Better to be dead than alive when the Romans came crashing in with their swords. Better to leave them with a thousand corpses rather than a thousand captured rebels to parade in chains past their Emperor. Better to be dead than a slave. That's what they decided, when they all went home and killed themselves."

"But you . . ."

"A Greek merchant bought me. He gave me the name Thea; taught me to read and write. He was kind, really. Most of my masters were kind. It hasn't been a bad life." Her voice was even.

"The blood?" Looking at her blue bowl.

"My people have an old proverb." Lightly. " 'An eye for an eye, a tooth for a tooth.' And blood for blood, because I should have died with the rest of them; I should have been brave like my sister and fallen on a knife, but I ran like a coward and I've been paying back in blood ever since. Is there any wine left?"

"No."

"Pity." She levered herself up, grasping at the wall. Like a priestess carrying a sacrifice she picked up the bowl and swayed out the door. Arius, only slightly steadier on his feet, ducked after her. She was kneeling by a camellia bush, draining the bowl out into the earth. He stood by awkwardly, feet planted apart for balance.

"There." She rose too quickly, staggering, and he caught her by the shoulder before she fell. The light of the distant lamps revealed that she was tall, the top of her head level with his eyes, and as angular as a doe. The point of her shoulder was sharp under his hand.

"Good luck to you tomorrow." She offered a smile. "I'll be watching."

Her eyes were black, dilated too far. He'd seen them before, those eyes. The same brave desperate gaze—on the Amazon he had slain in the arena. A nerve prickled along the back of his neck.

Careful.

"Good night," he said roughly, and left her.

THEA

THE next day, when it seemed too bright and glaring to believe that the previous night had ever happened at all, I watched Arius kill Belleraphon.

It was brutal, stomach-turning, utterly unforgettable. He strode out quietly, dwarfed by Belleraphon's strutting, preening elegance, and then launched an attack of such savagery that my knees buckled in the stands. Belleraphon's grin slid away as his shoulder was laid open; he began to fight in earnest, but it wasn't enough. Arius's sword took the top half of his shield, took another wide cut out of his ribs, took half the fingers on his left hand. Belleraphon's dancelike grace was hewed away a piece at a time, cut down to raw desperation, and even that wasn't enough. He wavered, a broken, bleeding thing, and he died on Arius's sword.

The Colosseum rose with a roar, stamping for him as they had stamped only last week for Belleraphon. They screamed, they shouted, they wept, they tore gold from their fingers and silver from their purses to rain down on the solitary figure in the sand. Men cuffed tears from their eyes and swore he was the god of war come on earth to walk among men. Women tore their *stolas* to bare their breasts, sobbing that they would love him forever. In the Imperial box, the Emperor nodded approval. Arius threw his sword into the sand, and they shrieked their love for him.

Miserable, in the middle of such glory? No one would ever believe it.

Three

❦❦

LEPIDA

BEAUTY is fate's gift—and every time I looked in my mirror, I knew Fortuna loved me.

I dressed carefully: lilac silk to set off my black hair, a chunk of amethyst on each hand to showcase slender fingers, strands of amethysts on silver wire emphasizing the length of my neck. Lovely—and then I had to ruin the effect with a hideous brown cloak over the top, and that long-faced, blank-eyed Thea at my back.

"I'm not carrying that." I wrinkled my nose at the basket she held out to me.

"Slave girls carry baskets on the way to the forum, Lady."

I took it grudgingly, looking in the mirror again. At least no one would recognize the beautiful Lady Lepida Pollia when she went incognito to the gladiator barracks. "Get behind me," I hissed at Thea as she fell into step at my side.

"Slave girls on the way to the forum don't walk behind each other," Thea said, impassive. "They walk in pairs."

That gawky sunburned slut never smiled at me, but I always felt the smile lurking, just the same. I sniffed and hurried ahead, away from the rows of gracious marble villas and toward the seedier district on the edge of the Subura where the gladiator schools were. Even a warm summer day couldn't make Mars Street pretty.

A perfumed slave boy tried to leave me waiting in the ante-room, but I gestured to Thea and she tossed him a copper that got me admitted. No one kept Lepida Pollia waiting. I was shown into a narrow room with a writing desk, and behind it the fat *lanista* in midtirade.

"—abusing your followers? Hurling wine cups at powerful fans, say, when they beg for souvenir locks of your hair? Or pitching drunken young patricians into the Tiber when they challenge you to a match?"

Arius sat on a wall bench with a jug of wine in one hand, head thrown back. He drank off a swallow with his eyes closed, and I drew in a breath at the sight of his arms. Rough, brown, muscular, scarred—

Gallus still hadn't seen me. "I'm not averse to giving you your head, dear boy. A little money of your own, perhaps. Roaming privileges in the evenings. But only if you behave yourself, and—"

I cleared my throat. Gallus gave an irritable glance. "Have you been sent with a gift, girl? Put it over there."

"I'm Lady Lepida Pollia," I said, sweeping my hood back in a gesture that showed off my rings. "And perhaps I *have* come with a gift. We'll see."

I stole a glance at the Barbarian, but he took another swallow of wine without looking at me. Too dazzled, of course. Gallus bounded to his feet at once, bowing over my hand, offering me a chair, gesturing a slave boy forward to take my cloak. His eyes flicked past me, looking for my father, then looked back again with greater interest.

"It's dreadfully hot in here. My fan, Thea." I patted my forehead, and Thea came forward to hand me my peacock feather fan. The Barbarian was looking at me now, missing nothing, not even Thea as she faded back into the corner. I slouched gracefully, shrugging off my *palla* so he could admire my white shoulders. "Aren't you going to wish me a good morning, Barbarian?"

Gallus nudged him. Arius shrugged. "Good morning."

"I see you've had other visitors." I glanced around the room at the gifts sent by besotted fans: silver plate, a cloak of Milesian wool, a tooled sword belt. "My father sent the Falernian wine. I noticed at the banquet that you had a taste for it. Such a discerning palate for a barbarian!"

"Wine's wine," Arius said when Gallus nudged him again.

I made an airy gesture, showing off my bracelets. "Anyway, I've come to say good-bye. I'm leaving for Tivoli tomorrow. I found out that you won't be fighting again until fall anyway, so I might as well escape the heat."

"Quite," Gallus agreed, passing forward a little plate of candied pears. "No use wasting the Barbarian in the summer games, is there? Paltry little festivals, with the Emperor gone. Now, the Romani games in September . . ."

"Quite." Popping one, two, three little candied pear slices into my mouth. "Would you like me to get you a prime spot in the Romani games, Barbarian?"

Gallus prodded him. Arius looked at me unblinking, and I felt a little thrill. Such a granite face! I'd see it cracked someday.

"Of course he'd like that, Lady Lepida," Gallus broke in smoothly. "How kind."

I could hardly look at him. Arius folded his sunburned arms across his chest, and I imagined them around me instead. Would he hurt me? I'm sure he would. "Thank you," I murmured to Gallus. "Of course, if he ever wants to thank me, he should send a message to my father's house in Tivoli. Thea, my cloak."

Thea came forward. Was she staring at his arms, too, imagining them wrapped around her? I rather think she was. I gave Arius a last dazzling smile and took myself away. Gallus was berating him again before the door even shut. "—got that father of hers wrapped around her little finger, so you'll be polite the next time she—"

I smiled as we stepped out into the morning sun. "Excellent," I said. "A pity we're leaving for Tivoli, but perhaps it's better that way. Gallus won't let him fight in the summer games—so the Emperor and everyone will be clamoring for him in the fall. Just like he'll be clamoring for me."

"Yes, my lady."

"He does want me, you know." Thinking of that impassive gaze. "Not that he says anything, but he's never talked to a lady before, has he? Just whores and slave girls, like you. And by the way"—as we crossed the end of the forum back toward my father's house, dodging round the shouting vendors with their wooden trays—"I shan't be taking you with me to Tivoli."

"My lady?"

"I've decided to take Iris instead. She can do my hair and

bring me my breakfast, and you can stay here to run one or two little errands for me. Let's just say I want to make sure Arius doesn't forget about me." I smiled sweetly. Thea's long horse face was impassive. I'd have that face cracked, too, someday. "You won't mind seeing him again, will you, Thea? Not at all, I think. And you can walk behind me now."

I'M expensive," she said by way of introduction. "But I'll do you for free."

He recognized the blond curls, the soft painted face, the transparent lemon-yellow dress. Laelia, one of the city's most exclusive courtesans. "How'd you get here?"

"Your *lanista* showed me in." She perched beside him on the bed and favored him with a glittering smile. "I like gladiators."

He edged back along the bed as she ran a soft hand down his arm. "Madam—"

"Call me Laelia." She leaned against him, one hand tracing a circle on his knee. "I believe you're nervous, Barbarian. Never had a woman like me before?"

Never had *any* woman before. To another pair of eyes— darker eyes, maybe; quieter eyes—he could have said it. Not to these blue eyes, flickering with excitement.

"So tell me." She hooked one knee over his and rubbed her foot along his leg. "How do barbarians make love?"

Make love. How would he know, hauling rocks in Roman mines since he was thirteen? He'd seen how the Romans did it, laughing and panting and thrusting, with their friends cheering encouragement and their knives at the woman's throat. He'd seen it often enough. He knew how the Romans did it, all right.

Just once, he'd tried with a woman. A prostitute at the mines, when he was fifteen. He'd hurt her. He hadn't meant to—but she bolted. He hadn't tried again.

His every muscle coiled tight as a perfumed, painted mouth closed on his.

Stop, he told himself. But his hands clenched on her shoulders.

"You've bruised me." She looked up at him with a smile of parted lips and gleaming teeth. "Like it rough, do you?"

He rose, so fast he spilled her on the floor. Caught her by both wrists, heaved her up.

Hurt her, whispered the demon. *That's how the men do it.*

He flung her out the door before she could protest, kicking it shut with his foot. He sank down against the wall, raking his hands through his hair. On the other side of the door he heard a stream of shrill curses. He closed his eyes, pushing his head down into his folded arms. Waited for his muscles to stop trembling. Waited for his blood to stop roaring. Waited for the demon whispers to die down to simple, straightforward, uncomplicated murder.

Killing he could handle. Killing was easy.

THEA

M Y mistress and her father left the next morning in a welter of wagons and slaves and silver litters, and I was free. Free! The July sun baked me golden brown, the dust rose off the streets and choked my lungs, the sweltering nights gave me my usual nightmares, but I was free. No Lepida to trail with a fan and a handkerchief, no bee-sting jabs from her tongue. No Pollio with his moist hands in dark hallways. No work to do, since the exacting steward ceased tracking our comings and goings and retired to the circus to watch the chariot races all day. The male slaves slipped off to the taverns, the maids tripped out to meet their lovers, and no one cared a jot.

I went walking in the evenings when purple twilight cooled the air, sitting on hot corner stones listening to street musicians and parting with my few coins to pay for the pleasure they gave me. I even sneaked into the Theatre of Marcellus to hear a famous actress sing a round of Greek songs, memorizing her every graceful gesture to practice for myself in the heat-shriveled Pollio gardens. In my mind I could see my mother smile as she said, "What a pretty voice you'll have when you're grown." And then I'd fall silent and perhaps creep back inside to my blue bowl with the frieze of nymphs on the side, because my mother was no longer here to sing me lullabies, and over the years it had somehow become my fault.

I saw Arius the Barbarian, of course. His *lanista* flashed him all over the city like a prize stallion: dragged him into the theatre to watch the comedies, into the Campus Martius where everyone strolled to see and be seen, into the Circus Maximus to watch the chariot races. Wherever he went there was a hush of deliciously savored fear, a respectful drawing back, and afterward the buzz of speculation.

"He won't last the next fight," people scoffed in taverns. "Beating Belleraphon, that was a fluke."

"And the Amazons?" his fans retaliated hotly.

"Anyone could beat a team of women!"

"No, he's something special. Just wait till the Romani games in September—" The argument went on, even though he ignored his fans as if they were shadows and drank alone in taverns despite the hundreds who would have kept him company.

His face started to appear everywhere, painted badly on the sides of wooden buildings around the Colosseum. Crudely chalked graffiti greeted my eyes on alley walls: "Arius the Barbarian makes all the girls sigh!" Vendors hawked garish little portraits on gaudy ribbons. Taverns offered him free wine, and whores offered him free time. Arius, a slave and a barbarian, a man who would be cut up and fed to the lions when he died instead of meeting his gods in a proper tomb. Lower than sewer trash, but so important: His fights would calm the crowds when they grumbled too loudly over the Emperor's taxes, his presence would titillate the most bored patricians at dinner parties and keep them from scheming, his blood would be sold to epileptics as a cure for their foaming fits, and brides would fight for one of his spears to part their hair on their wedding day and thus guarantee themselves a happy marriage.

All of it would vanish overnight, of course, if he lost his next fight. And I wondered how long he would last.

"Savages never live long," an aging legionnaire said critically, slamming a mug of beer down on the table at a tavern where I'd gone to sing. "The Barbarian's just like all those tribesmen I came up against in Britannia—throws too much into every stroke. Savages always lose in the end because they can't keep their heads."

Quite correct, I thought. Men who want to die usually do, and Fortune's smile on gladiators is notoriously fickle. But . . .

I watched Arius stride through the forum, seeing the icy rigidity of his shoulders, the iron grip of the fingers clasped at the small of his back, the fierce impassive gaze he turned on the *lanista* who waddled complacent and perspiring at his side. Thin ice over savagery—a potent brew, and the fans lapped at it deliriously. The ice never broke, but stories persisted of the men he'd killed in street brawls, the taverns he'd wrecked in drunken rages, the fellow fighters he'd slain in sparring practice, and hopeful crowds turned up daily outside the Mars Street training courtyard in hopes of seeing it for themselves.

Yes. While he lived, while he lasted, he'd rise to the top.

"What's the news in Rome?" Lepida wrote to me after a careless description of Tivoli's cool winds and soothing rains, her success at local parties, the Tivoli girls she put to shame. I wrote back an inventive account of Arius's carousing, naming each and every fabled beauty who'd reportedly offered her services free of charge, and volunteering my personal opinion that he'd sampled them all.

"My, aren't you talkative," she wrote back snappishly. "Well, you'd better start delivering these right away, one per week. And don't think I won't know if you conveniently lose them."

"These" turned out to be a packet of letters: prewritten on expensive paper, sealed and scented, and addressed to *"Arrius the Gladiator"* in Lepida's none-too-literate hand. Dutifully I took one and made my way to Mars Street.

"Oh yes," Gallus purred. "Lady Lepida's maid—you have a delivery from your mistress? These noble ladies and their plotting! Never fear, I'll leave you in privacy." He disappeared, leaving me alone with the Barbarian.

For a moment we just looked at each other. "I have a letter from my mistress," I said crisply.

"I can't read," he shrugged. "Only fight."

"I've been charged to read it to you." I cleared my throat, retrieving the letter and breaking the seal. " *'My dear Arrius,'* " I read, feeling my cheeks flush. " *'How horibly dull it is up here in Tivoli with no games. I so much look forward to the gladitorial shows when I get back. I've perswaded my father to give you a prime spot. I do hope you haven't forgoten all about me. Lepida Pollia.'* "

I folded the letter up. "Reply?"

"None." He was leaning up against the wall, arms folded across his wide chest, gazing out the window.

"She won't like that," I said, and noticed incongruously how a scar behind his ear interrupted the line of his russet hair.

No answer. I curtsied, turned—

"Thought I saw you at the Golden Cockerel last week."

"Yes. The taverner likes me to sing."

I saw Arius there the following night, drinking. Deaf to me. Another letter the following week. "No reply," he said.

"All right."

"It's hot today."

"Hot?"

"Oh—maybe not. In Judaea it must get much—"

"No—no, it's hot."

Every week I came with another of Lepida's misspelled notes. Read them aloud. Then waited for the diffident word that always came.

"Cut yourself?" Indicating, one day, my neatly bandaged wrist.

"Yes," I said evenly, turning my hands over to hide my scars. Too late.

"Your wrists look like my back," he observed, and looked at me. Just eyes, gray eyes, and they weren't as cold as people said they were.

There was an old woman among the Pollio slaves, a Brigantian woman who did the laundry. I wheedled a song out of her, a song from Britannia. It was a lovely thing that haunted the ear, and the strange words were cool and slippery in my mouth. "A song about home," the old woman said. "Like all songs from slaves." The next night at the Golden Cockerel, at the dawn hour when the drunks were nodding and Arius drinking grimly in his corner, I sang the Brigantian song about home. Sang it low and soft so the melody slipped coolly through the torpid room, sang it so a damp island breeze freshened the congealed air, sang it to the top of Arius's head as he stared down into his wine. He never looked up, but—

"Where did you learn that?" he asked me the next time I came with one of Lepida's notes.

I shrugged. "From a slave."

He said no more, but I was starting to know the planes and shadows of his face, the flickers of expression that crossed his eyes . . . and I was well pleased.

THE heat was making him crazy. The boredom, the inactivity, but mostly the lazy shimmering heat. He dreaded the arena, woke up swearing when he thought of the applause on his head, but the thought of the approaching games was getting better. Anything was better than feeling his own blood boil inside his veins.

He prowled out into the courtyard, where the midday sun made mirage pools on the packed sand, and got a wooden practice sword. He stripped off his tunic and drilled—relentless mechanical drills that satisfied his body if not his temper. The trainer paired him with a Greek for a practice bout, and Arius didn't wait for the Greek's salute before bringing his sword down in a vicious side sweep.

"Lay off!" The Greek jumped out of the way. "It's just training!"

Kill him, whispered the demon in Arius's head.

He launched forward. The Greek brought up his own blade, and wood met wood with a flat crack. The Greek's sword broke off at the hilt in a spray of splinters. He leaped back and Arius leaped with him, smashing his sword hilt into the Greek's nose. The Greek toppled, and they rolled in a flaying tangle across the courtyard. Arius got his hands around a sweating throat, gritty with sand—

Kill him. Kill him.

"That's enough, dear boy."

He blinked.

"Save yourself," Gallus said languidly from the shade of the doorway. "I want you fresh for the Romani games in September."

Finger by finger Arius unlocked his hands. Sat back. Rolled to his feet. He was bathed in sweat.

"You bastard," the Greek growled, "you broke my nose!"

Kill him, the demon whispered inside Arius's head. *You want to. Kill him.*

He turned his back and walked away. All along the courtyard he could feel the sour eyes of the other fighters. On the street side, on the other side of the bars, were the curious stares of passersby. He wondered how long it had been since he had lived without strangers watching.

There was no wind, but the sweat on Arius's skin had already evaporated. A violent pang of homesickness stabbed him, a longing for cool rains and green hills, for sweet mists that kissed the skin and soft winds rustling in the oak groves. He was tired of barren skies and hot, lifeless air. The heat would wither him into a dry soulless husk long before he ever grew old.

He turned away, aiming a vicious swipe at the air. A crowd had already gathered at the side of the courtyard, peering through the bars and laying bets.

Kill them.

He was about to turn back into the barracks when he caught sight of Thea through the bars. She was standing at the corner of the courtyard, a little apart from the crowd, a basket balanced on her narrow hip and a rope of dark hair hanging over one shoulder. On her way to the forum, probably. But pausing—pausing and watching him with her grave, quiet gaze. He gazed back. She had one of those damn bandages around her wrist again.

He didn't know why—but he brought up his sword and saluted her.

Hail, he heard the gladiators roar out in his head. *We salute you from death's shadow.*

He swung the blade in a graceful arc, halting the point a quivering inch from the sand, then followed through with a thrust at an imaginary enemy, a dodge back, a turn and then a feint. A slow and elegant dance with the sword, the sun heating his back, the sand gritting under his feet, every muscle in his body flowing as smoothly as warm honey. Thea's eyes never turned away.

Show-off, sneered the little black demon.

He whirled, bringing the sword high over his head and slamming it deep into the sand. It vibrated back and forth, the hilt humming under his hands, and he turned his eyes to Thea's.

The crowd was applauding, but the sound was far away. He had made her smile.

A NOTHER letter from my mistress." Thea lifted her brows. "Do you care if I read it? You know what she sounds like by now."

He shrugged, struggling to thread a needle he'd borrowed from a slave. The sleeve of his tunic had a jagged tear.

"I won't bother, then." Thea folded her arms around her own waist. "Any reply? She keeps asking me peevishly why you don't say anything."

"She's got eyes like a ferret. Tell her I said that."

Thea's face opened up into laughter. "She'd slap me sense-less, but it would be worth it."

A little silence. Arius got the needle threaded, tugging his torn sleeve across his arm where he could get at it. "Surely the slaves do that for you," Thea observed.

Arius shrugged again. "I hate asking Gallus for anything."

"Then you'll need to learn to mend properly. You're going about it all wrong, you know."

Arius found himself laughing. Rustily. "Never learned to sew."

"I'll teach you."

"All right." For the first time he took her into his little cell, watching her touch the stone wall, the back of a chair, the rough blanket on the bed. "What?"

"It's not what I expected. Austere." She turned, letting out another smile. "Needle?"

"Here."

"Good. Now sit down."

"Why?"

She placed her hands on his shoulders and pushed him down into the chair. Her voice was playful. "Because I'm the teacher, and the teacher has to loom over the pupil. First of all, that tunic has got to come off. You don't mend something while you're wearing it."

Self-consciously he shrugged out of his tunic. He still wore his training kilt underneath, from that morning's sparring, but he felt naked. One side of Thea's mouth flicked up, but her hands were businesslike as she turned the tunic inside out. "You'll need to trim the stray threads. Do you have a knife?"

"Gallus doesn't let me have anything sharp."

"Don't suppose I blame him. Just tuck the threads in and lap the edges over, then." Showing him. "Now take the needle, and use a roundabout stitch like this."

His stitches were crude next to hers. "It's no good."

"Did Vercingetorix beat Julius Caesar on his first campaign? Try again. Careful, you'll break the needle if you hold it so hard. It's not a sword, Arius."

His name was sweet in her mouth. She leaned over his shoul-der, her work-hardened hand gentle as she readjusted his grip. He felt her breath whispering on the back of his neck, the plaited ends of her hair caressing his bare arm. Her skin was smooth and cool in the stagnant heat. The little cell suddenly seemed much hotter.

The needle broke in his hand.

He jumped up then, knocking her back against the bed. "Get out."

"What?" Half-sprawled across his rough blankets, she looked puzzled. "Arius—"

"Go away." He said it brutally. Before the demon could whisper, *Hurt her.*

Something in her face shuttered. The second woman he'd thrown out of his room. Only this one left without a word, quietly and on her own two feet.

He banged the door behind her. Sank his back against the latch, head in his hands, and listened to her quiet footsteps retreating down the hall. Now she would have gone through the door, now the gates would have shut behind her, now she would be walking back toward the Pollio house and her blue bowl . . .

He yanked the door open. "GALLUS!"

"Yes, dear boy?" His *lanista* appeared in the hall, groomed and jeweled for a party, a pretty slave boy holding his pomander.

"Don't let her back in here again. Ever."

He slammed the door, and the demon laughed.

Four

⚜

THEA

"CAREFUL with those bracelets, stupid!"
The festival of Volturnalia was past, and my mistress was back.

"What a summer!" She stretched like a cat, impossibly pale and smooth and lovely. "Tivoli is so beautiful in August; not a bit hot. Too bad you had to miss it. Goodness, Thea, you do look brown. All dry and baked like a saddle. Anyway, you'll never guess what the Emperor's done! Marcus had the news before anyone. He's divorced his wife! Emperor Domitian, that is. Packed her off to Brundisium or Toscana or somewhere. Can you imagine? She probably had a lover—they're talking about that actor, the one named Paris who plays at the Theatre of Marcellus. I can't see an Empress with an actor, so it's probably just talk, but they say Domitian had him killed anyway. He's a *very* jealous husband."

"Shall I unpack now, my lady?"

"Yes. Marcus is coming to dinner tonight, so leave out the yellow silk. Don't bother with jewels; no need to look beautiful for Marcus." She regarded her betrothal ring impatiently, then her gaze flicked up to me. "So, Thea—"

"The jasmine perfume, my lady?"

"Don't change the subject, Thea. How did your little summer errand go?"

"He didn't get the last three letters."

Her fine black brows drew together. "If you lost them—"

"No." I busied myself with her perfume bottles. "He wouldn't see me."

"What do you mean, wouldn't see you?"

"I went to deliver a letter." I spoke tonelessly. "He told me to get out."

"What? Why?"

"I don't know."

"You idiot, you've ruined everything!" Lepida hauled back and slapped me across the cheek. "I should have known you'd mess it up somehow! How dare you!"

She whirled away from me, storming up and down the room in her bright silks. "And how dare *he*! He's nothing; he's just a gladiator. Doesn't he know who I am? I'll tell Father to throw him to the lions, I'll—" Her eyes shot back to me. "He has someone, doesn't he? Who is she? Some patrician whore? Some boy tribune?"

"No. He just—doesn't like people."

"Oh." She paused a moment in her pacing. "Perhaps he's just—shy?"

"Well . . ."

"Who would have thought it? The Barbarian is shy. I suppose it stands to reason. I mean, he can't have had anyone like me before. Maybe something can still be done." She flung herself down elegantly on the couch, piercing me with a needle-sharp glance. "Not that I'll be asking *you* to run any more messages, the way you've botched things."

As soon as I bowed out I sent up a prayer of thanksgiving. The God of the Jews is hard, merciless, a joker—but occasionally He relents. Yes, Lepida Pollia was back and there would be no more singing for me in taverns—but I wouldn't have to see Arius anymore. And surely when I didn't have to see him— swinging a sword two-handed across the training courtyard, with his gray eyes meeting mine over the blade as he saluted me . . .

Fighters. A bad choice for—well, for anything. I knew all about investments after living in the Pollio house. Gladiators are bad investments. They die too quickly.

"Thea!" A large, moist hand plastered over my elbow, and I

looked up into Quintus Pollio's jovial eyes. "Thea. Just the thing
I need."

W RAPPED in a coarse cloak with a deep hood, he got as far
as the Aurelian Gate.

"Hey, you." A clerk frowned at him peremptorily. "No
skulking out like a criminal; let's see your papers all right and
proper—wait, I know you!" A double take. Too late, Arius covered the gladiator tattoo on his arm. "Saw you in the arena.
You're the Barbarian! What are you—"

Arius hammered both fists into the clerk's middle, and ran.
Six guards brought him down in the middle of the dusty road.

I should've had a sword, he thought disjointedly as they
dragged him back to Mars Street by the elbows. *They'd never
have gotten me if I'd had a sword.*

"Yes, thank you," Gallus said coolly, passing money out
among the guards with a liberal hand. "He'll be chained during
training next time . . . hamstrung a guard? With his teeth? Perhaps this will ease the pain." More money changed hands, and
four of Gallus's thugs locked manacles onto his wrists and
ankles. Arius knew, hearing the sickeningly familiar rattle of
the chains, that there weren't going to be any strokes or smiles
this time.

As soon as the gate shut behind the grumbling guards, Gallus turned and smashed him twice across the face with a heavy
jeweled hand. So there really was muscle under all that pendu-
lous pink flesh.

"Stupid boy!" the *lanista* hissed, and he launched a string of
gutter invective straight from the slums.

"Your origins are showing, Gallus," Arius commented, and
another blow rocked his head back against the wall.

"So you made your grand bid for escape, eh?" Gallus spat.
"And where did it land me? Out of pocket, that's where it landed
me! *Stupid* boy!" Another massive blow.

Arius tasted blood in his mouth, and felt a surge of maca-
bre cheer. Beatings and chains and curses; here was a coin he
could deal in. "Go to hell, Gallus." He bared his bloody teeth in
a grin.

This time one of the *lanista*'s huge thugs came and did the punching. "Damaging your investment, aren't you?" Arius inquired dizzily.

"Oh, I'm beyond protecting my investment." Gallus's eyes were kohl-rimmed slits. "My investment's already disappeared down the drain. Care to know why, Barbarian? Because the Emperor's decided to make war on the Chatti. He's leaving for Germania to join his legions, so who do you think will sponsor any games in September when he's not here to see them? I doubt there will be any games at all. And that means that all through this summer when you drank yourself senseless, *I lost money!*"

"Too bad," Arius commiserated, and a hard palm split his lip.

"You'll still fight, boy. Maybe not in the Colosseum, maybe not with rose petals and silver coins showering down on your head, but believe me, you'll fight. At every two-bit arena with mangy lions and old gladiators, at every molding row of stands where people will pack in to watch you die, you'll fight. You'll recoup all the money I lost on you. And outside the Colosseum where there's no one to keep track of the rules, they don't bother with rules at all, so when you die with your guts hanging down around your knees and a sword punched through your back, I'll be there to watch. And I'll smile, *dear boy*, because you're a bloody waste of good air."

"Not as big a waste as you," Arius said with dizzy cheer. "You rancid tub of lard." He screwed his eyes firmly shut as Gallus's thugs moved in.

He slept on his stomach that night, his back laid open almost to the bone by a rope soaked in brine. As his good humor drained away into agony, he imagined a cool hand on his forehead and a warm alto voice soothing him to sleep.

THE Colosseum stood empty that fall, and the gladiators of the big training schools kicked their heels back and took life easy. But fighting filled the streets, and in the thick of every fight was the Barbarian.

There were crumbling arenas where the sand was threaded with weeds and the seats packed with the dregs of the slum districts, hard shifty-eyed men who applauded only when the blood spurted, and never called mercy for brave losers. But when the Barbarian hewed a giant Spaniard in two with a single stroke, they roared to their feet in a howling storm of approval and flooded into the arena like the sea.

There were seedy taverns where the tables were cleared away so the knives could come out, and losers' bodies were dumped in the Tiber. When the Barbarian jammed a pair of slender knives up the nose of an Italian sailor, he was bathed in wine and hoisted around the room on the backs of his fans.

There were dark alleys in the slum districts where the arena was staked out with knives and street fighters killed each other over a few handfuls of copper coins. The Barbarian was pitted against three knife-wielding brothers from the Subura, and when all three lay still around his feet he turned and drove his sword through the foot of a complaining fan.

He fought when his trident-mangled sword arm was muffled in a sling, when a knife hilt had broken two of his fingers, when a slash across his forehead blinded him with blood. He fought with half-healed bones and torn muscles, black bruises and torch burns. He fought with swords and shields, with knives and nets, even with his naked hands as he demonstrated one warm autumn afternoon when, to howling applause, he crushed a man's windpipe with his thumbs.

He was the hero of the mob, the favorite of the slums, and the plebs of Rome poured their money uncomplainingly into Gallus's hand so they could pack into shaky stadiums and hang on his every move. They told their children he was a devil, they counted his scars and tabulated his kills; they howled and shivered and came back screaming for more. They whirled him, bloody and tired, to the taverns where he sat showered with wine and hung on by whores, lurking sour and murderous in his lonely corner and coming out of his lethargy only to lash at any fan who pressed too close.

The black demon in Arius's head ran joyously through a knee-deep river of blood and howled its happiness.

Five

⋐⋑

THEA

THE Empress?" Through the thicket of greenery in the conservatorium I heard the resonant voice of Senator Marcus Norbanus. "I have no idea if she'll be reinstated, Lady Lepida."

"But you know everything about the Imperial family." My mistress's sweet tones. I was down on my knees scrubbing the tiles of the fountain, and I couldn't see her face, but I could just picture the breathless way she looked up at her betrothed. "So tell me . . ."

They promenaded to the other end of the conservatorium, but I could still hear every word. Marcus Norbanus may have been nearly fifty, but he had a fine clear voice, trained to carry to the farthest corners of the Senate house. "I've counseled for reconciliation. The Empress is popular, and with her reputation for virtue, no one believes her guilty of adultery except the Emperor."

"What about Lady Julia? They say there's trouble between her and her husband—will they separate, too?"

"No," Marcus said briefly. "Julia is . . . odd, shall we say. Fragile. She needs a protector. She looked to me for a time, after her father died, but I'm too old."

"You're in your prime!" Lepida's laughter made nothing of his forty-six years.

"No, I'm old." Suddenly his voice turned serious. "Do you want to marry me, Lady Lepida?"

That was too much for my curiosity. I lifted my hands out of the fountain and peered cautiously through the greenery. I saw my mistress's rich black hair, and Marcus's aquiline face brought down nearly on a level with hers by his crooked shoulder. Like his royal grandfather Augustus, he was not tall.

"You don't have to marry me, you know," he said as Lepida opened her lovely mouth. "I'm old, I'm hunched, and I'm set in my ways. No, don't interrupt. I spend half my time at the Senate, and the other half in the library. I write treatises, I despise parties, and I have a son two years your senior. Certainly I'm no match for a pretty young girl."

"I did wonder, Marcus . . . why remarry now?" Lepida's tone was demure, but I knew she was dying for an answer. "After so many years divorced?"

"I prefer to be alone." Marcus shrugged his crooked shoulder. "And even if I didn't, not many women would have a reclusive old wreck like me." I wondered if he had ever felt bitter about that, in his youth. Or even now.

"But with your rank, your education, your lineage—"

"Ah, yes, my lineage." A note of dry amusement entered his fine voice. "My imperial blood may have been come by illicitly, but I *am* the last surviving grandson of Emperor Augustus. Emperor Titus regarded me as harmless, but his brother has a more suspicious nature. Domitian likes to inconvenience me, and there are few ways to inconvenience a bachelor like forcing him to marry." He gave a courtly bow. "Especially to a beautiful girl like yourself, who is better suited for a young man."

I read neatly through that bit of flattery. What better way to keep a suspected rival down than to humiliate him— and what would humiliate a proud and austere senator like being saddled with a giddy child for a wife? Many middle-aged men might take brides of fifteen, regardless of Rome's snickering, but not a man like Senator Norbanus. No one snickered at Senator Norbanus, but thanks to an Emperor's spite, they would now.

Lepida, of course, missed the subtext. "So the Emperor *chose* me for you?" I could hear her nursing this bit of Imperial favor to her bosom. "Well, if he wants it—"

"No." Marcus's voice turned serious. "If you'd prefer another— and I'd understand if you did—then I'll refuse the match."

"You'd defy the Emperor?" Her eyes were very blue against the white *palla* she'd wrapped around herself in the fall chill. "For me?"

I took my eye away from the greenery. Poor Marcus Norbanus. Even a grandson of the shrewd Emperor Augustus could fall prey to a pair of sincere blue eyes. I busied myself quickly with the fountain tiles. Quintus Pollio was holding another banquet for the gladiators in a week's time, and there was already plenty to do.

LEPIDA

Y OU know, I've made up my mind about Marcus," I told Thea in the bathhouse, stretching myself out on the marble massage slab. "I think I'll marry him after all."

"My lady?" Thea's fingers kneaded my back. She might be gawky, ugly, sly, and rude, but she did have magic hands.

"Marcus. He may be old, but that just makes him easier to manage. I'll have him eating out of my hand in no time."

"Hmm." Thea sounded polite as usual, but I was never certain she wasn't making faces behind my back.

"Even if he's old and ugly and hunchbacked, he's still a senator," I continued. "And royal. Well, sort of royal. And I don't have to stay married to him forever—he'll just be my stepping-stone. Once I'm Lepida Pollia the beautiful senator's wife, moving about in all the patrician circles with governors and generals to choose from, well, I can take my pick, can't I?" Propping my chin in my hand. "Oh, I'm just full of plans. I can see everything unrolling out in front of me, exactly the way I want—more on the left shoulder."

"Yes, my lady."

"Be gentle. I'm still feeling bruised." What bruises, though! Two nights ago Father had hosted another banquet for the gladiators, and the Barbarian had once again been the guest of honor . . . I had the slaves mix Father's wine twice as strong as usual, and he never noticed when I slipped off the couch into the dark garden, where the Barbarian stood swaying on his feet and looking up at the cold distant moon.

"A lovely moon," I'd whispered, and I kissed him . . .

"I finally got him," I said to Thea with satisfaction, and turned on my side on the massage slab so she could reach under my arm.

"My lady usually gets what she wants," Thea observed. I twisted for a look at her, frowning, but she looked as blank as ever. And she had a point, didn't she? I usually *did* get what I wanted, and I wanted the Barbarian. In the dark garden his hands had landed on my shoulders, perhaps to push me away, but his fingers dug into my flesh and his teeth had drawn blood from my lip.

"It was all terribly thrilling." I lifted my arm so Thea could massage my side. "He's such a brute. He'd have dragged me off and had his way with me, if his *lanista* hadn't come out just afterward." Too bad . . .

"Sandalwood oil or jasmine, my lady?"

"Jasmine. I wonder what Father would do if he found out—" I giggled, arching my back. "He'd be furious. But really, what's the difference between what I want and what all those patrician ladies want?"

Of course it would be an enormous scandal—a young girl of good birth, seduced by a gladiator. But didn't that all just make it more thrilling?

"And really, why should absolutely everything go to Marcus?" I mused aloud. "Why shouldn't *I* get something? I know enough to act scared on the wedding night, and bring a little bag of chicken blood to the bed like all the brides do, in case the husband's too drunk to perform. But this way I'd have something else to bring to bed. Something to think about while I've got boring old Marcus draped all over me." I closed my eyes as Thea dabbed jasmine oil behind my ears. "I'd have a pair of big strong arms to think about instead of—"

"My lady," Thea interrupted me—*interrupted* me! "I don't want to hear about it."

"You don't?" My eyes snapped open. "Why is that, Thea? You're no Vestal Virgin. I've heard you panting under my father often enough."

"I'm sorry, my lady. I spoke out of turn." She busied herself among the perfume vials and massage oils. "Would you like your robe, now?"

"I know why you don't want to hear about it, Thea." I smiled, feeling a little thrill of satisfaction inside. Finally something had cracked behind that long blank face of hers. "Because you're jealous. Yes, you are. You've got a little crush on the brave, savage Barbarian, haven't you? Were you hiding behind a bush last night, watching when he kissed me? Were you just aching and wishing it was you?" I uncoiled languorously, rearing up so close I could feel Thea's breath on my face. "Shall I tell you what it's like, Thea? To be crushed by those hard arms, yanked off the ground by those callused hands, scraped by that rough jaw—"

Her face was like wood, but her eyes hated me.

"Poor little Thea," I smiled. "I'll give you a few coppers next time we go shopping, and you can buy one of those garish little portraits the vendors hawk by the Colosseum. Hang it around your neck on a ribbon, and sleep with it under your pillow—"

"Will that be all, my lady?"

"Yes, you can go. I'm quite finished with you." For now, at least. Once I had the Barbarian in my bed, I'd make her watch.

G ALLUS had begun letting Arius out in the evenings. He tried running, but these days he was recognized before he got ten steps. No use. Easier just to get drunk.

"Water," he bit out, ducking through the door of the Golden Cockerel, a flood of his fans banging raucously after him. "Wine. Food." He flipped a coin at the tavernkeeper.

"No, no, everything for the Barbarian is free! Such a splendid fight this afternoon! When you disemboweled the Greek—"

"Forget the food." Arius flung himself down at the corner table. "Just wine."

Drink and fight. Blood and wine. *Drink the blood, dear boy, spill the wine; it's all the same thing.* He stared into the mug.

"Careful," someone whispered nearby. "Just last week he broke someone's jaw for getting too close—"

Drink and fight. *Take it, swallow it, choke on it; it's all you get.*

The mug made a fine crash against the opposite wall. His fans cheered and followed suit, nine more mugs shattering to the sound of drunken applause. He could have pitched them all out into the darkening street.

Then a section of brown tunic and a neat work-hardened hand blocked his vision. "Arius."

He knew the sound of her voice before it had finished his name. "Get out," he said quietly.

"For God's sake, I've spent half the night tracking you down. My mistress won't let me back in the house until I've found you. The least you could do is be civil."

He curled his fingers around the wine jug.

"I have a message to deliver." Thea's voice was toneless. "My mistress wants you to meet her in the Gardens of Lucullus tomorrow at midnight. She's already bribed your *lanista*. You understand? Good."

For the first time he looked up, but she was already vanishing into the throng. He saw her briefly at the door, buffeted by a crowd of drunks as she slipped out into the street. He half-rose from his bench.

"Better hole up here for a while, Barbarian." The tavern-keeper thumped down another brimming mug. "Looks like the first of the winter storms is on its way. Only the pickpockets and the murderers are out tonight."

A crowd of plebs flooded in, struggling out of their cloaks and swearing. Arius grabbed his cloak, making for the door. A cluster of fans rose to follow him, but he rounded on them.

"You follow me," he said, "and I'll kill you."

Some followed anyway, but he knocked a few heads together, tossed a third man into the hearth, and while he was yelping and putting out his blazing hair Arius ducked out the door.

It wasn't raining yet, but it soon would be. He could smell it when he lifted his nose up to the iron-colored sky. The wind blew cold for the first time in months, and he shook back his hood. The first rain since . . . how long? He'd missed it.

He found Thea halfway down a tenement side street. Walking tall and straight, arms swinging easily at her sides. He caught up in a few strides. "Stupid," he said roughly. "Stupid to walk alone in this part of the city."

"My mistress is expecting me." She looked straight ahead, ignoring the dust that a spiteful breeze blew up against her face. "Lady Lepida Pollia doesn't wait."

"It's going to rain."

"No matter. I like rain."

They walked along in silence.

"You fought well today, Barbarian."

He shook the dust out of his eyes; the wind was picking up. More silence. They rounded a corner, ducked into a new gust.

"Who are you killing?" Thea's voice was barely audible over the pulse of the wind. "You don't kill for the fun of it. Or the applause. Or the money. So who are you really killing when you put your sword through all those Greeks and Thracians and Gauls?"

Gallus. The Emperor. The crowd. "Everyone."

"Even me?"

"Just—just once."

"Only once? Oh."

"The Amazon. Remember? She had—she had dark eyes—desperate, but not—and your eyes, they—" He stuttered to a halt, struggling for words. "Never mind."

"You killed her."

"She wanted it."

"What if I wanted it?" Thea halted in the blustering wind, tipping her head back. "Right now. Would you finish me off? I've been trying for years, a bowl at a time, but it's obvious I'm getting nowhere." She held out her hands, palms up. The scars along her wrists gleamed white. "Would you kill me, please?"

"What?"

"Here, I'll even start it for you." In one swift movement she stooped, dislodged a sharp stone from the road, and raked it down her wrist. Blood welled, sickeningly vivid in the gray light. "Finish it."

"No." He looked at her, looked and couldn't look away. He wasn't any good with words. "No."

For a moment she gazed back at him, her dark eyes as savagely miserable as the Amazon's. Then she pulled her bleeding arm close, cradling it against her breast like a baby, and pulled away. As she turned, her sandal strap broke and she tripped.

He caught her before he even realized she was falling, lifting her off her feet in both arms before she could sprawl across the hard stones. She caught at his shoulder, her work-hardened hand curling against the nape of his bare neck and leaking blood. He clutched her awkwardly off the ground as the wind tore at her hair, and he wanted her so badly.

He dropped her, and they stared at each other. Her mouth, he thought, would taste cool and sweet.

The first clap of thunder roared overhead, and they looked away. For the first time Thea seemed to feel the cold; she crossed her arms over her breasts and the sight of her bleeding wrist hit him like a stone barrier. "I—I should get this tied up," she said, and he nodded dumb agreement.

There were no shops, no taverns to duck into. Only a dark vestibule to a tenement house, the door barred. Arius banged, but no one answered. The wind picked up, blowing dust down the road in buffeting clouds, and he could see flickers of lightning beyond the distant edge of the Colosseum. He groped for words, any words. "Your mistress. She'll be angry?"

Thea looked at him blankly. "Oh. Yes. But—never mind, I'm used to it."

His arm brushed hers in the cramped doorway. They both jerked back. She bent down to fix the broken strap of her sandal. Her tunic molded flat against her spare body; he could see the supple brown curve of her waist, her back . . . He turned away.

Out of the corner of his eye he could see her hands swiftly tearing a strip from the bottom of her tunic and doubling it around her bleeding wrist. She tied it off neatly with the cord that fastened her braided hair, and the long plait unraveled down her back. She shook her head forward, and the dark sheet of hair hung past her waist, a wall hiding her face. Through the wall he could see flashes of her profile, her straight nose, her mouth.

He reached out.

In his head he heard a voice, too low and pleading to be the demon: *Don't hurt her.*

He stirred the ends of her hair with his fingers. The dark strands were silk against his palm and smelled like the coming rain. He gathered up a handful of her hair and carried it to his mouth.

She turned, eyes flickering toward him with a wary despairing hunger, and a sickening surge of memory flooded his mind: all the times in the arena when he had locked body against straining body, and the end had been a hot spurt of blood and a fading life. The Amazon died again in his eyes, turning into Thea, and he nearly told her to go away then and go away fast before he killed her, too . . . But then she leaned forward to lay her cheek against his throat and kiss the pulse behind his ear, and the arena disappeared, taking the blood with it. His hand tangled fiercely with hers; he felt her bones creak in his grip, and had to remind himself to be gentle. He had never been gentle with anyone in his life. He traced her lips with his thumb and then his mouth, felt her lips part beneath his own, and a stab of joy rocked him to the soles of his feet.

They slid against the wall to the ground, his cloak pillowing the stones under her head, and her hands slipped through his hair as he folded his body awkwardly into hers. He kissed the hollow of her collarbone, his hands following her back's pliant arc around to the soft curve of her breast, and something caught at his throat, something so alien it took him a moment to recognize it as happiness . . . Her skin was warm and sweet, and he never wanted to touch a sword hilt again.

T HE rain came down at last, drenched the streets, moved on. "Well, the *idea*—get out, you riffraff, off my doorstep!" An outraged voice trumpeted behind them as the vestibule door opened suddenly and torchlight flooded the doorway. Hastily they pulled their clothes about them and escaped in opposite directions, pursued by curses.

THEA

H E did not come to meet my mistress in the Gardens of Lucullus. She paced and shrieked for a while, her enticing sleeping robe billowing in the cool breeze that was perfect for trysting, but I heard nothing. Lepida raged all the way home, stiffing the hired litter-carriers of their tip and stamping back to her solitary bed, and none of it registered. *My Arius, not yours.* Mine for more than just one short hour in a cold doorway.

The house was asleep. I stole quietly through the dark halls, my heart knocking like a drum, and paused outside the door of the bathhouse. I stripped my hair out of its plait, covered my face with my hands for a moment because surely it couldn't be right to show this much happiness . . . and then I stepped inside.

Before my eyes adjusted to the darkness, I knew he was there. Before the faint rustle reached my ears, I knew he'd risen from the corner where we'd first met. Before my fingers touched flesh, I knew his hands were outstretched toward mine.

"Thea?"

"Yes?"

"Nothing." His hands gripped mine, engulfed them. "Thea. Thea."

He bent down, scooping me easily off my feet, and I shook my hair forward around his face, making a private cave just for the two of us.

Sanctuary, I thought. After that I didn't think at all.

Six

❦❧

"WELL, well." Gallus arched his plucked brows, stroking the arm of one of his slave boys. "Aren't we in a good mood this winter. No broken chairs, no smashed mugs, no ears lopped off my fighters—my wine cellar is all but untouched—why, I don't even think you've put a knife through a patron's foot for at least a month."

"Stuff it," said Arius. But amiably.

A busy winter. No more seedy arenas or back-alley rings; the Colosseum had been thrown open to the mob. The Emperor had come back to Rome just long enough to reconcile with his Empress before heading back up to Germania in a foul temper, but the games-loving Spaniards were in town and eager to be entertained. They packed into the tiers in their unaccustomed furs, shivering in the keen cold winds, and Arius fought for them. He fought Serpicus, the trident fighter with live snakes on his helmet; he fought Lupus, a German in wolf skins; he fought a Spaniard imported from Lusitania to uphold Spanish honor. They all met their ends in the Colosseum, to the sound of frenzied cheering. "For God's sake, can't you get yourself wounded?" Thea groaned. "Then for a nice long month or two you'll get to lie in bed with no sharp things trying to poke your life out, and maybe I'll get a little peace."

"No, you wouldn't." He lifted her up, squeezing her so hard her ribs creaked. "I'd drag you to bed with me."

"Mmmm." She kissed the scar that interrupted his eyebrow, making his flesh shiver. "I like the sound of that."

"Thea." He cupped her chin in his hand, tilting up her face. "Stay away when I fight."

"Lepida makes me come."

"But I don't want you watching when—" He broke off, but the sentence continued itself silently. *I don't want you watching when I'm killed.*

He lowered his face into her hair as she wound her arms around his neck. The next week, fighting a Gaul, he took a trident through the shoulder.

The Gaul took Arius's sword through the mouth.

"I still won," Arius pointed out to an irate Gallus as the barracks doctor cleaned and bandaged the triple wound.

"Yes." Frowning. "And since you can apparently fight with your right hand as well as your left, I'm not canceling your bout next month. You have *commitments*, dear boy, so don't think you can cry off just because someone pricked you with a trident."

"Bastard," Thea fumed that night. "I'm going to learn how to hex, just so I can put a curse on Gallus."

Arius threw back his head and laughed.

"Don't laugh; it's not funny. Well, I suppose it is, but . . . I take it back, about wanting you to get wounded. I'll worry more than ever, since you're fighting in another fortnight. Does it hurt?"

"It'll still carry you to bed." He scooped her up to prove it.

"You could just let me *walk* to bed." Thea snuggled her head against his shoulder.

"I'm a barbarian." Murmuring against her throat. "We always carry our women off like sacks of grain."

"If you're capable!" She poked his bandaged shoulder.

"Capable?" He flung her down across the bed, tickling her until she shrieked.

"All right, all right, I take it back! Stop it, you'll kill me!"

"Good," he growled, and covered her mouth with his.

Grabbing moments with Thea was surprisingly easy. There was hardly a day she couldn't snatch an hour away from running

errands in the forum and steal up to Mars Street. As the nights
got longer and darker, she began slipping out of the house and
through the garden gate to meet him. "Stay out of sight," she
warned, her bare arms prickled with gooseflesh in the cold. "If
Lepida sees us—"

"You shouldn't come, then. Not safe." He drew her inside the
warmth of his cloak and gripped her tight, a tumble of incoher-
ent endearments running through his mind; all the things he
wished he were clever enough to say properly.

"What is it?" Her eyes saw right through him.

"Nothing." He pulled her close again. He didn't know how to
tell her that his knees dissolved every night when she ran
through the door of his cell to land laughing and breathless in
his arms. There were no words. All he could do was show her.

"Arius," she laughed when he wrapped his arms around her.
"I can't breathe."

He'd never had another woman before her, but that wasn't
why she turned his bones to water. That was just Thea herself.

YOU'RE softening," Gallus said with disapproval. "Yes, yes,
I know you're still packing them in, but I know you, boy.
You've gotten cautious, that's what. And caution doesn't win
points in the Colosseum." Sighing. "It's the Pollio slave, isn't it?
Don't look so surprised, dear boy. I know she's giving you
something else besides letters these days. Well, better Lepida
Pollia's slave than Lepida Pollia, but still . . . if she's the one
who's making you lose your form, I've half a mind to send her
packing—"

Arius had both hands around his *lanista*'s throat before Gallus could blink. "Don't," he said. "Or I'll squeeze."

"That's the spirit!" A rapidly purpling Gallus patted Arius's
shoulder. "A little more of that in the arena, please. You can, ah,
let go of me now, dear boy."

He hated to admit Gallus was right, but Thea wasn't good for
him. Not that he'd told her so, but he'd lost his edge. Still, his
luck had held so far. Every time the games attendants dragged
a fallen enemy off through the Gate of Death, he'd been able to
think, *a few more weeks with Thea.*

"I'll bet you say that to all the ladies," she teased him one
night when he said as much. " 'A few more weeks with Sulpicia,

with Cassandra, with *Lepida*—' " She shrieked as he tipped her over onto her back, trapping her between his arms like a mouse under a cat.

"None before you," he whispered into her ear, "and none after."

"None before me?" She cocked her head in genuine interest.

He shrugged. No need to tell Thea about the demon, and what the demon whispered that a man should do to his women. Thea and the demon didn't belong in the same room. He smoothed a hand over her face, and wasn't afraid of hurting her anymore.

Some evenings she sang for him, drawing his head into her lap and stroking his hair as she crooned the melodies of Greece and Judaea and Brigantia. Her rich alto resounded in the pit of his stomach, washing up through his spine and sinking into every muscle until he fell asleep wrapped in the music of her hands and her voice. "Witch," he told her. "That voice of yours is a wand."

Sometimes they lay with their hands entwined on the pillow between them, silent as the circles of standing stones that marked the holy places in Brigantia, and her eyes swallowed him up whole. "What are you thinking?" he asked, as his hand memorized her cheek, her throat, the fall of her hair. She always shook her head, pressing her body hard against his so there was no space left between them, and they fell asleep intertwined like the roots of a tree. When he woke, her eyes would be open already, and her mouth curved in a smile that made him shiver with pleasure.

Sometimes she traced the map of scars on his body: the ragged lattice of whip marks over his back, the puckered marks of stones and lacerations on his feet, the sharp lines of blades and tridents marking his shoulders. "And this one?" she would ask.

"Slave driver broke my elbow with a club."

"And this?"

"Knife fight in the Subura."

"And this?"

"The tattoo for Gallus's fighters. Supposed to be crossed swords."

Thea peered at it. "Looks like crossed carrots." She fingered the scars and the tattoo, smoothing them gently so he felt clean and young and not too bitter to be happy.

"Don't fancy her myself," a Thracian told Arius, watching

Thea swing out into the street. "Not enough hip on her. That mistress of hers; the Pollia girl—now there's a sweet mouthful."

Arius knocked the Thracian's head against the wall, but not with the black fervor of the past. The demon whined on its leash but seemed very far away.

THEA

"YOU'VE got a lover, haven't you?" Lepida asked suddenly one evening as I stood behind her combing her hair.

My pulse leaped, but I kept the silver comb moving. "Pardon, my lady?"

"A lover, Thea. A man. You do know what those are?" Oh, she was foul-tempered this winter. "Who is he?"

"He?"

"Oh, don't give me that blank look. You know exactly what I'm talking about." I saw her blue eyes narrow in the mirror. "No secrets between maid and mistress. Tell me."

You'll have to give her something. "How did you know?" I asked, low-voiced.

"It's obvious, really. Dreaming through your errands, smiling into the soup. And you were gone far too long at noon today for a simple shopping trip. So—who is he?"

"Um. He's—" Damn her sharp eyes. I pulled the comb through her long black hair again, wishing I could yank it all right out. "He has a tavern. In the Subura."

"A tavernkeeper in the slums? Oh, Thea, what a prize. What else?"

"He has, um, black hair. He's from Brundisium. He has a scar over his knuckles. From when a drunk pulled a knife."

Lepida laughed. "And does he want to marry you? No, let me guess: He's married already!"

I took my cue, muttering, "Well, she's gone most of the time. They don't get on."

"I'm sure they don't. From gladiator to tavernkeeper, Thea—I always knew you had low tastes. In fact—" She twisted, eyeing me. "Lift your hair off your neck. Goodness, a bruise of passion?"

"He loves me hard," I murmured in Greek, and hid a smile of foolish happiness.

She caught it, and something in her face soured. "Run along back to your slums, then!" she snapped, and whirled back to her mirror.

Too close, I thought as I put down the comb. But to Arius that night, I just laughed. "Don't worry, I put her off the scent. Maybe it's a good idea she noticed. From now on whenever I run off to you, she'll think I'm running off to the tavernkeeper."

"So who's this tavernkeeper?" He bit my earlobe. "Can I kill him?"

He fought in the Colosseum a fortnight later. An enormous Trinovantian; a close and grueling fight. They slashed and battled across the sand for twenty minutes. I couldn't have moved to save my life, but Lepida was too busy sulking to notice my frozen figure.

"Really, I don't see what everyone makes such a fuss about," she pouted. "He's just a big ugly barbarian."

"The mob dotes on him," Pollio said absently. "Do admit, he's splendid. He's got the Trinovantian on his knees—"

But for all Arius's disdain as he stalked out through the Gate of Life, he was bloody and winded. And a voice in my head whispered, *How long before he's killed?*

I prayed at every temple in Rome. I visited witches and astrologers and fortune-tellers. I spent the coppers I had earned singing and bought charms by the armload. I wore down my knees praying to every god and goddess I'd ever heard of, and quite a few I hadn't. Arius was highly amused by my efforts, or pretended to be.

"You only believe in one God," he pointed out one long night.

"Yes, but my God is the god of the Jews," I said, curling against him under a scratchy blanket. "He'll look out for me because I'm one of the Chosen People, but He doesn't care a thing about you."

"I don't care about him." Arius ran his hand up the length of my back, leaving a trail of tingles and shivers. "So we're square."

"Who are your gods? Maybe I can pray to them."

He propped himself up on one elbow, looking down at me with the rare boyish grin that utterly banished his usual stoniness. "There's Epona. Goddess of horses."

"What can she do about the Colosseum?"

"Artio, then."

"Who's she?"

"Goddess of the forest. Also of bears," he added gravely.

"Be serious."

"There's Sataida. She's the lady of grief."

"That's better. I'll tell her not to kill you off and come paying me any visits."

"You'd grieve?" His grin slipped away.

I'd die.

I didn't say it aloud. That would be to tempt God, who doesn't like to take second place in any human heart. But Arius's sword-roughened hand slipped through my hair as if to feel my thoughts on his fingers, and then he caught me up so hard and close that I had no time for any thoughts at all.

A RIUS?" I whispered through the dark.

No answer. I felt the whisper of his breath on my bare shoulder.

Careful not to wake him, I turned my face into his hard chest. I closed my eyes against the blackness. And I spoke, softly and formally in the Hebrew of my childhood.

"Arius. Arius, Arius, Arius, I love you. I love you.

"I love the way you rub the scar on the back of your hand when you're nervous. I love the way you make a sword into a living part of your body. I love the way you burn your eyes into me, as if you're seeing me fresh every time. I love the black streak in you that wants to kill the world, and the soft streak that is sorry afterward. I love the way you laugh, as if you're surprised that you can laugh at all. I love the way you kiss my breath away. I love the way you breathe and speak and smile. I love the way you take the air out of my lungs when you hold me. I love the way you make a dance out of death. I love the confusion I see in your eyes when you realize you are happy. I love every muscle and bone in your body, every twist and bend in your soul. I love you so much I can't say it out loud in the daylight. I love you. I love you. I love you."

I breathed in the smell of his hair, the exact texture of his skin. Took him whole inside me. Murmured, finally, a prayer.

"God keep you safe."

And I slept.

Seven

※ ※

THEA

"ONE against six!" Lepida fanned herself prettily with one hand. "I can't wait. Goodness, when will they finish off those zebras so we can get to the fun part?"

My hands shook as I poured her wine. Distantly I heard the crowd roaring, the snap of the whips from the arena, the animal screams. The Agonalia games, celebrating the double-faced god Janus who ushered in every new year. A wild beast hunt raged in the arena below, striped zebras being hunted by teams of spearmen. But the zebras were just a prelude to the big show: Arius the Barbarian pitted against six Spaniards.

One against six, I screamed inside. *One against six!*

Lepida had talked her father into it. "I know it's against the rules," she'd cooed. "But what a fight it will be! The crowds adore desperation."

"Beat them." I'd seized my lover's face between my hands that night, hearing my voice rising and hating it. "Promise me you'll live. Promise!"

He held me hard, made love to me fiercely, but he didn't promise. Too wise for that. After three months with him, I should have been too wise to ask.

"Thea, hurry up with that wine."

I passed the goblet over with cold fingers. In the arena the dead beasts had been raked away, and the midday executions

were briskly progressing. Preparation for Arius and the Spaniards. I reached under my tunic for the faded ribbon I'd strung
about my neck that morning. Hanging from it were a dozen
charms and medallions, spelled to ward away violent death.
Purchased from old crones and astrologers, witches and
fortune-tellers, to buy my lover his life.

Dimly I heard the voice of the games announcer: ". . .
bring to you . . . champions of Lusitania . . . the SPANISH
SAVAGES!"

Out they charged to a surge of applause: six sleek and vicious
fighters, swords glittering in the sun, purple plumes nodding,
bowing and waving and strutting for the crowd. Their breath
puffed white in the cold.

So many. God, so many.

". . . and now . . . wilds of Brigantia . . . undefeated
champion . . . ARIUS THE BARBARIAN!"

They'd given him a little platform to fight on, something to
even the odds, and he sprang up on it hefting his shield. Utterly
calm, indifferent to the wild cheers raining down on his head,
indifferent to the cold. But so small next to that terrible horde
of Spaniards. So terribly mortal. I thought of Vercingetorix the
Invincible, who hadn't been so invincible after all because he'd
died in the arena like an animal.

The starting trumpet blared. The Spaniards swarmed up the
sides of the platform. As one the crowd in the stands surged
forward, shouting encouragement. My heart dropped into my
stomach like a stone.

He cut down the first two as they got to the top of their little ladders. But there were two more clambering over the
other sides, and their blades rushed to meet his with a bite of
iron.

The Colosseum was on its feet shrieking, and so was I. Once
I would have felt pity for the Spaniards, who wanted to stay
alive just as badly as Arius, but love had made me vicious and I
just wanted them dead. Arius hewed a Spaniard's sword arm off
at the elbow, and in the midst of all my terror for his life I felt a
rush of fierce pride in his skill.

He whirled and slashed, unable to move three feet on that
tiny square of space, but still cutting them down on four sides.
The crowd settled back in their seats to place bets, the odds
dropping. Just when I began to breathe again, it happened.

Such a little thing. He ducked a wild swing of a curved blade, and for a bare moment lost his footing. Teetered.

Fell.

He landed squarely on his back, only a few feet down, but I could see the breath go from him in a rip. I saw his lips skin back as he gulped a convulsive breath, already raising his blade, and then the Spaniards were on him. Three Spaniards delirious with triumph, their bright weapons raised—and even so he managed to stab one through the knee before disappearing from sight.

I heard Lepida's fidgeting cease abruptly. I heard Quintus Pollio set down his goblet. I heard every spectator in the Colosseum inhale.

I dropped the flagon, feeling the wine splash across my feet as I leaped forward, falling against the marble railing and marshaling all the power in my lungs.

"MITTE!" I shrieked, and every Roman within a hundred yards turned their heads. "MITTE, MITTE, MITTE!" Let him live. Oh, God, let him live.

And because it was a fine afternoon and the games had been very good that day and the Barbarian really had fought splendidly, other voices joined mine. "Mitte! Mitte! Mitte!"

When I saw a bruised and bloody Arius drag himself grimly to his feet, my own limbs gave out underneath me and I hit the ground. Roaring filled my ears and something granite-cold cracked open inside me, melting like ice in the rain.

"Thea? Thea, whatever is the matter with you?"

I looked up dizzily. My mistress's face was a pale irritated oval. "Sorry, my lady."

"Screaming in public—a slave never speaks unless spoken to." Her sharp-toed sandal prodded my side. "Get up."

I levered myself up, clinging to the railing. The blood roared so loud in my ears that when Lepida poked at the ribbon around my neck I could only look at her vaguely.

"Well, well, what's this? Charms, Thea? So many of them, too. Whatever for?" She turned over a copper amulet inscribed in Latin on the back. " 'Warding away the bite of all weapons and blades.' And 'Invoking the protection of Mars against violent death.' Goodness, I don't beat you that hard."

"My tavernkeeper," I muttered, collecting my scattered wits. "He's gone to the legions—I just want him to be safe—"

She waved me back, sinking back into the cushions of her chair as Arius limped out leaning on a spear and the Spaniards took their bows. She sulked as the arena attendants raked the sand, fidgeting and tapping her gold-sandaled foot against the floor, and finally announced she had a headache and it was too cold to sit outside and she was going home at once, and I didn't even listen to her pouting because all I could think of was Arius.

I trailed her home, changed her dress for a robe, fanned her and massaged her scalp and fetched her barley water and waited in agony until she dismissed me, and then I ran all the way to Mars Street. "Arius," I panted to the pretty slave boy who opened the door. "Arius." It was the only word left in my brain.

"I'm sorry, he's not—wait!"

Arius sat, shoulders slumped and head drooping, in the middle of the infirmary, filthy with dust and bleeding in half a dozen places. He held a wad of rags against an oozing slash on the back of his neck while the barracks doctor fussed around him and Gallus scowled over a writing tablet. A dozen fighters lounged, watching with curiosity or downright satisfaction as the defeated Barbarian was patched back together.

I must have made some sound, because he glanced up. I saw the mess of cuts and bruises the Spaniards had made of his face and all my precarious calm shriveled away. I fell across the room, meeting him halfway, and turned my face against his ripped shoulder when the tears flooded my eyes.

Dimly I heard him slap the doctors away, snarl an obscenity over my head at Gallus, and heave the wad of rags at the snickering gladiators. He couldn't quite pick me up—pain hissed through his teeth when he tried—but he lifted me until my feet skimmed the ground and retreated into his little unlighted cell. Then he just held me, rocking me quietly in the cold dark while I clutched him and sobbed with all the hysteria I'd promised myself I'd never show him.

"Are you all right?" I mumbled at last against his chest.

"Just bruised."

"Liar." I took his hand in mine, kissed the two splinted fingers, ran my palms over the purple bruises that marked his arms and shoulders, felt him wince as I touched his side where the ribs had been broken. "What will Gallus do now?"

"Throw me back in. Prove I haven't lost the edge."

"You have lost the edge. It's me. I make you soft."

"Sssshhhhh."

"Games," I said, feeling the hysterical thread swell inside me again. "Games and games and more games—never-ending *games*—" My voice cracked.

He kissed me long and desperately, and I swayed against him in the dark, hopelessly loving the hard curve of his skull under his hair, the strong arc of his neck, the strength of his arms. "You lost today," I whispered. "You'll lose again, no matter how good you are."

"Stop, Thea."

The ragged cry ripped out of my throat. "I'm going to lose you, and you tell me to STOP?"

"No." He gripped me hard, pulling my head against his shoulder. "I'll live. I'll get a *rudius*."

"It's been years since an Emperor's given the *rudius*—"

"He'll give one to me. I'll give him a fight to knock his eyes out. Then we'll leave, get out of here—"

"I'm a slave. I can't go with you."

"I'll buy you." His voice was a low rush in my ear. "My prizes—enough to buy you three times over. Then when I get out of the arena—"

"You'll never get out. You'll die first—"

"I won't." He tangled his hands in my hair. "Thea, I promise. I'll live, and we'll get out of Rome. Find ourselves a mountain in Brigantia—"

How long did he talk, telling me about the house we would build, the children we would raise, the cool sweet air we would breathe for the next fifty years? I don't know. But he had never talked so long before, and underneath the harsh grate of his voice I heard for the first time the indefinable rhythms of his native language. And I wanted it: the green mountain, the half-dozen strong and russet-haired children, the sweet Brigantian air no Roman had ever breathed. And I wanted Arius. Arius old, with gray hair and no fresh scars.

"Hold me," I said, and his arms locked around my waist, soldering our bodies together until it was dawn.

D ON'T dawdle, Thea. We have a thousand errands to run." Lepida tapped the side of the litter, addressing the bearers sharply. "The Forum Romanum."

Her bearers, six matched blond Gauls, heaved the litter up onto their shoulders and set off into the morning crowd. I fell into step behind, humming under my breath. The winter air was sharp and cold, and the shouts of the vendors carried easily from street to street. Now that Lepida was safely in front of me, I let out the smile I'd been smothering all morning.

He's going to buy me. I'll be free. The freshest of the knife scars on my wrists had faded to clean pink lines, and I was happy. I didn't even realize I was singing until Lepida poked her head out of her litter and snapped at me.

"Stop that warbling, Thea." Tapping the side of the litter, so the bearers lowered her to the ground. She pushed back her emerald green *palla*, blue eyes scanning the crowd. "Wherever can he be?"

"Are you meeting someone, my lady?" A handsome young aedile or dashing tribune, perhaps? Yes, she *would* meet a man in the middle of the forum in broad daylight, with her marriage to Marcus Norbanus only a few weeks away.

She sent me to buy a little bag of candied fruit from a vendor before the Temple of Jupiter, and I wondered happily if Arius was arguing now with Gallus, persuading him to buy me. Gallus would moan and complain of course, but he wanted to keep his star fighter happy . . .

My mistress was deep in conversation—with a man, of course. No handsome aedile or dashing tribune; just a middle-aged man with a bald head and a coarse-grained toga. Business then; not pleasure. I wiped my smile away for later, and bobbed a silent curtsy as I handed over the candied fruits.

My surprise, when the bald man reached up and squeezed my hip, was total.

"This one?" he asked Lepida in a harsh, common-accented voice. "No beauty."

"Perhaps not, but she's got a good strong back. Isn't that more important in your line of work?"

My eyes flew up to Lepida's. "My lady?"

She picked through the candied fruits, still addressing the bald man. "And she's literate, you know. In Greek as well as Latin."

"Don't expect me to pay extra, Domina. Letters are no good to a whore. How old is she?"

"Fifteen. But experienced, I assure you."

"No!" Words tumbled frantically out of my mouth. "My

lady—I've served you well! Whatever I did, I'll never do it again, I promise. What did I do?"

Lepida's cool voice overrode me. "When she couldn't get customers, she serviced the gladiators for free. You see why I have to get rid of her."

"Maybe." A shrewd glance. "But you can't dispose of her, Domina. She's your father's to sell, not yours."

"My father never interferes with my doings. And besides, I'll give you a very good price for her. Say two thousand sesterces?"

"Done." He dropped a purse into my mistress's sugary palm.

I whirled and ran. Right into one of Lepida's litter-bearers, who wrapped my elbows in heavy hands and wrestled me down to the ground.

"No! No no no—"

"Be careful with her." Lepida tossed aside the purse that had bought my life. "She's a sly one. Half a chance and she'll slip the noose."

"Oh, I've been handling these girls for years." A flat palm stung my cheek. "Quiet, girl, or I'll have you whipped. Understand?"

Arius. Arius, where are you?

Just a few tenement blocks away, in his room on Mars Street. Dreaming of our mountain.

"You won't be selling her here in the city?" Lepida's voice again, dim through the blood that pounded in my ears. "I'll not have her embarrassing me here in Rome."

No. No. He'll come, Arius will come and he'll kill them all—he promised *me—*

"I do my business down south. Ostia, Brundisium, the port cities. Waterfront brothels pay well for Roman whores."

"Good." For the first time Lepida turned her gaze on me. "Well, Thea, I told you I wouldn't put up with it. Sneaking out of the house to carry on with gladiators—"

"You had me followed," I said hoarsely.

"Hardly. Just peeked out my window at dawn a few nights ago to see if you'd come back from your mysterious all-night errand. And there you appeared! Such a passionate farewell, too . . . I already had my suspicions, of course. Especially after that charming display at the games. When I saw all those magic charms of yours . . . *Not* very clever, dear."

The Gaul who held my elbows loosened one hand to scratch his cheek. I wrenched an arm free and hit my former mistress a savage blow across the face. One blow, before the bald man's hand shot out to seize my hair and snap my head back so hard the tears sprung to my eyes. "You didn't tell me she was vicious," he objected.

"No matter." Lepida climbed back into her litter, my hand-print scarlet across her cheek. I saw her pull out her little gold hand mirror and examine her face coolly. "She's your responsibility now." The silk curtains dropped shut, hiding her from view.

"Stand up, girl." The bald man frowned. "Can you under-stand me?"

Ostia. Brundisium. Port cities, waterfront brothels, unwashed men.

Just six hours ago I'd lain in Arius's arms and dreamed that nothing could ever hurt me again.

I made another despairing lunge toward Mars Street, and was wrestled down to the ground. I drew breath to beg and got a mouthful of dust. Sandaled feet stepped around me in the street: a party of tribunes enjoying a good laugh, matrons draw-ing their skirts aside, slaves who looked away before they could catch my bad luck.

My new owner surveyed me clinically. "Better put the chains on her," he rapped out to the big servant at his back.

They locked the manacles around my scarred wrists. I turned my face away and howled into the earth like a dying animal.

B UY her?" Gallus paused, lifting his pen from his account slates. "Dear boy, you don't have to buy her. You've been getting what you want without that, haven't you? Why buy a cow when—"

"My prize money would buy her three times over."

"Your prize money? Dear boy, who does the managing around here? Who does the organizing, the planning, the marketing?"

"Who does the dying?"

"But you're not dead, are you?" Gallus tapped soft fingers on a rouged cheek. "Well, you have been quite well behaved lately.

I suppose you deserve a reward. Win your next fight, and we'll see what we can do."

"Done."

Arius waited by the garden gate that night, but Thea didn't come. Well, she wasn't always able to get away from that ferret of a mistress. The bed seemed very empty without her. He missed the warmth of her body curled inside his, her fingers laced through his, her hair falling over his arm. He smiled, and it no longer felt unnatural.

He sparred the next afternoon with the trainer, then sat back to watch the beginners hack and slash at each other. "Keep your feet planted," he called out to an Oriental boy with a trident. "Here, let me show you—" and found himself drilling them, as his brothers had drilled him. As he would drill his sons some-day, his and Thea's.

"Barbarian," one of Gallus's pretty slave boys piped from the shade. "Your lady's here."

Arius sent the practice sword thudding point-down into the sand and swung into the corridor. He pushed open the door to his little cell, grinned to see her standing at the narrow window slit with her hood still drawn up over her face. "Thea, are you—"

He stopped.

"So sorry," said Lepida Pollia, turning and pushing the hood off her high-piled black hair. "Thea couldn't come."

He backed away instinctively, as if a viper had just reared up in his path.

"Is that any way to treat an old friend?" Lepida gracefully shook off her cloak, revealing a jade-green gown and a rope of pearls around her neck. "We were once such good friends, Arius. I remember a certain banquet at my father's house when you were *very* friendly—"

"Where's Thea?" The words grated harshly on his ears.

"Why, she's gone." Lepida perched on the edge of his bed, cocking her head like an inquisitive bird. "Quite gone, my dear Arius."

Something cold uncoiled in the pit of his stomach. "What do you mean?"

"My father sold her. The slave trader took her out of the city—oh, yesterday morning, I think."

Slave trader. "Took her where?"

"Now how would I know that?" Lepida examined her gold-lacquered nails. "I don't concern myself with slaves."

The room whirled and turned white. Exactly the same effect, he thought dimly, as being crashed across the head with a shield boss.

"—I know you were fond of her, of course," Lepida was chattering, "but she wasn't worth it. Really. She let every man in the house cover her."

Thea. Thea with her eyes half-closed as she sang, Thea laughing up into his eyes at night, Thea kissing him in a dark doorway and showing him how to be gentle. Thea.

"—I was really quite put out when you took her over me, you know." A soft little hand touched his arm, kneaded it. "But I think I could be persuaded to forget. Are you in a persuasive mood, Arius?"

Thea. Thea. Thea.

He reached out, curving his hand around Lepida's face. Her blue eyes sparkled, and she turned to sink her teeth playfully into his thumb.

"You—utter—bitch." He sank his hand into her hair and threw her against the wall.

She staggered, rebounding, and before she could lift a finger he'd seized up the knife on the bedside table and flung her across the bed.

"Where's Thea?" Blade pricking the soft white throat. "Where?"

Lepida heaved in a breath to scream and he covered her mouth with a hard hand. Sharp little teeth sank into his palm, no longer playful, but the demon was roaring in his blood and he felt nothing. "I'll carve you like a roast," he whispered. "Where is she?"

Lepida heaved uselessly under his weight, spitting threats against his hand.

He ripped the knife through her high-piled hair. Wrenched a severed black curl loose and jabbed it in front of her eyes. "I'll shave you bald as a leper. *Where is she?*"

The blue eyes spat poison over his palm.

He sliced off another handful of her hair. "Where is she?"

"In a whorehouse, that's where she is!" Lepida spat when he removed his hand. "A whorehouse, any whorehouse in the Empire where savages pay for their sluts."

Another fistful of silky black hair slithered to the floor. *"Where?"*

"Do you think I know? Do you think I care? She's miles away, that's where she is—servicing every brute in Ostia or Brundisium, and you'll never see her again!"

Another white explosion rocked his eyes, and Lepida Pollia let out scream after scream as he carved her hair to pieces. Her necklace snapped, pearls falling with a soft rattle like rain on an upturned shield. It took five of Gallus's thugs to pry his hands off her throat.

"Lady Lepida!" Gallus fluttered. "My sincerest apologies— the severest punishment will be—"

She shoved him away. Hideous now, Arius thought disjointedly, with her face mottled red with fury and her hair shorn within an inch of her scalp. He saw her mouth open, spitting vitriol, but nothing reached his ears. Even when they packed her out the door, still shrieking her vengeance, and Gallus laid into him, he didn't hear a word.

H E fought three Moroccans in the Colosseum the following month, and it was a fight no one would ever forget.

He slipped his blade through the ear of the first, then stove in the skull of the second with the boss of his shield, and when the third dropped his sword and raised a hand for mercy, he curled his fingers into hooks and ripped out the man's throat with his bare hands.

The mob carried him shoulder-high through the streets that night, breaking windows, breaking jugs, breaking heads, and he smashed and roared and caroused at the fore. He hoisted an entire barrel of wine over his head to drink, he shattered a drunk's jaw for stepping on his foot, and when a prostitute wound an arm around his neck and kissed him, he kissed her back and drew blood from her mouth. The winter dawn showed cold and steel-gray before Arius staggered back toward Mars Street, spikes of pain driving through his temples, his tunic stained with somebody's blood.

"So you're back," Gallus said coldly. "I should have you knocked on the head like a rabid dog."

Arius swayed, indifferent.

"But we can consider ourselves blessed, dear boy, for two

reasons. First, Lady Lepida Pollia evidently has elected not to inform her father of your appalling behavior. Or else we'd have had the Pollio guards knocking on our door calling for your blood. And second, the Spanish governor sent this, as reward for a splendid fight." He held up a heavy purse. "Keep the purses coming, gladiator, and I'll keep you. Hear me, boy?"

An eruption of animal snapping and snarling drowned him out. "Dogs," said Arius, weaving. "Killing something."

"I'm not finished with you yet. Come back here!"

Striding unsteadily across the street, Arius waded into the writhing mass of dogs. Growls became yelps as he booted them out of the way, and they fled snarling. All but the one they'd attacked: a silky little gray bitch covered in bite marks, one leg a tangled ruin. He dropped to one knee and pried up a cobble to crush its skull.

But the bitch had huge eyes that stared up into his. Dark, desperate eyes.

He dropped the cobble and scooped her up, careful not to touch the mangled leg.

"No vermin in my barracks." Gallus drew the folds of his tunic aside as Arius brushed past. "It's probably diseased."

Arius banged his door shut on the querulous words. He laid the bitch down on his bed and stared at her a moment. "You'll be dead by tomorrow."

He was surprised when the dog chewed feebly on his extended finger. Useless little thing. It would be kinder to wring her neck. He got some scraps from the kitchens, coaxed her to eat.

"Thea," he said, and his voice sounded loud in the still room. "Is that what I call you?"

The bitch started at the sound of his voice, the thin silky skin quivering in the cold room.

"No. Too scared to be a Thea. She wasn't afraid. Not of anything."

Except the night he'd lost his first fight, when she burst into the middle of the barracks with eyes like holes burned into her face and sobbed in his arms, saying that she couldn't bear to lose him . . .

"No name. You don't deserve a name—you'll be dead by morning—"

The nameless dog gnawed on a corner of his pillow as Arius buried his face in the bedclothes and wept.

THEA

I opened my wrist with one firm stroke of the knife, watching as the blood dripped out of the vein. No blue bowl anymore, just a common copper pot, but my wrists were latticed with fresh knife scars and I sleepwalked through my days with the old mists clouding my eyes.

"Thea!" The harsh shout of my pimp. "Thea, get down here!"

I tied off my wrist indifferently and rose, straightening the dark robe and saffron-dyed wig that marked me a common prostitute. I'd worn them for two months. I smelled like a hundred unwashed men: sailors, galley slaves, tavernkeepers. In Brundisium, over two hundred miles from Rome, we had all kinds.

"Thea!"

I swayed as I started down the rickety stairs, but it wasn't the bloodletting. I only drained a drop or two at a time these days. I wanted to lay my wrist open to the bone, but I didn't. There was a fierce little presence kicking inside my belly, planted during those few snatched hours in the cold barracks cell that had once been my heaven. Arius's child. It appalled me—but when I poised the knife over my wrist, the knife that would release a quick rush of blood and take the child with it if I bled enough, my hand stilled. *Bring a child into this life?* I told myself savagely. *A girl to be a whore like her mother? A boy to die in the arena like his father?*

But I couldn't kill it. Even if I wanted to, I didn't think it would die.

No child of Arius the Barbarian would ever be scared away by a little blood.

PART TWO

JULIA

In the Temple of Vesta

Gaius is dead. Executed for treason. My husband, my cousin. Dead.

I had to watch. His eyes accused me when the guards took him away. He is dead. I am alone.

"New rubies, Lady Julia?" Marcus asks me on his next visit.

"A gift." They wind my throat, a noose of scarlet flames. "From my uncle." He likes me in red. Not green. "My wife wears green," he said once. "And I hate her. You should wear red."

"He means the jewels for an apology," Marcus says quietly. "He does not hold Gaius's sins against you."

"Sins? What sins?" My voice sounds shrill. The words pour out, a torrent of them, and when I babble about voices in the shadows and eyes in the corners, Marcus looks troubled and draws me to sit on a marble bench in the atrium as he speaks of lighter things. He has been a great comfort to me. Sometimes he reminds me of my father.

"Grieve for Gaius," Marcus tells me. "No one will punish you for grief."

Gaius was never easy with me. After the first week or two he kept his own bed, and we met only at the dinner couch where he would look at me strangely and I would realize I had been muttering again, and biting my nails until they bled. He was angry with me when I refused to eat in his

sumptuous new triclinium with the carved golden beasts on the wall. "I see their eyes," I said in a small voice. "They watch me."

"Gods, Julia!"

But I've always seen eyes. My uncle's eyes most of all. He tells me I am to call him Uncle and not Lord and God. "Even a Lord and God must have someone who is not afraid."

But I am afraid. And he is lord and god, at least of my world.

"Like slates," I tell Marcus dreamily. "His eyes are like slates."

He looks troubled again. "Are you . . . well, Lady Julia?"

Vesta, holy mother, goddess of hearth and home. How I envy your Vestals, whispering about the temple in their white robes, untouched by any man under pain of death. I would have liked to be a Vestal. Here I am always safe, and I see no eyes at all.

Vesta, watch over me. I have no faith in anyone but you.

Eight

❧❧

LEPIDA
A.D. 88

EVEN my new pearls didn't console me.

"Get out!" I flung a scent bottle at Iris. "I can't stand your stupid flat face. Out!"

She fled, wailing. What a bovine slut. She turned my hair into a haystack every time she touched it. I'd send her to the slave market and find myself a new maid, that's what I'd do. A senator's wife deserved no less.

But what did it matter if my hair looked like a haystack? What did it matter, with *no one there to see me*?

"Lepida?" The familiar knock at my door. "I heard a crash."

"Just a perfume bottle, Marcus. Iris knocked it over." I arranged my face in a winning smile.

My husband entered, kissing my cheek in greeting. Ugly and out of place in my pretty blue and silver bedchamber, and smelling like ink as usual. "Down in the library again, Marcus?"

"I can't find Cicero's *Commentaries*."

"The slaves don't put your things away properly. You should take a firmer hand."

"No need. Poking through the shelves, that's half the fun."

Fun. Lepida Pollia, the toast of Rome, married to a man who poked through scrolls for *fun*. "How sweet," I murmured.

"And you?" His eyes caught mine. "Have you been keeping yourself amused?"

"Half my things aren't even unpacked yet. As for the city—"
I waved a hand airily. "Well, Brundisium may not be Rome, but
I imagine I can find something to do. There's a new production
of *Phaedra* at the theatre. Oh, and I bought more pearls. They
were so pretty I just couldn't resist." Dimpling.

"Buy what you like." He smiled. "See? I told you the quiet
would do you good."

"Perhaps you were right." I held my smile steady.

"Paulinus is coming for dinner tonight. And a few friends.
It'll be quite a party. You'll like that, won't you?"

Quite a party. Marcus's serious son Paulinus, and a few old
men droning on about the Republic. When for four years I'd
shared dining couches with senators, with provincial governors,
with the greatest patricians of Rome. "Of course I'll enjoy it,
Marcus. I'll tell the cook to make up some of that venison with
crushed rosemary that Paulinus likes."

"I've asked him to come early. Sabina loves his stories
before bed."

"You both spoil her," I chided. "She's got a nurse to tell her
stories."

"Can I help it if she likes Paulinus's better?" He kissed my
cheek again—ugh, that inky smell!—and quietly limped out.

I waited until he was safely out of earshot before I threw
another perfume bottle at the door. I hate Marcus! I hate him, I
hate him, I hate him!

PAULINUS Norbanus lowered his sword as his opponent doubled over. "You all right, Verus? Did I—"

"Hah!" Verus straightened, whipping his blade up at Paulinus's throat. "Knew you'd fall for it. Yield?"

"Yield."

They sheathed their swords, loping out of the heat of the
practice ring back toward the Praetorian barracks. "You've got
to go for the kill, Norbanus. Augustus's great-grandson? You're
just a baked clam."

Paulinus grabbed him in a headlock, and they wrestled
across the sunny courtyard. A pair of sparring Praetorians
dodged out of the way, swearing amiably. "Yield," Paulinus
panted, thumbs jammed into Verus's windpipe.

"Yield, yield."

They ducked into the Praetorian baths, stripping off their sweat-stained tunics and collapsing gratefully in the hot steam of the *laconicum.* Verus groped through the billows of steam for the wine decanter. "Going to Marcellus's dinner party tonight?"

"I can't." Paulinus swiped a towel across his forehead.

"Got another party?" Verus grinned. "Maybe an intimate dinner for two?"

"Nope."

"Oh, come off it. It's that singer you've been tagging after—Antonia?"

"Athena. And no, it's not her."

"Don't blame you; she's a nice piece. Pricey, though. Expects lots of little presents. How much is this intimate little dinner for two going to cost you?"

"It's my father, you ass. He's in town."

"Your father, eh? Didn't think he ever came out of the Senate."

"Don't you know anything? Senate's out for the summer. Like school." Paulinus waved the bath attendants away as they approached with oil and strigils. He never felt comfortable letting slaves scrape him down. Soldiers should look after themselves.

"Maybe I'll pay your singer a visit for you. Tell her how much you miss her, while you're off listening to all those backbone-of-the-Empire types declaim the virtues of the Republic in Alexandrine verse." Verus groaned as the bathhouse attendant dragged a strigil across his back, scraping away the sweat. "Or maybe I'll say you're paying court to that toothsome stepmother of yours."

"Hey," said Paulinus.

"Oh, don't start. I'm just expressing my heartfelt admiration for that absolutely mouthwatering creature who happens to be your legal *mother*—"

Paulinus flung a towel at him. In the ensuing scuffle, a tray of bath oils was knocked over. Paulinus waved the slaves back, neatening the little vials into soldierly rows.

"You know—" Verus flopped down on a marble slab, beckoning the masseur. "I've never thought your father would wed a girl a third his age. My father, now, that old goat's on his fourth. But yours—"

Paulinus drew the strigil down his arm, sloughing away the

sweat. He could remember thinking the same thing. "Father—this Pollia girl—well—she's a child," he had blurted out five years ago. "I'm sorry, I shouldn't—"

"A natural observation." His father smiled. "I know what people are thinking—old lecher, young girl. I don't mind giving people a laugh."

A rush of angry color flooded Paulinus's cheeks. No one was going to ridicule his father while he was there. "Who's laughing?" he demanded.

"Everybody," said Marcus dryly. "Don't bristle, boy."

"But if they're saying—"

"They're saying I've lost my head over a girl young enough to be my daughter. They don't know that the Emperor ordered it, rather against my wishes. Though I think we may do well enough together, Lepida and I." Marcus smiled. "I have no illusions, Paulinus. Not at my age. But Lepida likes me well enough, and that could be pleasant."

Paulinus was uncomfortably aware that his own mother had not really been . . . pleasant. "Pleasant?" his aunt Diana had snorted once. "Paulinus, she was a bitch on wheels."

"Aunt Diana . . ." but he hadn't really been able to refute that. He had only been three when his mother divorced his father, ten when she died, but even so he could remember her shouting and throwing things. Once, he recalled, she had dumped all one hundred forty-two scrolls of Livy's *Ab Urbe Conditi* into the atrium fountain. "Not a very good edition anyway," his father had remarked calmly.

Well, if his father wanted a little peace in his old age, then he could have it with his son's blessing, and no one was going to laugh. Not in front of Paulinus Vibius Augustus Norbanus, anyway.

Verus was still talking, voice muffled against the marble massage slab. "I know you're touchy about letting your father help you—though I don't see why; if he were my father I'd have begged a prefecture by now—but if you won't ask him for a transfer to the front in Germania, get one for me."

"Still dreaming of war and glory on the Rhine?"

"Every night. I wake up just as the Emperor's awarding me a laurel wreath and a triumph. If only we'd been with him at Tapae!"

"Sounds like they managed to cut a swath without us."

"Well, Domitian's taking after Emperor Titus, I'll say that for him. Get Rufus Scaurus talking about his campaigns with Titus in Judaea; he'll tell you the best stories—"

When Paulinus was a boy, his great dream had been to save the Emperor's life. To leap in the path of a poisoned arrow, drag down a charging assassin, slay an entire barbarian horde. Silly boyish dreams. Yet . . . to serve, just to serve! "To be a Norbanus is to serve," his father had taught him. To make his father proud would be better than any laurel wreath or triumph.

"Hey, wake up. Time to go bow and scrape to Father and his lovely, *lovely* wife." Wink, wink. "I'll give my regards to Antonia for you."

"Athena."

"Maybe I'll give her something else, too—"

Paulinus flung a scraper at him.

"LINUS!"

The cry went up as soon as he stepped over his father's threshold, and something assailed his knees. Paulinus laughed and leaned down to hug his four-year-old half-sister. "You've grown up, Vibia Sabina! Practically a lady." He ruffled her brown hair and she giggled. She was little, bird-thin, and bright-faced, and her birth had delighted him; he'd always wanted a sister. She was frail, and she fell into mild bouts of epilepsy, but her giggle was delightful. Marcus watched them both with a smile as he limped across the atrium with its blue-tiled pool and intricate mosaics.

"Sabina, where is your curtsy?" Lady Lepida glided in, all rose-red silk and pink pearls. Such a pretty little thing herself; Paulinus could hardly believe she was Sabina's mother. She looked too soft and doe-eyed to lift a child in her arms, let alone bear one. Sabina's little monkey face straightened, and she broke away to bob solemnly. He saluted her, Praetorian fashion, and winked.

"Much better," said Lady Lepida. "Run along, now. Marcus, your guests are here."

Sabina disappeared in a flash of yellow, her mother a bird of paradise gliding behind her into the triclinium of gray-veined marble. Marcus turned in Lepida's bright wake. "I'm sorry I didn't write earlier, Paulinus. A sudden arrival, I know."

"I did wonder. Change of plans?"

"Yes," said Marcus briefly. "I'll explain later. Now, I believe you know most of my guests. Drusus Aemelius Sulpicius, Aulus Sossianus, that obnoxious young Urbicus from the *septemviri*—he's clever, though . . ."

His father's dinner parties were infrequent and pleasantly similar. The same low-voiced guests reclining on their cushions, the same simple supper, the same white-bearded orator declaiming Greek verse (why were Greek orators always white-bearded?), the same philosophical banter back and forth across the couches. When he was a boy, these dinners had always bored him cross-eyed. They still did, but now he knew his father's table fed the best minds in the Empire. Once anyone started quoting Plato (and they always did) Paulinus was utterly lost, but there was something comforting about lying here on the cushions watching his unassuming father so easy among the great minds of Rome. Comforting knowing that your father was just as brilliant as you thought he was when you were a boy.

He looked better these days. Neater, more distinguished. Lady Lepida's influence, of course. Paulinus looked over at his stepmother.

She reclined against the cushions eating grapes from a silver bowl, the taut line of her throat very young and unprotected somehow. She'd barely said a word all evening. Paulinus felt a rush of sympathy for her. Naturally she must feel out of her depth, married to such a brilliant man. She really was very young—twenty-one, only two years younger than himself. And she hardly looked any older than she had at sixteen when he had first seen her in the red bridal veil. He smiled at her across the table.

LEPIDA

I hadn't been so bored since—well, I don't know when. Boring Marcus and his boring friends and that boring Greek orator and all their boring speculation about the Fate of the Empire. Every time I thought they were finally winding it up, someone would start up again on Plato. Or one of Marcus's awful treatises.

"I found your views on the declining birth rate quite interesting, Norbanus," Senator Sulpicius or Gratianus or somebody boring would say, and off they'd go for another hour, talking about Marcus's awful boring treatise, which I'd had to *read* last year just to keep him happy. Of course they all pressed him to read aloud from it, and thank goodness he refused, even though I could tell he was bursting with conceit. How simple he was. They didn't care anything about his treatise; they were just hoping for another free meal. Anyone could see that. Anyone but my stupid husband.

Paulinus was the last to leave. He insisted that Marcus take him upstairs first to say good night to Sabina. Just sickening, the look on their faces as they gazed down at the little bed. I didn't see why they were so fond of her. She looked nothing like me. One could hardly even take her out in decent society, not the way she fell into seizures in public places. Twitching, foaming brat. I should have known any child of Marcus's would be deformed. And she was Marcus's child; I'd made sure of that.

"I thought it went very well, my dear," Marcus said as we waved Paulinus out at last.

"Yes, darling." I smiled, and he raised my hand to his lips. I leaned forward and kissed him, and he cradled my face in his hands.

"Stay with me this evening?" I said archly. I had my own bedchamber—I'd insisted on it!—and Marcus never presumed without my invitation, but I allowed him regular access. These little shows of affection kept him happy, and my bills paid.

"My pleasure. After I've told Sabina her bedtime story."

Sabina, always Sabina. He doted on that stupid child. I sometimes wondered if having her hadn't been a mistake. It wouldn't do to be replaced in his affections by my own daughter, would it? But I smiled and murmured, "What a good father you are," and kept on smiling until his footsteps had faded off into her room, and then I poked my tongue out in his direction.

I stamped off to my bedchamber, regarding my reflection in the polished steel mirror as Iris stripped the pins from my hair. The rose-red gown suited me. I had the complexion for red, and not many girls did. Even the Imperial Lady Julia had looked sallow under her red bridal veil. My bridal veil, now . . .

My wedding day had been an enchantment. The white gown, the crimson veil, the procession, the sacrifice at the shrine— everything was perfect. Well, except for Marcus; he just looked old. Still, I found I could ignore him quite easily. At a wedding, the bride is the star. I even had a pair of gladiators to duel in my honor.

No, not the Barbarian. He'd been whisked away by his *lanista* on a tour of the provinces. Afraid of me, no doubt, and what I'd do if he dared show his face in Rome. Well, he should have been afraid. I would have thrown him to the lions without a moment's hesitation, and I still would. If he'd dared show his face at my wedding—!

Well. It was a marvelous day. Simply marvelous. But the night . . .

Marcus by rights should have carried me over the threshold, but he was too old and feeble. Paulinus carried me instead, and then everyone bowed out and left me alone with my new husband in the dark bedroom.

"Your hair—?" As I slid my red veil off, Marcus had gestured to the tumble of short curls that it had taken Iris and her hot tongs most of the morning to create. After Arius sheared me, I'd kept my head carefully covered until the hair grew a little.

"Oh, I got dragged off into a dark alley by a very nasty old woman with shears." Artlessly. "My hair is probably adorning some bald matron's wig at this very moment." That was the story I gave my father, too, when I came home from the gladiator barracks with my hair chopped within an inch of my head. Oh, I could have gotten Arius thrown to the lions, but I'd have had to explain to Father why I'd gone to his room in the first place, and even Father's indulgence had limits . . . No. Better to deal with Arius in my own time.

But by the time he'd come back from his yearlong tour of the provinces, Father had been promoted from organizer of the games to praetor—and I had no chance. Well, I'd get my revenge someday. I always did.

"At least they only took your hair." Marcus had been properly concerned, and I gave him my most bewitching smile. His eyes softened, and he took my hands. "Lepida, let me make something clear to you," he said as he sat down beside me. "What happens here is for you to decide. If you want this marriage to be in name only for a while, I understand that."

"Don't be silly, Marcus." I made my voice rich and teasing. "I want to be a proper wife. With children . . ." I embroidered on those themes for a while, and watched his eyes get soft, and as soon as I leaned over and kissed him, well, that was that.

It wasn't horrifying at all. Nothing to turn anyone's hair white. Marcus was just what I expected. Gentle. Tender. Considerate. A little *too* considerate. I don't want to be treated as if I'm made of glass. I like a little . . . handling. But of course I sighed and gazed up at him adoringly and said he was wonderful, and he never suspected that when I closed my eyes it was because I couldn't look at his bare crooked shoulder without being disgusted. But it was worth it, because he let me do anything I wanted. Go anywhere I wanted. Spend anything I wanted.

I sighed and ran the silver comb through my hair. What glorious years those were. Marcus trudging off to the Senate every day and me running off to dinner parties every night. Really, sometimes I felt quite fond of Marcus. I hadn't thought to stay married to him so long—I could easily have moved on to someone younger and handsomer within the year—but I learned fast that a permissive old senator is better than a jealous young soldier.

"You don't mind if I go out?" I always made sure to ask him every so often. "I do love parties and plays, darling. I'm just not brilliant and intellectual like you."

"No, you're young and lovely and utterly charming." He kissed my cheek. "So go enjoy yourself." I always thanked him sweetly before whirling off to my round of parties. What parties! Wine and music and handsome men who paid me compliments, men who pressed around my couch and told me I was beautiful, men who wouldn't have looked at me the year before, but who all wanted me now because I was Lady Lepida Pollia and I had a dozy old husband who let me do whatever I liked, and I'd made myself into the most beautiful woman in Rome.

I learned how to paint my face so I looked elegant rather than provincial. I learned how to knot my *stolas* carelessly at the shoulder so the silks looked as if they were about to slide off altogether. I learned how to sway and lounge inside those silks. I learned how to laugh with my eyes and promise unspecified delights with my lashes. I learned the drawling court jargon that revealed at once who was in the know and who was not. I learned that my father was considered rather gauche, really, and it was better not to be seen with him by anyone who counted.

I learned about the potions one could swallow to prevent children. I learned that a married woman could do anything she pleased as long as her husband didn't care, or at least didn't see. Oh, I learned a lot.

"How can you bear to leave Sabina?" Marcus asked me, hanging besotted over the cradle after our daughter was born.

"I don't want to smother her, darling." And off I went in jade silk or sapphire, revealing more of my shoulders than ever— thank goodness the baby hadn't thickened my figure!—to meet with senators and soldiers and tribunes, because a married woman with a child indisputably her husband's can do whatever she pleases.

"I've waited so long for you," Lucius Marcellus groaned, and Aulus Didianus, and that rather marvelous African trident fighter who never spoke much but was more than ready to *handle* me. I was quite put out when Arius killed him in the arena.

Marcus never suspected a thing. That was another lesson I learned. And how wonderful it all was, the parties and the jewels and the banquets and the men. Lepida Pollia, the toast of Rome. I'd always known it would be that way. Always. No less than I deserved.

And then—over. All of it. Stuck in Brundisium, a pretty little seaside town with airy summer villas and a sapphire-blue harbor and far too many exotic languages reverberating around its docks; a hundred leagues from Rome. And Marcus—ever-amiable, ever-obliging Marcus—suddenly a stone wall.

Iris's voice broke in on my thoughts. "Your sleeping robe, Domina?"

"Yes." Suddenly I was sick of the red *stola*. Red the bridal color, the color I'd worn when I'd married Marcus. Marcus, whose fault it was that I was stuck here.

Iris clumped away, and I contemplated my reflection in the polished steel. I looked utterly enticing. My hair had even grown out again, down toward my waist in a shining blue-black cascade. How could my husband refuse me anything?

WHAT happened then?" Sabina murmured, yawning.
          "We'll finish the story tomorrow, sweetheart. You're half asleep."

"No'm not . . ." She yawned again, and Marcus stroked the

feather-brown hair. It was as silky as Lepida's. He smiled, thanking his wife silently for giving him Sabina. His first wife hadn't wanted children; Paulinus had been an accident for which she'd heaped blame on Marcus. "Well, I hope it's my fault, Tullia," he had said, trying to make a joke of it, and she had grabbed up a marble bust of his father and heaved it at him.

"Well, I'm not Tullia," Lepida had teased in her rich voice. And in the first year of their marriage: Vibia Sabina.

"Good night," he told his daughter softly, and withdrew.

"Marcus?" Lepida called as she heard his footfall outside. "Darling, do come in. It's cold in that corridor."

What warmed him was her smile of welcome as she turned from her mirror, her black hair loosed down her back and the dimple winking in her cheek. "Sit down, Marcus. I've heated some wine."

He smiled back, and let her draw him into the warmth.

Nine

❧❦❧

THE bout was a Thracian with a net and trident, famed in Sili-
cia but shaking with nerves to be facing the Barbarian in the
Colosseum. Arius killed him fast and indifferently with a blade
through the shelf of the jaw and stalked out through the Gate of
Life. The fans cheered, and the demon went yawning to sleep at
the back of Arius's mind.

"Very good, dear boy." Gallus hardly looked up from his
accounting as Arius came back to the barracks doctor for his
usual examination. "Go get drunk if you like. Try to be back
before dawn, will you?"

There was the usual riot of games fans at the tavern, the
usual smash of wine jugs and windows. They knew to keep
their distance—it was July, the streets boiling under a blazing
brass sun, and everyone knew the Barbarian's temper was
black and short in the heat of summer. A girl approached him
with a nervous giggle. "I'm Fulvia," she said breathlessly as he
drank straight from an ale cask. "You're the Barbarian, aren't
you?"

He looked at her. Blue eyes. Fair hair. She'd do.

"I saw you today in the arena. You're a wonderful fighter—"

Arius jerked a thumb toward the stairs where the innkeeper
let him use a room. She giggled and raced for the bed. An unde-
manding girl. She didn't mind when he turned his face to the

wall afterward and fell silent. None of them did, those dozens of girls who had shared his bed these past years. They seemed disappointed if he talked, as if talking took the mystery away. They wanted the Barbarian brooding and silent and intact.

That was all right with him. He didn't want to talk to girls anymore. Not ever.

He used to see Thea everywhere. Every dark braid of hair had been hers, every narrow hip balancing a basket. His hopes had leaped and crashed a dozen times a day. Agony, but he missed it. Agony was better than forgetting.

Her face slipped his mind now, the exact arrangement of eyes and nose and mouth escaping him. He sometimes sat with his eyes squeezed shut, trying to remember until his head ached. If he forgot her face, he'd forget everything: the way she'd touched his scars, the way she'd coaxed him to talk, the way she'd convinced him that things like demons and blood and nightmares weren't real.

She was probably dead by now.

He left the blond girl soon after, padding silently through the stinking back alleys to Mars Street. Gallus's thugs let him in without a word: the star gladiator had no curfew. Gallus even gave him a small allowance. It had all become very civilized, except for the killing part.

His dog yipped as he came into the room. She lay curled on his pillow, gnawing a hole in a leather gauntlet. "That's the third set of gauntlets this year," he growled.

The gray bitch wagged her tail and hopped nimbly down to the end of the bed. She'd lost a leg to that pack of street dogs, but managed quite well on the other three. He lowered himself into bed with a groan, abused bones protesting, and the bitch curled herself neatly behind his knees. "You've got a nose for the soft spot, haven't you? Worthless dog." He tweaked her silky ear, and her dark gaze reminded him helplessly of Thea.

THEA

G RAY gown, silver bracelets, braided hair: my armor.

"Thea?" Penelope poked her head of gray curls into my neat little chamber. "You know you're to sing at the faction party before Senator Abractus's dinner?"

"Yes, I'm all ready," I answered, twisting a last bracelet into place and looking for my lyre.

"Larcius is lending you a big slave for an escort. Those charioteers can get rowdy."

"Dear Larcius," I smiled. My master. How I loved him.

After Lepida Pollia discarded me like a stained dress, I'd gritted my way through three months in a waterfront brothel. Three months of sweating grunting men: endured until they finished, forgotten as soon as they left me. My growing belly saved me; my pimp forced potions into me to make the child slip, but I vomited them up. When my belly made me too unwieldy for whoring, my pimp clouted me over the ear and looked about for someone who might take me off his hands. I was bundled off to a rather lovely little villa overlooking Brundisium's busy forum and was soon gazing at my plump and pink-faced new master. Just another pimp, I assumed.

But: "My steward tells me you have a lovely voice, child." The pleasant patrician voice surprised me, and so did the kindness of the eyes that assessed me. "He heard you singing on the windowsill of some deplorable waterfront establishment. What he was doing down in that quarter of town I shan't ask, but whatever his recreational tastes, his musical judgment is almost as good as mine. Tell me, can you sing 'Cythera's Eyes'?"

After an hour's recital in the sunny little atrium, my delighted new master—not, apparently, a pimp—called for the plain freedwoman who was more or less his wife. "Penelope, wait until you hear the newest acquisition. What's your name, child? Thea? She's marvelous! Who would have thought? She'll have to have lessons right away. A voice like that has got to be trained, nurtured, polished—can you play the lyre? Lessons for that, too. We'll launch you as a singer. Think of it!"

"Oh, shut up, Larcius," Penelope laughed. "You're confusing the poor girl."

She explained it all as she helped me move into a little room so airy and clean that I felt every bit the dirty whore in it. "Larcius buys musicians, you see. It's his hobby—'Larcius's Stable.' This house is stuffed full of flutists, drummers, lute players, a boy choir. Don't give me that look, dear, the choirboys are for *singing* in this house. Nothing but the best for Larcius; he's got a very good eye for talent."

"What's in it for him?" I said cautiously.

"The pleasure of hearing you sing." She patted my hand. "And you needn't worry about any of *that*, my dear. He doesn't bother the slaves. He's got a stuck-up wife in Rome, not that he ever goes to the city, and here he's got me. Now, when is the baby due? A few months? You just put your feet up—"

My baby came early, screaming like a demon and wringing me out like a wet tunic and my new master could hardly wait to begin my instruction. "You'll have to study this closely, child— Aristoxenus's *Harmonics*. It's critical that you understand enharmonic microtones—"

"Larcius, really," Penelope chided. "She only finished pushing a baby out thirty-six hours ago. And that's a big baby there," she added, eyeing the puce screaming bundle that was my child.

"Very big," I'd said feelingly.

"But she doesn't even understand the difference between the highest note of a *parthenios aulos* and the lowest of a *hyperteleios*!" Larcius protested.

"I want to begin my training," I broke in before Penelope could protest again. "I want to start now." Arius's son had come into the world howling the house down, chewing ferociously on his own wrist, his hair already showing in russet-colored spikes along his soft head, and I could hardly look at him without a knot of love and longing and pain rising in my throat. Much easier to think about the notes of a *parthenios aulos* than about what I could possibly name my new son.

Larcius plunged me into work. He bought me singing lessons and lyre lessons, criticized my technique minutely, taught me the tricks of performing. "Don't pander to the audience, Thea. Bring them in to you." How did he know so much? He was a patrician trained in Roman law who had never performed for an audience in his life. "Do admit, though," he said when I argued. "About music, I'm always right."

Penelope bathed me in milk to bleach the brown out of my skin, washed my hair in sage and elderflower decoctions to give it gloss, anointed my hands with butter to soften the old calluses. "You're an artist now," she said as she taught me the rules of fine dining and elegant conversation. "You'll need a performance name. Something cool and dignified, I think. Calliope, perhaps, or Erato—the muses of epic verse and poetry . . ."

So I went from Leah of Masada, to Thea of Arius, to a nameless waterfront whore, to Larcius's newest nightingale—and on the whole, life was good. All Larcius's musicians wore a little welded copper ring carved with his name, but otherwise his ownership sat lightly on us. So lightly, it was hard to believe five years had gone by. Five years of singing lessons, of practicing with my lyre, of chatting to guests and arguing with Larcius over song interpretations. Five years of musical engagements: intimate suppers demanding hushed love ballads, rowdy faction parties where only cheerful drinking songs would be heard. Five years.

As I'd done every night for the last five years, I finished armoring myself in my gray gown and silver bracelets, collected my lyre, and went to check on my sleeping child before going out. He was just five now, and he had a name, but it wasn't his father's. I never, ever thought of his father anymore.

I hear you've been paying court to a lute player recently. Or was it a dancer?"

Paulinus rubbed his jaw self-consciously. "Do you know everything, Father?"

"I keep my ears open, boy." Marcus's voice was amused.

"She is a very great artist," Paulinus said firmly.

"I have no doubt of her artistry, whoever she is." They turned out into the vine-veiled garden, Paulinus shortening his stride to meet his father's patient limp. Ferns glowed green in the sunlight, the blue-tiled fountain trickled placidly, and slaves moved past with jugs and baskets of laundry. They all had a smile for their master. "Isn't it time you married?" Marcus continued. "I should like a daughter-in-law."

"Bring a woman into the Praetorian barracks? The household gods would shatter."

"She could live here while you were on duty. The house is big enough for two."

"Is it?" Paulinus said doubtfully.

Marcus laughed. "Lepida's not the jealous sort. She'd be glad of the company."

"But she has friends of her own, doesn't she?"

"Yes." Briefly. "Not always the kind of friends I'd wish for her. A girl her own age, in the same house . . . it would do her good. And it would do *you* good, boy."

"A bachelor like you, singing the praises of marriage?" Paulinus smiled.

"I am now."

Paulinus looked at his father: the image of his austere Imperial grandfather in simple rough tunic and sandals, radiating contentment. Marcus smiled. "Care for some grapes? We've a fine harvest this year. So the steward says, anyway." He paused by the trellised vine climbing around the garden's pillars. "I'm trying to learn more about grapes. Thinking of writing a treatise, comparing the decay of the Republic to the decay of the vineyards in the fall. But I don't even know if vineyards do decay in the fall. All I know is that ripe grapes appear on my dinner table regardless of season. Here, try these."

Paulinus tried a grape. Sour and seedy. "I read your last treatise, on the declining birth rate and its solutions. Bit over my head, of course." He perched on the marble rim of the fountain. "What did the Emperor think of it?"

"The Emperor?" Marcus found another withered cluster of grapes. "I'd be surprised if he's heard of it at all."

"Emperor Vespasian always read your treatises." Paulinus quietly slipped half his grapes into the fountain behind his back.

"Domitian is no great reader. And if he does get around to reading it, I doubt he'll look on me with any favor. He dislikes political speculation."

"It's just proposed solutions for the birth rate. What's political about that?"

"He may see it as a criticism that he has failed to produce an heir."

"Oh." Paulinus digested that. "The Empress—well, ten years married and nothing to show but a few miscarriages. He'd be within his rights to divorce her—but you pushed to have her reinstated, so you must have thought her a wiser choice than . . ."

"Than?" A dry look. "It's not the Empress you're asking me about, is it, boy?"

"Well—it's none of my business, I'm not denying that—but even down here we get rumors . . ."

"You mean the rumors that Domitian has turned his gaze toward his niece Julia."

"I didn't think anything of it. People talk. But—well, he did execute her husband for treason . . . and Emperors have married their nieces before. Emperor Claudius's fourth wife—"

"Who poisoned his mushrooms. Not a very good precedent to follow."

"Well, Julia wouldn't poison anybody's mushrooms. I remember that much about her from when she was a child."

"Yes. The Emperor is quite fond of her."

". . . How fond?"

"It doesn't do to believe too many rumors." Marcus stirred the grape leaves with a gentle finger. "The Emperor executed Julia's husband, and since then has endeavored to make it up to her through his own rather abrupt brand of kindness."

Paulinus remembered the little princess who had been his childhood playmate: a solemn straw-haired girl, always the willing standard-bearer in his games. "I didn't really think those rumors could be . . ."

"Then why did you ask?" The dry tone returned.

"Well—my friend Verus, he's served palace duty. He didn't believe any of the rumors, either, but he said—" Paulinus stopped. "He said—you could see Lady Julia shrink. Every time the Emperor came into the room. Like she was afraid of him."

"Oh, she is," said Marcus. "But she's terrified of everything. She still sleeps with a lamp in her room, because she can't bear the dark. And even when Domitian is being kind, he sometimes frightens. These rumors, perhaps they only gained credence because Lady Julia herself believes in them."

"Believes in—?"

"You haven't seen Julia since you were ten years old. She's . . . not the same since her father died. She was always fanciful, but now she talks of eyes in the dark and sings to voices that aren't there." A pause. "The slaves say she starves herself. The Emperor had to have her forcibly fed, and she collapsed into hysterics and tried to tear her own hair out." Marcus's stern senator's gaze flicked up to his son. "This is for your ears only, Paulinus."

Paulinus nodded, swallowing. "What are you saying? You mean Lady Julia is—"

"Mad," said Marcus. "Though I like to hope she's only floundering out of her depth in a world too sophisticated for her. I could say the same for Lepida."

Lepida? Paulinus seized gratefully on the change of subject. "Why did you bring her all the way down here, Father? I heard she was the toast of Rome."

Marcus grimaced. "These grapes are terrible." He tossed the cluster into the fountain. "Your stepmother may look lovely and worldly, Paulinus, but she's still very young. Her freedom went to her head, and she fell in with—well, a fast crowd. I should have stopped it, but I didn't want to deny her her youth just because I'm old and tired and want to spend my evenings in a library. And she looked so happy, skipping off to her parties. It's hard to deny her anything."

Paulinus had a sudden vision of Lepida, laughing and oblivious in the middle of a viper pit. "What happened?"

"We dined at the palace every week. I shouldn't have taken her, but she begged so prettily . . ."

"And?"

"She caught the Emperor's eye," Marcus said simply.

A brief pause. "Oh," said Paulinus.

"I didn't think anything of it, at first. He watched her, but he watches everyone. But then last month Lepida received an Imperial invitation: dinner at the palace, without me."

"What did you do?" Fascinated.

Marcus shrugged. "Sent word back that she was ill, and would be going to the sea to recover. We left for Brundisium that evening."

Paulinus collected his thoughts. "How did she take it?"

"Stormed and cried a bit." Marcus lowered himself to the fountain rim beside Paulinus, resting his hands on his knees. "I don't think she realized what that invitation meant. She's an innocent in some ways. All she knew was that I was taking her away from her parties and fun. But she's settled down this past week."

"But Father, you don't even seem to hold it against him—the Emperor, I mean. That he tried to have your wife."

"Oh, he tries to have everyone's wives. Domitian likes anything in a *stola*. But unlike many of our previous Emperors, he doesn't much mind if a woman—or her husband—says no. There are always plenty of women in the world for him. He's back in Germania beating the Chatti now, and has probably forgotten Lepida exists."

"I don't understand him."

"Who understands an Emperor? An Emperor, Paulinus, is a man accustomed to absolute and godlike power. A man who plans for the good of thousands too often to consider the good of one. Even the best of Emperors is like that; even Emperor Augustus the God, our ancestor. Domitian is no Augustus; he's tricky and odd-tempered like all the Flavians. And he's no god.

But I've seen eight men wear the purple, and Domitian wears it better than many. I wasn't much impressed with him as a boy, but he's turned into one of the best administrators I've seen, and a fair general as well." Marcus looked at his son. "Will you do something for me, Paulinus Augustus?"

"Anything, sir." Formally.

"Watch over Lepida for me. I don't like to leave her, but I'm due back in the Senate in two weeks. She'll need company."

"On my honor." Paulinus snapped his best salute, realized he still had the grapes in his hand, switched hands, and nearly lost his balance on the fountain rim. "Well, you can count on me," he offered.

"I couldn't ask for more." Marcus smiled. "Now, what do you say we find ourselves some wine instead of these terrible grapes, and make a proper toast?"

"As you wish, sir."

They wandered out of the atrium, pacing identically with their hands clasped behind them, the twisted shoulder brushing the straight.

LEPIDA

I was destined to be a royal mistress. "Lady Lepida Pollia the Emperor's mistress"—how much better than "Lady Lepida Pollia the senator's wife." From the moment I first laid eyes on Emperor Domitian, I knew he'd be mine. All I had to do was, well, get him.

"My wife, Caesar," Marcus had introduced me at my first Imperial banquet. "Lady Lepida Pollia."

I curtsied very low. "Lord and God." That was how he liked to be addressed: Lord and God. I wouldn't mind being addressed as Lady and Goddess. Yes, I would like that *very* much.

I watched him all night, while Marcus droned on about taxation. Domitian was not unattractive. Tall. Heavy-shouldered. Ruddy-cheeked. A military air, but not so stiff-necked as Paulinus. Distant with his noble guests, laughing with his generals. As for his Empress, well, she might as well have been a statue for all the attention he paid her.

Not that she was my only competition. I'd heard the rumors

about Domitian and his niece. If the rumors were true—if she had drawn him away from his once madly adored wife—then she had to have something remarkable.

Well, I watched her all evening and saw nothing fascinating. A wispy child: flaxen-haired, straight-bodied, wide-eyed, and silent. How pathetic. And how *strange*. After huddling on her couch like a rabbit for nearly two hours, she suddenly got up and wandered to the far end of the dining hall, muttering to herself. Conversation came to a complete halt as the Empress rose, took hold of her arm, and led her back to the couch. "Eat, Julia," Domitian ordered impatiently, and she attacked the plates like a starving dog, cramming food into her mouth until her cheeks puffed. Never taking her round colorless eyes from her uncle, as if she feared he'd stab her with a table knife. Domitian turned back to his generals and didn't glance her way for the rest of the evening. I ignored Julia after that, too, and soon she was hardly coming to the Imperial dinners at all. The little freak.

Marcus had an inexplicable sympathy for her. "She was always frail," he said after one evening when Julia had spent the entire meal coughing into her wine cup and gabbling nonsense words whenever anyone tried to talk to her. "Poor Julia."

"Poor Julia," I agreed. A freak, and mad. Even if the Emperor ever had been interested in her, he certainly wouldn't be now. High time for someone new to move in. He had many mistresses, but none who lasted.

I'd last.

"Lady Lepida." His dark eyes focused on my purple silk *stola*, just a shade lighter than his own Imperial cloak. "How regal."

"Thank you, Lord and God." Instead of demurely dropping my gaze, I boldly stared back at him.

"Do you sing, Lady Lepida?" He addressed me abruptly across a roast peacock later that evening.

I savored the little lull in conversation as heads turned toward me. "No, Lord and God," I said in the low, rich voice I'd practiced in the atrium as a girl.

"Pity." He turned away, snapping his fingers for the wine decanter, and I leaned forward to call after him.

"They say gods have keen ears for music."

His eyes lingered as I turned away casually, sliding over on my back and bending all my attention, all my charms on the dining companion at my right hand, a young tribune who nearly upset his goblet in his eagerness.

Another gaze lingered besides Domitian's: the long dark eyes of the Empress. Pretending to be amused. I knew she was writhing with jealousy.

The following week, a summons. An Imperial freedman in white lawn and gold bracelets, with the announcement that I, Lady Lepida Pollia, was invited to dine alone with the Emperor the following evening. I yawned my thanks as if I'd had a thousand such invitations before, and as soon as he bowed out I danced with joy, whirling around the conservatorium like a giddy girl.

Giddiness, of course, had to be put aside at once. There were weapons to be assembled: blue to emphasize my eyes, or red for drama? The pink pearls Marcus had given me on my wedding day, or my sapphires? Musk perfume, or rose? I took out every gown in my wardrobe and reduced the bovine Iris to tears before I decided on bloodred silk, with gold bracelets on both arms and one ruby at my forehead. Sophisticated, sensual, alluring . . .

"Lepida?"

"I'm resting, Marcus." Dreaming, as Iris lacquered my toenails scarlet, of the jewels Domitian might clasp about my throat.

He struck the door open, and I hastily assembled my sweet smile.

"Marcus? What—"

He cut me off. "You've received an invitation to dine? From the Emperor?"

"Well—yes." Which one of the slaves had told him? I hadn't planned on letting him know at all. He was better off in his usual cloud.

"You're planning to go?" His eyes took in my scattered rouge pots and perfume bottles, the open jewelry chest, the gowns thrown over every chair.

"How can I refuse the Emperor, Marcus?" I said in my sweetest tones.

Marcus reached out and traced the line of my cheek. "Iris," he said, "would you carry a message to my steward? Tell him to send to the palace at once. Lady Lepida has been taken ill."

I sat up with a jolt. "What?"

His voice carried over mine. "In fact, she is so ill that we are leaving at once for Brundisium in the hopes that the sea air will restore her health."

"Marcus, you can't—"

"Yes." Stroking my cheek. "I can."

He gave me a lot of twaddle after that about how innocent I was, how I didn't realize what such an invitation meant. How it was time I left my wheel of parties and went with him to Brundisium to visit Paulinus that summer. How the Emperor would forget all about me.

"No!" I cried and stormed at Marcus, and when that didn't work I kissed and cuddled him, and when that didn't work . . . why didn't it work? *Why?*

"I'm sorry, Lepida," he repeated as I climbed unbelievingly into the litter that would carry us down the Via Appia to Brundisium.

Sorry? He hadn't even *begun* to be sorry.

It wasn't too late. Not yet. I could still persuade him to take me back to Rome.

"Iris." I turned away from my bedroom window with its view of Brundisium's blue harbor. "Get out the pale pink *stola* and the pink pearls. No perfume, he hates perfume. Tell the steward that I want fresh flowers in the outside triclinium, arum lilies and pale pink roses. Lute players in the alcove. A plain dinner; you know he likes simple foods . . ."

CATCHING fish, Sabina?" Marcus smiled down at his daughter, plumped earnestly on her knees by the fountain in the garden, trailing her fingers in the water.

"Petting them." She stretched out toward a flicker of iridescent scales. "Trying to pet them," she corrected herself.

"Let me help." Marcus dropped to his knees beside her. "I'll shoo them toward you, and you can pet them all you like. But gently."

She trailed one finger down a carp's gray-scaled back. A quiet girl, his Sabina. Excitement brought on her seizures.

They swished the water back and forth. Marcus wondered if his grandfather Augustus had ever paddled his feet in a fountain with his own daughter. But Augustus's daughter had ended badly, dying alone and in exile. And his adopted sons had all died before him: murdered, poisoned, drowned. All young. All dead. Marcus stroked Sabina's shiny brown hair; thought of Paulinus's straight soldierly bearing and serious eyes. Better not to be an Emperor.

Sabina looked up at him and smiled, and for a moment his heart chilled. Julia had looked like that once, when she had been four years old and toddling after the adventurous Paulinus like a baby legionnaire. Happy and trusting and whole . . .

"Father?" Sabina's voice. "Father, you let the fish get away."

Marcus looked down at Sabina. "I did, didn't I?" He smiled again as she skimmed her hands through the water. Better not to be an Emperor.

LEPIDA

THE evening came off beautifully. The dinner was superb, the flowers lovely; the lutes chimed softly in the hidden alcove. The triclinium, all austere gray-veined marble and simple cushions in the republican style, was far too plain to be fashionable, but it worked to my advantage. In my pale pink *stola* and pearls I was the center of the room, framed by the window overlooking Brundisium's jewel-blue bay.

"I hope you didn't promise Sabina a story?" I toyed with a stray tendril of hair. "I was thinking about retiring early this evening."

"I'd planned to start my new treatise," Marcus said mildly, but with a gleam in his eye. "I suppose it can wait."

"Good."

A weighted silence. Just as he reached for my hand, I murmured casually, "Marcus . . . have you given any thought to going back to Rome?"

"I'm glad you mentioned it." He bent his graying head to fold a kiss into my palm. "I've made plans to go back."

"You have?" I flung my arms around him. *Jewels, banquets, lovers, Emperor . . .* "Oh, Marcus, I adore you!"

"Lepida." He pulled away to look into my eyes. "Sweetheart, you'll stay here. It's time you slowed down a bit. Sabina hardly sees you—"

"Sabina doesn't need me!"

"Yes, she does. It's partly for her sake that I've decided to leave you both in Brundisium. The sea air is good for her. I've asked Paulinus to look after you both. He'll squire you about if you're bored."

I leaned forward, twining my arms about his neck. "You can't leave me," I murmured in his ear. "I'll miss you too much. Won't you miss me?" And when he opened his mouth to answer—if only I could get him to stop *talking*!—I kissed him.

"Still want to abandon me?" I murmured much later. He couldn't say no now. I'd sleep with him every night if I had to; I'd tell him his ugly crooked body looked just like Apollo's, but he *was* taking me back to Rome.

"It's hard to leave you." He smoothed my throat. "But I'd rather be a trifle lonely than see you swept away on a whirlwind."

"What's that supposed to mean?" Even after five years of marriage I couldn't break him of speaking in those stupid riddles.

"Nothing." He kissed my cheek. "I leave next week."

I sat bolt upright in bed, clutching the sheet. "What about me?"

"I'm sorry, Lepida."

That's all he would say. Through all my arguments, my tears, and my kisses, that's all he would say. *I'm sorry.* I still couldn't believe it. He couldn't say no. Not Marcus, as malleable and obliging as my father.

But he did. He left me without a backward glance.

"Will he be back soon?" Sabina said wistfully.

"Who cares?" I snapped, and stamped back inside. Back to the stupid boring house in the stupid boring city, where stupid boring Paulinus waited earnestly to entertain me. "I have a headache," I snarled at him, and then my stupid boring daughter distracted them all by bursting into tears and then collapsing in a twitching heap. I retreated upstairs as they fussed over her, and flung myself across my couch.

It wasn't too late. It couldn't be too late. Domitian was gone, yes, back to Germania and his armies. But I'd get him—it wasn't too late for that. And it certainly wasn't too late to teach my husband a lesson.

Ten

⟨⟨❦❦⟩⟩

"WILL I see you after Lappius's dinner party?"

"I'm afraid not." Paulinus dragged himself reluctantly out of bed. Gods, he'd be late for duty. "I'm not going."

"Why not? He's your cousin, isn't he?" Athena smiled, propping her folded arms on the rumpled pillows. "Half the Praetorians are begging invitations. He sets the best table in Brundisium."

"He's never had much use for my father and me." Paulinus shrugged into his tunic, reaching for his sandals. "Thinks we're both duty-bound sticks."

"Perhaps that's why I like you." Athena kissed the back of his neck.

"Are you singing?"

"Yes." She reached for her own robe. "So why aren't you coming? It's one of the last real parties of the season."

"I'm under orders from my father to keep my stepmother cheered up. She's been very downcast since he left for Rome."

"Your stepmother?"

Paulinus glanced at Athena, but she was absorbed in tying back her dark hair. "Lady Lepida Pollia. You've heard of her?"

"How could I fail to hear of one of Rome's brightest stars?" Her marvelous alto voice was dry.

"Are you sure you—"

"I'll see you next week. I'm to sing at Senator Geta's party." Her smile was bright, telling nothing, and Paulinus wondered— not for the first time—how well a man really knew any woman, even if he shared her bed. Athena had been an easy companion for the past year; a tall dark girl hired to sing for a Praetorian barracks party, who had impressed him by settling a fight between two drunken tribunes, tactfully putting off an amorous centurion, and joking in Greek all at the same time. One of Praetor Larcius's stable of slave musicians; a good companion and an easy lover. He would have said he knew her well. But now her mouth was drawn in a hard line and he had no idea why. "What are you—"

"Next week," she said cheerfully enough, dismissing him, and he shrugged away his puzzlement. Women were odd creatures.

It was an easy ride to his father's villa. Paulinus took his horse on the long route around the harbor, enjoying the smell of salt on the warm breeze, the cheerful shouts of the vendors by the waterfront, the bright tunics of the women against the blue of the harbor. Even the thief who tried to steal Paulinus's coin purse looked cheerful, shying off with amiable curses when Paulinus touched his sword hilt in warning. Paulinus was already smiling as he reined up his horse outside his father's villa, and the smile broadened to a grin as Sabina tumbled out to meet him.

"I watched for you all morning," she said, tugging her hand free of her nurse and running to his side. "Can I pet your horse?"

"Of course. His name's Hannibal. My crazy Aunt Diana gave him to me when I joined the Praetorians."

"Why is she crazy?" Sabina reached timidly toward the broad nose.

"Because she's very beautiful, almost as beautiful as you, and rather than get married she ran off to the countryside to breed the best horses in Rome. Hannibal here is one of her finest. Would you like a ride?"

She beamed and held up her arms. He scooped her up, plopped her into the saddle before him, and wound her fingers through the mane. "Hold on tight." She shrieked joyfully as he kicked Hannibal into a slow lope.

They'd ridden up the street and back three times when

Paulinus's stepmother appeared in the garden gateway. "You're both children," she observed, shading her eyes from the hot morning sun. "Sabina, get down at once."

Paulinus dismounted, lifted Sabina off, and bowed all in the same motion. "Lady Lepida." He looked at her with a new curiosity: the woman who had caught the Emperor's eye.

She turned in a rustle of silk. "Come in."

Sabina grabbed Paulinus's hand and dragged him inside. "Can I show you my new doll? She's Cleopatra. I named her after Father's stories about the Queen of Eeejit—"

"Don't pester Paulinus, Sabina," Lepida broke in. "Go find your nurse."

"That's all right, I don't mind—" But Sabina had already dashed off.

"Now she'll be wanting a pony. Marcus spoils her dreadfully." Lepida draped herself across the couch. "So. Have you come to keep me entertained?"

"Um. My father did ask me to keep an eye on you."

"And report back to him on my progress? What a good soldier." She sighed, fiddling with a black curl. "Well, I'm absolutely bored to tears."

"You must miss him." Paulinus was touched by the wistfulness on her face. What would it be like, having a girl look wistful when you were gone? Maybe it would be nice to have a wife at that.

"I'm screaming for something to do, but there's just not much in Brundisium. Absolutely everyone's moving back to their town houses, and then there's me. Stuck in a villa with a four-year-old child."

She looked unexpectedly like Sabina, bored and pretty and very young. "Come to a dinner party tonight?" Paulinus offered impulsively.

Her blue eyes flicked up to his. "A party?"

"My cousin, Lappius Maximus Norbanus. You've probably never met him—he doesn't bother with us much; thinks Father's a terrible bore, I'm afraid. But he's just been made governor of Lower Germania, and he's hosting a huge farewell banquet."

She gave him a slow open-lipped smile, and he could see suddenly why the Emperor had taken a second look. "Really?" She danced across the room, standing on tiptoe to kiss his cheek. "What should I wear?"

"It doesn't matter." He bowed over her hand with all the gallantry he could muster. "You'll still be the most beautiful woman there."

THEA

A party like any other. Tinkling laughter, jeweled guests, wine in silver cups and grapes in golden bowls, couches heaped with tasseled cushions and musicians plucking softly at lyres. I waited in the anteroom until I was summoned, in the lull between the cakes and the cheeses, and then I swirled forward with my warmest professional smile: Athena, the nightingale of Brundisium's fashionable set.

A good crowd. Brundisium's patricians weren't always polite; I'd been to parties where my voice was drowned out by the buzz of conversation, and parties where the men whistled at my bare arms and didn't listen to a note of the music I'd worked so hard to prepare. But this was a polite gathering, and they listened appreciatively as I strummed the first chords on my lyre and launched into "Song of Eos." In the second verse I saw Paulinus on the far couch, a female figure in blue beside him, and I knew then what a professional Larcius had made of me. My voice never quivered when I laid eyes on Lepida Pollia.

She was staring at me with those peacock-blue eyes I remembered so well. A great lady now, her silks draped with a flair she'd never achieved as the daughter of a games organizer. Sapphires about her neck the size of grapes. Her lacquered fingernails twitched once on the velvet cushion, and then her smooth smile blinked back into place. I remembered that smile as she tugged the curtains of her litter shut, the scarlet print of my hand marking her face.

Somehow I finished the song, and the next.

"Marvelous!" Paulinus led the clapping as I bowed. They came to me afterward with congratulations, as I laughed and chatted as Penelope had taught me and Lepida reclined on her couch, her blue eyes never leaving mine over the rim of her wine cup. I longed to cross the room in one long stride and smash her pretty face into the mosaics.

"I believe you have never met my stepmother, Athena." Paulinus tucked my unwilling hand into his arm, bringing me to her couch. Such a dear boy—so many patrician men talked over my head as if I were a statue—but why did he have to be so polite now? "Lady Lepida Pollia."

I extended my fingertips. The hand that clasped mine was as white and pampered as ever.

"Such an interesting performance," she drawled. "Athena—a Greek name? Surely you aren't from Greece."

I unreeled a fluid line of my finest Greek, and saw her flush. She still couldn't speak Greek. I would have bet she still couldn't spell, either. In any language.

"Athena's Greek is far better than mine," Paulinus was saying, oblivious. "She's from a noble family in Athens."

"I would have guessed the slum quarter of Jerusalem," Lepida murmured. "How long have you been singing in Brundisium . . . Athena?"

"Oh, five years or so."

"Before that?"

"Here and there." I sketched an airy professional gesture. "Enjoying myself."

"Indeed. A great pity Brundisium has no arena, so you can't enjoy yourself at the games. I hear you have a great passion for gladiators."

"I prefer music to blood, Domina."

"But the games are so thrilling." She stretched a languid hand for a cluster of grapes. "Why, just last week in the arena Arius the Barbarian lost a hand to a Turk. That must have been a sight. Grapes?"

"No, thank you." I kept my face still. Oh, God, she was lying, she had to be. I listened for all the news from the Colosseum; I would have heard if Arius had lost a hand. She had to be lying. I'd have to make inquiries among the grooms and the litter-bearers, just to make sure—they always followed the games . . .

A little smile flicked her mouth, and I blindly turned toward Paulinus, smoothing a stray fold of his white lawn synthesis. "Still coming to dinner tomorrow night?"

"I thought we agreed next week?"

"I have a cancellation tomorrow."

"I'm afraid he can't come tomorrow," Lepida broke in smoothly, insinuating a hand into Paulinus's elbow. "He's promised to take me to the last play of the season."

He looked down at her. "I did?"

"You did." Her eyes never shifted from mine.

"All right. Next week then, Athena?"

"Next week might be tight, too . . ." Lepida traced one finger along Paulinus's hard shoulder.

"Then perhaps at the barracks party next month." I drew my arm from Paulinus's, giving his hand a last small squeeze. "If you wish to hire me for any little entertainments of your own, Lady Lepida, then talk to Praetor Larcius. The great music patron; you've heard of him? Well, perhaps music isn't quite your forte. He handles my career. Be sure to book at least three weeks in advance. I'm in *great* demand these days."

"You always were. Among a certain set."

I smiled. She smiled. I strolled away.

"Do you know Athena?" I heard Paulinus ask his step-mother.

"No," she said easily. "I've never seen her before in my life."

My breath came short as if I'd dashed a mile. But I had another party to sing at, and no time to think about Lepida Pollia. Even if I was a singer and a success, I was still a slave—and I couldn't go home and grind my teeth and weep into my pillow the way I wanted to. I had to make music and smile prettily for whatever guests had hired me from Larcius . . . and sometimes that sat as heavily as the slaps and jabs of my days as Lepida's shadow.

A lovely evening, Paulinus," Lepida yawned as they climbed out of the litter. "Have a drink before you head back to your barracks."

"I'll just look in on Sabina."

"As you like."

Sabina was fast asleep, curled around a straw-stuffed horse, eyes tight shut. Smiling, Paulinus smoothed the hair out of her eyes and then slipped back into the hall.

The house was dark and quiet, the slaves long gone to bed. The smell of jasmine drifted up from the atrium on the hot summer night. Paulinus felt his way down the back stairs, down the hall, past the library. And as he passed the last room—his stepmother's room—the door eased open. He reached out to close it, and stopped.

His stepmother stood by the bed, her back to the door. A pile of discarded sapphires gleamed on the bedside table, and her hair was a loose black sheet down her back. He hadn't realized what beautiful hair she had.

She stretched languidly, and the light from the single lamp played over her white arms. Her blue silk robe had slipped off one shoulder, and as she gave a little ripple of her back it slipped off the other and drifted down to settle over the floor.

Paulinus closed the door. And his eyes. He took a step back, stumbled into a vase, grabbed it hastily to keep it from falling, and knocked over a statue of a bathing Aphrodite. The crash was appallingly loud. He took off down the hall.

He went to see her the next day. Only the proper thing to do. Hadn't his father asked him to look after her? He was just following orders.

"Paulinus!" She stretched out a soft hand. "To what do I owe the honor?" She wore Nile-green silk with a single massive pearl at her forehead and another on her hand.

He found himself stuttering.

"Nervous?" She led him into the atrium, sinking down into the cushions of her couch. "Why? Going to visit that singer, maybe?"

He reddened. "No—I—well, that is—"

"Really, I don't know what you see in her." Gesturing him to sit. "Years ago she used to be my personal slave."

"But—you said that you'd never met her."

"I lied." Lepida rang for wine and refreshments. "She's cleaned up since those days, but she's still the same little whore. Wine?"

"Um. Thank you." He looked at his stepmother as she leaned forward to pour him a goblet. He had never imagined Lepida's soft mouth saying words like that.

"Oh, yes," Lepida continued casually, stretching a pale arm along the cushions. "She serviced every man in the house, including my father. Including *your* father. Sweetmeats," she added to the slave who appeared in the doorway.

"My *father*?" Paulinus choked on his wine. "But—he never—he doesn't—not slaves. It's not his way. He wouldn't think it was fair." How had he gotten himself into this conversation? It wasn't *fitting*.

"Oh, I imagine it was her idea. A few smiles, a few sidelong glances—the same way she hooked you, I imagine." Lepida dropped her pointed little chin into the palm of her hand. "Just think, Paulinus. You and your father have shared the same girl . . ."

He stared at his stepmother. Her perfume wove through his nose. Some strong musky scent. Her fingertips glided along his knee.

He jumped to his feet. "I should go." His voice sounded hoarse in his own ears.

She tilted her head to look up at him, her blue eyes calm. "Guard duty?" she said, and the husky note in her voice was gone. If it had ever been there at all. "What a pity. Do say good-bye to Sabina before you go, or she'll mewl all day."

Lepida stood on tiptoe to brush her lips against his cheek. A stepmotherly kiss.

He still flinched.

LEPIDA

OH, excellent! He was nervous already. Wondering just what was going on. Let him wonder.

He really was handsome. Tall and straight and sun-browned, a direct gaze, black hair that curled vigorously no matter how hard he tried to flatten it down. He'd look like Marcus when he was old, but he was young now. Young and strong, and there was no hump on *his* shoulder. Yes, quite handsome. I'd never noticed before, until I saw Thea draped all over him . . . and it had all given me the most marvelous idea.

Paulinus didn't come see me for nearly a week. Dull days. The slaves were irritable. The shops were closed due to some dreary holiday. The skies clouded over in the first hint of fall, turning the famous blue harbor into gray slate. Sabina moped, running to the window every time she heard a horse outside. "'Linus promised he'd play with me," she sighed.

"He's playing with me now," I explained. "Grown men like Paulinus don't play with little girls."

"But he promised."

"Men are liars, Sabina. Now go away." I gave her a swift clip around the ear, and she fled, wailing. Children really are tiresome.

Boring days, but I survived. All part of the plan. I counted four days, then made sure to bump into Paulinus just outside his barracks.

He was bare-chested and sweaty in a training kilt, just come from exercising. When he saw me, he halted as if he'd hit a wall. "What are you doing here?"

"How rude, but I'll overlook it. I'm going to Senator Halco's banquet tomorrow—the last good party of the season, and I need an escort. Pick me up tonight."

"I—"

Drifting closer, I wiped his forehead with my bare hand and surveyed the film of perspiration on my fingertips. "Goodness. All sweaty."

I left him standing there, looking after me. Stunned, no doubt, and wondering how it all happened.

A LL dressed up," Verus whistled when Paulinus emerged in white lawn synthesis and signet ring. "Who's the lucky lady? Athena?"

"Lepida." It popped out of his mouth before he could stop it. "That is, my stepmother asked me—I'm escorting her to a banquet this evening. That's what I meant."

Had Verus given him an odd look as he backed out the door?

"Paulinus," Lepida greeted him, gliding across the marble floor. Scarlet silk draped against every curve of her body, and a single massive ruby gleamed at her throat. Her eyes were outlined in kohl, her lips colored carmine. He wondered how he could ever have seen her as childlike.

The banquet was all bright lights and bright gowns, loud voices and louder music. Hired dancers and acrobats, a blur to his eyes. Roast flamingo and dormice rolled in honeyed poppy seeds; all ashes in his mouth. Lepida shared his dining couch, laughing and flirting and talking with everyone except him. But under cover of her *stola*, under cover of her conversation, her foot caressed his.

"Senator, how delightful! Do show me—" She reached across Paulinus's back to examine Senator Halco's sapphire ring, and her breath whispered across his neck.

"Lady Cornelia, your hair! However did you manage those

curls—" She turned over for a better look, and the tips of her breasts brushed his shoulder.

He remembered nothing about the banquet. Nothing but his father's wife making love to him in a thousand tiny ways.

"A delightful party," she enthused as they streamed out of the house with the other guests. Dawn lurked around the corner, but she was still bright-eyed. "To think I thought Brundisium was going to be boring. I haven't had so much fun in years." Her fingers kneaded his arm.

He handed her up into the litter. She arranged the folds of her *stola*, allowing him a glimpse of bare white ankle, and he was helplessly certain that she wore nothing at all under the clinging silk.

She shot him a glance under black lashes. "You'll take me home, of course."

"I've got guard duty in two hours."

"Skip it."

"I can't. My centurion—"

"You'd leave me alone in the small hours of the night, just to avoid a scolding from your centurion?" Blinking innocently. "Whatever would your father say?"

Father.

His father, bent and quiet and kind-eyed. *Lepida may look lovely and worldly, but she's still very young . . . watch over her for me.*

Paulinus wanted to die.

"Climb in." Lepida flung herself back against the cushions. "I'm getting cold."

He climbed in.

She tapped the side of the litter. It swayed like a ship as the bearers rose and lurched out into the street. She twitched the green silk curtains shut, cutting off the light from the streetlamps and turning the litter into a dim shadowed box. Paulinus crammed himself into the far corner, blood pounding in his own ears.

"So silent, Paulinus." Her voice had an even greater effect in the dark. "Too much wine?"

"No," he managed. "Against the rules, before guard duty."

"Do you always follow the rules?" Her sharp-nailed little hand found his wrist.

"Yes," he clipped. "It's safer."

"Oh, but safe is so boring. Safe is so . . . safe." Her painted mouth found his.

Her arms twined around his neck like snakes, and her teeth drew blood from his lip. But when he leaned in toward her she tugged back, teasing his lips with her tongue, working her belly against his. He kissed her with a stifled groan, ripping the silk away from her breasts with shaking fingers. She wrenched his tunic up, her legs twining around his hips as her musky scent twined through his brain, and as he fell into her he felt her smile.

Afterward he turned his back. He wanted to die.

"Well, I do believe we're home." Lepida pulled her red *stola* around her naked body and slipped down out of the litter. "Coming, Paulinus?"

"Don't," he said dully. "Don't."

"Coming?"

He looked at her. Her cheeks were flushed pink, her eyes sparkling, her milky throat rising out of the torn *stola* like a flower stem. She grinned, tongue flickering over her lips, and he felt a dull ache on his shoulder where she had left bite marks.

"Yes." The word was as heavy as lead in his mouth. "I'm coming."

He followed her into the house like a dog.

Eleven

❦❦

THERE was a boat, Paulinus knew, that carried the souls of
the dead to the underworld. A dark boat rowed by a grinning,
skull-faced ferryman. Paulinus's own boat was a bed, white and
airy and beautiful as a cloud, and the lovely black-haired girl
who stroked the oars in it was carrying him to hell faster than
any skeletal ferryman.

"You know how many men I've had?" Lepida rippled her
back under Paulinus's hands. "I started with a gladiator when I
was fifteen, so I wouldn't have to go to your father a virgin
bride. I told your father the bruises came from falling down the
bathhouse steps, and he believed me. What a fool!"

"Don't say that," Paulinus muttered. "He's not a fool. He's
brilliant—and he's honorable—and he's everything I've ever
wanted to be, so don't—"

"You want to be an ugly hunchback?"

"Don't insult him." Paulinus was shaking. "Don't you
dare—"

"Oh, the dutiful son rears his ugly head. Well, dutiful son, if
you love your father that much, then get out of my bed."

She was sprawled on her side, the sheets pushed down
around her hips, her hair half-covering and half-revealing her
breasts, her mouth parted in a smile. He couldn't move.

"I didn't think so." She slid down onto her back and crooked a finger at him. "Come."

He came.

LEPIDA

I could make Paulinus come to me just by twitching an eyebrow. I could sink my nails into his back and watch him arch up in agony and ecstasy. I could bite him and caress him, and whether it was pleasure or pain he came back for more. Paulinus the immaculate, the good; Paulinus the soldier, the saint; Paulinus my stepson: enmeshed and enslaved and utterly under my spell.

How wonderful.

What fun it was, making him dance to my tune. I made him brush my hair and oil my back, I made him run my errands and carry my parcels. I kept him waiting in uncomfortable places, summoned him and sent him away again, pouted when he shouted at me and giggled when he wept. I made a tryst with one of his friends at the Praetorian barracks and summoned Paulinus to catch us in the act, feeling his eyes behind the crack of the door hating me as I moaned and writhed under another man—and that night he still came crawling back. Who would have thought that men tortured by guilt could be so much fun?

"Skip guard duty," I commanded when he pulled away and reached for his breastplate.

"I can't."

"I said, skip guard duty." I spider-walked my fingers up his spine and laughed as he came back to bed with a groan. He missed quite a few of his Praetorian duties, thanks to me. And then he missed his punishment details.

"This has to stop," he muttered thickly. "It's wrong—shameful—"

"Oh, but that's what makes it fun. If you want someone tame, run back to that sticklike singer of yours and see if she can squeeze you into her busy, busy schedule."

He glowered at me helplessly, but he didn't run back to Thea. Oh, no. I was better than Thea. Finally someone had realized that.

* * *

NOT here!" Paulinus pushed me away as I drew him off behind a garden statue at a dinner party.

"Why not?" I flexed my fingers along his chest.

"They'll—they'll see!" Not so far off were the sounds of well-bred laughter and soft joking, footsteps and rustling gowns. "If they catch us—"

"Isn't that part of the fun? Doesn't it . . . excite you?"

He opened his mouth in horror, but I snaked upward to suck on his lip and draw his hand inside my *stola*, and there was no more argument.

We weren't caught. But we could have been, and what a scandal it would be! A senator's wife and her stepson? The laughter would follow Marcus all the way into the Senate. "Did you hear about Norbanus's wife? Yes, the fool left her alone in Brundisium and now the son is doing his father's work for him!"

Oh, yes, that was exactly what they'd say. As I never hesitated to tell Paulinus.

"You'll ruin him, you know." I leaned back on my elbows, tracing my toes over the small of Paulinus's back as he pulled away from me. "His career. His writing. His standing in Rome. All gone." I snapped my fingers. "Marcus Norbanus, cuckolded by his own son. It would destroy him."

"You think I don't know that?" His voice was muffled.

"I think you do. Fascinating, isn't it? You won't give me up for your own father." I coiled myself against his back, reaching around to smooth my hands over his chest. "What if he walked in right now? What if he saw the two of us together like this?"

"Stop it."

"Imagine his face." I put my lips very close to Paulinus's ear. "He limps in, tired from a long day. All he wants is to kiss his lovely wife and invite his beloved son over to dinner. And what does he find? His beloved son riding his lovely wife, rutting with her, right in his own bed, so close he can hear them both *moan*—"

Paulinus wrenched away, knocking me back against the sheets, and swung around with his fist raised.

"Are you going to hit me?" I murmured. "Oh, do. I might enjoy it."

He faltered. I threw my head back and laughed. He fell on

me with a strangled curse. I wound my body around his and branded him with my teeth.

H E hated her.
    He hated the leap of triumph in her blue eyes every time his feet dragged him unwillingly toward her bed. He hated her little pink tongue flicking catlike over her lips. He hated the cruel, casual words that fell so easily out of her lovely mouth.

He couldn't stay away.

"You all right, Norbanus?" Verus tossed out at him one evening at the barracks. "You don't seem yourself these days. That singer giving you hell?"

Athena. He hadn't gone to visit her in a month. She seemed cool and colorless beside Lepida's fiery insolent dash.

Sabina was wistful. "You never play with me anymore."

Centurion Densus was more blunt. "Snap out of it, Norbanus. Or I'll have you on punishment detail till Saturnalia." Centurion Densus was a legend among the Praetorians; graying but still vigorous, a hero who had once fought off a mob in the terrible Year of Four Emperors and saved the life of a young Empress-to-be. Paulinus had looked up to him like a god. Now he couldn't even meet the centurion's eyes.

In his sleep he heard Lepida's sly whispers. He saw her demure and shy on her wedding day under the red veil; saw her shameless and hopelessly tempting on his father's bed. She lived under his skin like a thorn.

"You hate me, don't you?" she asked suddenly one evening after he'd finished in sweat and despair.

He turned his face away.

"Yes, you do. Whatever for?" She propped her chin on her hand. "Because I've cost you your honor? What a bore. Why is it always the woman's fault if a man loses his honor?"

"No," he jerked. "My fault."

"Well, at least you're honest." She curled her finger around his ear. "So if it's your fault you've lost your honor—such a quaint phrase!—then why hate me?"

"Because you don't care," he said baldly.

"Neither do you, darling." She pinched his earlobe between her lacquered nails. "Or else you'd leave me right now. And you can't, can you?"

He opened his mouth—and paused. The pause stretched out into minutes.

"Didn't think so." She crooked a slender white ankle around his chin. "Kiss my foot, Paulinus."

He bent his head, pressed his lips against her instep—and saw his father's eyes. Her skin tasted like honey and betrayal.

THE letter fluttered from his hand, and his stomach rushed into his mouth. He barely made it to the *lavatorium*, throwing up again and again.

"My dear Paulinus," Marcus had written in his firm unaged hand. *"The Senate has finished its wrangling over the problem of the drains and the new aqueduct and the declining birth rate (at least briefly) so I am coming home to visit. You may expect me—"*

"I thought I'd see you this morning," Lepida yawned as Paulinus appeared in the atrium. She was still wrapped in her white sleeping robe. "Got one of these, did you?" She waved a roll of parchment between the tips of her fingers.

"He's coming back."

"Yes, so I read. Care for some barley water?"

"No." His feet took him across the room and back, across and back. "He's coming back."

"Will you stop repeating yourself?" She arranged herself among the couch cushions.

"Lepida, it's got to stop. Now." He could see the slaves clustered in the anteroom beyond the atrium, whispering behind their hands.

"Why?" She reached out and caught him by the wrist. "Won't you miss me?" Her other hand found his knee.

"Don't," he whispered. "Don't do this to me."

"Do what?" Her fingers slid up his thigh, higher. "This?"

He closed his eyes with a groan, hearing the slaves scatter.

PAULINUS!" Marcus gave an open-handed wave out of his litter. "Give me your arm, boy. I've been riding in this contraption since dawn and I'm stiff as a board."

Paulinus handed his father down before the gate and was enveloped in a one-armed hug. The familiar smells of unpressed linen and fresh ink enveloped him. He buried his burning eyes briefly in the humped shoulder. The gray morning was crisp and cool, but his face flamed.

"Good to see you, boy." Dusty and beaming, Marcus looked him over. "You look tired. Are they working you too hard in those barracks?"

Paulinus felt his ears burning. He was spared an answer when an armload of scrolls fell out of the litter. "Did you bring a whole library, Father?"

"Not at all. Just Seneca's meditations, a little Cato, some Pliny, Martial's satiric verses—gods, there goes the rest of them. Here, take these. No, take them all while I give my daughter a kiss."

Sabina skimmed out of the house like a bird. "Father, Father!" She swarmed up into his arms.

"Miss me, little one?" Marcus kissed her soundly. "I missed you, too. And I believe I've got a present with your name on it."

"A pony?" she asked eagerly.

"No, I couldn't fit one in the litter. Just a very pretty set of coral beads. Guaranteed to make you as beautiful as your mother."

"Marcus." Lepida floated down the stairs in green silk and her wedding pearls. "Home at last!"

Paulinus dropped his armload of scrolls and bent clumsily after them. He could see her cooing into his father's ear, her face fixed in a breathless smile . . . how could she do it? Less than an hour ago she had been writhing underneath him, limbs locked around his hips, nails leaving long cat-scratches in his back. How could she do all that, and still look his father in the eye and say, "Welcome back"?

"Welcome back." She kissed her husband on the cheek, and her eyes slid over his shoulder to rest on Paulinus.

He didn't think he could ever look at his father again.

At least it was finally over. It was over, and his father would never know. Not even Lepida would try anything with his father in the same house . . .

Her blue gaze locked with his over the dinner table that evening, and she ran her tongue around the rim of the wine cup.

He knocked over a bowl of grapes.

"Careful, there." Marcus caught the bowl before it could slide off the table. "Are you feeling all right, Paulinus? You don't look well."

"They keep him so busy at the barracks, darling." Lepida

stretched to refill her husband's wine cup. "I've hardly seen hide or hair of him for two months. Sabina is quite desolate at the way he's been neglecting her."

"I'm—I'm asking for a transfer," Paulinus blurted out. "There's a company of Praetorians with the Emperor in Dacia—"

"Just when I've come back?" Marcus protested.

"Surely there's no rush." Lepida gave her slow white smile.

Paulinus rose, nearly upsetting the grapes again. "I should get back to the barracks." He grabbed the bowl just in time.

"Stay." Marcus rose, too. "I'll put Sabina to bed and catalogue those new scrolls, and you can entertain Lepida with all your tales of valor."

Paulinus's heart dropped into the pit of his stomach.

"You'll do all that cataloguing this evening, Marcus?" Lepida's eyes never shifted from Paulinus. "It will take all night."

"Better get it done now. If I leave the scrolls out the slaves will insist on putting them away, and then I'll never be able to find anything."

"I have to go." Paulinus hated the note of entreaty in his voice.

"Stay." Lepida's soft hand descended on his arm.

Go. Go before you wish you were dead.

He followed her.

M ARCUS only meant to take a moment organizing his scrolls—his first evening home, after all, and he should spend it with his wife and son. But he sat down for a moment to look at the new copy of Martial's verses, and that reminded him of a line he'd read in Catullus so he went rummaging to find that . . .

"Father?" a little voice piped from the door. Marcus smiled at his daughter, already dressed for bed in a little white robe.

"Don't worry, Vibia Sabina, I'll come to kiss you good night."

"No, Mother sent me. She took me aside today and said she had a surprise for you after supper, so"—he could hear Lepida's voice through his daughter's—"if you weren't out of your library an hour after dinner, I had to come fetch you to her chamber *immed'ately.*"

Marcus laughed. "Then I abandon Catullus and surrender to the ladies of the house."

Sabina tugged him by the hand through the library doors, little bare feet pattering the mosaics, and up the stairs toward her mother's chamber. "I like Mother's room. It's all blue an' silvery an' it has a bed like a shell. She let me play on the bed today, with her jewels. When she was telling me how to bring you down."

"Did she?" He'd been right, bringing them all to Brundisium—he'd never seen Lepida play with her daughter like that before. But she'd been hardly more than a child herself when she bore Sabina. Now she was growing up.

They halted outside Lepida's chamber door. "To bed now, little one," said Marcus. "I'll come tell you a story later." He smiled, watching Sabina's nursemaid tug her away down the hall, and pushed open the door of Lepida's chamber. Her bed did look like a shell, all veiled in white and silver—he always thought Lepida could have been a pretty mermaid inside it, curled shyly inside her hair.

It was then he heard a groan. Hoarse gasps. A cry inside the veiled curtains.

For a moment he thought of attackers—burglars through the window. He took a limping step forward, drawing breath to raise the alarm, and saw more.

A soft white body. A hard brown one. Intertwined limbs. A sweep of blue-black hair across the pillow. A Roman-nosed profile arching toward the ceiling, mouth open in a silent rictus of agony, or release. Pale hands clenched around straight young shoulders. The couch vibrating under the rocking bodies.

Paulinus.

Lepida.

As he gazed numbly, the intertwined bodies rolled and it was his wife on top, his wife raking her nails down his son's chest—his wife who tossed her black hair out of her eyes and looked calmly over her shoulder at the doorway.

Lepida.

Paulinus.

That was when Paulinus opened his eyes. Dark eyes, a Caesar's eyes, dull and stupid with lust. Then his gaze fell on the door, and his face snapped open with an almost comic shock.

"Father!" Jerking away from Lepida, he tumbled off the edge of the bed to the marble floor, scrabbling too late for a sheet to cover his nakedness. Lepida did not scrabble. She leaned back on her elbows with a little cat's smile.

"Father, I—"

Quietly Marcus closed the door. There was no fury, no betrayal—only stone crumbling into dust.

Twelve

❦

"FATHER, please—" Paulinus tumbled through the door of the chamber into the hall, still tying the cord of his tunic. "Let me explain—" His face felt stiff, a marble mask. Slaves were gathering, blurs in his eyes, but his father's figure was razor-sharp. "If you'll just let me—"

"It can wait." He felt his father's eyes, but couldn't meet them. "I promised your sister a bedtime story."

"Father, you have to believe me." His voice felt too high, but he couldn't stop it rising. "I never meant—I never planned—"

"Oh, I believe you." Marcus gave a flick of his fingers, and the slaves scattered. Behind him, still visible through the half-open door, Lepida had retrieved her robe and sat down humming at her dressing table to brush her hair. Marcus ignored her utterly.

"I'm not trying to—" Paulinus wrenched a hand through his sweat-damp hair. "I'm not saying it isn't my fault, but—"

"Please."

"Please what—"

"I don't want details."

"But I have to—"

"No."

Paulinus knew that "no." He'd not heard it since he was four-teen years old and whining to go to Baiae for a festival. It was his father's Senate voice, the one that cut like an edge of steel. Paulinus's voice stopped at once, chopped off in his throat.

"Your cousin Lappius is in Agrippinensis by now. In Germania." Marcus's voice was low and even. He stood quite still; no different than ever in his tunic and sandals, but something had happened to the corners of his mouth. "A change of scene might do you good. Lappius thinks I am an old fool, but he likes you. He'll be glad to have you for a month or two."

"I'll leave tomorrow." Paulinus felt a tortured thrust of eagerness. "As soon as I speak to Centurion Densus—"

"I'll arrange it."

"Then—then I'll leave now."

"I think you should."

"Oh, gods, Father—" Paulinus's voice cracked. He tried to force out the words *I'm sorry*, but it was so hopelessly inadequate. He stared at his father, standing so gray and bent in the hall, and tried to keep from weeping.

LEPIDA

IT was a good hour before I heard my husband's hesitant footstep outside my door. "Come in, Marcus," I called out, picking through a dish of candies. "The sooner we get this over with the sooner I can get some sleep."

He limped in, old and shabby and broken as one of Sabina's decrepit old dolls. He managed to look me in the eye, but the lines about his mouth had reappeared.

"You're late," I greeted him.

"Putting my daughter to bed."

I smiled sweetly, popping three little candies into my mouth. Let him make the opening gambit.

"Are you in love with my son, Lepida?"

I stared. "What?" Of all the opening gambits I'd expected . . .

"Phaedre loved Hippolytus." Marcus seated himself wearily on my blue silk couch. "I doubted you had any such feelings, but it's best to eliminate all possibilities."

"You're such a romantic, darling. In love with *Paulinus*? Don't be absurd. Who's Phaedre?"

"No one you know."

"Your Paulinus was terribly amusing, but he's far too much

like you for comfort. Well, in some ways, that is." I shook my
hair back so Marcus could see the marks Paulinus's mouth had
left on my throat.

He closed his eyes. "If you'll allow me another silly question, Lepida? Not an original one, I'm afraid. Just 'why?' "

"Isn't it obvious? If you hadn't been so tiresome about taking
me back to Rome—"

"Ah." He rubbed the high bridge of his nose. "I should have
known. I presume you'll divorce me, then?"

"Why would I want that?"

"Why else would you put on that charming little spectacle
upstairs?"

"Just to teach you a lesson, Marcus. You did deserve one,
didn't you? After swooping me out of Rome just when I caught
the Emperor's eye—"

"The Emperor." He actually laughed. "Catch him with my
blessing, Lepida."

"Oh, I intend to. But I can hardly catch myself a lover unless
I've got a husband, can I? Men don't like unattached
mistresses."

"Get another husband. I'll return your dowry; you could
marry anyone you liked."

"Could I? When I'm just a middle-class rich girl back in my
father's house? The best I could catch the first time around was
you, and then I was a virgin."

"I'm afraid that's your problem, Lepida." He looked at me
coolly. "I won't have you in the same house as my daughter."

"*Your* daughter? How can you be sure, when I was entertaining every worthy Roman citizen in the city behind your back?"

"Oh, Sabina's mine. You're a creature of society, Lepida, and
society says that the whoring doesn't start until the children are
born."

His detached tone caught me off-guard. And his expression—as if he were studying an interesting legal concept instead
of his own wife. I tossed my head. "Well, you'll have to put up
with me, Marcus. Because I'm not going anywhere."

"You thought you'd open my eyes, Lepida? They're opened.
And I don't particularly like what I see—can that possibly surprise you?—so I intend to divorce you. Do you understand
Roman divorce, my dear? All I have to do is speak the words
and have you gone from my house. But you needn't worry," he

added. "I'll let you keep your dowry. You gave a fine performance. Worth a few thousand sesterces, even if you did your best to corrupt my son."

His eyes were cold and hooded, his voice a slow patrician drumroll. How dare he look at me as if he were an Emperor and I were an insect?

I let the smile drop. "No, Marcus. No divorce. You'll go back to Rome, and you'll take me with you, and you'll pay all my bills, and you won't ask questions when I come in at dawn smelling like the Emperor. That's what you'll do. Or I'll ruin you."

"Try," he said calmly. "You'll ruin yourself."

"Do you understand the courts, my dear?" I leaned forward, nailing his eyes with mine. "Courts are made up of men. Susceptible, sympathetic men. I know men, Marcus. I fooled you, didn't I? And Paulinus, the upright honorable soldier. The men in those courts are no different from any others. I can make them believe me."

"Believe what?" He dissected me with his eyes. "An unfaithful wife? How many of those do you think they see every week?"

"But do they see this every week?" Straightening, I covered my face with my hands and let my shoulders heave. " 'Paulinus made me—I never wanted to, never; he's my stepson! But he forced me, and when I went to Marcus afterward he just laughed—he said it was part of a wife's duty! I knew it wasn't natural, not the—the things Paulinus made me do—but I was so frightened—'

"Seen enough?" I lifted my head. "Why, Marcus. You're looking at me as if I had snakes for hair."

"I wish you did." The words came with a kind of wonder. "I'd have had better luck with Medusa."

"If you divorce me, I'll have Paulinus charged with rape. The courts *will* believe me, Marcus. They'll believe me when I tell them Paulinus raped me and you agreed to it. They'll believe me when I say that I turned to other men because I was mistreated. They'll believe me when I say that Sabina isn't your child at all, but Paulinus's. When I'm done, you'll just be a dirty old man who couldn't wait to get his hands on a fifteen-year-old girl and her money. Paulinus will just be a rapist who the Praetorians can't wait to be rid of, and Sabina will be an incest-born bastard."

I leaned back, smiling. "As for me, I'll be divorced and free and rich, and my father will breathe fire at you for daring to hurt his little girl, and I'll be married again in no time. Because I'll be sure to get all of your money as well as mine, darling. I think the Emperor will allow that—he's never been fond of you, after all. So you see, it really is to your advantage to keep on my good side."

He didn't bother begging me not to do it. He just looked at me, and his eyes were wondering. "What is it you want?"

"Your cooperation. Your compliance. Your silence. That's all. We don't even need to live together, or hardly at all. Just enough for appearances' sake." I rose, yawning. "Goodness, it's late. I believe we've said everything there is to say, don't you? If we're leaving for Rome this week, I've got a lot of packing to do."

He sat as still and silent as a catacomb, staring out in front of him with blind eyes. Yes, this was the way it should be—I was the Empress and he the insect. It was enough to make me feel positively benevolent. I stooped and brushed my lips carelessly across his cheek. "Don't despair, darling. If you don't sulk too loudly then perhaps I'll slip back into your room now and then. You'd like that, wouldn't you?"

He caught my wrist as I drew a finger down the side of his face. "Madam," he said formally, "I'd sooner bed a snake."

I felt my smile slipping. He limped out.

THERE was just enough light from the half moon for Marcus to see his son riding through the stable gates. Riding north for Agrippinensis, far away in Germania. His breath showed in faint puffs on the cool night air, and the slump of his shoulders was visible even from the window.

Lappius will welcome him, Marcus thought. *He'll fill Paulinus's days with parties, and his nights with hired courtesans. The matrons of Agrippinensis will throw their daughters in his path, and perhaps he'll make a hasty marriage in hopes of forgetting. But he won't forget. He'll throw his window open on those freezing German nights and sit shivering till dawn, thinking of Lepida and wanting to fall on his sword. Oh, Paulinus—*

The moonlit road was empty now, and the night was cold. Marcus closed the window.

"Do you require anything, Dominus?" The household steward hovered.

"The truth." Marcus turned. "How long?"

"A few months." The steward hesitated. He had been running the Norbanus household for twenty years, and Marcus knew his every expression. He gestured the man to go on. "I would have written, Dominus, but Lady Lepida threatened . . . the slaves are all afraid of her. She's—not a kind mistress."

One more thing he had not known about his wife.

"Good to have the young master in Germania, Dominus. He'll get over it soon enough."

Would he? "Thank you, that will be all."

On the desk was the rough draft of Marcus's new treatise, completed a week before he came home. Proposed improvements to the existing inheritance laws. Marcus unrolled the scroll until he reached the words he had proudly penned the night before.

To my wife.

A surprise for Lepida, who didn't understand his treatises any better than Paulinus, but who had done a fine job pretending how much they meant to her.

Marcus reached stiffly for a pen. He cut the nib down to a fine point and uncorked the ink. He scratched out the dedication in two precise lines. No scribbling. Scholars didn't scribble. Scholars didn't scribble and senators didn't weep, so he set the scroll aside to dry and folded his hands.

LEPIDA

Lepida!"

"Lady Lepida!"

"You're back!"

I flung my arms out: the star guest at one of Lady Lollia Cornelia's sensational dinner parties. "Darlings, it's been desolate without you."

They hastened to assure me that it was Rome that had been desolate without me, and I wafted in on a wave of adulation. Ah, this was what I'd been missing: the parties, the suitors, the jewels, the gossip . . . I made three trysts that night. Kept two, left the third waiting. How much fun it would be to coax him back into good humor next time!

"The Emperor has taken himself back to Dacia," Marcus told me, not bothering to look up from his scrolls. "He'll be gone a long time, I'm afraid."

"Oh, don't worry. I'll find plenty to do until he comes back." I swanned out just in time to see Sabina scurry behind a pillar. She avoided me these days. If I said a word to her she just stared back with huge eyes. How had I ever borne such a child?

"She's an utter idiot," I shrugged to Aemilius Graccus over bedside wine. "Just like her father, really. What a pair." I collapsed into laughter as he improvised a wicked little impromptu verse on the subject of my idiot husband and daughter. All Rome was laughing by the end of the week.

"I'm fair game," Marcus told me pleasantly. "Sabina is not. If I hear another verse about my daughter, I'll have you in the courts regardless of what pretty stories you threaten to tell. Is that understood?"

"Oh, yawn," I drawled—but I kept Aemilius's little versifications away from my daughter after that. Better not push Marcus too far.

We dined weekly at the palace through that fall, but without Domitian's powerful presence it wasn't the same. The Empress was far too impeccable a hostess to be entertaining—oh, how I quivered when I saw her emeralds, though!—and Lady Julia was as silent and twitchy as Sabina. Grown ugly, too; wasted away into a positive stick. Hadn't she once petitioned her uncle for permission to join the Vestal Virgins? Best place for her. What man would want her now? But the Vestals wouldn't take widows, even Imperial ones. Pity.

Oh, I was full of plans. I was back in Rome and life was good, and everything was falling into place exactly as I wanted it. *This* was what I'd been born for!

THEA

PAULINUS left Brundisium at the end of that October without a word to me—it wasn't like him, but I took it with a shrug. Some crisis in the Praetorian barracks, maybe. He'd been very distant and preoccupied lately, hardly visiting me at all. Perhaps some crisis in the family—any family with Lepida Pollia was bound for havoc. Or perhaps Paulinus was tiring of me. That was all right, too. I liked him, but there were one or two other young tribunes already angling for my company. They embarrassed my master.

"You're a musician, child," Praetor Larcius chided me. "An artist. You should have an audience, not—clients."

"I prefer to think of them as suitors, Dominus." Having been a whore, and not so long ago, either, I knew the difference between a suitor and a client. Besides, I might not be able to choose the audiences I sang for, but I could at least choose the men who courted me, and it was something. Slaves have to make do with whatever choices life allows them. "What's wrong with entertaining the occasional nice young officer?"

"Yes, but you only entertain them if they give you expensive presents."

"I have a son to save for," I shrugged.

"But that kind of thing can give a singer a bad name." Sighing. "You might be a slave, but that doesn't mean you won't want to marry someday."

"I don't ever want to marry." The law didn't recognize slave marriages. Husbands and wives could be separated when a master died, and never see each other again.

Larcius's bright eyes saw through me. "What a cynic you are, child."

"Yes, I am, Dominus." I dropped a kiss on his plump hand, feeling a little ashamed of my occasional flash of resentment. So there might be times I didn't want to sing for his friends, times I just wanted to curl up with a book or take my son for a walk like an ordinary girl. I *wasn't* an ordinary girl, I was a slave— and a slave lucky enough to have a very kind master.

"Well, perhaps it's best you don't want to marry," Larcius was saying. "I can't think of a man anywhere who would marry you with that beastly child."

"What's he done now?" My son was five years old, and he was a horror. An absolute horror, and he looked just like . . . never mind.

Too late.

A mistake, thinking about Arius, though it wasn't as bad as

it used to be. Wasn't like getting torn apart with white-hot pincers anymore; no, the pincers were cold now. Instead of tearing, they just . . . probed.

It was all the *memories*, I thought irritably as I bowed away from Larcius. The way they didn't fade, not the least little bit. I could still remember the rough texture of his jaw. I could still remember his every scar, drawing my imaginary fingers over each puckered line. Arius kissing me, Arius bloody and shaken in the arena, Arius surprising me with his short deep-chested laugh. Arius, stamped into my bones.

In my early days on the waterfront, all I'd thought about was getting a message back to Rome, to my lover. "I am in Brundisium; come and take me away." But I hadn't had money in those days, not enough to send a letter. Later on, when I had money and sent a wild passionate letter on the Via Appia north, I had no response. Weeks of waiting, breathless and heartbroken. No response. Why had I been surprised? Arius couldn't read. Gallus sifted all his mail, and he had no reason to pass on any letter of mine. I'd softened his prize gladiator, made him human and that much more likely to die. Gallus had probably chuckled over my letter and then torn it to scraps.

I wrote no more letters. What good would it do? Even if Arius somehow got one, he'd never be able to come to me. I'd never get to Rome, because Larcius loathed both the city and the stuck-up wife who spent his money in a vast house on the Aventine, and he'd made his nest in Brundisium instead. So I stayed in Brundisium, too, singing and smiling, entertaining the occasional nice young patrician, getting belated news of my lover's fights and breathing easier every time he beat the impossible odds again.

Forget him.

That's what I prayed every night, even now. *Oh, God, let me forget. Let me forget. It's easier that way. It's easier to forget and stop the aching.*

But God, the cosmic joker, had said *No*. Never forget. Know everything about him, down to the bottom of his soul. Have the knowledge, when you can't have him. Have the memories, when you can't have him. Have a son with his smile, when you can't have him.

And He was just, because I'd known all along that to love a man more than God is to play with fire.

* * *

A PPALLING place, isn't it?"
      Arius shrugged as Gallus twitched the curtains shut on
the ox-drawn palanquin. He'd been to Germania before, during
his first provincial tour after he'd sheared Lepida Pollia bald
and Gallus had judged it wise to leave the city for a time. Five
years later it looked the same: cold and crude and new.
Wind-lashed huts clung to barren hillsides, and in the valleys
the Roman towns looked bright and garish. Shackled tribesmen
worked fields full of icy mud, turning flat accusing eyes on
Arius when he passed.

      "They're a sullen people, these Germans." Gallus snuggled
deeper into his furs. He had made such a killing on Arius's last
tour of the provinces that he had judged it time for another.
"Absolute barbarians—just like you, dear boy. Don't try to run
away again, will you? I'll shackle you if I have to."

      Arius had tried running away, during that first tour. His face
and his gladiator tattoo had given him away within five miles,
and after that Gallus kept him watched whenever they left Italy.
He didn't try running anymore. Not much to run for.

      He fought four bouts through the arenas of Germania that
winter, taking on champions in wolf skins and champions in
horned helmets, and he left them all dead. After his bouts Gallus rented his presence out at dinner parties where he met governors and legates, charioteers and senators, painted patrician
women who took him eagerly to bed and soft-eyed boy tribunes
who tried to do the same. But he liked to duck out of the stifling
banquet halls into the dark frosty gardens, looking up at the roof
of stars that seemed much bigger and sharper than they ever did
through the haze and smoke of Rome. Germania. Gaul a little
to the left, and Britannia a little to the left of that.

      Agrippinensis. Not much of a city. A bout with a German,
then a banquet at the crude new palace of Governor Lappius
Norbanus. The walls might be wooden instead of marble, and
the lamps might smoke from rough German oil, but there were
oysters in wine sauces, lark tongues braised in herb butter,
pastries stuffed with olives and cheeses . . . and mead from
Britannia, cold and frothing and lethal. Arius swallowed it
down, remembering his brothers getting roaring drunk on cold
mead, and watched a great many young tribunes get roaring

drunk on it, too, at the governor's banquet. The governor's young cousin, he saw with grim amusement, was drunkest of all. A Praetorian—those soft palace guards could never hold their wine.

"I saw you fight today," the Praetorian challenged. His face was flushed, his white lawn synthesis already wine-stained, eyes bright with hostility. "Left it a bit late, didn't you?"

"Still won." Arius didn't look up from his plate.

"I wagered a hundred denarii on you. If you'd lost—"

"By Jove, Paulinus." Governor Lappius descended on his young cousin, all beaming smiles and false ringlets. "Don't terrorize our guest. He'll rip you to bits with his bare hands, and there's not one of us who could stop him." A wink at Arius. "Don't mind my young cousin, Barbarian. Broken heart, you know."

"She could have written me," Paulinus was muttering, swaying as the slaves helped him back to his own couch. "Not a bloody word—faithless cow—"

"Poor Paulinus," said the governor, amused. "I'd best send him to bed before Saturninus pounces on him. That's Saturninus there"—importantly—"governor of Upper Germania, you know. He fancies boys, especially drunken pretty ones like Paulinus. He'll be gone in another year anyway. Saturninus, that is." Lappius adjusted his wig, chest swelling as his noble guests watched him chatting so cozily with Rome's greatest gladiator. "Here's a tidbit you won't hear back in Rome, Barbarian. Saturninus will be dunned out of the governorship by year's end! Domitian doesn't like boy-fanciers, you see. Imagine that! A pretty youth's better for buggering than any girl, and you'll not find more than a handful of men in Rome who don't agree with me, but for once our Emperor's one of them. When I think of Emperor Nero and his boys! Well, it's a new era, and men like Saturninus are certainly out in the cold." Lappius pointed to a tall, balding, militarily erect patrician who sat frowning over his wine. "All he's got to drown his sorrows in now are drunken young men like Paulinus! When he's dunned out of the governorship and it's all the news in Rome, Barbarian, tell them you heard it first from me—"

"You think I care," said Arius, "who governs any of your wretched provinces?"

Lappius's smile slipped, but he hitched it back into place.

"Excellent," he said brightly. "The dancers are ready. Lovely, aren't they? Any of them are yours, of course, if you want them."

Arius returned to his mead, indifferently watching the lithe brown bodies writhing nude across the mosaics. From Agrippinensis to Taunus on the morrow. A Dumnonian champion awaited him, having publicly sworn he would send the Barbarian screaming to his gods. Arius half hoped he would.

DECEMBER melted into January, marking a drunken, miserable winter for Paulinus. The drunkenness and misery vanished overnight when the news came roaring to his cousin's palace: Governor Saturninus of Upper Germania had launched a revolt. He had proclaimed himself Emperor, and at the head of an army of legionnaires and tribesmen he was on his way to Agrippinensis.

Thirteen

❧❧

"UPPER Germania now!" Senator Scaurus murmured. "What's next? Gaul? Spain?"

More murmurs. Business had conducted itself as usual in the Senate House, the rebellion barely mentioned. Saturninus was dismissed as an upstart, a disappointed old soldier with a few blue-painted natives trailing in his wake. But more senators than usual had lingered after the conclusion of business, clustering together in the marble tiers as they nervously fingered the purple borders of their togas.

"If Egypt goes then we'll be blockaded—"

"—and with the Emperor off in Dacia—"

Scaurus's voice again, low and panicky. "I say we negotiate with Saturninus now. Pacify him. Who knows what may happen? Do we want another year like the Year of the Four Emperors, senators falling to the wayside right and left because they sided with the wrong claimant? Do we—"

"The Year of the Four Emperors." The voice of the god Augustus's grandson cut through the commotion like a knife. Eyes turned toward the gray-haired figure sitting some distance separate, drawing idle circles on the marble rail with a pen. "I wondered when someone would mention that. Twenty years ago, and still none of you can speak of it without quaking."

"Easy for you to say, Norbanus," Scaurus snapped. "You

don't scrabble for your life like the rest of us when the heads start to roll. What do you know about quaking?"

"I know that my son is in Lower Germania as we speak." Marcus was still looking down at the pen. "I know that he has a touch of Imperial purple in his veins, just as I do. I know that Governor Lappius appointed him unofficial commander of Lower Germania's legions—in deference to his name. Which means that when Saturninus makes his account of those who threaten him, Paulinus will head the list."

A little silence. Marcus Norbanus labored to his feet, old and tired in his senatorial toga, his face fallen into crumpled lines and his shoulder very stooped. But his voice still reverberated around the Senate, and everywhere the little clusters of frightened men turned toward him.

"The Year of the Four Emperors. The year after Nero; the year of Galba, Otho, Vitellius, and Vespasian. Most of us remember it quite vividly. I certainly do. Galba confiscated our family estates, Otho sent my father a polite invitation to commit suicide, and Vitellius threw me in a cell where I spent three months nursing a dislocated shoulder, reading whatever books my few remaining friends could smuggle me and wondering if I would be assassinated. And when Vespasian marched in and decided I was harmless enough to be let out, I was verminous, orphaned, paupered, crippled, and alone—since most of my family had decided to divorce themselves from the 'protection' of my Imperial name."

Rustling. Marcus smiled wearily.

"So yes, I remember that year. A year of greedy usurpers who murdered, rioted, and dragged Rome through hell. We look at Saturninus and wonder if he's another Otho or Vitellius. We look around at Egypt and Spain and wonder if there are any more Othos or Vitelliuses out there, waiting to pounce. Some of us will start wondering how fast we can get out of Rome. Some of us will start wondering if we can cut deals with Saturninus. Some of us are wondering if we can play both sides and come out on top whoever wins. And I guarantee you"—his eyes drifted across the rows of senators—"that some of us are wondering if we can't just let Domitian and Saturninus kill each other off, and grab the throne ourselves when they're dead."

One or two pairs of eyes flickered.

"But, wondering aside, none of us wants another Year of the

Four Emperors, do we? Not I. I have a son to lose now, and a daughter, and if a dungeon cell turned my hair gray at thirty-three then imagine what it will do to me at fifty-three." Another ripple of muffled laughter. "Even those of you who secretly think you'd make a better Emperor than either Domitian or Saturninus—do you really want another war? I don't think you do. Not when you count the cost." Marcus's voice rose suddenly, snapping out to the far reaches of the room. "But that's what you're giving us—war—every time you meet in frightened little groups and whisper about the wisdom of giving way. You pave the road for war, and I won't have any part of it because *I—hate—giving—way*." The eyes of Augustus the God bored through them all. "Not to an ambitious little runt like Saturninus. So until you're ready to throw your undivided support behind Domitian—because undivided support is the only thing that quashes ambitious little runts with armies—until you're ready to do that, fellow senators, I'm going home. I'm going home to see my daughter, and wonder if your bickering has doomed her to be spitted on a German pike."

In utter silence Senator Marcus Vibius Augustus Norbanus limped out of the Senate.

"FATHER?" Sabina tugged at Marcus's hand.

"What?" Her *palla* had fallen back, and he tugged it forward up over her hair. Even if the winter winds hadn't been biting keenly around their faces, the altar of Minerva was a stern marble place. No one approached bareheaded.

"Why do the gods like *white* bulls better?"

The pontifex glared, leading the bull forward, and Marcus put a finger to his daughter's lips. Laughter surged wildly in his middle. White bulls, white swans, white sows—why *did* the gods want their sacrifices white? With so many mothers praying for sons in Germania, on one side of the rebellion or the other, there was hardly a white animal left in Rome. Limping out of the Senate house, he'd gone straight to the market in search of a sacrificial beast, and paid an exorbitant sum for a scrawny bullock whose haunches wouldn't have fed a family of five. "The gods just want blood, Sabina."

The pontifex led the bull forward to the temple steps. Two more priests murmured prayers, and the bull threw up its nose at the stench. The steps were red-brown and sticky. Sabina looked nervous but she had asked to come—"I want to pray for 'Linus, too"—and he allowed her to hide her face in the folds of his toga as the knife descended. The bull bellowed, going to its knees, and Marcus came forward to bathe his hands in the stream of blood. "Minerva, protect my son," he said. Confused images of the sturdy four-year-old guiltily confessing he had put a beetle in his mother's wine cup, the boy bursting with pride in a brand-new Praetorian breastplate, the man writhing agonized under Lepida's raking nails. "Minerva, goddess of soldiers. A thousand bulls, white or any other color, if you bring my son home safe." Clasping his scarlet-gloved fingers as the priests chanted and the bull died. "Blood for blood."

WE'VE done what we can." Commander Trajan shrugged. "Now we wait."

Paulinus glanced sideways at his second-in-command: stocky, fit, square-shouldered, some twelve or thirteen years older than Paulinus, wearing his breastplate like a second skin. Trajan commanded the tautest and fiercest of the legionnaires in Lower Germania, and by rights he should have commanded the offensive against Saturninus. But Paulinus's cousin Governor Lappius had insisted hysterically on appointing Paulinus unofficial commander of both legions, against all rules of military rank, and Paulinus—suddenly sober again after a month of wine and hazy self-recriminations—had not refused. He could not rejoice, not when civil war lay around the corner—but he could not halt the small voice in his head from singing, *Commander of two legions! Commander of two legions!* Not that Trajan had been happy about it.

"I need you," Paulinus had said bluntly. "I don't know this country, I don't know your soldiers, and I don't know the terrain. You'll be my second."

"Yes, Commander." Stiffly. "I am happy to serve under you."

"Bull," Paulinus had said. "But can I still rely on you?"

Trajan's forthright eyes surveyed him. "Are you a pansy like your cousin?" he sneered, and they had been friends instantly. Trajan had done much of the work on the town's hasty defenses, advising Paulinus where the cohorts might best be placed— Paulinus's main contribution had been to stop Trajan from throttling Lappius, who even now was crouched back in his crude wooden-walled palace and moaning.

They waited now on their horses, side by side, wrapped in heavy cloaks and breathing white into the frigid air. Before them stood the smart ranks of legionnaires, leaning on their shields and chatting among themselves.

"So why are you out in Germania instead of serving your cushy palace berth?" Trajan asked idly. "What's your poison, Norbanus—women, family, or debts?"

Paulinus hesitated. "Women," he said. "Family, too, come to think of it."

"I'll take a rebellious province and a horde of screaming Germans any day."

"So would I." Paulinus flipped a bit of his horse's mane to the other side of its neck. Somehow, on the brink of battle, Lepida seemed very far away. He couldn't picture her clearly, not here with the smell of snow and steel and mud in his nose and the chink of shields in his ears. It was a masculine smell; she had no place in it.

Trajan squinted up at the sky. "Sun's breaking out."

"Good." A sunny day, a battle, an attempt to save the Empire from civil war . . . perhaps he'd even die, and then his father might be proud of him again.

A lathered horse skidded to a halt before him, spraying icy mud from its hooves. The scout tumbled off and saluted. "Commander, Saturninus has been spotted. The Eleventh and the Fourteenth march from the northwest."

"Auxiliaries?" Trajan rapped out.

"No sign yet, sir."

"Good." Paulinus loosened his sword in its scabbard. "Deploy first division."

Yes. A very good day to die.

"Advance!"

THE shield formation had broken, Saturninus's men leaving their disciplined rows for individual battles. The snow was scarlet and the battle raging. Paulinus sat tense and narrow-eyed, trying to take it all in. "Advancing on the south side?" he barked out as Trajan pulled up his squealing horse with a skid of hooves on slush.

"Holding ground." With the reins doubled around his fist and a sword in his hand, Trajan looked like Mars come to earth. They had to shout over the cries of wounded men, the battle yells of victorious legionnaires, the thump of hooves and metallic clash of shields. "No sign of Saturninus."

"He's back there." Paulinus pointed to a knoll by the river-bank. He could hardly keep still in his saddle. He dripped sweat inside his armor, wishing for Trajan's calm, longing to charge in and fight as the legionnaires could. "Keeping well back."

Trajan added a few choice comments about their enemy's appearance, ancestry, and sexual tastes. Paulinus laughed grimly. Aides hovered, waiting to be deployed, but there were no orders to be given now. Just a hard slugging match.

The sun had broken through the clouds, and it beat down on the battleground in hard glittering rays. Under the onslaught of armored feet and sunlight, the grunts of battling men struggling back and forth with their armored shoulders locked fast against each other, the hard-packed snow was breaking down into slush. A legionnaire—Paulinus's, Trajan's, Saturninus's, who could tell—slipped in the bloody slush and died screaming, fish-hooked on another man's *gladius*.

"Do you think we—"

A long bubbling howl cut him off. They both spun around toward the woods.

"Savages." Trajan spat out strings of curses. "May they rot in Hades—"

Paulinus spurred his horse up a steep embankment, trampling the body of a legionnaire who had fallen with a spear through his eye in the battle's first minutes. "Hades," he echoed.

"What do they look like?" Trajan shouted up.

"Chatti, probably. A good eight hundred. Clubs, wolf skins, tattoos." Paulinus raised his voice to his aide. "Sound the signal."

The trumpets blew short blasts, and the legionnaires braced in their lines. The Chatti coursed down out of the trees like wolves, howling murder to their foreign gods. A champion at their forefront, waving a stolen Roman shield on which the unlucky legionnaire's head had been mounted, screamed a challenge out to any man brave enough to approach. The tribesmen behind him took up the howl, crying for blood like a pack of wild animals run out from some arena of hell. A distant cheer went up among Saturninus's men. Paulinus fingered his sword hilt, blood drumming in his veins. Closer they ran. Closer. Toward the frozen snake of the Rhine. Paulinus was done waiting—he'd charge into the thick of it and take their champion himself, mount the man's head on his own shield and send him gibbering back to his demon hell . . .

"Minerva," he murmured to the goddess of all battle strategy. "Be with us."

His grip tightened. The howls assailed his ears as the dark swarm flooded over the frozen river.

Except—the river—

"Oh, gods," he whispered. "Oh gods, yes!" Not Minerva, but Fortuna—Fortuna, goddess of luck, who had just passed over his head in a rustle of golden wings.

"What?" Trajan wheeled his horse, already looking back toward the battle.

The second wave of Germans surged out over the frozen river as Trajan surged up the embankment. Paulinus almost thought he could hear the ice creak—and then it broke. A cluster of Germans shrieked as they plunged into the frigid water.

"The sun," said Trajan unbelievingly. "This crazy sun."

Howling abated as the Germans fell back. They regrouped. Sallied forward again. An entire shelf of ice fell away, and the front rank of savages disappeared into the Rhine. Even over the clash of battle they could hear the screams, the splashes, the sounds of drowning. The head mounted on the champion's shield bobbed loose, grinning up at the sun as the champion himself drowned gurgling in his bearskin.

Paulinus whirled on his aide. "Sound the attack. Press Saturninus back against the hill." His aides scattered, grinning, and trumpets began to bugle. Trajan let out a whoop. Paulinus leaned down from the saddle, plucked up a spear, hefted it.

Trajan grinned. "Shall we?"

YOU'RE alive!" Lappius mopped at his round face. He looked ten years older. All about him fluttered the slaves and the women, wide-eyed at the sight of the two grimy soldiers in their midst. "By Jove, if you'd died in this rebellion—Paulinus?"

"He's dazed," Trajan said over Paulinus's head. "He made himself a hero."

Paulinus blinked. He was alive. He didn't quite believe it.

"—cut his way up the hill toward Saturninus himself—"

A party of Lappius's young courtiers grinned at Paulinus, slapping him on the shoulder and mouthing congratulations. Paulinus looked through them in a fog, thinking of Saturninus. Just a soldier who wanted real work instead of cattle shows and sullen natives . . . He'd had some idea of killing Saturninus himself, but he came up the hill and found that the man had stabbed himself through the gut. He'd stared up at Paulinus, his eyes full of blood, dying slowly, and Paulinus drove a *gladius* through his heart to put him out of his agony. Trajan found Paulinus with his back to a tree and Saturninus's severed head beside his hand.

"—The Fourteenth is slaughtered, and the Eleventh is running. They'll be lucky to get off with decimation."

He found himself wishing Saturninus had killed him instead. There was Lepida to face, now, and his father, and even the battle hadn't restored anything. Everything was hard again. In the middle of the fight it had all been simple.

"—hunting down the last of the savages, but I'll wager not one in ten got out of the Rhine—"

A fat woman in a pink *stola* moaned relief and fainted. The slaves fluttered ineffectually around her. Paulinus stared at her plump white legs until Trajan grabbed his arm and tugged him out again. The rest of the day—the rest of the week—moved by in a whirl. Trajan hunted down the rebellious legionnaires with relish. Saturninus's hacked-apart body was publicly displayed outside the governor's palace and left to rot: a warning to all other would-be usurpers. Everywhere Paulinus and Trajan rode, the citizens clapped and the legionnaires banged their shields. "Stop wincing," Trajan grinned. "We're heroes."

"Will you stop saying that?" Paulinus growled.

"You're a funny one, Norbanus. Most of us dream about being heroes."

"You're the hero. I'll see you with a good post if it's the last thing I do."

"Me, a paper-pusher?" Trajan hooted. "I'm an army man, pure and simple. Let's get drunk and look for whores. Boys or girls for you?"

"Girls," Paulinus said hastily.

"Take my advice." Trajan grinned again. "Girls may be prettier, but boys are less trouble. Don't suppose you'd care to—"

"No, not my style." Paulinus was used to the offer by now. Half his friends and most of his superior officers preferred boys or young soldiers to their wives.

"Pity. Still want to get drunk?"

"Gods, yes."

A letter arrived from Paulinus's father, sent by fast courier. A single sheet of parchment, a single line of writing. "*Well done, boy. Marcus.*"

"Hate me!" Paulinus shouted down at the letter. "Disown me! Don't *congratulate* me!" He crumpled the letter up and threw it across the room. Then spent the next hour smoothing it out. Lepida wrote nothing.

After a week, the Emperor marched in.

"Norbanus, is it?" The famous Flavian gaze made Paulinus's knees brace. He stared fixedly past the Emperor's ear. "I know your father. You'll join me for dinner in two hours." He turned to Lappius. "Bring out the traitors. We'll deal with them now."

"All of them, Lord and God?"

"The officers. The legionnaires will be decimated; that can wait until morning. Prepare the officers for execution." The Emperor's purple cloak swirled as he took off briskly across the courtyard. Twelve Praetorians, six secretaries, a cluster of generals, a handful of slaves, and Lappius Norbanus trotted in his wake.

"So that's how a Caesar handles treachery." Trajan whistled. "I like his style."

Paulinus lowered his voice. "He didn't even hold trials."

"Who needs 'em? We know they're guilty." Trajan flicked a speck of mud off Paulinus's shoulder. "Go spruce up, pretty boy. You're having dinner with the world's most powerful man."

The world's most powerful man hardly looked up as Paulinus ducked into the Imperial presence and snapped off his sharpest salute. "Norbanus," he said perfunctorily. "Sit. Eat. Camp food; I hate eating soft on campaign."

Paulinus sat, tangling his cloak around the stool legs, and helped himself diffidently. He ate for ten minutes in silence as the Emperor bolted his food, dictating a letter to a pair of secretaries between bites, and sifted rapidly through a heap of correspondence. The hard soldier's bread and plain stew looked strange sitting on Lappius's golden plates. Rather like Domitian himself, who sat on the silk cushions in the leather breastplate and rough tunic of a legionnaire and rapidly flipped through a dozen frayed old folders of paperwork. Paulinus eyed him covertly: the man his father had pronounced both a good general and a great administrator; the man who decimated entire legions and was kind to a mad niece; the man of whom great depravities were whispered and who had looked with interest on Lepida, and who now sat before him in a plain tent wearing less silk and gold braid than his own secretaries.

The Imperial gaze flicked upward at that moment. Paulinus flushed and applied himself to his dinner. Too late.

"So, Norbanus." The Flavian voice dragged Paulinus's eyes obediently upward. "You're a tribune in my Praetorian guard."

"Yes, Caesar. I've been stationed in Brundisium."

"Mmm." Domitian snapped for a secretary and dictated a quick postscript. "Centurion Densus's command?"

"Yes, Caesar." Wondering how the Emperor had known *that* off the top of his head.

"I know all my Praetorian commanders," Domitian said as if he had read Paulinus's mind. The Emperor had a broad ruddy face like an amiable shopkeeper, but Paulinus didn't imagine that those black eyes missed much. "Your father is Senator Marcus Vibius Augustus Norbanus."

"Yes, Caesar."

"You are his only child?"

"I have a sister. Four years old. She likes apricots." Paulinus closed his eyes. "Why did I just say that?"

"You're nervous." Unexpectedly the Emperor smiled. "We Caesars have that effect on people. Have some wine."

Paulinus sipped gratefully.

"So. You weren't stationed here in Germania?" Stamping various documents.

"No, Caesar. I was on leave. My cousin Lappius appointed me commander of the legions over my objections."

"Your objections?" The black eyes probed.

"I wasn't a good choice. I knew nothing about Germania, or Saturninus and his legions. I could never have managed without the help of Legate Marcus Ulpius Trajan. I recommend him in the highest possible terms."

"He will be rewarded in due course. But you were in command."

"It wasn't much of a battle. If the Rhine hadn't thawed—"

"I dislike the word *if*." The Emperor melted a stick of sealing wax in a candle flame. "*If* the Rhine hadn't thawed—what of that? Fortuna favored you. You won."

"Just don't expect me to do it again." It popped out of Paulinus's mouth. "Um. That is to say—"

Domitian laughed. "Are you trying to get yourself punished rather than rewarded?"

"No, Caesar."

"I hear you killed Saturninus yourself." Secretaries went scrambling as Domitian tossed out a load of letters and scrolls.

"He committed suicide."

"You could have claimed the credit. No one would have known."

Paulinus shrugged.

"Spar with me sometime." Abruptly. "I need the practice."

"Caesar?"

"Yes, I know how to use a sword." The pen wove in an elaborate parry before swooping down to sign a dispatch. "I'm dismally out of practice, since my sparring partners always allow me to win. An irritating habit. Would you allow me to win, Tribune Norbanus?"

"... No ..."

"I thought not." Domitian slid a hard thumb under a seal and rapidly scanned another letter. "So. You spared me the trouble of putting down Saturninus and his legions myself. For that I thank you."

"Thank you. I mean, you're welcome. Caesar."

"It was not much of a rebellion, and I doubt it would have gone far. But you have saved me the trouble of subduing an angry province. And yet I cannot give you a triumph. Mutinies, even defeated ones, cannot be made much of." Still scanning the letter. "Thus I find myself indebted to a man I cannot reward. How interesting."

Another pause. Domitian glanced up from his letters and looked Paulinus in the eye. Paulinus looked back. He didn't know what to do with his hands.

The Emperor tilted his head at the servants, the guards, the scurrying secretaries. "Leave us."

They filed out, whispering.

"I am putting your cousin Lappius forward for the position of consul next year. He's a fool, but a fool can do relatively little harm as consul." Domitian's hands stilled for the first time, dropping the pen and thoughtfully tapping the desk. "Commander Trajan will have another military post that promises much action. I reward loyal men. I need them around me, for the day when some assassin tries for my life."

Paulinus remembered the mess hall rumors: *The Emperor's scared of his own shadow—*

"I know they say I'm afraid of my own shadow." Domitian mirrored Paulinus's thoughts again, and he jumped. "But with half of ten previous Emperors dying by the knife, I would be foolish not to fear assassins. It's a dangerous job, being Emperor." Domitian contemplated his fingertips. "I'm not asking for pity. But one gets . . . tired."

Paulinus felt an unexpected twist of sympathy. "I don't envy you, Caesar," he said candidly. "People might assume I want your job just because my great-grandfather was an Emperor. But I wouldn't have it for anything."

Domitian looked at him sharply, opening his mouth. He closed it again, sharpness fading into speculation. "You know—" thoughtful—"I think I believe you."

They traded glances again, in simple curiosity.

Domitian nodded once and reached for a sheet of parchment. He wrote out a rapid page, then stamped the Imperial seal at the bottom and tossed the still-wet document across the table at Paulinus.

Paulinus skimmed the formal phrases. *". . . we hereby recognize Tribune Paulinus Vibius Augustus Norbanus . . . in reward for his loyalty and devotion . . . award the title and responsibilities of—"*

He blinked. Jumped back. Read more carefully. *"Award the title and responsibilities of—"*

He lifted his eyes, astonished. "Caesar—it's too much."

"I'll be judge of that."

"Surely there must be more qualified men—"

"Of course there are more qualified men. They will all loathe you for jumping over their heads and try to undermine you at every turn. Accept that position, and you make a hundred mortal enemies. Do you want it?"

"Well—of course I want it, but—"

"Then why are you trying to talk me out of it?"

"I'm not trying to talk you out of it, Caesar. I just think that—"

Domitian's black eyes were amused. "Didn't anyone ever tell you not to contradict an Emperor?"

Paulinus felt his mouth opening and shutting like a fish's. His ears were roaring. "Well. I didn't mean to contradict you. Caesar. I just—"

"Good." The Imperial hand extended. "Congratulations, Prefect."

LEPIDA

I really was glad that Saturninus's little rebellion fizzled out in Germania. He wouldn't have made a good Emperor at all. Everybody knew he liked boys, and where would that have left *me*? So I was quite relieved, along with the rest of Rome, when the rebellion had been crushed. There was a little bonus in it for me: Domitian would be sure to come back to the city at long last, and I had a new flame-orange *stola* encrusted with gold embroidery that would dazzle his eyes . . .

"To think your son is the hero of the hour!" I trilled to Marcus over a rare supper. We scarcely saw each other now, keeping to our own wings of the house and meeting only for form's sake. I was considering buying a house of my own, in a more fashionable district than the Capitoline Hill.

"'Linus is a hero," Sabina piped.

"No he's not, darling. Paulinus is an earthworm masquerading as a man." I smiled at Marcus. "The apple doesn't fall far from the tree, does it?"

He looked through me as if I were made of glass. And he didn't tell me The News. I had to learn from Gnaeus Apicus, my latest lover.

"Praetorian Prefect?" I sat bolt upright in bed. "The Emperor's appointed Paulinus as Praetorian Prefect?"

"Astonishing, isn't it? The boy can't be much older than you"—Gnaeus pinched my breast—"and he's only served as a tribune. High jump for one so young—"

Praetorian Prefect. One of the most important posts in the Empire. The Emperor's eyes and ears. Watchdog, spymaster, commander of the Imperium's private army . . . Paulinus, suddenly one of the most powerful men in Rome.

"Marcus, why didn't you tell me?" I said sharply when I got home.

He never lifted his eyes from the scroll he was reading. "One of your lovers was sure to give you the news."

I curled my lip and stamped off. How dare he keep me out of the know like that? News like this was enormous. I hadn't planned to keep Paulinus on my string once he came back to Rome, but things were different now. He was the Emperor's right arm now. He could get me an invitation to the palace every night of the week! Unless he'd forgotten me . . . but I didn't really think so. And if he had, I'd make him remember in a hurry. I'd better write him a letter right away, to remind him.

Perhaps I should marry him. Would it be legally possible? Rome had such tedious laws regarding incest.

"My dear Paulinus . . ."

PART THREE

JULIA

In the Temple of Vesta

The flame on the altar is two flames. My eyes are hazy. Hunger. It makes me weak. Light-headed. Distant. A thousand miles away from this body I hate.

"You're too thin, Julia," he frowns at me sometimes. Well, even a Caesar cannot have everything. I eat when he tells me to, and when he is gone I go to the lavatorium and vomit it all up. I have not taken food in a week. My body will disappear.

My half-sister Flavia writes to me. Even from as far away as Syria, where her husband is governor, she has heard enough to be concerned. "I've heard some very strange rumors, my honey," she wrote in her breathless slapdash hand. "People do love to talk, don't they? Our uncle must have raised taxes again, to have them making up such things. But enough gossip. Are you well, Justina? You don't sound at all like yourself."

Justina. Our father's pet name for me when I was little. Justina, because I looked as grave as a judge. No one calls me Justina anymore—no one except Flavia, who is a thousand miles away, and must not be allowed to worry.

Marcus worries. Something has made him unhappy, but he still finds time to worry for me. "Eat something, Lady Julia. Keep up your strength." He thinks I am mad.

"Goodness, child, you really are much too thin," the Empress said to me last week. Her manner toward me has never changed: calm, regal, polite. If anything, she looks at me with faint pity.

Because of my uncle? Or because I am mad?

I ate a little, when he was gone in Germania. But now he is coming back. I had a letter after Saturninus was killed, and what was in it melted the flesh from me in the space of a moment. But then I looked at the letter again, and there was nothing in it but brusque pleasantries. Do I imagine it all? The images—they are so disjointed. I close my eyes and the only thing unwavering is the flame.

Vesta, goddess of hearth and home, ask the Fates to cut my life short. It is taking much too long to starve.

Fourteen

❧❧

THEA
BRUNDISIUM, A.D. 90

MY master was plump, bald, smiling, and airy, but two deep
lines appeared on either side of his mouth when he was
angry and turned him from a harmless praetor to a cold and
furious judge. The two lines were very deeply graven today as
I came into the sunny little atrium to stand before him on his
silver couch. This was going to be bad.

In a few clipped words he told me. "I'm so sorry, Dominus,"
I said in low tones. "It won't happen again."

"You've said that before, Thea. It always happens again."

"I'll be more careful this time, Dominus. I promise."

"I've lost a good deal of money. And it's more than money."

"I know." He'd never been so angry before. I winced.

"You know how rare Assyrian double pipes are?" Larcius
glared. "I had to import them all the way from Thebes! Bought
from the most tightfisted old haggler of an Arab the world has
ever seen! And where are my Assyrian double pipes now?
Smashed to smithereens by that ghastly child of yours!"

"He was playing gladiator," I said weakly.

"He's gladiating me out of house and home," Larcius said
darkly. "And it's not just the pipes. He gave one of my choirboys
a bloody nose yesterday."

"He was just roughhousing. It's just—well, he plays hard."

He loves me hard . . . I turned the thought away. "He's waiting to apologize now, Dominus. He's very sorry."

My son came in on cue. His hair was plastered flat with water, he reeked of soap, and he wore the least destroyed of his tunics. He didn't really look meek, as I'd hoped, but he had achieved a sort of foreboding silence. "Vercingetorix." I prodded him to stand in front of Larcius. "You have something to say to our master."

Vix scuffed a hard bare foot along the mosaics. "Sorry."

"For what?" Poking him again.

"Dunno."

"The pipes!"

"I said I was sorry."

"And the fight with the choirboy?" I prompted.

"Weepy whiny pussy," he said scornfully. "I'm not sorry for that."

"Vercingetorix—" I hissed.

"I see," said Larcius. "Go away, you horrid child, and try not to break anything for the rest of the day."

My son scuffed out, scowling. "I'm sorry, Dominus," I sighed. "I promise I'll beat him."

"I've never seen it do a bit of good, but feel free. He's reducing your inheritance, you know."

"My—inheritance?"

A smile broke through Larcius's frown, and he waved me to a stool before the couch. "That was the other reason I wanted to see you, child. I've changed my will to include you."

"You have?"

"You'll come into some money when I die. Your money—did you really think I would keep all your earnings? I've invested them for you. Except the amounts I've deducted for young Vix's breakages. He'll be freed along with you," Larcius added a little dubiously, "when I'm dead. And I'm glad I won't be around to see the havoc he'll unleash on the civilized world." He smiled as I flung myself forward and pressed my cheek against his plump hand.

"Thank you! Thank you, thank you—you're the kindest master, Dominus—"

"Yes, yes. Go beat that dreadful child of yours, and then practice your scales. I still want to hear a smoother line on the last verse of 'Silver Sea.'"

"Yes. Yes, I'll practice." I bowed and all but danced out of the atrium. Free after he died! Larcius would live a long time, please God—but someday, by the time Vix was grown, we'd both be free. With a little money to start a life of our own. I could work for myself for a change—sing the music that I wanted, turn down the clients I didn't like, stay home if I didn't feel like performing . . .

The house was a cheerful racket of people: Larcius's slaves, his famed choirboys, his flute players, his lyre players, all herded into some kind of order by Penelope, the plain freed-woman who loved him like a wife. She seized my arm as I floated past, her curls vibrating with exasperation. "Thea, Vix was caught in the courtyard playing dice with beggars again—"

Vix yowled as I took him by the ear and dragged him back to my cozy little room on the first floor. "OW! I wasn't doing nothing! He was an old legionnaire, and he said if I won a round of dice he'd show me his sword! You know that kind of sword's called a *gladius*? Can I—"

"No, you cannot have a *gladius*!" I smacked him, and he bounded ahead of me down the hall, stabbing and feinting at each statue as he passed it. I reeled him in again. "And that was a dreadful apology to Larcius, Vix. He'd be within his rights to *sell* you."

"Think he'd sell me to a gladiator school?" Vix socked one scarred fist against the other. "Then I'll learn how to cut 'em! I'll take 'em apart! I'll—"

"You're going to my room, not a gladiator school." I twisted my hand into his russet hair and dragged him down the hall. He tried out a few new curses culled from the docks, and I smacked him a little wearily as I hauled him into my room. He'd decided this year that he was too big to sleep with his mother and had moved out to sleep in the choirboy loft. I doubted the choirboys thought it an improvement. My son was big for seven years old, and his hard little sunburned body already had a lot of scars: from a battle with a local bully, from a game of Julius Caesar and the Gauls, from a tavernkeeper who'd beaten him for steal-ing beer. My son Vix, short for Vercingetorix. I'd thought of naming him—well, naming him something else—but the name hurt my throat. So he was Vix.

I wouldn't have been able to keep him if Larcius hadn't bought me from the waterfront brothel. Whores didn't get to keep their children. My pimp would have ordered him left out on the hills to starve with all the other unwanted babies, no matter what I might have had to say about it. My son, left to die on an abandoned hillside when he was only days old. The thought of that still made me shiver.

"You gonna thrash me?" He caught the momentary softness in my eye.

"Not today. But you'll stay here the rest of the day. And no dinner."

He flopped down on my bed, grinning. He didn't know who his father was, of course—few slave children had legitimate fathers. Vix never dreamed that his was Rome's greatest gladiator. He would have loved that, my son who dreamed of ringside glory and gravitated toward weapons like a moth toward a candle. Brundisium had no arena, thank God, and this my son regretted deeply. If I told Vix his father was Arius the Barbarian, he'd get to the Colosseum if he had to crawl every step of the way. And that I wouldn't do to Arius. Let him think it ended with us. Never let him know that, two hundred miles away, he had a seven-year-old son growing up into a tough little russet-haired copy of himself. Never let him know, because it's the knowing that kills.

ROME

"Anaumachia!" Gallus drew eager figures on his account slates. "A sea battle for the Saeculares games! Oh, won't that draw the crowds. Ever seen a naumachia, boy? They flood the Colosseum with water pumped out of the Tiber, and bring in warships manned with gladiators. Can you swim?"

Arius drained the last drop of wine from his mug. "Yes."

"Good, good. I've seen quite a few good gladiators get knocked into the water and simply sink. Pity if that were to happen to you."

Arius hurled a toneless obscenity and swung out.

"You'd better be going to practice!" Gallus's voice followed him down the hall: "You're not so young anymore, you know. You can't afford to get complacent!"

In the new training courtyard that had been built with his prize money, Arius fought four practice bouts. By the end he was winded and panting. No, he wasn't so young anymore. Thirty-three? Thirty-five? Old enough to wake up every morning feeling so exhausted, so crippled and abused to the core of his bones, that he could barely hobble out of bed. Thirty-five years or so, eight of those years spent in the arena. A long career; three times the length of most gladiators. His fights were scheduled months in advance, his fortune—Gallus's—had been made several times over. He was feted and cheered wherever he went, he dined at all the great patrician houses, his name was a household word among fighters and spectators alike. They said he was the greatest gladiator Rome had ever known.

Eight years, he thought dully. *Eight years*.

"Another bout?" the trainer asked, respectful.

"No."

"You wouldn't last another bout, you flabby savage," came a hoarse little voice from the sidelines. "You're getting old, Barbarian."

"Not too old to heave you over the wall, dwarf."

"Better a dwarf than a numbskull." Hercules made a rude gesture. Blue-eyed, bearded, audacious, and three feet tall, he fought comic preludes in the arena to Arius's fights.

Arius snagged a towel and swiped his forehead. Hercules eyed him disapprovingly. "You're breathing much too hard."

"I'm drunk."

"You're always drunk. You're a sieve. Here, have some more. Thin as piss, but it's got a good kick."

They drank sour wine in amiable silence: Arius slouched against the wall, eyes closed to the sun; Hercules with an absurd sunshade over his head and his feet dangling high off the ground. An odd sight, but too familiar to attract second glances. Everyone knew that the Barbarian and the dwarf were inseparable.

"Hello there," Hercules had introduced himself a year ago in his odd hoarse voice. "I'm new. You must be the meat."

Arius had blinked. "The what?"

"The meat. The crowd's main meal. Me, I'm an appetizer."

A mutter of warning drifted over from the next table: "Better watch who you're callin' meat, little man."

"That's what he is," Hercules said coolly.

"You've got a mouth," Arius growled.

"I've worked freak shows, arenas, and provincial fairs," said the dwarf. "The gigs are all the same: make people laugh, and try not to get your teeth kicked in. I'm good enough at the first, but not the second. As you say, I've got a mouth. So if a dwarf is going to get beaten up"—an elaborate bow toward Arius—"why not get beaten up by the best?"

Arius had found himself smiling. Rustily, but still smiling. He pushed his wine jug across the table at the dwarf. "Want to get drunk?" And they'd gotten drunk.

Hercules peered out from under his sunshade. "So what's this I hear about a sea battle? I suppose you'll be cast as Neptune the Almighty and I'll be cast as you. They always cast me as you, now. I'm much prettier, but I've got that sour scowl down pat. Plus," he added, "my cock is bigger than yours."

"That so? Dwarf?"

"The gods give all dwarves extra inches below the belt," Hercules intoned, "to make up for the extra inches we're missing above."

Arius smiled. "So if I'm Neptune for this sea battle, what are you?"

"A tadpole. And tadpoles, my savage friend, live to swim away while all the big fish get eaten up."

"Mmm."

"Maybe it's your time to get eaten up," said the dwarf cheerfully. "The crowd's certainly panting for it. The only thing you haven't done for them by now is die."

"Mmm." Arius's dog came hopping up, curling neatly by his feet and chewing on his sandal laces.

"Useless thing," Hercules said. "She gnawed my good gauntlets to bits yesterday. Can I kick her?"

"Would the Hercules of legend kick dogs?"

"I'm not him, and good thing. He was a bonehead, by all accounts. But it does make a good performance name, doesn't it? What was your name before you were Arius the Barbarian?"

Arius smiled. "Eurig."

"*Eurig*?"

"Eurig."

"Arius is better," Hercules said. "*Eurig*. Gods, that's unkind."

"Can't hardly remember it."

"Good thing, too, Eurig." Hercules chortled, polishing off

the last of his wine. "This wine's terrible. Let's go to the Blue Mermaid and get drunk there."

"Maybe you'll find a whore who'll believe that story about dwarves and their extra inches."

"You want to compare, Barbarian? You just whip out your sword and I'll whip out mine . . ."

Fifteen

❦ ❦

LEPIDA

WHAT a bore.

I didn't want to see the Barbarian star in the naumachia, but the Saeculares games were *the* event of the season, so go I did. In white silk with a collar of fabulously worked Egyptian gold about my neck, carrying a peacock feather fan with a quartet of Moroccan slaves at my back. The day had dawned clear and hot, and the Colosseum was packed to the sky. The plebs cheered the victorious legionnaires, they cheered the German prisoners, they cheered the sacrifices of the white bulls to Jupiter and the black bulls to the gods of the underworld. The Emperor, with his new Praetorian Prefect riding in splendor at his right hand, received a huge ovation. Paulinus had the place of honor at the Emperor's right hand in the Imperial box, and I looked at him speculatively. Nearly a year and a half since I'd last seen him; he'd been busy in Germania mopping up the mess after Saturninus's rebellion. Over a year but he hadn't forgotten me, judging from the torrent of stiff letters that ranged from the slavish to the enraged. Today I might be watching the games from the box of the Sulpicii (three or four of them were my lovers) but by the next festival, I'd be seated beside Paulinus in the Imperial box.

The cheer that greeted the Emperor had been full of excitement. But nothing—nothing matched the madness with which the crowd greeted the Barbarian as he tore into the galleys and gave them their blood.

"Sink it! Sink it!" the plebs were shrieking, and Arius was busy obliging them. Four galleys had begun the naumachia, two blue-sailed for the Spartans, and two red-sailed for the Athenians. One of the red-masted Athenian ships was burning merrily. The Barbarian was climbing above the fire, watching as his enemies below scrambled with buckets.

"Watch out!" Publius Sulpicius shouted at my side, forgetting all about me for once as the Athenian galley heeled over, but Arius regained his balance on the mast and rode the topmost spar down, ropes doubled around one fist and his sword ready in the other. *"That's it! That's it!"*

He was good. Gods, he was good. I went to the circus now more than I went to the games, not liking to see a man cheered who had once sheared me bald and walked away living. "I don't see what all the fuss is about," I said loudly as the Barbarian dived headfirst off the sinking mast into the manmade sea, but no one was listening to me and anyway I *did* see what all the fuss was about.

Arius surfaced on the opposite side of the Athenian war galley with his sword between his teeth like a pirate. He grabbed for an oar and hoisted himself up onto the deck, spitting his blade into his hand and wading in. Long before his fellow gladiators stroked up in their galley for a share in the glory, the Athenians were running in panicked circles and the red sails were burning. I caught my breath as Arius emerged from the carnage. He had an arrow stub protruding from one shoulder and half his hair was burned off, but set against the background of flaming sails and heaped corpses he could have been Mars come to earth. He never looked back at his fellow gladiators, moving in to finish off his victory. He just took a shallow dive into the water, resurfacing with an energetic splash as he unlaced his mail sleeve and let it sink, then scrubbed the ash and blood off his face. Ignoring the screams, the shouts, the crash of sparks and burning timber, he turned on his back like a boy paddling in a swimming hole and floated, eyes closed against the blue sky.

I felt my eyes sting, and realized I wanted to weep. My stomach was clenched into a knot and my hands trembled. The applause, the screams, the falls of silver coins and the showers of rose petals lasted a full hour as the Barbarian drifted on his back in the middle of a sea battle, with his eyes peacefully shut—and I had never wanted anyone more. Why had he not wanted *me*? Why had he picked Thea with her rough hands and her sunburned face? Why not me? Someday I'd have the answer from him, along with his guts coiled and steaming from his belly.

"The *rudius*," one of the Sulpicii pageboys whispered, and suddenly everyone was saying it, the whispers mounting through the tiers of the Colosseum.

"The *rudius*—he'll get the *rudius* now—the Emperor will give him the *rudius*—!"

The Barbarian opened one eye and shook the water out of his ears, squinting up at the Imperial box where the Emperor had risen and was stepping forward.

A RIUS heard his sandals squelch as the Praetorian escorted him up the marble steps. Squealing women rushed to soak their handkerchiefs in the puddles. He heard the word rudius. The wooden sword? It had been years since he'd dreamt of a *rudius*.

"Bow," the Praetorian hissed, jabbing a spear haft into his back. Arius jerked his head toward the most powerful man in the world.

"So." Emperor Domitian's eyes raked him. "This is the Barbarian."

"Yes, Caesar."

A small frown flickered in the Emperor's forehead.

"Lord and God," hissed the Praetorian.

"Lord and God," said Arius.

"Well fought, Barbarian. I've watched you for eight years—a long time. Why have you not hung up your sword?"

"I'm a slave, Lord and God."

"They say slaves are cowards." The Emperor reached out idly and snapped his fingers. A slave came forward with a silver tray. On the tray—

Arius's breath stopped.

"A *rudius*." The Emperor tapped the plain wooden blade. "For you, perhaps. Shall we see?" He snapped his fingers again.

A tubby little man bustled forward. He had a fringe of ring-lets around his bald head and a Greek freedman's robe. "Nessus," said the Emperor. "You read the future as easily as the rest of us read the alphabet. What does this man's future hold?"

Arius looked from the astrologer to the *rudius*, and back to the Emperor.

Nessus held out an imperious hand. "Palm, please." He peered at the lines, chanted a line or two of mystic gibberish, poked at the sword calluses and scars. Then he peered back at Arius's face. "How interesting."

"Interesting?" The Emperor leaned forward. "What do you see?"

"I see—well, Lord and God, it's a very strange hand. I see three deaths."

"Three?" Emperor and gladiator spoke in unison.

"Three. Odd, really—most of us only get the one, don't we? He will die once by fire, once by the sword, and once as an old man."

"You see no *rudius*?" The Emperor's broad ruddy face was inscrutable.

"Um." Nessus flicked a nervous glance at Arius. "Well, no."

Arius felt a dull jolt. The drifting rose petals seemed to freeze in place.

"Pity." The Emperor settled back into his golden chair. "I would have said he's earned it by now. Take it away," he told the slave.

Dumbly Arius watched his freedom disappear.

" 'By fire, by the sword, and as an old man,' " Domitian mused. "How interesting. Well, it's a prophecy worth testing, isn't it?"

For a moment their eyes locked, and silent words were exchanged.

You want to kill me, don't you? said the Emperor.

I'll slaughter *you.*

Prefect Paulinus Norbanus looked back and forth between them. "Caesar?"

Domitian waved a casual hand. "Take the Barbarian back to his barracks, and send the Imperial physician to tend his wounds. We won't cheat the gods of his first death. The death in the arena."

* * *

"GOT it out of your system, now?" Hercules ducked. A mug shattered on the wall where his head had been. "I don't see what you're so sore about. You wanted to die. You've been moping around trying to die for eight years. And now, hey, it won't be long. Not when the Emperor's got that curious eye of his on you." Hercules ducked a bowl. "Quit hurling crockery, you big bully. You're scaring your dumb dog."

Arius snarled, scooping her up with one hand and disappearing into his room. He banged the door but could still hear the voices outside.

"We'll never be rid of him now." Gallus, hoarse from the choking Arius had given him for chuckling at the predicament. "If it weren't for the fees he brings in . . . Well, may all the gods bless the Emperor. I'm rich for life."

"Get away from my door, Gallus!" Arius roared through the keyhole. *"Or I'll rip your head off!"*

"Always knew all that fatalism was a sham," Hercules remarked.

Months of hair-raising battles followed. Arius's fights had long been formalized, set far in advance, and not since the early days had he ever been scheduled for more than four fights a year. Now all the rules had been swept away, leaving only one: he fought in whatever way would amuse the Emperor. He fought with his left arm lashed behind his back, fought on a bed of hot coals with only a pair of sandals to keep him from burning, fought when bloodied and dizzy from wounds. He'd been pitted naked and unarmored against a chariot full of archers, pitted with only a short knife against a black-maned lion, pitted on horseback against two maddened bulls.

He survived.

How many times did the crowd freeze in place, inhaling a common breath as he dragged himself out from under a lion's carcass or a wrecked chariot? How many times did he lock eyes with the Emperor in a duel that ended, over and over, in a draw?

Arius lost count.

"Are you trying to get killed?" Hercules rasped. "The Emperor's little innovations are bad enough, but you don't have to glare at him afterward. Have a thought for me! As long as you're alive I'm immune, just like the dog. You die, and we'll both be begging for scraps and getting kicked when we don't move fast enough."

"It's not up to me whether I live or die." Arius shrugged. But sometimes he wondered if it was.

"Is it magic?" Gallus asked, oh so casually as Arius sat with his eyes shut against the wall bench in the barracks courtyard after a savage fight against a Cretan. "Did you swallow some Druid potion back in Britannia to make yourself invincible? One hears of such things."

"Nothing like that," Hercules returned before Arius could speak. "It's immortality. He's been made immortal."

"By who?"

"By you. By the crowd. By the Emperor. You've all made him immortal. A god among men."

Arius rolled his eyes, taking a swallow of wine. "Rubbish," snapped Gallus.

"'Tisn't rubbish. You've only yourselves to blame. Don't come crying to me when he finally decides to turn his wrath on you." The dwarf grinned manically. "He won't come for you first, though. He'll go for the Emperor first. 'Lord and God,' hah. Domitian's only a god because he calls himself one. Won't he be shocked out of his Imperial purple sandals when he realizes he's been playing cat and mouse with the real thing? Oh yes, our Barbarian here will take care of the Emperor first. Then he'll come for you. He'll come for you in the dead of night—"

"I'll have you flogged, dwarf." Gallus stamped off in a whirl of perfumed linen.

"You know the funny thing?" Hercules turned his cynical gaze back to Arius. "Sometimes I think you are immortal. Imagine that."

Arius drew a circle in the sand of the courtyard with his foot. His shoulder ached sharply where a leopard had clawed him to the bone in his last fight.

"Arius the God." Hercules smiled down at the nameless dog. "Funny, hey girl?"

She whined and attacked a leather glove.

Sixteen

꘎꘎

THEA

"DEAD?" I spun around. "Lady Julia—she's dead?"

"That's what I heard." Penelope wrinkled a sympathetic nose. "She's taken the last ferry."

"But . . . how?" I asked. "She was only twenty-three or four. Not so old. How did it happen?" Two of the laundresses had gathered close in the atrium to hear, and a new lyre player from Corinth.

"Well—" Penelope shrugged. "One hears it was a fever. But I heard it might have been suicide. She stabbed herself in the stomach—"

"She stabbed herself in the stomach, all right, but not for a suicide." One of the laundresses lowered her voice. "She had a mite of trouble, if you know what I mean, and she tried to cut it out."

A murmur of speculation. I turned away and walked to the center of the atrium where a hard winter rain was running off the roof gutters into the little blue-tiled pool in the middle. Dead. Lady Julia was dead. I leaned my forehead against the marble pillar, breathing in the smells of fish and tar that the rain brought from the harbor. I hadn't known Lady Julia, but I'd caught her eyes once on a bright morning by the shrine of Juno, on her wedding day, and I'd looked at her gold-embroidered robes and flame silk veil and silver-shackled arms, and wondered why I pitied her. Even more strangely, her pale little three-cornered face had turned and found mine, and I saw that she'd envied me. Me, a sunburned slave girl who carried fans and scrubbed floors. She'd envied *me*. Why?

Well, we all knew why, didn't we? Or thought we did. We heard the rumors, even in Brundisium. I remembered her, pale and drained beneath the red veil as she walked into her uncle's arms for the ritual bride theft . . . and I saw the bridegroom who had to use both hands to wrench her away.

"So she died aborting a child," I said, very calm. "Whose child? The Emperor's?"

"Oh, ugh." The lyre player wrinkled her pretty nose. "Her own uncle?"

"You shouldn't repeat foul gossip," said Penelope severely. "The Emperor is brokenhearted, so they say. But that's no cause to repeat anything filthy." She retreated in high dudgeon.

"Brokenhearted," I wondered aloud. "But over a niece, or a mistress?"

"I heard she was his mistress sure enough," one of the laundresses shrugged. "And he's mad with guilt now, because he made her get rid of the child."

"Why?" I put my hand out from under the atrium roof into the rain. The storms this month had ruined the Lupercalia festivals. "Domitian needs an heir, so why order her to kill his child? She may be his niece, but Emperors have married their nieces before. He could make the Senate accept both her and the child, if he wanted."

"So he didn't want to," the lyre player shrugged. "Emperors are funny."

So they were.

ROME

"THERE will be some loss of dexterity." The doctor unwound the bandages on Arius's hand. "Especially in the last two fingers. Too much wear and tear over the years. How many times have you broken those fingers of yours?"

"I don't know." Arius flexed his hand experimentally.

"What was it this time? Sword hilt?"

"Shield boss."

"My sympathies." The doctor frowned. "Mind you rest them for a few weeks. Or they'll just snap again like dry twigs."

"No fear." Arius curled the injured hand inside the strong one. "I'm on break."

"Yes, that's right. Imperial moratorium on all festivals and games, was that it?"

"Mmm."

"For the Emperor's niece. She was in Cremona, you know, and with all the heat up there the funeral rites had to be carried out immediately. Oh yes, the Emperor was quite wild when his niece came back to Rome in an urn."

Arius had a sudden inner picture of Domitian knocking the funeral urn flying with one sweep of his arm, mouth opening in a silent scream, and then falling to his knees to sweep up the greasy white ashes with frantic hands. Arius blinked the image away.

"Done yet?"

"Oh, yes, quite done. Well, I'd best be getting along." The doctor paused a moment, flushing. "My wife—she's a great fan of yours. Would it be possible . . ."

"Talk to my *lanista*." Gallus charged enormous sums for little wooden medallions bearing a portrait on one side and a lock of hair on the other. Not his own hair; the barber's or the page-boy's or even Hercules's, clipped and dyed reddish. "Anyone who's willing to fork money over for mementoes of you, dear boy, deserves to be fleeced." Arius was for once in complete agreement.

"—She'll be so pleased," the doctor enthused. "She's so excited whenever I get a call to patch you up. Dines on it for weeks. Well, rest that hand! We want you fit for the next games, whenever the Emperor comes out of this black mood of his."

Arius turned away as the doctor bustled out. He flexed his fingers. No, they weren't all they once were—they wouldn't straighten fully anymore. But he could still curl his hand around a sword, and that was what counted. He could pick up a sword tomorrow if he had to. He didn't need any rest to win.

I don't need anything *to win, you son of a bitch.* It wasn't the doctor he was talking to.

The Emperor crawled into his head again. The cool look on his face at Arius's last fight, when he'd ordered his guards to tie Arius's left arm up behind him.

Challenge.

Was there something in Domitian's gaze these days? Something besides the challenge? Something like . . . fear?

"Fear?" Hercules had hooted when he ventured to say as much. "Why would the Emperor of all Rome be afraid of you?"

Arius shrugged. "He's got it in for me."

"Oh, right. Millions of subjects to jerk around, and he spends all his time and energy torturing you. You're getting vain in your old age, Barbarian."

Arius supposed the dwarf was right. He doubted Domitian woke up nights dreaming of him, not the way he woke up dreaming of Domitian. Dreaming of Domitian's ruddy, enigmatic face and his invisible challenges.

But was he imagining the look on the Emperor's face every time he picked himself up off the sand next to the carcass of his latest opponent, and looked up at the Imperial dais?

Why are you still living? he imagined Domitian saying.

Because you want me to die, he said back.

What are you?

"Nobody," Arius said aloud. "Nobody, Lord and God." And bared his teeth.

THEA

Y ou're moving up in the world, child!" Larcius bustled beaming into the atrium where I sat practicing a new song on my lyre. "I've been contacted by the Imperial chamberlain. You're to sing at the Imperial banquet for the Emperor when he arrives in Brundisium next week! Not the only one of course. They've got fire jugglers in from Crete, and an orator from Thebes, and of course Cleopatra—"

"I'll hardly be noticed if they've got Cleopatra." She was a little golden dancer, the sensation of Brundisium, who commanded high prices for her dancing and even higher ones for her more intimate favors.

"They'll slip you in between the fish and the cheese," Larcius agreed. "Still, anyone with ears will know they're hearing real music. What will you sing, child? I think 'Cythera's Eyes' is a bit sentimental for the Emperor, what about 'Goddess Fair'?"

"Too intellectual." I smiled. "He's a soldier, probably likes jolly straightforward tunes."

"Something with a chorus, then. They'll sing along if sufficiently drunk. You're wasted on soldiers, child."

I let Larcius pick all my music, and when the night came and he had changed it all twice over, Penelope finally shooed him away and let me prepare myself. In honor of the occasion I put away my trademark gray gown and chose a dress of black Indian silk checkered in gold around the hem. Gold bands in my coiled hair, gold bracelets above and below the elbows, kohl discreetly lining my eyes. The armor that turned me from Thea into the cool, serious, intellectual artist who was Athena. Sometimes I looked in the mirror and didn't see myself at all. There had been a brown girl once who loved a gladiator, but she was long gone.

"Mother!" Rouge pots and perfume bottles vibrated dangerously on the table as Vix crashed through the door. He barreled through the choir singers, the lute players, the rest of Larcius's stable who were readying themselves for evening engagements. "Mother, can I go to the dog fights? Last time a deerhound tore out a mastiff's throat and there was blood 'n' guts everywhere and—"

"You are certainly not going to the dog fights."

"Aw—"

"No arguing!"

Vix flopped down scowling next to my dressing table, and a bottle of rose water went *smash*. "You gonna see the Emperor?" he asked.

"Yes. I'll tell you all about it when I come back."

Vix shrugged. Gladiators, not Emperors, held his fascination. "Staying late?" he said hopefully.

"Not too late." I ruffled his hair. "You'd better be in bed by the time I get back, or I'll beat you till you scream."

"Why are you so mean to me?" he complained. "I get beat on more than any of the others."

"The other children aren't half as evil as you, Vercingetorix."

"You wait till I'm big. Then you won't whale on me anymore. I'll be a big mean gladiator and then you'll have to be nice to me." He bounced around the dressing table swinging an imaginary sword, and I felt a pricking in my eyes. All he needed was a wooden practice blade and a dusty practice arena, a pair of gray eyes and a half-smiling salute . . . I stretched out an arm and pulled Vix in close, smelling the sea salt that meant he'd gone for an illicit swim in Brundisium's harbor and exposed himself to half the diseases of Italy.

He wriggled free, messing up my hair. "Quit kissing me."

"Only if you're good."

"I'll be good, I'll be good."

"Likely story," one of the slave women snorted.

A hired litter took me to the palace in Brundisium where the Emperor had yesterday arrived. I'd never sung at the palace before, and I craned my eyes eagerly as I alighted. But as legends go, it was a disappointment. Domitian's grief did not accord well with luxury: The mosaics were neglected, the statues dusty, and half the rooms unlit, so I scuttled after the Imperial steward tripping over my own feet in the dark. Shown into an empty anteroom curtained off from the banquet hall, I was left to wait. The fire jugglers were performing, tossing burning brands from hand to hand, and then the next course would be brought in.

"Thea," Cleopatra the little dancer greeted me. Golden curls danced on her shoulders, and her sinuous body was draped in scanty pink gauzes and spangles. "Can you lend me your earrings? One of mine just broke, and I can't go before the Emperor with bare ears."

"Everything else is bare, why not the ears?" But I surrendered my gold drops with a smile. Cleopatra and I often crossed paths at banquets and dinner parties, and she was always friendly. "Just don't leave them on some man's bedside table this time."

"If I do, the Emperor will just buy me new ones." She dimpled. "My mistress bribed the chamberlain to tell him I look just like Lady Julia. He'll keep me after the banquet, just you wait."

"I'm sure he will," I agreed.

She winked. "Let's peek!"

At first I thought I wasn't seeing right as I peered around the curtain into the triclinium. Just a dark hole. But I blinked, and then I saw that everything was black. Black marble walls, ebony dining couches heaped with black silk cushions, dark-skinned African slaves in black tunics ushering dishes in and out in ghostly silence.

"Cheerful," I observed. The conversational hum was subdued, the lamps flickered fitfully, and even the bright silks and
jewels of the guests seemed muted by the black gloom.

"At least you'll match." Cleopatra twitched a fold of my
black dress, then craned her pretty neck past the folds of the curtain. "Is that the Emperor? On the first couch there, in the
breastplate?"

"No, that's Prefect Norbanus." Paulinus looked fit and
healthy, wearing the signet ring and chain of his new office with
ease. Power sat well on him—I couldn't imagine that his new
position had changed him from the sweet boy I'd known. I
hadn't seen him since he'd left so suddenly for Germania, in the
campaign that had made his career.

"So that's the Emperor next to him? In the black tunic?"
Cleopatra patted her curls. "Well, I'll lift his eyes out of that
wine cup!" She burst into the triclinium on cue, a phoenix flash
of color and music in the blackness, arching and rippling and
twisting. The Emperor's dark eyes held only a flicker of interest
as she fell at last into a graceful heap before his couch, but a
flicker was enough.

"You're next," the steward called me.

I'd be a dull stick after Cleopatra's antics—the Emperor
barely looked up as I glided in with my lyre. But Paulinus gave
me a friendly smile of recognition, and I remembered what
pleasant company he'd always been. I gave a little extra bow to
him and stepped up onto my pedestal, waiting until the slaves
were done serving the next course. Even the *food* was black:
blue-black oysters from Britannia, black bread studded with
olives, purple-black plums heaped in onyx bowls . . .

I got a ripple of applause and started on my first song. Lively
mindless music Larcius scorned, but this black party needed a
little cheer. I sang for Paulinus, who liked a good tune, but he
looked up at me only now and then. His brows were furrowed,
and he bent all his attention on Domitian, talking in coaxing
murmurs. Could they possibly be friends? Emperors didn't have
friends, especially not Domitian—even as far south as Brundisium we heard of his increasing conspiracy sweeps, the fre-
quency of his treason trials. Of course, any intelligent ruler of
Rome feared assassination: At least half of the previous ten
Emperors had been murdered.

The Emperor was heavier than when I'd first seen him up close, at his niece Julia's wedding. His hair was thinning across the top, but his cheeks still had a ruddy flush. His black synthesis was unembroidered; he wore only a seal ring for jewelry. His black plate was untouched and his goblet three quarters full. Not just an austere man; gloomy. But some whispered comment of Paulinus's got a smile out of him, and his smile had charm.

I finished my song, and there was a halfhearted little ripple of applause. Not a lively crowd, but I could hardly blame them. I adjusted the tuning of my lyre, and one of the senators addressed himself valiantly across the black plates at his Emperor.

"Lord and God, we've heard a good many rumors from Judaea lately. More rebels in Jerusalem?"

"Easy enough to crush, if there are." The Emperor gave an indifferent shrug. "A limp-spirited people, Jews."

I'd heard worse than that in my life, certainly. But a demon seized me.

"In your honor, Lord and God," I said sweetly, bowing, and struck up the opening chords of a Hebrew song I'd learned in childhood.

From the corner of my eye I saw the Emperor's chin jerk, and I sang on. I caressed every word of Hebrew, letting the rich tones linger around this overheated black room as they had once lingered around the stones of Masada.

Applause rippled out as the last note faded. I smiled right into the Emperor's eyes.

"Singer." His voice cut suddenly through the applause.

I bowed. "Lord and God."

"Your name?"

"Athena, Caesar."

He looked at me long and hard, as a man of power can afford to look at a slave. He looked so long and hard that people began to whisper.

I wondered if I'd signed my own death warrant.

He extended his hand. "Come."

I came.

"Sit."

I sat. On the couch of honor right beside him. Whispers rose to ripples.

He sat back, eyes fixed on me unreadably. Black eyes, as black as the walls. "Talk."

And I talked.

Y OU sing well."

"Thank you, Caesar."

"I'm not praising you. I'm praising the voice the gods placed in your throat. 'Athena'—why a Greek stage name for a Jew?"

"My master felt that 'Athena' suited me. Serious, dignified."

"Yes, you are that."

"Thank you."

"I don't like Jews."

"Hardly original, Caesar. No one does."

"My brother did. Titus. He had a Jewish mistress, Queen Berenice of Judaea."

"Ah, yes. 'Titus the Golden and his Jewish whore.' Or as the Jews see it, 'Queen Berenice and her foreign gigolo.' We always looked down on her for it."

"The Jews looked down on Titus?"

"Of course. We, after all, are the Chosen People. He was only an Emperor."

"He was always the golden one."

"You were jealous of him?"

"You presume too much. Wine?" He offered me his own cup.

"Thank you, Caesar."

By midnight, the guests were staring openly. The Emperor hadn't addressed a word to anyone but me in more than an hour. His voice was bland, unfathomable. My own came out in cool counterpoint. I hardly knew what I was saying. Over the conversation our eyes locked, unblinking.

" 'Athena'—the Greek Minerva. Minerva is my household goddess."

"The goddess of wisdom? Very wise. War might always be around the corner for an Emperor, but wisdom's harder to come by, Caesar."

"You should address me as 'Lord and God.' "

"Does everyone call you that?"

"My niece Julia did not. She was an exception. Not you."

"I'll call you 'Lord and God' if you want. But don't you think it slows down the conversation?"

"An Emperor is never in a hurry."

"As you wish. Lord and God."

"Are you laughing at me?"

"Oh, no. Lord and God."

"I won't be laughed at by a Jewish slave. You may address me as Caesar. Can you get through that without giggling?"

"Yes, Caesar."

Two hours after midnight. A troupe of weary jugglers came out again to entertain us. Slaves brought out a hastily prepared dish, little cakes enameled in black sugar. Behind a pillar in the anteroom, I saw the slaves gawking. Guests stirred uneasily, no one knowing if they should interrupt us or not. I didn't know if I wanted them to.

"This chamber—why all the black, Caesar?"

"It frightens my guests."

"You want to frighten your guests?"

"It's useful. I judge people on how well they handle fear."

"But everyone is afraid of an Emperor."

"You aren't."

"I passed your test, then?"

"For the time being. Should I reward you?"

"My friend Cleopatra would tell me to ask for jewels."

"I don't give women jewels."

"I don't want jewels, anyway."

"Then what do you want?"

"Strings for my lyre. The imported kind, from the gut of a Cretan bull. They're the best."

"I'll send some tomorrow."

"Thank you, Caesar."

"The first time I've ever given a woman bull guts."

"At least it's original."

Four hours after midnight. The banquet should have ended long ago. Everyone yawned and dozed on their couches. Slaves drooped against the walls, trying to keep their eyes open. Musicians sawed tiredly at their instruments, recycling music heard at the beginning of the night. More people gathered in the anteroom behind the black curtains: I saw that Larcius had arrived with a worried Penelope. But no one dared to leave.

"My niece Julia. I suppose you've heard of her death?"

"It's a great loss, Caesar. Rome's loss."

"Don't mouth platitudes at me."

"I'm not. I saw her once. She looked kind."

"When did you see her?"

"At her wedding. I was fifteen."

"I don't remember her wedding."

"Well, it was a short marriage."

"She was very . . . she had a delightful giggle, when she did giggle, which wasn't often. Shouldn't have died. My astrologer Nessus said she wasn't supposed to die so young. He's never failed me before."

"One hears she wanted to be a Vestal Virgin."

"Spiteful dried-up old priestesses. She'd have been wasted on them."

"Perhaps."

"She was—she was a great comfort to me. And now everyone keeps shoving blond girls at me, as if she had been my mistress. Filthy-minded fools."

"People like to talk, Caesar. What's the use of having an Emperor if you can't make up filthy rumors about him?"

"Did any of your former masters sell you for impertinence?"

"No, I'm usually very tactful. But you did tell me to talk."

"So I did. I can't think what got into me. I don't usually like loose talk. And anyone who slanders my niece's memory, I'll hang."

"Then you'll execute a good many harmless gossips."

"Traitors."

"Innocents."

"They're all innocent when they're dead."

"It's no use arguing with you, is it?"

"Correct."

Dawn. Most of the guests had gone to sleep on their dining couches. The others, glaze-eyed and crumpled, nibbled at drying oysters in curdling sauces. A pageboy in a black tunic dozed on his feet, head drooping over the wine flagon. Even Larcius nodded in the anteroom.

The Emperor rose. His guests came to attention with a start. As soon as he took his black Flavian gaze off me, I realized how exhausted I was.

"A delightful evening," Domitian said carelessly to the room at large. Without so much as a glance toward me, he was gone.

All the eyes turned to me then. Wondering what he saw in me. Because while it wouldn't have been uncommon for the Emperor to take a fancy to a singer at a party, it *was* uncommon that he hadn't simply set me aside for later with a word. It wasn't like Domitian to keep important guests waiting while he talked to slave girls. It wasn't like Domitian to talk to *any* girls at length. He had no great use for women outside his bed; everyone knew that.

But he had talked to me half the night as if no one else in the world existed, and suddenly everyone was crowding around me with sleepy but shining eyes.

"—my dear Athena—"

"—such a delightful performance—"

"—one of the great artists of our city—"

"Now that's enough." Larcius bustled to my side. "It's been a long night. Home at once, child."

A well-manicured hand tapped my shoulder, and I turned. An imperial freedman, marked with the official purple insignia. "Lady Athena?" he said in an educated drawl.

The room was avidly silent. I was *Lady* Athena now, was I?

He bent and whispered in my ear for a moment. I nodded. He bowed very low, a bow reserved for the Emperor—or those closest to him.

Seventeen

THEA

"YES, more than a month now and no sign he's tiring of her!" one of the slaves whispered outside my room, having just carried out an armful of my dresses. She'd run into two more laundresses and they'd at once put their heads together. For the last month, no one at Praetor Larcius's house had been able to talk of anything but me.

"I heard he took a courtesan from Madam Xanthe's establishment—" Another of the slave women.

"Yes, and sent her back within the hour. He keeps our Athena all night!"

"She's not beautiful like those courtesans. What's she have, that he doesn't tire of her?"

I didn't know, either. "Why?" I asked once, but Domitian only shrugged. He sent for me a minimum of five times a week. I invariably stayed the night and walked back to Larcius's house in my sandals, yawning at the spring dawn.

The laundry woman: "Sshh, she'll hear you!"

"No, she won't. She's been up all hours, doing God knows what, and she'll sleep till midday."

In fact I was sitting up on my sleeping couch, my hair hanging down the back of the loose Greek chiton I wore to bed, chewing on the end of a stylus and trying to write a song. Domitian rather liked the music I wrote myself—"You might even write something good someday," was the way he phrased it.

"You know he *talks* to her? You suppose she advises him—the voice behind the throne, and all that?"

Silently I laughed. I had no influence over Domitian at all; he'd left me in no doubt of that. "Don't plan on meddling in Imperial affairs," he'd said coolly on my first overnight stay at the palace. "I never ask my women for advice. A rule for living that follows 'Never anger the gods' and 'Never bet on gladiators.'"

I already knew about that last one.

The slave women again: "You think he'll tire of her soon?"

Even if he did, my future was assured. There would be many men in Brundisium wanting to hear what in my voice had so fascinated the ruler of the world. Everywhere I went I was courted and congratulated. Only Larcius seemed concerned.

"I hate to see you like this, child." Embarrassed. "You're a singer. An artist. Not a courtesan."

"The Emperor knows that. He gave me lyre strings, didn't he? Enough to keep me playing until I'm fifty."

"Don't be tiresome, child. You know what I mean!"

I smiled. A bit of insolence in that smile was borrowed from my son, but I couldn't help it. Larcius sighed. "Well, I hope you know what you're doing. You're missing a great many engagements, you know. Centurion Densus and Lady Cornelia Prima asked for you to sing for their eldest daughter's wedding, and they've always been some of your favorite patrons—"

"Tell them no." My Imperial lover didn't like to share my time. In a way it was refreshing—the Emperor had singled me out, and as a result I didn't have to be subservient to anyone anymore. Except him.

The melody I was trying to write unstuck itself in my head and flowed out of the stylus. Rather nice. It would go well with the text of an old Greek poem that I had in mind. Maybe I'd get a word of grudging praise out of the Emperor: "Not good, but not bad, either."

"Thea?" Penelope burst in, her gray curls vibrating with exasperation. "Thea, that child of yours is beating up Chloe's son again—"

By the time I rushed down the hall in my bed robe, Vix's roars were filling the house.

"Call my mother a cheap whore!" Vix and Chloe's son were lurching about the atrium swinging at one another. *"She's not either cheap! She's very expensive! She's the best! Your mother gives it away for FREE!"*

They fell with a crash into the tiled atrium pool. Vix came up spluttering and roaring, still swinging. I grabbed him by the doubled-up fists, hauled him out of the pool, made the appropriate apologies, and dragged him down the hall again. "You cannot keep going around picking fights! What did Chloe's son say to you?"

"That you were the Emperor's whore."

"I *am* the Emperor's whore, Vix!" Dragging him into my bedchamber.

"Yeah, but he said you weren't no singer! Said you'd do anything for a copper. Said—"

"No excuse. Bend over." I got out the worn birch switch, and Vix let out a bloodcurdling scream.

"Vix, for God's sake, I haven't even *hit* you yet."

"So get on with it." He grinned.

I gave him a dozen good whacks across his wet rear. He yelled as if I were removing his gizzard with a fork. Not that he was really in agony; he just yelled on principle. I wasn't really angry with him, either; I just hit him on principle. I had to do something to prove I wasn't an utter failure as a mother.

"So if you're the Emperor's whore, when does it get good for me?" Vix straightened amiably as I put the birch switch away, rubbing his behind. "Will he take you to the games? I could go to the games! Sit in the Imperial box up close—"

"You are not going to the games."

"Am too! I'm gonna be a gladiator someday—"

"You are not going to be a gladiator!"

My people have an old saying about the sins of the parents being visited on the children. I used to think that was all nonsense. Just imagine.

N OT a bad song," said the Emperor. "Less banal than usual."
"That's what I thought you'd say." I laid my lyre aside.

"Do you care what I think?"

It was very late. The lamps guttered low, casting shadows over the Imperial bedchamber. A plain bedchamber, reflecting

Domitian's plain tastes: no silk hangings on the walls, no velvet cushions on the sleeping couch, no jewels in the marble eyes of the little Minerva that stood in the corner.

I reached for my night robe and pulled it over my head, not pushing back the blanket until I was dressed. He didn't like to have me lounging naked on his bed. "I won't have any woman brazening around my chambers like Cleopatra," he said shortly. "Unless I say otherwise, you'll keep yourself clothed like a decent woman."

He was already reaching for his portfolio, light gleaming through the thin spot in his hair. He was sensitive about that thin spot, I'd found. He frowned as he squinted over a scroll, but it was an absent frown; he was in an approachable mood this evening. "Plans for the harbor?" I asked. "Or a new arch?" Everywhere Domitian went, he built: harbors, arches, roads, aqueducts, temples, all rising to the glory of the Flavian dynasty.

"The harbor."

"It's going very slowly, isn't it?"

"The engineers say they need another year. I estimate three."

"More like four, I'd say. The auspices are pointing toward another flood."

"You know more about harbors than I do?"

"No, but I've lived in Brundisium a long time."

"And I never take a woman's advice."

I shrugged, arranging myself to wait in silence, but after a moment he gestured at me to continue talking.

"I'm not sure what you want me to talk about, Caesar." Lightly. "Why don't you tell me a story instead? Your thrilling victory over the Germans at Tapae, maybe?"

"I despise telling stories."

"That's a change. Most men love to bore me with their tales of valor." As soon as the words were out of my mouth, I realized my mistake. He didn't like being reminded about the other men I'd entertained before him. That was one reason why I hadn't told him about Vix.

His black eyes looked at me consideringly, as if my skull were made of glass and he could see through it to the little russet-haired boy in my head. A fly buzzed, and his hand snapped out casually, trapping the fly on the pen's sharp tip. He never missed. The courtiers liked to joke about his kills, laying bets on how many flies could stack up on his pen by the end of a long summer afternoon . . . but the jokes had fear behind them. Perhaps just because he was Emperor. But perhaps not. I was never entirely easy with him despite my frankness of speech. And I hadn't told him about Vix . . .

I changed the subject.

"Will you be going back to Rome soon, Caesar?"

"No. To Tivoli for the summer."

"When will you be leaving?"

"Why?" He sharpened his pen. "Looking to be rid of me?"

"Maybe I'm looking to be rid of all the sycophants in my drawing room." A flood of them every morning now, begging for a word with me. Senators murmuring tactful words about governorships for themselves and posts for their sons, poets writing me verses for patronage, old soldiers hoping for a place in the palace guard—even young men stupid enough to think stealing the Emperor's mistress the ultimate coup. You'd think it would be exciting to be the hub of all that attention, but it was surprisingly dull. A little sad. All those greedy eyes.

"Don't worry," said Domitian, breaking my thoughts. "As soon as I'm tired of you, the sycophants will be gone. I suppose you'll be sad when the day arrives?"

"No."

"I used to value honesty in women. I'm beginning to reevaluate that opinion."

"Shall I go, Caesar?"

"No." He drew the sharp tip of his pen down over my forehead, my nose, my lips. "Come here."

As a lover, he was brisk and unsentimental. So far he hadn't exhibited any strange needs or unusual demands; in fact his only stated request was "Refrain, please, from pretending ecstasy. I find it distracting." He was thick-bodied but agile, with a sprinkle of graying hairs curling crisply on his chest: a vigorous forty years of age. In bed most men look like fools to me, but Domitian was no fool.

When he was done I reached for my robe. "It's near dawn," I said. "I should go."

He lay against the pillow, his eyes unreadable. "You should."

I was a singer and I knew how to read an audience. I'd been a whore, and I knew how to read men. But I looked at Domitian and I never knew what he was thinking. I'd seen him sign death warrants with a casual flourish, I'd seen him throw his head back and shout laughter at some unexpected joke, I'd shared his bed and looked into his black eyes across a pillow—and I did not know him at all.

I tied my sandals, collected my lyre, and slipped into the hall. Behind me the lamplight outlined the Emperor's harsh-cut nose, the half-folded eyelids that camouflaged the sharp Flavian gaze. The "bed-wrestling," as he called it in his more jocular moods, was done. He was already busy with his scrolls.

An easy man? No. A likable man? Not even that.

But not a boring man.

I was rarely summoned to the palace in the morning, but when the freedman knocked on my door after breakfast I didn't argue. To my surprise I was shown not into the bedchamber but the tablinum, where my Imperial lover was half-hidden by a mountain of paperwork. "Come in," he said, stamping his seal ring at the bottom of some document or other. "Close the door."

The interview, where I received the first shock of the day, was brief and businesslike. A smirk hovered around the freedman's mouth as he ushered me out, and I knew that soon everyone in Brundisium would be whispering that the Emperor had paid off his whore at last and what did you expect with a common singing Jew. I drew a fold of my veil over my head and hurried through the atrium, threading through a crowd of slaves and hangers-on. I bumped squarely into the second shock of the day—a shock wearing a ruby-red *stola* and smelling of musk.

"Watch where you're going," she snapped, and pushed past me.

"Lady Lepida?" I said.

"Yes, what?" She turned and looked at me for the first time. I pushed the veil off my face, and as her skin flushed a mottled red I felt an obscure gladness that I was wearing my new gown of spangled amber silk banded in gold around the hem.

"Thea?" Her eyes darted over the amber beads around my neck, the chunks of topaz in my ears, the inlaid gold circlet that caught up my hair. "What are you doing here?" I could see her mind whirling, fast as the wheels of the chariots around the circus.

"I'm working." I made a vague gesture that showed off my gold rings. "What are you doing here in Brundisium?"

"Visiting my stepson—he's just come south from Germania, not that it's any of your business—"

"Oh, but Paulinus isn't here just now." I set my earrings dancing with a small toss of my head, feeling a swell of savage satisfaction in my middle. "Some business at the Praetorian barracks, no doubt. Come back tomorrow?"

"How do you know? What are you doing at the palace, *Athena*?" Lepida glared, groping for her calm. People about us were beginning to stare, and she lowered her voice. "Prefect Norbanus is a close personal friend of the Emperor's, and if he hears how you've spoken to me—"

"Well, Paulinus is a close personal friend of mine, too. I'm sure he'll forgive me." I used my superior height to look down my nose at her, a trick that worked just as well now as it had in the past. Maybe a little better, since now my gown was just as fine as hers and my jewelry finer. "And the Emperor, well, he'll forgive me anything these days. You weren't hoping to see him? He's very busy with the harbor plans just now. The pressures of his position are infinite." I sighed, getting into the spirit of things. A stout matron in a plum silk *stola* looked at us, whispering behind a beringed hand to her husband. "Infinite pressure, but my poor darling bears up so well. Better luck tomorrow." I turned on the heel of my gold-trimmed sandal as if ready to swirl past.

Her sharp-nailed little hand dug into my arm. "What do you mean? You don't know the *Emperor*!"

"Oh, but I do. He's devoted to me." I smiled, planting every word like a dart and raising my well-trained voice to carry. A group of nearby lictors glanced over. "Hadn't you heard? Athena, the Emperor's new songbird? His new mistress?" I twirled, spinning my gold veils. "Me."

Her face turned green. I'd never seen anyone's face turn green before, and I watched with interest. Just like an unripe cheese. Lepida opened her mouth, closed it, opened it again. I cut her off, loosing my last and biggest dart. Everyone in the atrium was staring now. "In fact, when the Emperor retreats to his villa in Tivoli for the summer, he'll be taking me with him. *Alone*."

I smiled again, fondly, into her gaping face. "Do feel free to call before I leave for Tivoli. We have so much to say to each other. Oh, and you needn't feel embarrassed about calling on a common singer. I get so many distinguished visitors now . . . Have a lovely day, Lepida Pollia."

A beautiful moment. Oh, what a beautiful, perfect moment. But as I proceeded out of the palace and down the street, glee gave way to puzzlement. The Emperor was taking me to Tivoli. Where he took no one.

Why?

"Time to pay me off?" I'd asked him crisply, threading my way through the usual bustle of slaves, pages, and secretaries in his tablinum. Perhaps if his farewell present was generous enough I could buy my freedom from Larcius . . .

"I'm not paying you off yet," he said disinterestedly, sealing up a scroll and handing it to a slave. "I'm taking you to Tivoli for the summer. We leave in five days."

I must have looked quite comical, standing there with my mouth open. He looked up in some irritation, but then he rose and walked around the desk toward me, his mouth flicking upward into one of its rare, charming smiles. "No, Athena, I rarely joke." He picked up my hand, surprising me again. Outside of "bed-wrestling," he rarely touched me. He lifted my fingers to his lips as if to kiss my hand, but then he leaned down quite suddenly and bit the side of my palm.

"Pack light." Without missing a beat he resumed dictating to one of his secretaries, who gave me an awed look as I left the room in a daze and bumped into Lepida.

I blinked the image away, looking down at the little crescent of pink marks on the side of my palm. Barely visible in the sunlight.

Well. I really had better be getting home. If I was leaving for Tivoli in five days, I had a lot of preparations to make.

Eighteen

⤜⤛⤚

"So what is a high-powered government official like Praetorian Prefect Norbanus doing escorting his master's mistress to an assignation?" Athena teased. "I hope it's not a demotion."

Paulinus laughed. "I think I'm the only person the Emperor trusts to get you there without trying to seduce you," he said cheerfully. In a smoke-blue *stola* with lapis lazuli combs holding her dark hair, reclining in an Imperial litter curtained in plum silk and borne by six impassive Nubians, Athena looked every bit an Emperor's mistress. Paulinus felt a moment of faint envy—he'd enjoyed her company long before the Emperor, after all . . . not that Domitian knew that. He banished the thought, steering his horse up to the litter's side. The road had been cleared before them, dew already drying. His cohort of Praetorians chattered easily behind, hoisting their spears across their shoulders and swearing amiably at the spring mud underfoot, glad as Paulinus was himself of a pleasant ride on a sunny blue morning.

"Since I'm off-limits now, you might as well call me Thea," she said, fanning dust away from her face. "That's my real name, after all."

Paulinus blinked. "I didn't know that."

"Of course you didn't. Men don't talk to their mistresses. Only to their friends."

"So the Emperor doesn't talk to you?"

"Well, *he* does." Athena—Thea—sounded reflective. "But he's different, isn't he?"

"He is," Paulinus agreed.

"And he values you very highly." Thea propped her elbow against the plum silk cushions. "You haven't had many breaks from Dacia these past few years, have you?"

Paulinus shrugged, feeling the red plumes nod on his helmet. "I'm just a watchdog."

Thea smiled, her lapis earrings swinging against her throat. "He uses you hard, doesn't he?"

"Yes," Paulinus said seriously. "But it's a great trust."

"I suppose it is. Trusting you with his wars and his women . . . One doesn't think of Emperors having friends, but he's made a friend out of you, hasn't he?"

"No." Paulinus smiled down at his horse's dappled neck. "You can't be friends with a man like him."

"Why?" Curiously.

"Oh, he's just—" Paulinus fumbled for words. "If you could see him at the front, you'd understand. He's not like those generals you see droning heroics over cups of warm wine and never getting close enough to smell it. He's right there in the thick. The legionnaires, they'd do anything for him. He's one of them. A soldier."

Thea cocked her head. "People say he's a god."

"Maybe he is. If there's any man on earth who's a god, it's him." Paulinus looked sideways at her. "What do you think?"

"Oh, I'm a Jew," she said lightly, fanning herself. "We only believe in the one God. Anyway, it's strange to think of sharing a bed with a god, like Leda or Europa."

"I—well, maybe it's none of my business, but—" Paulinus felt himself reddening, and looked down at his horse's mane.

"Paulinus." The low, rich voice was amused. "I will never tell the Emperor that you used to visit me for anything more than my music."

"That wasn't what I was thinking of." Though it was something of a relief, no doubt about that. "It's the rumors about him. Don't believe everything you hear."

". . . I see."

"The rumors about his niece," Paulinus burst out. "Filthy rumors, and he just snorts and says that gossip lives on no matter how many people you execute. But people shouldn't talk about their Emperor that way. Just because he was kind to her—"

"Did you ever meet Lady Julia?"

"Not since I was a child. By the time I got my appointment as Prefect, she was living in Cremona, for her health. She was mad, you know—I saw the reports from the previous Prefect, who kept files on everyone in the palace. She went about muttering nonsense, starving herself, crawling off to the Temple of Vesta to try to sleep under the altar . . . Even when I knew her as a child she was strange. She'd scare herself to death with the things she dreamed up out of her head. She wasn't—wasn't *normal*, although I'd never tell the Emperor that. He won't hear a word against her. He never had any children of his own, you see, so he took her as a daughter instead."

". . . But she died of an abortion, didn't she?"

"No." Paulinus remembered the private report he had read, the description from the doctor in Cremona who had afterward fled in fear of his life. "It was suicide—she cut her stomach open. She lingered, and the infection— After that, people *would* say it was a botched abortion. My father was there; he tried to put the truth out, but who listens to the truth when lies are more interesting?"

A rather uncomfortable silence lapsed after that. Athena shifted on her cushions, rearranging the plum silk curtains to shield her face from the sun. "I saw your stepmother in the palace a few days ago, Paulinus."

She'd sought to find a less awkward subject. Hardly her fault she'd found a *more* awkward one. "Lepida?"

"Yes. She said she was coming to see you."

"Well, she didn't." Paulinus leaned down to brush a bit of dirt off his boot. "She's—we're not really on good terms. I see her sometimes, but . . ." He trailed off again.

"Personally," Thea said in candid tones, "I'd rather be on good terms with a viper than Lepida Pollia."

A mile or two of silence. Thea's painted fan moved slowly back and forth.

"Lady Athena—Thea." Paulinus felt his voice burst out of him. "Have you ever been—well—I mean—have you ever—really *wanted* someone? Wanted them like water in the desert—even when you knew all their faults, every single one—and it didn't matter?"

He saw a deep swell of pity in her eyes, and looked away. "Yes," she said. "Yes, I've wanted someone like that."

". . . How long did it take to forget?"

She shook her head slowly, the fan ceasing its motion. "I didn't."

"You didn't?"

"No . . . Maybe if I'd married and settled down, but—" A shrug. "You should marry, Paulinus."

"Oh. Well, it's not me. It's—it's my friend—Trajan's his name—"

"Of course."

He found it easier to ride ahead of the litter, after that, than meet her eyes.

THEA

GIVEN Domitian's taste for simple living, I was surprised at the beauty of his villa in Tivoli.

It was a jewel of white marble: colonnaded walkways and terraced gardens, urns of lilies and pools of quiet water, rippling mosaics and silver nymphs in niches. A luxurious and solitary hideaway tucked a mile or two from the exquisite town of Tivoli; a place where a man with no privacy could be alone. Domitian had arrived a day or two after me, and for once there were no crowds of courtiers or busy secretaries. Except for silent slaves, the Emperor of Rome and I were utterly alone. Strange.

"We'll dine on the terrace," he ordered me. "One hour."

I dressed carefully in a pink-marbled room that might once have been Julia's, choosing a plain white robe with a silver girdle under the breast, my hair hanging down my back and no jewelry but Larcius's welded copper ring on one hand and a single massive pearl on the other. How nice to take a break from my careful performance toilettes. I pushed the rouge pots and fingernail varnish aside, and glided out to the terrace on bare feet. Two silver couches were drawn up beneath a shaded willow tree, underlaid by the rushing sound of the river below.

The Emperor was already waiting, leaning back on one elbow on his couch as he glanced over a pile of scrolls. "A Vestal Virgin," he remarked, noting my white robe.

"No, just a girl on vacation." I climbed up onto my own

couch, tucked my feet up under me, and helped myself to the
dishes the silent slaves brought out in a noiseless stream. Ostrich
eggs, flamingo tongues, fallow deer in rosemary, sugared hazel-
nuts, pastries in cream, an old red wine in a jeweled flagon—
quite a change from Domitian's usual meals of beef and bread
and beer. There were other changes, too, I noticed. Silk cushions on the couches when usually he despised silk . . . solid silver dishes when he usually ate from clay . . . and instead of the
usual wool tunic he wore a barbarically colored robe of some
exotic eastern silk.

He glanced up, then, and caught my eyes. "Admiring me?"

"Yes," I smiled.

" 'Yes.' " He tasted the word. "You'd say that to any man.
How many have you had?"

"What?"

"How many." His gaze unsettled me: not quite expressionless,
not quite detached. "Come, Athena, take a guess. A hundred?"

"I don't know." Evenly. "Now, I have only you."

"Excellent reply. Glib, convincing, and noncommittal. You
could be a senator, if you weren't a whore."

"I—"

"What are you, twenty-four? You must have had a young
start."

"Caesar—"

"How young? Twelve? Thirteen? When did you learn to lie
so well?"

I set down my goblet. "What a beautiful view you have. May
I look?" I went to the edge of the terrace without waiting for an
answer. There was a sullen streak of red in the sky, all that was
left of the sunset, and a moon coming up over the roof of the
villa. I looked down, past my bare feet. The terrace had no rail,
just a sheer marble edge dropping fifty feet or more to the
smooth-flowing river.

"Dangerous," said Domitian, behind me. "Isn't it?"

"Yes." I turned and looked at him. "But I've got good
balance."

He gazed back for a moment, then rose and crossed the terrace to my side, his barbaric robe crackling. "A lovely view," he
said. "In the morning the mist comes up off the river in a cloud,
like Jupiter when he came to Danae. Quite beautiful." He stirred
my hair with his fingers.

"Did you come here often with Julia?" I blurted without thinking.

"Julia?" He said the name as if he'd never heard it before. "No. She didn't like the terrace—afraid of falling. Not like you."

He wrapped my hair into a rope around his hand. "But you're not Julia, are you?" Gazing absently out over the river, he pulled my head back with a jerk that brought tears to my eyes. "Julia wouldn't stand on the edge."

The pressure on my scalp eased as his hand loosed my hair. I stood frozen as he traced the side of my neck, stroking it almost, this man who never touched me casually. I felt his hand running the length of my neck, felt him breathing behind me, and I was still stupidly surprised when he seized me by the throat and squeezed.

"Are you afraid?" he asked, and his eyes were those of a curious child's.

My toes scrabbled on the bare edge of the terrace. "No."

"You're lying." His hands hardened on my throat.

"Maybe."

"You're terrified."

"No."

"Do you know what I do to liars?"

I was beginning to get a fairly good idea. We swayed on the bare edge of a fifty-foot drop. I was going to fall.

And fall I did—on my hands and knees, on hard marble as he swung me away from the edge. I dragged air through my bruised throat in rattling breaths. I looked up at him.

He regarded me for a moment. Then he smiled, that charming Flavian smile that softened his grim face. "You'll admit it," he said cheerfully. "You'll admit it—that you're afraid. Time for bed."

He scooped me up in one hard soldier's arm.

I woke slowly. Bruises. Pains. A man's hand on my bare shoulder.

I wrenched away, nearly tumbling off the bed. But the man was a fair-haired Greek in a slave's rough tunic, and he smiled at me in a friendly sort of way. The Emperor was nowhere in sight.

"Who are you?" My voice rasped in my own ears.

He just smiled again and began to straighten up the room,

putting the pillows and sheets back in order. He paused when he picked up the dress I'd left on the floor, wrinkling his nose at the stains.

"Throw it away," I said.

He looked at me with such immense sympathy, standing there with the ruined dress in his big hands, that I turned my face away. He'd probably seen it all before. I didn't protest when he picked me up. I doubt I could have walked alone.

He carried me into the little green marble bathhouse that adjoined my bedroom. The pool was already steaming hot; someone had lit the coals. He dunked me in the warm water and bathed me like a baby, scrubbing me with a soft cloth and combing camellia oil into my hair. His fingers were gentle on the bruises.

"What's your name?" I asked.

He smiled, and lifted me out of the pool. Patting me dry with a towel, he wrapped me in a robe and carried me outside. I shook my head quickly.

"No, I don't want to go—not the terrace—do you know where the Emperor—"

He made reassuring noises, gesturing around the empty terrace. There was only one couch drawn up, only one bowl and goblet laid. Below the marble edge, the mist was rising up off the silver river—Jupiter coming to Danae. Beautiful.

I covered my face with my hands.

Dimly I felt the big slave settle me on the couch. He gathered up my wet hair, and I felt the teeth of a comb stroking through the damp strands.

I rocked back and forth in the warm May sunshine, my eyes squeezed shut against my palms.

"Hello, my dear."

I looked up so sharply I nearly fell off the couch. But it wasn't Domitian. It was a little rotund man of about thirty, round-faced, a fringe of ironed curls over his forehead.

"I'm Nessus," he said, beaming. "The Emperor's astrologer. You must be the new concubine? Very pleased to meet you. And no, the Emperor isn't here. Gone on some official business, I believe. He should be gone all day."

I nodded a stiff greeting. I couldn't form a single word, but Nessus didn't seem to notice, plopping down on a carved stool opposite my couch and sticking out his plump sandaled feet.

"Athena, isn't it? Knew it was some sort of goddess. You've

met Ganymede, I see. That's him combing your hair. An apt name, isn't it?"

I looked up at the slave, who smiled over my shoulder. Ganymede—"beautiful youth"—it was apt. He had dark-blue eyes and wheat-colored hair and a form like a golden Apollo. His hands were very gentle. "Thank you," I said hoarsely.

"He's a mute," said Nessus. "Naturally mute, as it happens, though it hardly makes any difference since the other slaves in this villa have had their tongues removed."

I looked at the little astrologer. "You're no mute."

"Yes, well, I'm not a slave. As good as one—no one wants an astrologer these days, so I'm bound to my Imperial pension. Are you going to eat those rolls?"

I pushed the food toward him. "Why—why does no one want an astrologer?"

"Because it's against the law, of course. The Emperor has officially exiled astrologers. But he has found my services useful all the same—quite natural; I *am* the best—so he has found it convenient to keep me at his side. It's a good job as they go: The food is delicious, the wine plentiful, and the pay regular." He smeared honey on a roll. "Now your story. I'm quite famished with curiosity."

"I'm a singer. He saw me, he liked me, he brought me here. That's all."

"You must learn to put a little verve into your storytelling, my dear. Don't be afraid to brag. I myself am an inveterate bragger. There must be something special about you, or he'd never have chosen you in the first place. What's your secret?"

"My secret?" I curved a hand around my throat. "I don't remind him of Julia."

"Ah." Nessus's bright little eyes flicked in quick sympathy to my bruises. "A strange girl, Julia. Such a fragile thing, but she stood eight years of his—" He cleared his throat hastily. "That is, she wasn't as fragile as she looked. Could have bowled me over with a feather when she died. I would have sworn it wasn't her time to go. I'd read her horoscope, you know. Well, she took fate into her hands, she did. Some people can do that." He sighed and bit into a peach.

"You read her horoscope?"

"Yes. And her palm, too. Tell you the truth, I like palms better than stars. Not so much mathematics involved."

"Could you read mine? I want to know how soon he'll get tired of me."

His gaze flickered at my raw voice. He held out his plump little hand and I gave him mine.

"I'll forgo the mystic chanting and hand-waving I usually do at times like these." Nessus's eyes raced over my palm as matter-of-factly as a clerk reading a scroll. "The past first . . . a hot place, hot and dry. A six-pointed star—ah, indicating the race of David! so the hot place must be Judaea. A city full of death, bodies piled three and four—yes, Judaea does have some unpleasant history. Let's skip that part. Afterward, new cities and new people; a new name. Music; that's a constant. Runs through the hand like a gold thread. A few old hatreds. Old loves, too, goodness. A warrior, I see—carved his way deep into this little hand of yours. Applause around him like a cloud; does that mean anything to you?"

"No," I said hoarsely. "Keep going."

"After the warrior, a child—oh, don't stiffen up, I won't tell. More children, but that's edging into the future. Yes, a whole mess of children."

"Whose children?" Not Domitian's children, not his, oh God, not his. I thought of the Egyptian paste of auyt gum and acacia tips that could block conception; the tinctures of pennyroyal and rue that would end a pregnancy if the paste failed. Whores' tricks, learned in my time on the waterfront, and I'd use them gladly. No child of mine would ever be Domitian's.

"Doesn't say whose children. It's a palm, not a genealogy. Now, there's a crown at the base of the finger. We both know who that is. The lines here are cross-hatched—a time of trial approaches."

"How long?" I whispered.

"I don't know. Some time, I believe. A period of hardship, outcome uncertain. More than that—" He folded my fingers over my palm and pushed it back at me. "A gnarled past, m'dear, and a gnarled future. I'm sorry."

"Some time?" I repeated. "How much is *some*? A long time?"

Ganymede patted my head.

"It's times like this I hate seeing the future." Nessus pushed the plate back at me. "Here. Have a bun."

Nineteen

&⁊&

THEA

GANYMEDE prodded me into going shopping. I visited the more fashionable of Tivoli's shopping forums, and even with a veil over my face everyone knew me.

"My lady, some perfume?"

"Some rouge from India?"

"Silks to make your skin glow!"

I walked woodenly through the forum, pointing at whatever I wanted. I chose things that would keep their value, gold figurines and ivory ornaments, things small enough to be carried out the door in a hurry. Ganymede trailed at my heels like a patient dog, carrying the growing mound of packages. Pleb women whispered behind their hands at me; patrician ladies arched their plucked brows; a pair of legionnaires elbowed each other. Everyone cleared out of my way.

Jewels. I walked into the nearest shop, pointed at a tray of rings, and before the shopkeeper's bemused eye began to load them onto my bruised hands. Two or three per finger, gold and silver and pearls—

"Bracelets, my lady?"

"Yes." I slid handfuls of ornate bands over my arms until I looked like a shackled criminal, then clasped three or four necklaces about my neck. "The Emperor's stewards will see to your bill," I said, and walked out with my king's ransom. The

ransom that might buy me a future when the Emperor tired
of me.

Please, let that be soon.

I crossed the road toward the nearest seat, a cool marble
block by the Temple of Jove. A cart pulled up sharply to avoid
hitting me, but no one swore or shook their fist. I was the
Emperor's woman; who would touch me? The red-and-gold
armored Praetorian who marched at my back wasn't there to
protect me, but to keep me from running away.

Ganymede made an inquiring noise. "Yes," I said, sitting.
"Yes, you were right to drag me out. It's lovely." Even lovelier
to be on my own, to know that the Emperor had gone back to
the city and might not be back until the next evening . . .

I lifted my face to the wind. A beautiful breezy day. Not
cold, although I had my wool *palla* clutched tight around my
shoulders. A perfect day.

I huddled deeper into my wool and my jewels.

"Ganymede! Ganymede, is that you?"

I looked up. Ganymede, a beaming grin breaking out over
his face, thrust my packages aside to step forward and bow
excitedly before a little woman in yellow who was climbing
down from an elaborate gold-trimmed litter.

"Yes," she said, "I'm delighted to see you, too. I wish I still
owned you, Ganymede; I've not had a good massage since losing you. Oh, who's this?" Her dark eyes turned on me.

"Athena, Domina." My manners asserted themselves, and I
rose.

"I am Lady Flavia Domitilla." Her warm little hand raised
me from my curtsy. "I live in the villa just over the hill there. Or
rather I live there now; my husband used to be governor of
Syria. But the Emperor's recalled us at last, so I'm determined
to settle down and be a proper Roman matron. The Emperor,"
she added casually, "is my uncle."

So she was that Flavia Domitilla: Emperor Titus's other
daughter from his first marriage; Domitian's second niece. Less
interesting and less gossipworthy than her half-sister Julia, since
she had married well and produced the correct two sons. Which
meant that—hmm—it was perhaps the mother of the future
Emperor who stood opposite me with the charming Flavian
smile on her rosy face.

"You must come up and visit me at my villa sometimes," she

was chattering. "It's no more than a fifteen-minute jog by litter, and I adore company. I'm afraid I can't pay calls on you, since my uncle detests callers."

I blinked. Visit? A patrician woman, a Flavian princess, no less, inviting her uncle's whore to drop by? Did she even know what I was?

"Oh, this is luck!" She clapped her soft hands. "I've been simply dying for a look at you. You're quite lovely, aren't you? I certainly didn't hear wrong about that."

"The Emperor—told you about me?"

"Of course not. He never tells anybody anything. But slaves talk, even the mute ones. I've heard so much about your singing, you must sing for me sometime. You play the lyre, too? Oh dear, is that a bruise?"

I looked at her sharply, searching for veiled curiosity. But she regarded the blue mark on my wrist without avidity.

"I fell out of my litter, Domina." I pulled down my sleeve. How much did she know about Domitian, this patrician lady in yellow who wore her Flavian charm all around her like perfume from India? How much had her half-sister Julia told her?

Have you inherited your uncle's tastes along with his eyes, my lady?

"Ask Ganymede to make you his special salve." Flavia gestured, and I fell into step beside her as she moved down the street with the blind confidence of one for whom crowds always clear a path. "He makes a lovely-smelling paste that's very good for cuts and bruises. He was constantly mixing the stuff up for my half-sister Julia. She was always falling out of litters."

I looked at Lady Flavia Domitilla, and her black eyes regarded me shrewd and unblinking from her cheerful Flavian face.

I curtsied again. "Thank you, Domina."

"Oh, good heavens, just make it Lady Flavia." Patting my arm. "Well, I'm afraid I must dash—far too much to do this morning. Do remember to drop in."

Another flash of yellow, and she was gone, her Praetorians trailing behind her like a comet's tail.

By evening the Emperor was back. "I'll be coming and going all summer. Get used to it."

"Yes, Lord and God."

"I thought we had agreed on 'Caesar.' "

"Yes, Caesar."

"Because you Jews only believe in one god, don't you? So when you call me 'Lord and God,' well, you're either lying or you think I really *am* your one God."

"Would you like some wine?"

"No, I would not. Which is it, Athena? Am I a god, or are you lying to me?"

"No matter what I say, you'll tell me I'm lying."

"Perhaps." He lay back. "So what is this one true god of yours like?"

"He's harsh. But just, too."

"Does he take mortal wives, like Jove?"

"No. He is male and female both."

"No wonder the Jews are such a crushed people. Tell me, do you fear this womanish god of yours?"

"Yes. I do."

"But not me." He took my hair in his hand and brought me down against the edge of the sleeping couch. I turned my face in time, so my cheek hit the sharp corner instead of my eye.

"Why?"

I had nothing to give him.

L ONG days. Sun burning. Mostly alone, as Domitian flitted back and forth to the city on Imperial business. I took endless shopping trips, endless baths. Worried about Vix, doubtlessly causing trouble for Penelope. Read my horoscope, drawn up by Nessus. The stars gave the same bad news as my palm. Nessus looked apologetic, and Ganymede stroked his hand and crooned wordlessly. Could they be lovers? Anybody'd love Ganymede, mute or not.

Domitian, in between working on new legislation, was writing a manual on hair care. Had thin hair himself, God help you if you mentioned it. I recommended an elderflower rinse to improve shine, but was told to be quiet. An Emperor penning hair advice? Well, we all need hobbies. Emperor Tiberius played with slave girls, Emperor Claudius studied the Etruscans, Domitian wrote about hair. His other hobby was lining the slaves up below the terrace and shooting arrows between their outstretched fingers. He was very good; never missed unless he wanted to. In a bad mood, he liked to be accurate. In a good mood, he liked to miss.

I sang songs for Larcius. Saw him large and pink and approving; Penelope, too. She said to get more sleep. Larcius said I sounded hoarse. Too much choking, I told him seriously, and he understood. Then he disappeared, and I woke up and realized I'd been dreaming.

A month gone already. Only a few more months of summer left, then Domitian would be returning to Rome and I would go back to Brundisium, back to my boy, back to Larcius and his gentle voice. A few months. Going very slowly.

"Nessus tells me you've met my niece, Flavia Domitilla."

"Yes, I have."

"A featherbrained girl, just like her mother. A Christian, of all things. Do you know what they are? A ratlike people who scuttle in catacombs and paint fishes on walls. I've contemplated removing Flavia's sons from her care, but they seem to be good Romans thus far."

"Are they to be your heirs, then?"

"Correct. Since my wife has failed to provide alternatives. Are you looking to provide one yourself? I hear you've had at least one child—"

"Farmed out," I lied quickly. "I don't like children. I've never even seen it." *Oh, God, let him believe me.* The thought of Vix in this monster's hands—

"Open your eyes," breathed Domitian, "and tell me you're afraid of me."

"No."

"I can smell it on you."

"No."

Long nights. Moon burning like hot silver. Never alone. Long, long nights, full of strange things. The sharp pen he used to spear flies out of the air; used for other things. Soft bracelets on chains, fastening my wrists to the sleeping couch. Questions. "It hurts? No? If I shift the edge deeper—" Blank-eyed and busy-handed, a scientist among his experiments.

Childish, to think the brothel was bad. Too unimaginative to be bad. Tiring, but not bad. Bad is a cheerful voice at midnight, saying, "Afraid now? Hours left to work on that!"

Jars and jars of Ganymede's ointment.

"It's not bad yet, Thea." Julia scolded me gently in my dreams, robed all in white like a Vestal Virgin. "Wait eight years for bad." *Julia, I wronged you. Believed you were mad. Might be mad, myself. Did he like to watch you when you slept?*

A second month gone by. So slowly.

"You're looking pale, Athena," Flavia Domatilla greeted me. "Not enough sun. I don't care what these die-away beauties say, sun is for soaking up, not fleeing from like a horde of barbarians. How is the Emperor?"

"Very well, Lady Flavia." She never asked further than that, and I never elaborated. "How are the boys?"

She brightened. "Running wild, brown as Arabs, and declaring they'll never go back to the city as long as they live."

"And your lord husband?" I'd met Flavius Clemens, a pale gentleman who was certainly aware of my profession, but who accorded me the same exquisite courtesy he extended toward every woman, from his wife down to the lowest body slave.

"He's much better for all this fresh air. I declare, I'm never going back to the city, either. I'm having such fun, ripping up this villa and putting it back together. I just had the mosaics done last week."

I looked at the floor, finding the pattern of two iridescent-scaled fish repeated in circles. "Lovely," I said. "The fish . . . they're a Christian symbol, aren't they?"

"I see my uncle's told you about my little peccadillo." A dimple appeared in her chin as she smiled. "Yes, I'm a Christian. My mother's freedman Thrax was, and given the way my mother's husbands came and went, Thrax was nearly my father, so I suppose something stuck. I embarrass the Emperor greatly, I'm afraid. It's no secret, even though I make all the right genuflections in public."

"You—you might want to be careful, Lady Flavia," I said diffidently. I liked her, she was more than courteous to me, but the social gap between us was still enormous. "The Emperor said he might—might take the boys away, if they weren't raised as good Romans."

"Oh, but they are. Besides, he'd never take them away. Because where could he move them but into the palace with him? He dislikes children far too much for that. In the end, he'll just dismiss my beliefs as an irritating little hobby. Really, that's all it is. Who's to care if I take food baskets to some of my poorer brethren now and then?"

Her placid tone aroused my immediate suspicion. Flavia went far beyond food baskets, surely. Were all the slaves swarming around her pretty villa really just slaves? Were all the ragged children begging at her door really just beggars? Secrets ran in the Flavian family, for its kindest members as well as its cruelest. But she never asked mine, and so I'd never ask hers. She was already chattering on about something more innocuous.

"—so you've had Nessus draw up your horoscope? It's bound to be right; he's the best astrologer in the Empire. A pity my faith doesn't permit me to consult astrologers. Isn't he a dear? I may consult him anyway. He's always been thankful to me, ever since I lent him Ganymede for a massage. I never got Ganymede back, of course; Nessus spun some meaningless prophecy to keep him. My faith doesn't permit me to approve of boy-lovers, either, but I must say they are happy—"

Did me good, listening to her. I think she knew it, too. Always urged me to come again, and never asked questions. Had she learned that lesson with Julia?

I thought about Arius.

A hard body blazing heat through a blue tunic. Hair a true red in the sun. Knotted muscles flowing like warm honey. Scars on the back of his hand, on his forehead, on his shoulder. I had nearly as many myself, now. Odd little white scars, made with odd little toys in places that wouldn't show. Not visible scars made with swords.

A hard face. Broken nose. Cloud-colored eyes. Slash of a mouth. Eyebrow interrupted by a knife-line. Male smells: sun-warmed leather, iron, sweat, arena sand. But not blood, somehow—not blood. Blood washed off.

Hard hands, warm hands that gripped a wine cup some-times, or a sword, or a throat. Or they just—touched. For joy's sake, not for pain's.

Go away, Arius. Go away and leave me alone.

THREE months had passed. Cool autumn breezes touched even the summer warmth of Tivoli. September around the corner. Fall was here. Fall was here.

"Time for Rome again," Domitian remarked over dinner. "Pity. It's been a delightful summer."

"Delightful," I murmured into my wine goblet.

"Sarcasm doesn't become you, Athena." He was in a good mood, however; my punishment was mild. "Well, sarcasm or not, you've served me well. A delightful summer companion. How shall I reward you?"

"You've rewarded me enough, Caesar."

"With my divine presence?"

"And with all the presents you've let me buy for myself on your credit."

"Yes, you did get rather greedy among the jewelry shops. The Jew coming out in you, no doubt."

"No doubt." *Send me home, oh please send me home.*

Domitian pushed back his dinner plate, rising with a rustle of exotic silk and going to the naked edge of the terrace. He looked healthy and fit, color glowing in his cheeks, the hint of that charming smile rarely leaving his mouth. He regarded the river for a moment, then swung around. "Come here."

I came.

He placed an absent hand on the nape of my neck, and I felt my toes curling over the marble edge. I wavered, and he smiled.

"Shall I pull you back?" he said.

I knew beyond a shadow of doubt that if I said yes, I'd go over the edge.

"No." I looked him right in the eye. "I'm not afraid of heights, Caesar."

For a moment I thought I was going over anyway. But as he'd done on our first night here, he swung me away from the brink and let me fall to the marble floor.

Then he stepped forward and lowered his sandal over my splayed hand—not hard, just firmly enough to hurt. My littlest finger, the one with Larcius's slave ring, rested directly beneath his heel.

His last gift, I thought frozenly. *All the lyre strings in the world, and no fifth finger to reach them. He'll take my music—*

His foot tapped on my finger a moment. Then he knelt with the swift grace that sat so oddly on his thick body, and when he picked up my hand I saw he had a dagger.

I struggled, of course. But he prisoned my hand in his hard

fingers, and the blade flashed—and it took me a moment to realize that for once there was no blood and no pain.

The plain welded ring with Larcius's name clattered onto the
marble in two pieces.

I stared at it.

"Cheap thing," said Domitian, sheathing the dagger. "Un-
worthy of a brave woman."

My finger had a white band instead of a welded copper one.
"You're freeing me?"

"I thought you might care to wear this instead." He flipped
open a small filigree coffer by the dining couch, and turned
with his hands outstretched, gesturing for me to turn. I caught
sight of a silver band before he looped it close around my throat.
Looking down I could just see a shiny black stone—jet,
maybe—nestling in the base of my throat. "It's—it's beautiful."
He allowed me to buy whatever I wished, but since the lyre
strings, he'd never chosen anything for me himself.

He made no reply, just beckoned over my head. When I
looked up there was a blacksmith in the door, soot-stained and
out of place on the elegant terrace.

"Weld it closed," said Domitian. "It doesn't matter if you
burn her."

"What?" I twisted my head to look at him. "Weld—"

"A more elegant version of that tawdry ring," he explained
genially. "I added the stone out of whimsy. A black stone. Consider it my eye upon you. I like to mark my belongings."

I felt the blacksmith's rough hands at my neck, hooking the
silver band. "But—but you said—"

"I arrested Praetor Larcius on grounds of treason," Domitian
said carelessly. "He was permitted to commit suicide, after the
trial. The possessions of traitors are forfeit to the Imperium, of
course. You now belong to me."

"Larcius." I forced the words through stiff lips. "No. Oh, no—"

"Yes. I didn't think I'd find you so interesting, not after three
months. But there's something in you I seem to like, and on a
long-term basis I prefer to own rather than rent. You'll return to
Rome with me in a week."

The silver was hot on my neck, softening, welding together.
I barely felt the burn. Inside I was cold as frost. Larcius. Larcius
dead.

Oh, God—*Vix*—

"You know I've built a new palace? Nearly completed. I'll use it for public functions . . . and for the Empress's quarters. You'll move into her old rooms next to mine in the Domus Augustana—that's my private palace. You know, I had a statue of Minerva carved with your face for my private temple? Perhaps you really are a goddess. It would be foolish to let my very own goddess slip away from me, wouldn't it? And I've never been a fool."

Vix. Where was Vix now? *Where was my son?*

Domitian traced my neck, his eyes turning blank and absent. "I like to play games, you know. With my chamberlains, my senators, my guards. It's easy to make them afraid of me. Even my wife's afraid under that marble face of hers. But you aren't. You and one other—you know who? He's not even a human being. Just a slave, another animal like you. A gladiator; the one they call the Barbarian. Can't be a god, no matter what they say. Just a barbarian. But he doesn't fear me, either, you know. And he survives—survives everything. Stands on the edge and looks—looks up at me—and looks—but we'll take care of him. We'll see him when we get back, in the first games of the season—and that will be that. There is only one lord and god in Rome—and a goddess; I can put up with that, Athena."

There was more pain, more pain that I hardly noticed, because the blacksmith had stepped away and the silver had cooled. Cooled to a solid band around my neck that would never, ever come off.

Twenty

❦❦

THEA

So it's to be a family parade," Flavia groaned. "Which means triumphs and rose petals and trumpets and those ghastly games. I've been Imperially summoned back to the city," she explained as I looked blank. "Me and my husband and the boys. My uncle must feel the masses need a little pomp and spectacle. Maybe they grumbled too loudly about his last levy."

"But Paulinus says he's very popular."

"Oh, with the army; they think the world of him. But the Roman plebs just want a tax cut and lots of chariot races. Therefore, if one raises the taxes one must spend elsewhere. Usually on pomp and spectacle." Flavia gave a small, dry smile. "I'm only a feather-brained Christian, my dear, but I do know how these things work."

I was starting to learn, myself.

"Well, the boys will be happy," Flavia said. "I'm afraid to say they simply adore the Colosseum. Maybe I can leave them with their father and plead a headache before the blood really starts to flow. That's what Julia and I always did. Oh, dear, I do miss her." Flavia sighed, rather sadly. But she looked up at me and smiled again. "I'll miss you, too, Athena. You've been marvelous company."

"Why don't you call me Thea, Lady Flavia?" My hand strayed up to the lump of jet—Domitian's eye—that sat at my throat. "I'm going to Rome, too."

And I would be seeing the games.

ROME

U NDER the Colosseum, Arius could already hear the crowd.
        "Feisty today, aren't they?" Hercules observed. The dog,
curled up on Arius's cloak, snored oblivious.

Methodically Arius stripped down and readied himself. The
blue kilt. The greaves. The mail sleeve for his fighting arm,
embossed all over with what some wealthy fan had imagined were
barbaric symbols. At the familiar routine, the demon woke and
stretched inside him, not snapping at the leash as in the old days
but still looking around with a certain interest. Arius stretched,
reaching for his sword. A sword with beautiful balance and a
special left-handed grip, forged just for him. Being the best had
its privileges.

"It's time." Hercules reached for his own sword, a miniature
copy of Arius's.

The cheering was louder. Dust sifted down from the ceiling
as they wound through the dim passages. Just outside the cages
of doomed Christians, Gallus cornered them.

"Ah, so glad I caught you. Good luck today, good luck. You
do know you have two fights today, don't you, dear boy? Yes,
just wanted to be sure. And in case there are any other surprises,
well, don't be surprised!" Gallus patted Hercules on his diminu-
tive head, ran a hand along Arius's bare arm, and disappeared
with a wink of jewels.

Hercules looked after him. "Is it just me, or has that bastard
got something up his sleeve?"

"It's just you." Arius turned his head up, catching the sound
of the applause again. In the cage behind him, the Christians
moaned and crossed themselves.

Today, he thought, *today's important*—and wondered why.

THEA

A splendid parade. How could it not be? I sat in my cur-
        tained litter in the back, but I still saw it all, peeking
through the black silk curtains.

Rose petals. Banners. Trumpeters—a modest number, since

it was no military triumph we were celebrating, but simply the festival of Volturnalia. Praetorians, rank by rank in their red and gold. Paulinus, back from the German front and looking very noble on a black horse, much cheered. Flavia and her husband in litters, smiling and bowing as only royalty can smile and bow. Emperor Domitian himself in a gold chariot, flanked by Flavia's proud sons. The younger boy was Vix's age. Then there was me, in a silver litter with the curtains fluttering just enough to let them catch a glimpse of a purple silk gown, a flash of silver and amethysts, a bare white ankle on black velvet cushions . . .

My head ached.

I kept seeing Larcius, as I'd last seen him. A fond kiss good-bye, as I left for Tivoli. Never dreaming the Emperor would swat him aside like a fly, simply to get possession of me. Why? He certainly didn't need to; could have bought me outright—but a man like Domitian would always rather swat than buy. I wrote to another praetor in Brundisium who had once been fond of my singing, begging for details of Larcius's death, and he replied in a brief stilted letter. Larcius had been convicted of treason in a mockery of a trial—but as Domitian said, he had been allowed to commit suicide. He'd hosted a final dinner party for all those friends not afraid to be tainted by his association, but really it would have been a farewell to his musicians. I could see it easily: Larcius in the place of honor with Penelope at his side, listening to his choirboys, his lute players, his singers perform one last time. He would have given each performance its due, stopping afterward for a final kind word, a few coins, perhaps a last criticism. Behind the curtain the slaves would all have been weeping wrecks, but they would have performed their best for him. Bidding his guests farewell, he had apparently retired into his bedroom, where he had climbed into a perfumed bath and cut his wrists.

I had not a shred of doubt that Penelope had held his hand till the end, then taken the knife and joined him.

What will happen to the household? I wrote the praetor, frantic for Vix.

"Traitors' wills are nullified, and their possessions forfeit to the Imperium," came the reply. "Praetor Larcius's brother purchased the bulk of his estate back from the Imperial auctioneers, except the musicians. Please don't write to me again, Lady Athena."

So much for the pleasant household that had turned me from a prostitute to an artist, given me and my son happiness. Larcius's brusque brother did not care for music, but he would surely have bought Vix along with the rest of the household slaves. Big strong boys were valuable; stable hands until they grew, and then guards or litter-bearers. At least my son was safe . . . until he began making trouble.

Which meant he wouldn't be safe for long.

Oh God, who knew when I would see him again?

"Lady Athena." The guard repeated himself, impatient. The litter had stopped; curtains swept aside. Incense. Priests. More trumpets. More cheering. I got down—and saw the Colosseum. A vast charnel house, blocking the sun.

When I stumbled, Ganymede leaped forward, steadying me. Dear Ganymede. My appointed body slave now . . . and Nessus somewhere behind us in the crowd of freedmen, following wherever Ganymede went.

"All right," I murmured, and stepped out. Up the marble steps, never mind the headache—walk. Right behind Lady Flavia, no doubt planning herself a headache before the main show. The two boys behind, hopping with excitement. Then Paulinus with a girl in red on his arm. Behind the Emperor with the wife he hated at his side—the Empress, tall and dark and all emeralds, gazing through me. Up through a marble hall to the Imperial box. Didn't think. Didn't think. Especially not about Vix, who might now be yowling under a beating from his new owner, not understanding that he could be sold on the slave market in a heartbeat.

The arena stretched in front of my eyes, all clean white sand. Not clean for long. No gladiators yet—they'd be below, waiting, praying. Arius would be there, but as many times as I'd tried to picture that in the past weeks—seeing him again, fighting in this arena, almost close enough to touch—blind panic closed around my head like a vise.

I turned my eyes away from the spreading oval of sand, rushing at a seat in the back. Ganymede stood behind me like a post. Hand on my shoulder, comforting. Before me sat Domitian, the boys on one side, his wife on the other; Flavia on the edge where she could sneak out, Paulinus—

"Athena," someone said. "What a surprise."

Lepida Pollia, Paulinus's guest, was seated right beside me.

* * *

MARCUS Norbanus had a grudging liking for the chariot races, since his cousin and friend Diana often dragged him to the Circus Maximus, but he didn't often attend the games. "A barbaric spectacle unenlightened by taste and informed by need," he sometimes said, and wondered at the sight of the mob bending to decrees they had howled objection to four days previous. Yet he did sometimes come, generally bringing a slave to hold his scrolls and quills so that he could work between the big fights, which he watched coolly. "Go to the games," Marcus said dryly, "to see Rome at its purest." As he went to the Barbarian's latest fight, he expected nothing more surprising than the usual victory and the mob's usual hysteria.

"Dominus." His steward spoke low-voiced in his ear. "I've just received word that Lady Lepida received an invitation to the Imperial box."

"That's of little importance," Marcus shrugged.

"Yes, sir, but she took Lady Vibia Sabina with her this morning—"

"To the *games*?"

"Yes, Dominus. And since she could not take Lady Sabina to the Imperial box—"

Rage boiled in Marcus's middle as he made his way to the high-walled section where the patrician women sat. A frail seven-year-old girl, taken to the games and then abandoned among strangers. He found his daughter crammed in a corner behind a cluster of Lepida's fashionable friends, dressed in her best and utterly forgotten as the painted women giggled and slopped wine and called down to the gladiators. Marcus made his apologies in a cutting voice and extricated his daughter. "Can we go h-home?" she hiccuped. She had a wine stain on her dress from where someone had dropped a goblet on her.

Marcus hesitated. He'd like nothing better than to take his daughter home, but crowds of plebs were pressing excitedly through every entrance, feverish with excitement. Even with the Norbanus slaves to beat a path, it would take a stifled, sweating hour to make their way home—and nothing brought on Sabina's fits like crowds. "We'll leave after the Barbarian's fight when the crowd quiets," he decided. "Until then, you can sit quietly and rest, Vibia Sabina."

But there was no quiet to be found in his box.

"Ow—leggo, leggo—"

"Quintus?" Marcus entered, brows raised, and saw his steward struggling with a slave boy.

"Pardon, Dominus, I caught this one trying to sneak in—" a sudden howl as the boy twisted and got his teeth into the steward's wrist, darting for the entrance, but Marcus's hand shot out and caught the back of the young neck.

"So," he said mildly, "what are you? A slave, I think. Who is your master?"

The boy made a good break, but Marcus had anticipated it and dug a grip in the rough tunic. The boy scowled again: he was perhaps a year older than Sabina, russet-haired and sunburned. Sabina gazed at him, wide-eyed.

"Where do you come from? Tell me, boy," Marcus ordered as he saw the young jaw jut, "or I'll turn you over to the magistrates."

"Brundisium." Sulkily.

"So far? Did your master bring you?"

"My master's dead. I hitched a cart to Misenum, then kept going on." The boy shrugged. "All the roads come here."

"All roads lead to Rome," Marcus agreed. Sabina giggled at his side.

The slave boy looked sullen. "I just wanted to see the Great City."

"I see. And you could not start with the chariot races?"

"Those are for pussies!"

Sabina surprised Marcus by giggling again. "Father," she tugged his sleeve, "can he stay?"

"If he has the stomach for it." Marcus found his daughter a low stool well back from any view of the arena and nodded at the boy. "Keep out of the way and keep quiet, but watch if you like."

"Can I?" The boy bowed for the first time, grinning. "You got a good view, Dominus. I didn't miss the gladiators, did I? Took me forever to sneak in—"

"Quiet," said Marcus, amused.

"Sorry, Dominus." The boy ducked a bow again, not sounding terribly sorry, and settled by the rail.

"What's your name?" Sabina ventured.

"Vix." He looked down at the little silken presence at his elbow. "Vercingetorix, actually, but that's kind of a mouthful."

"After the Gallic chieftain?" Sabina glanced at Marcus. Just last week her tutors had reviewed Vercingetorix in their account of Gaul's conquest.

"He was my father." Bragging.

"He died over a hundred years ago."

"He was my grandfather," Vix amended.

"You really ran all the way from *Brundisium*?"

"Yeah, I used to belong to this old guy, but he died, and I didn't want to go to the slave market."

Sabina's eyes widened. Vix expanded under her gaze.

"It was rough getting out of Brundisium. I stole a chariot, right? And the driver comes after me with a whip—"

Marcus looked at the two children: his daughter; tiny, quiet, clean, and pearled, and the slave boy, filthy, foul-mouthed, grinning, and mendacious. *Dear gods*, he thought. *My daughter's made a friend.*

THEA

IUGULA!" Lepida shouted down at a gladiator begging mercy, her eager profile flushed pink, and for a horrid moment I had a feeling that I should be standing at her back with a peacock-feather fan. A wave of sickness caught at my throat.

Lepida settled back, fanning herself pleasantly as blood spurted on the sand. "Still no taste for the games, Thea?"

In the arena a Moroccan was beheading a Gaul. "No," I said. "I'm merely bored." Closing my eyes.

"Bored? But it's so thrilling!" All around us in the stands people were on their feet, waving, shouting, shrieking. Flavia's two sons were fascinated. Domitian watched with an expert's detached eye. Paulinus's gaze wandered restlessly, looking anywhere but at Lepida. His hand rested on her armrest, a bare half inch from hers as if afraid she'd burn him.

Paulinus and Lepida? Nothing shocked me anymore. Poor Paulinus.

Poor Gaul. Dragged off flopping by his heels.

"Well!" Lepida ate a stuffed grape leaf, sucking her pretty

fingers. "I can't wait to see what's next. What *is* next, Paulinus?" She traced his wrist with a scarlet-lacquered nail, and he jerked. "Oh, of course. The Barbarian." She smiled at me.

I stretched my mouth into a blind smile. "And how is your husband, Lady Lepida? Shouldn't you be sitting with him?" Words tumbled off my lips, any words. "Don't tell me you've run through his money already."

Lepida opened her mouth, but then there was a flutter of orange silk and a jangle of gold bracelets as Flavia rose. "Oh dear," she murmured. "I feel quite faint—the heat—you'll excuse me, Uncle? Boys, be good—" She disappeared.

"Do you feel all right, Thea?" Lepida's soft, solicitous tones. "You don't look at all well. Perhaps you should go home, too. Hmmm—where *is* your home, these days?"

"The palace." I had the pleasure of watching her face tighten and prepared a cutting little speech, but it died in my throat. Because the crowd's murmuring rose to a roar, and for the first time in a week the agony of worry for my son was drowned out as his father strode out onto the sand.

Arius.

I didn't realize my lips were silently shaping his name over and over, not until Ganymede touched my shoulder and made an inquiring noise. I smiled jerkily at him, but couldn't take my eyes off the gladiator who had once been my lover—passing so close to the Imperial box that I could count the scars on his back.

Dwarfed by that vast space, just as I remembered. Deaf to the applause, just as I remembered. More lines in the set brown mask of his face. But still tall and unstooped. Still refusing to strut or smile. Still beautiful.

God, he was so beautiful.

He didn't bow to the Emperor. Just jerked his head in a gesture reminding me abruptly of Vix. Then he turned away and lifted his sword, and I felt the old iron hand clamp around my lungs.

He fought a Thracian. The face was a blur in my eyes. All I could see was a pair of wicked little Thracian swords flashing in the sun and I couldn't breathe, especially when a curved blade clipped into Arius's leg and came out covered in blood. But then somehow one of those wicked curved swords went flying and Arius came forward in a fluid lunge. He fought more calmly now, his movements more connected, the arc of his blade more controlled. The Thracian fell screaming with a half-severed foot, speedily finished off with a thrust through the heart. I went through the motions of clapping.

"What a bore," Lepida pouted. "If he'd lose just once—"

Arius yanked off his helmet, raking his fingers through his hair and through my heart, too. He tossed his sword over to the arena guard, strode forward, and jerked his head at the Emperor again. Domitian, playing dice and playing mind games with two courtiers, wasn't even paying attention to the arena. But Arius paused, drawing out an odd moment, and Domitian looked at him. I saw the tension in the back of the Emperor's neck and remembered: *Even my wife's afraid under that marble face of hers. But you aren't. You and one other—you know who? He's not even a human being. Just a slave, another animal like you. A gladiator; the one they call the Barbarian.*

At last Arius tore his eyes away and turned toward the Gate of Life. I'd forgotten the exact dip and sway of his shoulders. Imagine forgetting that.

The murmurs in the stands changed to laughter as a trapdoor opened in the arena floor, and a tiny black-bearded figure skipped out. A dwarf, dressed like a miniature Arius. A comic performer. I didn't think I could ever laugh again.

Arius stopped a moment, bending his head toward the dwarf. He grinned at some joke, and my insides melted like a candle. So he'd found a friend. He needed friends.

He slapped the dwarf's shoulder, setting off again for the Gate of Life. But just as I began to relax, four arena guards stepped down and seized Arius. Another trapdoor opened in the floor and out came a half dozen green-kilted Brigantians with swords in hand.

WHILE the midday executions had been dragging on, the slave boy had been engrossed in telling Sabina about his adventures on the way to Rome, which apparently featured flying horses, three-headed dogs, and a gang of forty thieves. As soon as the Barbarian appeared, Marcus noticed, the boy fell raptly silent.

"Whoa. Oh, whoa." Sitting back with a whistle when the fight was done. "Whoa."

"What?" Sabina craned her neck. Marcus nudged her back, below the rail. She was too young to see anything the arena had to offer. She didn't seem to mind, though; her eyes were round as saucers from the slave boy's fibs, and she hardly seemed to hear the arena's racket of screams and clashes.

"The Barbarian." Vix sounded awed. "I knew he was the best, but he's even best-er than I ever thought. He's a *god*."

"He is very good," Marcus found himself agreeing. "I always make sure he has a fight after the Senate imposes a new tax. He calms the mob down for weeks."

Sabina blinked. "Who's the Barbarian?"

"Where'd you grow up?" Vix looked down at her. "In a box?"

"I'm not allowed to go to the games, usually. I have epilepsia," she explained, "and excitement isn't good for me."

"I never knew anybody with epilepsia." He eyed Sabina with more interest. "'Cept Julius Caesar, but I guess I didn't really *know* him. Y'know gladiator's blood'll cure it? I should give you some of my blood. I'm gonna be a gladiator, too, y'know."

Her eyes widened again. "Are not."

"Are too." The boy aimed a thrust at the wall with an imaginary sword. "I'll be even better than the Barbarian."

"You'll get in trouble."

"You get in trouble no matter what you do," Vix said sagely, "so you might as well do everything you can."

A philosopher, Marcus thought. What an appalling child. And Sabina looked entranced.

"Hey, they're opening the trapdoor." Vix leaned forward over the rail. "What's next?"

WHAT—" Arius twisted as the guards grabbed hold of his arms. "My fight's done."

"We've got orders," one of the guards said shortly. "If you know what's good for you, hold still."

They wrenched him around, two holding each side, and he saw a trapdoor open in the sand to disgorge a half-dozen green-kilted boys from Brigantia. Fanning out, swords held wide, toward a puzzled Hercules.

"No." Too late, Arius began to struggle.

Hercules looked around, confused. His comic act came next: "Arius the Barbarian mowing down the heathen," the heathen being played by twenty peacocks. But there were no peacocks in sight . . . just a half-dozen boys with their swords out.

"Oh," he said. "Oh."

The comic wooden sword dropped from his fingers.

He ran.

They fell on him.

THE boys fanned out into a circle, and Arius saw Hercules stagger. Run for an opening. Go down in a welter of rising and falling sword hilts.

From a long way away he heard himself cursing, felt himself wrenching at the guards. A blow fell across the back of his head and he went to his knees.

Panting and sobbing, Hercules wriggled free. Dashed for escape on his short legs. A howl of laughter went up from the stands as he made a great scrambling leap and tried to climb the wall.

They pulled him down.

Arius got an arm free and crashed his fist into the face of one of the guards. A shield boss clubbed down on Arius's shoulders, and he ate sand.

Hercules was screaming.

Arius erupted off the ground and took a guard around the knees. He clawed his hands up to the man's belt, and got his dagger.

Hercules was screaming his name.

Arius found a gap in the armor and stabbed. Blood pattered on his face. He rolled off the body, surged to his feet, and took a great lurching leap before three guards hit him from behind and he went down again.

For a moment his eyes got clear of sand and saw Hercules' face. A white oval pressed into the ground, two blind eyes filled with blood, a smeared mouth opening in a black howl.

Arius felt his mouth opening, his whole body cracking, and somewhere inside his head he howled back. A long unending scream consumed him, a dreadful backdrop to the thuds of the sword hilts against Hercules' body as the Brigantian boys leisurely beat him to death.

His vision went black as the demon reared its head and screamed.

They gave him his sword and let him go.

"Well," Marcus said mildly. "This is interesting." Beside him the slave boy hung open-mouthed on the rail.

Arius fell to his knees when they released him. The sword dropped from his hands.

Kill them, howled the demon, but it seemed very far away.

Couldn't breathe. He ripped off his helmet, flung it aside. His fingers curled in on themselves.

Kill them, whimpered the demon. He could imagine Gallus smiling, settling back in his chair. "That should bring out the old Barbarian," he would be saying happily. "Enjoy the show!"

Arius rocked back on his heels. The Brigantians gazed, panting, swords wavering in damp hands.

Arius spread his arms. His hands were bleeding from where the nails had dug in, but he felt nothing. "Kill me."

They stared at him.

"Kill me," he roared. "Kill me, you bastards!"

His voice echoed around the death-silent Colosseum. He flowed to his feet and took a ferocious step forward, spreading his bared hands. "Kill me!"

Muttering, forking the sign of the evil eye at him, they backed away.

THEA

IN the Imperial box we were frozen like statues: me with my hands pressed to my mouth to keep from screaming; Lepida with a handful of sweets halfway to her lips; Paulinus open-mouthed; the Empress shedding her usual calm to look surprised; Flavia's sons frozen in fascination.

Then Domitian erupted out of his chair. *"Iugula,"* he shouted as loudly as Arius, and turned his thumb in the sign for death.

A scream strangled in my throat as the Brigantians circled in. But Arius turned, his empty hands spread wide.

"Who's first?" he asked, his voice blasting us all. "Who'll take the first hack at the Barbarian?"

Their eyes flickered. They licked their lips. They looked at each other.

"Kill me!" He took a wavering sword blade and pressed it against his own throat. "Do it."

The boy dropped his sword.

Arius turned on the others like a lion, and five swords hit the sand. A half-dozen boys in the prime of strength backed away, their faces white as a senator's toga, as a single aging gladiator bore them slowly down with his eyes.

Then he began to laugh. He flung his head back and roared laughter up at the sky. He jumped lightly at the Brigantian boys, and they backed away shivering, rings of white showing around their eyes.

He turned his back on them and advanced on the Emperor—the Emperor, standing rigid at the front of the Imperial box.

"Care to take a crack, Caesar?" Arius shouted, spreading his arms. "You blood-sucking Flavian whore."

WHOA," said Vix. "That was stupid. He's in trouble now—"
"What?" Sabina rose from her stool, craning her eyes. "What's all the noise? What's—"

"I think it's time we left, Vibia Sabina." Marcus scooped her up, gesturing to the steward. All around, the crowd stood utterly silent, transfixed by the scornful gladiator. Dear Fortuna, what would the plebs make of this?

"What about Vix?" Sabina peered over Marcus's shoulder as he carried her out. "We left him behind."

"He'll be safe." Marcus had no desire to see what the Emperor would do to the Barbarian, and no desire for his daughter to see it, either. "Cling tight, Sabina."

"He stole my pearl haircomb," she said mournfully. "Do you think I'll see him again?"

THEA

As Domitian wrested a bow and a quiver of arrows from a guard, I fell toward him with some idea of throwing him to the ground. But I tripped and fell headlong, and he swiftly nocked and shot.

The shaft thudded into the sand between Arius's feet.

Arius laughed again. He strode forward, holding his arms out, offering himself up. Grinning.

Domitian shouted. No words, just a long bellow. He shot again.

The arrow wisped through Arius's hair. The next brushed past his shoulder.

Ordinarily Domitian could draw a bow with such precision that he could send five arrows winging between the splayed fingers of a slave fifty yards away. Today, not one of an entire quiver touched his scornful target.

Arius laughed again. I felt a bubble of hysterical mirth lurking at the back of my own throat. In the stands I heard a ripple of choked giggles. Domitian gazed wildly back and forth, looking for laughers amid an audience of fifty thousand.

Arius's laughter trailed off. He leaned forward. Nailed Domitian's eyes with his own. He spat into the sand.

"Guards!" Domitian bellowed, brick red. "Guards!"

A hail of spears rained down into the arena. Two struck a hapless Brigantian boy, who screamed and writhed. But Arius strode unhurriedly to the center of the arena to lay the crushed body of the dwarf on his shield, lift it up, and stride unhurriedly out through the Gate of Death. Not one spear touched him.

A silence fell over the Colosseum, a silence so dead and heavy that it froze fifty thousand people to stone. A few made stealthily for exits—one of them a fat man with a fringe of oiled ringlets. The Emperor's eyes darted to him, and a finger pointed to the man who had suggested that killing the dwarf would bring a better show from the Barbarian.

"Throw him in."

The stands erupted. Roman citizens leaped to their feet, ripping the air with their hands and baying for blood, and a dozen hands picked Gallus up and tossed him over the wall. Into the arena, where a half-dozen sobbing, hysterical Brigantians tore him to pieces before he could shriek the words, "I'll pay."

IN the arena Arius had felt immortality surging through his veins, but in the dark hall of the Gate of Death, immortality faded. He felt sand gritting in his mouth, he felt a sluggishly bleeding wound on his leg, and even the light weight of the dead dwarf was heavy.

Hercules.

In the bare hallway where the dead were dragged, he laid out the dwarf on his shield like they laid out the heroes of Brigantia. Straightened the crushed limbs, closed the eye that hadn't been gouged out, folded the little hands around their little sword. He dropped his own helmet at the dwarf's side, then his armor. A good time to put an end to Arius the Barbarian, who surely didn't have long to live anyway. He found a torch guttering in a wall bracket and held his arm over it until the blurred gladiator tattoo burned over black. The pain of the fire barely registered.

Arius laid the torch at Hercules' still feet: a pyre for a hero. Hercules would have liked that. He went up and down the hall, collecting more torches from their brackets, and piled them around the shield like a bier.

He turned away just as the dry wood of the floor began to kindle. He took off blindly, shivering, stumbling, rebounding off the walls. The halls were oddly empty—but then he'd never been inside the Gate of Death before. Maybe death was empty. Even so, any minute now the Emperor's Praetorians would come and put a sword through his gut. Any minute now—he stumbled around a corner, bounced off a scurrying slave carrying a pail of old meat for the lions, avoided a pair of guards, and ran down another corridor.

An orange blur rebounded off him. "Careful, there!"

His eyes focused. The orange blur resolved itself into a plump fair-haired woman in a flame silk *stola*, a dirty child slung over each hip. She regarded him sternly. "Listen," she said. "You haven't seen us."

"What?"

She beckoned behind her. "Come along." A stream of slaves passed, bearing filthy, big-eyed children on their hips or leading them by the hand. He counted more than thirty.

"What the—"

"You haven't seen us," she repeated, waving slaves and children past. "I'll pay you to forget. Same as I paid everyone else. You haven't seen us."

"I'm a dead man anyway." His body felt like lead. "Better get out quick. There's fire."

"Fire?" She sniffed for smoke; felt the stone wall hesitantly. "Where?"

"Back there." Waving over his shoulder. "The hall where they drag the corpses."

"What? Who are you?"

"Barbarian," he said, weary.

"Arius the Barbarian? I thought you looked familiar. That commotion I just heard up there in the arena—that wouldn't have anything to do with you, would it?"

"Sort of."

She gave him a shrewd look. "Are you on the run?"

"No." He spoke patiently. "I'm dead."

"You look alive to me." She sniffed the air again. "You know, I do smell smoke. Here, grab this child."

Arius grabbed. It was easier to obey. He felt little hands leech around his neck, and followed the orange gown up the dark passage. "Who you?" he slurred around a stone tongue.

"Lady Flavia Domitilla. The children are heretics, or at least their parents are. Christians and Jews sentenced to be thrown to the lions. I am arranging otherwise. Are you listening? Do as I say, and you'll get out, too."

The Emperor's niece. Arius supposed muzzily that that was why they weren't meeting any arena guards in the passages. An Emperor's niece could bribe people like that to stay out of the way . . . Slaves looked askance at them, hastening past with armloads of weapons or long rakes for the dead, but she calmly tossed coins at them and kept going.

The smell of smoke was much stronger now. The next pair of slaves didn't even give them a glance, just hastened back shouting for buckets.

"Here, open that door." He shouldered a heavy door open obediently at her order and came out into sunlight.

"Hand the children up into that wagon. Quickly. There you go, little one—no, no, don't cry, it's all right. Marcellus, drive." She sent the horses and their driver off with a slap, then whirled to beckon Arius. "Here's my litter. Get in."

He stared at the lavishly dressed woman, the silver litter, the velvet cushions and silk drapes. It was all too unreal.

"Get in," repeated Lady Flavia Domitilla. "Or do you want to be speared by Praetorians?"

"Wait a moment."

"But we haven't got—"

He reversed to the door, limped to the first turn of the passage, and putting two fingers to his lips let out a whistle. A moment later and the dog came trotting out, a half-chewed glove hanging from her teeth.

"We leave now," came Lady Flavia's voice from the litter. "Are you coming or not?"

He scooped up the dog and got in.

THEA

FIRE!"

"Fire!"

"The gladiator barracks are on fire!"

One of the guards seized my arm, hurrying me out of the Imperial box behind Domitian and the Empress. Craning my neck, I could see the smoke rising from the Gate of Death. Dear God—*Arius*—

I came dizzily into the square outside the Colosseum, under the shadow of Nero's colossal statue. People pressed in all directions, mothers locking frantic fingers around the wrists of their children, men shoving and shouting. The Praetorians assigned to my protection cursed and gripped their shields, applying armored shoulders to the crush, and I flattened myself back against the steps of the Temple of Venus. Over the frantic press of pleb heads I saw a bare flash of the Emperor, still snapping at his Praetorians, and then a hand closed around my wrist and yanked me into a vestibule in the temple's east wall.

"Hey," a very familiar voice said.

"*Vix?*" I gaped in astonishment at my dusty son, heart suddenly expanding out to fill my ribs, and then seized him in a fierce hug. As soon as I felt his solid weight against me I didn't think I could ever let him go again. "Vercingetorix, what are you *doing* here?" I whispered around the block in my throat.

"Ran away," he said, muffled against my shoulder. He sounded cocky as ever, but his rough paw found my hand under cover of my cloak and gripped it hard. "Larcius's brother, he's all right but his steward had it in for me. Put me to work in the kitchen yards, and there was this thing with the prize geese, and not that many of them got stolen, but the steward said he was gonna sell me to a salt mine. So I sneaked into a wagon train going north."

"Misenum to Ravenna, and then on to Rome?" I smiled into his hair. I should have known that no new master could keep my son in check. He looked so dusty and tired, his lip jutting as he tried so hard not to look like he'd been missing me—

I steeled myself and shook him till his eyes rattled.

"Hey—!"

"Hush, there's no time. For once you have to *listen* to me, Vix." I peeked around the edge of the vestibule. "They're already looking for me. Vix, you have to go—I can't keep you here." I paused, groping wildly. "Lady Flavia."

"Who?"

"Guard!" I seized the arm of the nearest Praetorian. Thank God Domitian was still absorbed with his own guards, on the other side of the Temple of Venus. "Guard, this slave boy has run away from Lady Flavia Domitilla's household in Tivoli. You must see him back to his mistress."

The guard eyed my dusty, scowling son dubiously. No doubt thinking of the sixteen-mile ride to Tivoli.

"Take him at once." I put all the haughtiness of an Emperor's mistress into my voice. "He is Lady Flavia's favorite pageboy, and she'll reward you handsomely for returning him. Take this"—I pressed a few coins into the guard's hand—"for your trouble."

"Yes, Lady." He tramped off toward his centurion to beg leave, and I whirled on Vix.

"Mother, I'm *tired*." His hand still gripped mine under my cloak—for years he'd been too tough to hold my hand in public, and now he was clinging to me. "My feet hurt an' I'm hungry an'—"

"You're being taken to Lady Flavia Domitilla in Tivoli," I cut him off ruthlessly. No time to hug and cuddle him, no matter how much I wanted to. "Lady Flavia, the Emperor's niece. Tell her—privately—that you're my son. Athena's son." I stripped a silver bracelet off my wrist, a bracelet Flavia had seen me wear often, and pressed it into his hand. "Give her this. Flavia will see you right, she's always got children running about." I kissed him hard, pushed some coins into his dirty hands, turned to see the Praetorian tramping back. "I hope Lady Flavia gives you a good beating for your disobedience, boy," I said loudly. "Praetorian, be sure you watch him. He's nothing but trouble."

Vix gave me a dirty look as the guard hauled him off. He twisted in the hard grip, and at the same moment a hand fell on my arm—Domitian. For a moment, my son and my Emperor locked eyes.

"Caesar!" I said brightly. "We should retreat—" and drew him away as best I could, until I could look back and see that my son and his keeper had gone.

I was lucky. Really very lucky. Domitian was in high bad temper, but he didn't punish me. Just had one of his stewards march me back to his private palace, the Domus Augustana, and dump me in a luxurious room to rot.

The fire in the gladiator barracks burnt itself out. Not much damage, as I found out later. Two things had been found among the ashes: the Barbarian's armor and shield. Divine fire, whispered the plebs, who talked of seeing him fly down to Hades. Praetorians, I would have said if anyone had asked me. Praetorians acting on Domitian's orders: killing the Barbarian and then burning the body. Only one lord and god in Rome.

Vix. I looked out from the balcony of my new bedchamber, over the panorama of Rome and beyond. *Vix, are you in Tivoli now?*

Arius . . .

Don't think about either of them. Only survive.

How I've gone up in the world. I've got a gold bowl to hold my blood now.

W E'RE leaving tonight," said Flavia. "For Tivoli. I've got a villa there; that's where we'll hide you. Do you know anything about gardening?"

"Gardening?" The burn on his arm was starting to hurt now, but mostly he felt tired.

"Yes, gardening. I need another gardener, and you need an occupation. And a disguise, while we give people time to forget that famous face of yours. Hmm. What do you think of 'Stephanus the faithful gardener'?"

"Mmm." The motion of the litter was putting him to sleep. The dog was already chewing on the silk tassel of the litter cushions. "If we get that far."

"Oh, but we will. No one will search this litter at the gate. I'm the Emperor's niece." Flavia smiled. "Why don't you go ahead and pass out now."

He closed his eyes. Arius the Barbarian left the city, dead to the world.

PART FOUR

❧❧

The Temple of Vesta

Now and then, Marcus comes to the Temple of Vesta. Not to give the goddess thanks—he can think of no hearth and home more cursed than his own—but to pray for Julia.

"I feel her here," he says. The Chief Vestal is his friend; she has a fierce spirit under her white veil, and the two of them have collaborated, once or twice, against some of the Emperor's harsher decrees.

"Perhaps she is here, Marcus Norbanus."

He holds his hands out to the eternal flame on its quiet altar. "Vesta, goddess of hearth and home, guard the soul of Lady Julia. She was always your servant."

Twenty-one

❦❦

LEPIDA
A.D. 92

IF you want a villa in Tivoli, by all means, buy one." Marcus barely looked up from his scrolls. "Any house you wish, as long as I'm not in it."

"Thank you, darling." Marcus could be rude to me, he could drill me with those marble-hard eyes, he could say blistering things across the breakfast figs on the few occasions we still met at home, but in the end we both knew who was in charge.

So, a villa in Tivoli. In Rome I had my own house on the most fashionable side of the Palatine hill, source of all Rome's finest parties and far from Marcus's quiet *domus* near the Capitoline library where he stayed with Sabina—but for summers, the fashionable needed another watering hole. Baiae had once been popular, but Emperor Domitian had a villa in Tivoli and now no one who was anyone went anywhere else. So I had my new villa with its huge circular triclinium and atrium cascading with flowers, with enough ancestral busts of Marcus's illustrious ancestors to make a show. Perfect for entertaining. I could fix it up properly during my mourning period this spring. Silver couches with rose silk hangings, intricate mosaics, perhaps some of those new erotic statues that looked so daring. A month to put everything straight, and everything ready in time for the summer season. No need to mourn longer than a month; Father wouldn't have wanted me sitting at home moldering in grief. A fever had taken him—

too tiresome, when he was just starting to climb the ladder and stop being an embarrassment to me.

"Sabina, will you quit lurking around like a sick rabbit? Do something normal." She spent a week or two with me every now and then, for form's sake. Marcus didn't like it, but I had to be seen with my daughter enough for propriety. "Go have a spasm somewhere else," I told her, and proceeded in my blue-curtained litter to the public baths where I had myself steamed and perfumed and oiled, soaking in the latest gossip. The Empress was involving herself in good works, the refuge of all neglected wives. There were rumors that the Emperor's niece Lady Flavia Domitilla was a Christian—"Yes, my dear, one of those dirty fish-people!" The new erotic poetry from Crete had been banned in the name of public morals, but for a fee private copies could be obtained. The Chief Vestal Virgin had been arrested for impurity—"Such a scandal!"—and had been sentenced to burial alive on the next holiday, while her lovers would be beaten to death by rods. *Stolas* were to be worn shorter, showing the whole of the ankle. Gray was fashionable, and hair dressed into a braided crest with silver ribbon. "Yes, that's what the Emperor's concubine Athena wears—"

"I don't like gray," I said sharply. "Much too drab." I turned on my side for a dusting of lilac powder.

Athena. Thea, that common little slut Thea, was still in my way. Swooped in on the Emperor before Julia's ashes were cold! Still queening it at Domitian's side over a year later. The courtiers jokingly called her the mistress of Rome, as they had once called Julia. *My* slave girl, the mistress of Rome!

Well, she wouldn't be for long. With my new villa in Tivoli, I'd be much closer to the Emperor. I'd get Paulinus to drop my name, escort me to a few more Imperial functions. Yes, that would do the trick. I'd still get what I was after.

Didn't I always?

"THE investigation of the Vestals I leave to you." The Emperor passed a packet of papers over to Paulinus. "If the Chief Vestal is corrupt, then so might the acolytes be. Corruption always filters down from the top."

"I'll see to it next week, sir." Paulinus saluted.

The Emperor smiled. "When can I break you of the habit of saluting me, boy?"

"Never, sir." Paulinus saluted again, grinning.

The Emperor waved him off with a tolerant hand and beckoned for the usual troop of secretaries. "Get on with you, Paulinus. It's nearly midnight. You soldiers don't have to burn the midnight oil like Emperors—"

"Good thing, too." Paulinus tucked the folder under his arm. "Good night, sir."

"Good night."

He did not, however, go straight to bed. Maybe soldiers didn't have to burn the midnight oil, but Praetorian Prefects certainly did. There were guard rosters to draw up, papers to be sorted and signed, letters to be answered . . . a great many letters.

By midnight Paulinus was rubbing his aching head. Eyeing his bed, he caught sight of a crumpled scroll at the edge of his desk, marked with a familiar brusque handwriting. He slid his thumb under the seal. *"To Prefect Paulinus Augustus Norbanus the Almighty Right Arm of the Emperor,"* Trajan had written in his ebullient upward-slanting lines.

Paulinus smiled and leaned back. Trajan had been transferred from the cold muddy woods of Dacia to hotter climes and hotter battles where sullen legionnaires, army cutbacks, and irate superior officers had not stopped him from amassing an impressive reputation. *"Envy me,"* Trajan wrote. *"Lots of wine, plenty of fighting, pretty girls, and prettier boys—and with the Chatti calmed down for good, you're stuck in Rome pushing scrolls around a desk. Is the Emperor treating you well, Bureaucrat?"*

Better than well. The Emperor worked him, loaded him, talked to him, joked with him, trusted him: a god, a master, a friend. A glimpse into a mind a thousand times more complex than his own. A burden of unbelievable good fortune.

"I'm coming back to Rome in a few months, and I'm dragging you to the Colosseum. It's been months since I've seen a good gladiator. I suppose we'll have to pay our regards to your family, but they aren't bad. I've found that your father is some kind of cousin on my mother's side. Everyone is well, I hope?"

Paulinus's mind skittered to a halt. Well? No, he didn't suppose any of his family were well. Sabina looked as sad as a sick puppy. His father was polite—unfailingly gentle, unfailingly courteous, never reproachful. *Hate me*, Paulinus wanted to shout. *Just hate me.* But instead of curses—

"Duties going well, boy?"

"Yes."

"The Emperor thinks much of you."

"Yes, well—yes."

"You don't look well. Rings under your eyes."

And claw marks down my back, and a bite on my shoulder, and an ache in my gut, all put there by your wife—hate me, oh gods, just hate me—

But the eyes were awkward and caring. Easier not to face them. He scarcely went home at all, now; just a visit every month or two for form's sake. "That pretty little Pollia cow," Paulinus's aunt Diana had said, disgusted. "It's not enough she's got her claws in you. Now she's driving you out of the family."

"You know?" Paulinus had been appalled. His aunt Diana lived out in the country with her horses, paying no attention to gossip. If *she* knew . . .

"Paulinus, everyone knows. Say the word, and I'll run the bitch over with my chariot."

Trajan again: *"No wife yet? I thought a sentimental chump like you would be an easy target. No doubt women are climbing all over the Emperor's right arm."*

"Where do you think you're going, Paulinus?" Lepida's voice, sinking as it always did straight past his brain through the pit of his stomach and lower so it was his own body that betrayed him as his mind wailed. She didn't have much time for him, with her parties and her banquets and her other lovers. But every few weeks she'd send a note—*"Tonight"*—and he'd stare at it for a day, swearing up and down that he wouldn't go, and in the end his feet would drag him to her door.

No, there weren't any other women. Lepida had burrowed under his skin like a fishhook.

I've wanted someone like that, Thea had told him last summer. And she'd never forgotten him.

Never. Never was a long time.

But time was time, and time could be filled. Paulinus closed his window on the beautiful spring night and its nightmares, and reached for a blank scroll. *"To Commander Marcus Ulpius Trajan, Judaea,"* he scrawled. *"All going well here in Rome . . ."*

A ND SO," Marcus wrote, *"it is this author's conclusion that the only possible solution for the success of the Imperium, the Senate, and the People of Rome is the system of adoptive Emperors."*

He put down his pen and sat back, massaging his thumb with his free hand. It was late; most of the house was asleep. He'd been writing for a good three hours.

"And for what?" he said aloud, idly. The Emperor had forbidden him to publish any more speculative treatises.

"Political speculation encourages freethinking among the masses." The black eyes had rested on him coolly. "My regard for your son earns you this warning, but the next time you publish advice on how my Empire should be run, you will face my disapproval."

Finis.

Marcus swept up the finished scrolls and folded them away into his desk drawer. *You can forbid me to publish, Lord and God, but not write. Or to think. Not even a god can do that.*

"Father?"

He looked up to see a little white-robed figure in the doorway. "You should be in bed, Vibia Sabina."

"I couldn't sleep." She edged a little farther into the library. "Can I come in?"

"Of course."

She ran across the room and climbed up into his lap: eight years old, but small for her years. Too small. Everything about her reminded him of a bird: the fragile bones, the pointed face, the fall of feather-brown hair down her back. He tucked her hair behind her ear, feeling the too-rapid pulse in her temple. "Another seizure?"

She shrugged. She had a very deep pride, his daughter— even to him, she hated admitting when the strange faulty connection in her mind gave way and threw her into one of her fits.

"Are you taking your medicine?"

"It doesn't work, Father."

"Then we'll go to another doctor."

"He'll just tell me to drink gladiator's blood. That's supposed to help epilepsy. Remember the slave boy named Vix who told me—"

"We live in the age of enlightenment, and I won't have you drinking gladiator's blood. I'm sure it tastes very nasty."

"I don't want to go to any more doctors, Father."

He smoothed her hair. "We'll talk about it later, then."

"I love you." She closed her eyes in perfect trust, and he felt a stab of guilt. *I'm not worthy of it, Sabina. Not a good father to you, or Paulinus.*

There was nothing of Lepida in his daughter, but there was something of Paulinus: the diffident but straight gaze, perhaps. Paulinus, who paid a dutiful visit every few months and winced whenever Lepida's name was mentioned, just as Sabina did. Marcus kept Sabina from her mother's company as much as possible, but he had already failed Paulinus. What would his Imperial grandfather have done? What would any decent man do for his children?

Watch them shrivel by inches, or ruin them in a stroke?

He fingered another scroll shoved to the back of a drawer—a long scroll, tightly written in his own hand, labeled *"Evidence."* A good many slaves had given testimony on that scroll, nervously affirming Lepida's misdoings over the years. But slave testimony might not be enough—every court of law knew slaves could be intimidated by a cruel master.

"Cast-off lovers," he mused aloud. Lepida might have some who were angry enough to talk. Or some with pressing debts—if he could buy their secrets from them, so much the better. He fingered the scroll.

I am the grandson of the god Augustus. I will not be saddled all my life with that evil she-viper.

Wait, another voice said—the voice of his wily Imperial grandfather. *Not just yet.*

TIVOLI

WELL, Stephanus?" Lady Flavia Domitilla came through the wet green garden, a shawl about her shoulders, hair gleaming in the orange light of the sunset.

Arius bowed. "Reporting on the north vineyard, Domina. The late frost took some of the grapes, and there's something on the vines—black stuff."

"Pity," she sighed. "Those vines make an excellent wine in good years. I'll have Urbinus take a look at them."

"I'll fix it," Arius said stubbornly. He found he liked gardening. It didn't much like him yet, but he'd find a way.

"So much for my wine." Lady Flavia clearly did not share his faith, but she smiled. "How you've changed, Barbarian."

He ran a hand over his hair, dyed dark with walnut juice. He'd grown a short beard, too, and his gladiator tattoo was gone under a burn mark. The only link between Arius the Barbarian and the gardener was the little three-legged dog limping devotedly at his heels. None of the other slaves appeared to recognize him, and in his hut behind the vineyard he could keep his distance from the rest of the household.

"As much pleasure as you take in wrecking my vineyards," Lady Flavia was saying, "you don't have to stay here. I was sure you'd want to move on. It's been more than a year, now."

He shrugged. "I don't mind staying." His own hut instead of a locked cell, wet velvet earth under his feet instead of bloody sand, birdsong instead of hungry applause—this place might as well have been paradise.

"You can go home, you know," Lady Flavia was saying. "Back to Britannia, if you like. I can arrange that."

"I know. But—it's not right. Not yet." He wasn't sure Britannia was still home. He'd dreamed of going back once, but that had been when he had Thea. Now, maybe a hut in a vineyard outside Tivoli was home enough. Or maybe he'd lived too long as a slave to feel comfortable making any decision about the future. "I'm not done here yet," he said at last.

"What are you waiting for?"

"I don't know." He sniffed the air, feeling ill at ease. "The gods'll let me know, maybe." Until then, days among the twining vines and nights before a fire with his dog were good enough.

"You are an odd one," said Flavia. "If you're not leaving us, I'll keep an eye on the vines myself. I'm staying here all year, instead of going back to Rome. Rome doesn't need me."

"And the Emperor?"

"He's well," she said calmly. "Restless, I think, since the wars in Germania are over and he's always preferred army life. But well."

"I'll take my leave, Domina." He bowed, snapping for the dog. "Good night."

Twenty-two

❧❧

PAULINUS tucked his helmet under his arm, raking his fingers through his sweat-matted curls. Spring had bloomed early and hot this year; after the heat of the midday sun outside, the House of the Vestal Virgins was pale and cool and still.

A middle-aged woman approached in a silent flutter of white robes. "Yes, Prefect? Have you come to pray?"

"Official business, madam." Paulinus handed over a scroll with the Imperial seal. "You are requested and required to assist me in all my inquiries."

"I see." The Vestal's eyes ran over his armor, the sword at his side, and the four Praetorians at his back. He felt very large and male and clumsy. "I will assist you myself. No man is permitted to walk unescorted on Vesta's ground."

"That won't be necessary." Paulinus caught sight of another Vestal, pausing curiously to look across the long atrium. "She can escort us instead." Always better to choose an unprepared guide. "Madam, please come with me."

The younger Vestal came, meeting his eyes straight on. "Is there trouble?"

"No. I just have a few questions." The last time this girl had seen a Praetorian, Paulinus remembered, was probably when the guards had appeared to drag away the Chief Vestal in chains, to be buried alive for breaking her vows. He smiled reassuringly. "No arrests. Just an informal inquiry."

She looked to the older Vestal, who nodded. "I will be pleased to answer your questions, Prefect."

"I'd like to see the House of the Vestals." *Get a feel for the place*, the Emperor had told him. "I've never seen the inside before."

"Then it wasn't you who conducted the arrest of our former Chief Vestal?"

"No. That affair was handled directly by the Emperor."

"And this?" She tilted her head. "A follow-up? To see if the rest of us have become corrupted?"

"Are you?"

She looked back at him. "How much do you know about the Vestal Virgins, Prefect?"

"Enough."

"I wonder." She turned, white veil fluttering, and led him down the long pillared atrium. Tranquil pools in the middle reflected rows of white marble statues, and Paulinus gestured his Praetorians back as he caught up to his guide. Her head reached his shoulder, covered by a white veil, and the white robes draped a slight body. She walked swiftly and quietly, hands folded at her waist, and her sandals made no sound on the marble floor. She led him away from the sunlight of the atrium, through a maze of marble corridors. "Our sleeping chambers."

She eased open one narrow door after another. The cells were bare, white-marbled, identical. One was occupied: a middle-aged woman sitting upright and staring at the opposite wall, barely breathing.

"What's she doing?" Paulinus asked, and realized he was whispering.

"Meditating." His guide closed the door. "When not occupied by our duties, we reflect upon the mysteries. Now if you'll follow me—this is where we eat."

Another bare room, empty except for a long carved table. Another Vestal sat before a plate of rough-grained bread and figs, eating without greed. She glanced over with tranquil eyes, then looked away.

"The schoolrooms." His guide stood back from another door, and he looked in to see two little shaven-headed girls bent gravely over scrolls. They wore white robes and coarse sandals: miniature copies of their elders.

"Why cut their hair?" Paulinus watched the girls confer over a tablet. With their clear young faces and shaved heads, they looked neither female nor male but something in between, something . . . not entirely human. Already they had the still movements and passionless eyes of the older Vestals.

"They shed their hair as they shed all other worldly possessions. When they become Vestals in full, it is allowed to grow back."

He wondered what color his guide's hair was under her veil. "They're very young."

"They come between the ages of six and ten, and spend ten years training." She shut the schoolroom door and set off down another hall. "Then they enter into ten years of service. After that, ten years of training the young in turn."

"What are your duties?"

"We prepare the flour that is used for all city sacrifices. We gather water from the sacred spring in our temple grove. Above all, we tend Vesta's fire—in a sense it is Rome's hearth." She smiled as they turned back into the central atrium with its double lane of white marble statues. "There are other duties, but I'm afraid I may not tell you about them."

"Fair enough." He studied the row of statues as he passed— former Vestals, he assumed. Young and old in their marble-carved forms; short and tall, fat and thin, but somehow they all looked alike. The carved Vestals gazing over the atrium with their serene marble eyes seemed no different from the living ones who passed below in their goddess's duties. His guide could have climbed up on a plinth, settled her white robes, and become indistinguishable from her dead sisters.

"Would you like to see the Temple?" she asked.

"Yes."

A round and simple room, nothing more. There was a discreet curtained area where wills and other important documents were stored—the Emperor's among them, Paulinus knew. But there were no mosaics, no ornamentation, no bloodstains from elaborate sacrifices. Just an undraped altar in the round temple's center, and a flame burning in a bronze bowl.

"The flame of Vesta." His guide's voice echoed quietly around the room. "The eternal flame. If it goes out, we are sub-

ject to charges of negligence." She walked to the altar and rev-
erenced the flame with a curiously liquid movement. Paulinus
stood silent. How many men were privileged enough to catch a
glimpse of this silent female place?

They don't need us, he thought. *They've created a whole
world without us. A good world.*

"Have you seen everything you wished?" His guide returned,
tilting her head up at him.

"Yes."

His Praetorians marched outside, but Paulinus found himself
lingering in the entrance. His guide seemed content to linger
with him, hands folded at her waist. Her lashes were pale—
probably her hair, too, under the veil. "You're happy," he asked
suddenly. "Aren't you."

"Yes. Are you?"

"Me? Of course."

"Of course. Will you be returning here, Prefect?"

He hesitated. He'd abandoned his note-taking halfway
through the tour of the temple, but every image was stamped
clear. There was no corruption here, no hidden vices, no oath-
breaking. But—"Yes," he said. "Yes, I'll be returning."

She did not seem surprised. "Until we meet again then,
Prefect."

"Paulinus Vibius Augustus Norbanus."

"I am the Vestal Justina," she returned.

"I'll be back." Formally. "Without my guards, next time."

"I am always here."

PAULINUS spent his summer in a saddle. Riding out to the
Praetorian barracks to supervise training. Carrying the
Emperor's dispatches back to the city. Journeying to Tivoli for
long fireside evenings at the Villa Jovis. Those summers alone at
the villa were good for the Emperor, Paulinus thought. He looked
happier, more relaxed, lounging easily on his luxurious couches
and rarely far from a smile. Thea's influence, probably. She was
constantly at his side in Tivoli.

"She's a wonderful girl," Paulinus said enthusiastically
one evening after she'd gone to bed.

"Correct." The Emperor's eyes turned inward, gazing at the
lamps. "She's a slave and I dislike slaves; she's a Jew and I dislike

Jews; she's full of secrets and I dislike secrets . . . still, there is something about her, isn't there?"

Paulinus smiled to himself. The words were harsh, but he heard the affection behind them.

"I'm glad he has you," Paulinus told her the next morning after the Emperor disappeared into the tablinum with his petitions and ledgers. "You're good for him, Thea."

"So I am." She twisted a spray of jasmine from the bush that climbed around the atrium pillars. "He leaves all his shadows for me, leaving the sunlight for the rest of you. He's very sunny when he wants to be, isn't he? Even to me sometimes. Just now and then, he'll go back to that brusque soldier I first met . . ." A shrug. "Disconcerting."

"He relies on you, you know."

"I hope you don't want me to beg favors for you, Paulinus. Domitian might rely on me, but he never takes my advice. He didn't even take my advice on his treatise about hair care."

"What did you advise him?"

"That it didn't become an Emperor's dignity to write a manual about hair."

Paulinus laughed. "Maybe he doesn't take your advice, but I can see why he loves you."

Her head turned, and for a stunned instant he thought he saw savagery flick across her eyes. But it disappeared so fast . . . and then she threw her head back and smiled brilliantly. "Oh, yes," she said. "Yes, he loves me. Who could doubt that? And I hear he's found a bride for you, now."

"Yes. A young widow of the Sulpicii—twenty-six, no children, bringing half of Tarracina and Toscana for a dowry."

"Are you talking of a wife or a horse?" A short laugh. "How stupid men are."

Paulinus blinked. "Have I displeased you?"

"Oh, no. How can you do that? You're one of the most powerful men in the city, and you don't see anything."

"Thea"—cautiously—"are you feeling well? It's been very hot lately—"

"So I'm ill now, am I? Well, it's a short step from sick to crazy. That's what you thought about Julia." She stalked back into the villa in a billow of saffron silk.

Paulinus wondered if he was ever going to understand women.

That afternoon Thea was gone. "Off shopping?" he asked the Emperor.

"Visiting my niece Flavia, probably." Not looking up from his scrolls. "Why don't you send a guard for her? I'll want her after dinner."

"I'll go myself," Paulinus smiled. Lady Flavia had joined his childhood games with Julia, too—he wondered if she'd remember him. Once they'd stolen a wine flagon from their mothers at the Circus Maximus and gotten drunk at the age of six . . .

The ride to Lady Flavia Domitilla's villa took Paulinus's bay mare an effortless fifteen minutes. He dismounted at the doorway, dismissing his Praetorians to the house and leading his mare around toward the stables at the back. He came around the edge of the garden—and stopped.

Thea stood in the dust of the stable yard, trailing her fine silks heedlessly in the dirt, her hair spilling down her back. She had both hands planted on the shoulders of a dirty russet-haired slave boy, and was speaking in low fierce tones.

"—don't care what your excuse is this time, you cannot go around knocking people down! You're very lucky to live here, and as long as you do so then you will obey Lady Flavia when she asks you to—"

"She's not my mother!"

"But I am, and I won't have you behaving like a barbarian!"

They glared at each other.

"Why don't you show me your new sword drills now?" she said in softer tones. "I really do want to see them, and—"

Paulinus took a step forward. "Lady Athena?"

The smile slipped off her face as if someone had wiped it away. "Paulinus? What—what are you doing here?"

"Who's he?" The boy turned his glare on Paulinus.

"He's no one," she cut in before Paulinus could answer. "Go back into the house."

"Mother—"

"Don't argue with me!"

The boy threw Paulinus another glance before turning toward the villa.

"Who's that, Thea?" said Paulinus levelly.

"He's no one. What's it matter to you?"

"It matters because I'm Praetorian Prefect and I'm supposed

to know what goes on in the Emperor's household. What goes on behind his back."

The belligerence faded out of her eyes, replaced by fear. "Vix doesn't matter to the Emperor. He's just a little boy."

"He's your son."

"I said, he's nobody."

"He's your *son*." A hesitation. "Surely he can't be the Emperor's?"

"God, no." Shuddering. "His father's dead. Does it matter?" Her eyes flicked up at him. "Vix lives here, with Lady Flavia. I see him when I'm in Tivoli. It's harmless!"

"Then why are you afraid?" Pause. "The Emperor doesn't know, does he?"

"No. He doesn't."

"Why? Surely he wouldn't care if—"

"I don't know if he'd care or not. I don't know. Maybe he'd shrug and say, 'Who cares if you have a bastard brat?' But maybe he wouldn't." Her eyes flicked up. "He doesn't like children. He doesn't like reminders that I've had other men before him. And I don't think he'd like seeing the proof that another man got a strong son on me when the Emperor of Rome has not. You know him as well as I, Paulinus Norbanus. What do you think?"

Paulinus's brain skittered to a halt.

"I've seen Vix three times in the past year." Harshly. "Three. When he learned to use a sword I wasn't here to applaud him. When he knocked Lady Flavia's son unconscious in sparring practice I wasn't here to thrash him. When he fell out of a tree and broke his arm I wasn't here to bandage him. But even three times in a year is better than nothing."

Paulinus looked at her.

"Don't tell." Her eyes pleaded nakedly. "Please don't tell."

He thought suddenly that out of all the months he'd lived by her side at the Domus Augustana, he'd never seen her face open up like it had when she smiled at the russet-haired boy.

"Oh, gods." He raked his hair out of his eyes. "I'm supposed to fetch you back to the Emperor's villa now. But I'll give you an hour. All right?"

A smile broke across her face. She looked more abruptly beautiful, standing there in her dusty robe with her hair hanging down her back, than she did decked in all her jewels. She stood smiling for a moment, happy as a child, and then she turned and ran into the villa after her son.

Paulinus wondered if he was falling in love with her. Gods, that would be inconvenient.

"Paulinus Vibius Augustus Norbanus!" He turned and saw Lady Flavia standing at the garden gate. "I don't think I've seen you since we were ten years old. Come into the garden where it's cool, and tell me all your news."

He started for the house. And realized that, for the first time in his three years as Praetorian Prefect and Imperial confidant, he had a secret from the Emperor.

Twenty-three

TIVOLI

T HE gardener known to everyone at Lady Flavia's villa as
Stephanus was just bending down to wash his face in the
water trough when a stone sailed out of the bushes and stung him
on the shoulder.

He turned in one smooth instinctive movement, knife leaping from his belt to his hand, and lunged. Among the prickly
bushes he caught a handful of rough tunic and yanked. Solid
weight crashed into his knees. He staggered, losing hold of the
tunic, and when he regained his balance he found himself looking at a nine-year-old boy.

"I knew you weren't no gardener," the boy crowed.

Arius let out a long breath. The cool autumn breeze had been
raising gooseflesh on his arms all day, but now he felt warm. His
body was never cold when it expected a fight.

"When gardeners get scared they drop their shovels and
swear. They don't go pulling knives and charging." The boy
crossed his arms over his chest, looking Arius up and down.
"Barbarian."

Arius grabbed for him. The boy skipped back out of reach,
grinning.

"I know you, boy." Of course there were dozens of slave
children running over Lady Flavia's spacious villa, but this boy
looked familiar. "You spar with Lady Flavia's sons."

"I know you, too. Saw you once in the Colosseum. Your last fight."

"You don't know what you're talking about." Arius bent and picked up his knife. "I'm Stephanus. One of the vineyard gardeners."

"I saw the Barbarian—"

"You're imagining things." Arius cursed his luck. He'd been so careful, keeping to himself behind the vineyard, hardly coming to the house at all except to make the occasional report to Lady Flavia. The other slaves of her household hardly saw him enough to know him as a gardener, let alone a gladiator. And now this boy who had barely seen him in either identity had recognized him.

"You got a three-legged dog, just like the Barbarian," the boy persisted. "And you got a scar on your arm, right where he had his gladiator tattoo—"

"Lots of people burn themselves. Lots of people have dogs, too."

"Hey, I know how the Barbarian moves! I *saw* him! Maybe I didn't recognize you at first 'cause of the beard, but I knew the first time I saw you that you didn't move like any goddamn gardener." The boy's eyes devoured him.

"Scram." Arius sheathed his knife and stalked back to the water trough.

The boy dogged at his heels. "Teach me."

"What?"

"Teach me! I want to be a gladiator."

Arius looked at him. "What kind of moron wants to be a gladiator?"

"I do."

"Go away."

"C'mon, you've got to teach me! I get lessons from the guards that teach Lady Flavia's kids, but they're all dozers. Been a year since I learned anything new."

"I said scram."

The boy lunged and took Arius around the knees. Arius hit the ground rolling, but the boy grabbed his wrist and tried his best at an arm lock. "Teach me," he panted.

Arius heaved a shoulder and sent the boy flying. In another second he had a knee on the boy's chest and a hand around his throat. The young ribs bent under his weight, but small hard fists plugged at his solar plexus. Arius twisted away and cut off the boy's air. The young face turned purple under its sunburn, but the boy didn't beg.

Abruptly Arius loosed his hold and sat back.

The boy sat up. "Got inside your guard, didn't I?" he wheezed.

Arius rose. "Come back tomorrow."

"Why not now?" Scrambling up. "I'm Vix."

"Stephanus."

"Oh, right."

"Whatever your theories," Arius warned, "don't go spreading them around to the other slaves, or I'll beat you bloody. Hear me, boy?"

"Kill me if I talk," the boy promised. "Start now?"

"Draw your knife," Arius said, wondering why he was doing this. "Too slow. You should be able to get a knife out of the sheath and into someone's stomach before they can inhale. Angle the blade in more."

"Like this? Hey, we're both left-handed. What are the odds?"

ROME

"—so he's sitting on his judge's chair in the courtroom"—Paulinus's hands sketched a quick picture—"and a pleb woman is swearing up and down that the inheritance should go to her and not to the plaintiff because he isn't her son and heir, as he's claiming. And the Emperor asks her, 'Is this the truth?' and she nods, 'Yes, Lord and God,' and he says, 'Good, then you can marry him. Right now, on the spot, and the inheritance will be shared between you.'"

The Vestal Justina smiled, her eyes crinkling. "And what did she say?"

"She fell to her knees begging to be let off. So the Emperor judged that the plaintiff was her son after all, and the inheritance went to him." Paulinus shook his head. "And do you know what he told me later? The Emperor, I mean. He said it was a trick he'd stolen from the legal records of Emperor Claudius. Claudius himself couldn't have pulled it off any better. That woman's face when he proposed she marry her son—"

Justina laughed, and Paulinus felt rich. She didn't laugh often. Smiled a good deal, slowly and quietly, but rarely laughed. He settled back in his chair with a sigh.

"Tired?" She looked still and cool in her white robes, blending against the pale marble walls.

"I'm always on the run these days." He smiled at her. "I wouldn't mind a day in your position—sitting still in a white room watching a flame."

"Oh, it's a bit more than that. But it is peaceful."

She was peaceful. He'd gotten into the habit, these past months, of dropping in on her. The Imperial investigations of the Vestal Virgins were officially closed, but he still visited every few weeks, just to talk to Justina. To sit in the public room, in full view as any Vestal must be when speaking to a man, and speak for a while in quiet voices about nothing very important. "I'm to be married," he said suddenly.

"I'd heard something of it. A girl from the Sulpicii family?"

"Yes. Calpurnia Helena Sulpicia. The Emperor is hosting our betrothal feast as soon as the augurs find an auspicious date. She's a widow—quite young, though, no children."

"Is that all you can say of your future wife?" Justina asked.

"I hardly know her. She seems pleasant, though, and I've got to marry someone."

"Do you?"

He shrugged. "If I stay unwed much longer, people will start thinking I prefer boys."

"Quite a few soldiers do." The cool voice was amused, and he shot her a sideways glance. For a priestess, she was prone to comments of distinct worldliness.

"My friend Trajan does," Paulinus said ruefully. "He says men are easier than women. He's probably right, too, but it's not the way for me. I'll marry Calpurnia Helena Sulpicia, and have sons." He looked at her. "Did you ever regret it—not marrying?"

She blinked. "Well—no, I was—I never even thought about it. I was, well, nine years old when I was chosen. I certainly wasn't thinking about marriage then. And then the Vestals swallowed me up, and I never looked back. Anyway, Vestals do marry sometimes. After they've served their thirty years and retired."

"Really?" It was his turn to be taken aback.

"It doesn't happen often—it's considered bad luck to wed a former Vestal. But our former Chief Vestal was planning to marry when she retired. She was executed instead."

Paulinus looked Justina straight in the eye. "She should have waited, instead of taking him as a lover."

"Oh, he wasn't her lover. They'd known each other for years, but she never broke her vows."

"The Emperor handled the case himself. Do you think he would have convicted her without ample evidence? You don't know how careful a jurist he is."

"You don't know how seriously Vestals take their vows." Her voice cooled.

Paulinus opened his mouth—and reminded himself it was impolite to argue with a priestess. "I would never wish to impugn the Vestals." Carefully.

"And I would never wish to impugn the Emperor." A crooked little smile tilted her mouth. "Let's not argue."

LEPIDA
A.D. 93

PAULINUS'S proposed bride was no threat at all to me. Lady Calpurnia Helena Sulpicia was as sturdy as a pony, with square hands and a snub nose. A year older than me, too. I'd worried considerably that I'd lose my stepson to some sly sylph of a fifteen-year-old, but this ample widow was not worth worrying about. I'd met her on a handful of occasions but had never spoken with her for long. Now the year had turned, however, and it was Lupercalia and the Lupercalia festival was a time for lovers, so the augurs had finally fixed a betrothal date for Paulinus and his little pony of a bride.

"My dear, what a very *interesting* gown," I greeted her as she entered my hall dressed for her feast at the palace. "Blue? Such a bold choice, with skin like yours."

"Thank you, Lady Lepida." Her voice was placid. "Could you check the clasp of my bracelet? It's come loose."

I bent over the clasp. Her sapphires were bigger, bluer, and better than mine—I'd worn blue for the banquet, too. "It's not loose at all." I searched her face, but the wide hazel eyes were innocent as a child's. No one would ever write odes to *her* gem-like gaze. I loosened the clasp of my *stola* to show a little more shoulder, arching my neck. "Paulinus will be late, of course. He's so taken up with his duties."

"I'm sure he is."

I was about to launch another attack—on her hair, this time;

an unremarkable mouse blond for all that it was tied up in knots of jewels—but I heard the uneven footfall behind me and turned to face Marcus.

"Lady Calpurnia." He smiled, kissing her hand. "I've just received a message from Paulinus; he's tied up in guard duties and says he'll meet us at the Domus Augustana."

Calpurnia nodded. She didn't seem disappointed, which displeased me. How much more fun it would have been if she'd fallen madly in love with him. I could have dropped a few hints here and there about his feelings for me, tortured her for months with the uncertainty of it all . . .

"Father!" Sabina skimmed in from the atrium. "Father, you forgot to let me fix your tunic."

"So I did." He bent down, allowing her to adjust the crisp folds. "Do I pass muster now?"

"Perfect."

"Your daughter, Senator?" Calpurnia turned toward Marcus, not me.

"Yes. Vibia Sabina, meet Lady Calpurnia Helena Sulpicia."

Sabina showed her gap-toothed smile. "I'm very pleased to—"

"Curtsy, Sabina," I snapped. "You're eight years old; you should know better."

"Lepida," said Marcus coldly, "she's nine."

"Well, if rudeness isn't adorable at eight, then it's not adorable at nine, either."

She curtsied. I saw her eyes shut for a moment, dizzyingly. "If you're going to have a fit, have it upstairs," I ordered. "I won't have you embarrassing our guests."

"Lovely to have met you, Vibia Sabina," Calpurnia said as my daughter sidled out. "I look forward to seeing you again."

"Now that that's over with—" I pulled my ice-blue *palla* up around my shoulders. "Shall we go?"

Calpurnia and Marcus looked at me. I knew the expression on Marcus's face quite well: cold, hooded scorn. Calpurnia's square face held disapproval. Who did they think they were? I ignored them on the ride to the palace, twitching the curtains of the litter aside and watching the plebs celebrate Lupercalia outside. Always such fun, with the wilder men racing about in loincloths cracking whips, and lovers stumbling from dark corner to dark corner. Last Lupercalia I'd had four men clamoring for my festival favors, and they'd made me a bet I couldn't take them all on . . . I had them all and two to spare! More fun than this Lupercalia looked to be. Marcus was already droning about Senate business, and Calpurnia was *encouraging* him.

The lights of the Domus Augustana blazed, drawing us in. Domitian usually hosted formal banquets at the new palace with its massive staterooms and extravagant fountains, but Paulinus had the honor of being feted at the Emperor's own private palace. Slaves leaped forward to take our cloaks; jeweled freedmen drew us down glistening passageways to the triclinium, which had been transformed into a vision of orchids and laurel and dazzling crystal and solid-gold dishes. For Paulinus, the Emperor had spared no luxury. He had even forsaken his usual plain tunic for a gold-embroidered purple robe worth more than a month's grain shipment from Syria.

"My friends!" Domitian came toward us, his ruddy face beaming. "Delighted to receive you. Marcus"—a friendly nod—"Lady Lepida"—a kiss to the cheek(!)—"the lovely bride"—a press of Calpurnia's hand. "You are all welcome!"

"So pleased," murmured the Empress, all emeralds and silver at his side.

"Sorry to keep you waiting." Paulinus strode through the doors, still shrugging the folds of his lawn synthesis into place.

"Never mind, never mind." Domitian threw a friendly arm around Paulinus's shoulders, and I wondered if the rumors were true—if he really was going to name Paulinus his heir. Last year a prefectship, this year an heiress, next year an Empire . . . Certainly Domitian was closer to my stepson than to anyone else in all Rome. *Emperor Paulinus Vibius Augustus Norbanus* . . . incest laws or not, I *would* marry my stepson if he became Emperor!

"Well?" Domitian said good-naturedly as Paulinus hesitated over Calpurnia's hand. "Kiss your betrothed!"

Calpurnia offered up her cheek. Flushing, Paulinus bent down and brushed it with his lips. His eyes flickered toward mine, and I shaped a mocking kiss at him. He flushed and looked away.

"Paulinus." Marcus stepped forward. "Good to see you, boy. It's been too long."

"Father."

They stepped toward each other, eyes not quite meeting as they hugged. Paulinus stepped back as if he had been burned, dull color rising high in his cheeks.

I giggled.

We'd barely arranged ourselves on the silk-cushioned couches before a stream of food and music and entertainers flooded in. Sugar-glazed fruit heaped high in silver bowls, whole roasted peacocks with their vibrant tail feathers still in place, honey-brushed pork stuffed with sage and rosemary and gobbets of its own flesh. Drummers danced before my eyes, and sweet-voiced choirboys from Corinth, and lithe brown acrobats climbing toward the ivory ceiling on each others' shoulders. Slaves shoved food onto our plates as soon as we cleared them, and Domitian roared at us to eat up, eat up. He gestured with the peacock's crispy, feathered neck, grease spots already staining his priceless purple robe, and I realized he was drunk. Old Falernian flowed around us like the Tiber, and as the heat gathered under my skin it seemed entirely natural to let my hair loosen and my *stola* slip off one shoulder. Now *this* was more like Lupercalia!

The Emperor was telling stories of Paulinus's bravery, shouting out that here was the best friend a man ever had, and he'd have the whole world know it. Paulinus was glassy-eyed, matching the Emperor goblet for goblet. Calpurnia's cheeks were flushed, her gown crumpled as she sprawled uncomfortably across her couch. The room was too hot and there was too much food and too much wine, but the music soared in a bright ribald stream and the Emperor loomed over us like a vast bloated god, so we shoveled food into our mouths and poured wine down our burning throats and coughed out bursts of hysterical laughter.

Marcus sat cool and chill beside me, and as I glanced over at him dizzily I saw that his eyes weren't on the Emperor or his son, but on the Empress. The Empress, equally cool and chill on the end of her couch, and gazing right back at him. There was something important about that tense speculating gaze, but the room was spinning around me and everything was hilarious and I couldn't stop laughing at Calpurnia's broad perspiring face. I tossed down another goblet of wine, half of it slopping over the mosaics, and flopped over on my back to laugh up at the ceiling. My *stola* slipped off the other shoulder, baring my breast, and Paulinus's glazed eyes fastened on it.

"A betrothal ring for the bride!" Domitian roared. "Paulinus, don't tell me you haven't given it to her yet? Here, let me." He fumbled for Calpurnia's shrinking hand and shoved a sizable ruby onto the wrong finger. "Betrothed! Time to kiss her again, Paulinus. No, no, not like that!"—as Paulinus planted a smeary peck on Calpurnia's lips. "I suppose I'll have to do this for you, too"—and the Emperor kissed Calpurnia, teeth mashing against her lips. Her muffled squeak disappeared into the mocking drumroll of the musicians.

"Caesar," the Empress said sharply, speaking for the first time all evening. "You're frightening the poor girl."

"Frightening?" The black Flavian eyes narrowed. "What would you know about kisses? Cold as an icicle—wouldn't melt in a volcano, you scheming frozen—"

The Empress rose from her couch, not a hair out of place. "Thank you for a delightful evening," she said at large. "Marcus, Lady Lepida. Prefect Norbanus, Lady Calpurnia. Good evening to you all."

"That's right," the Emperor muttered as she drifted out. "Get out of here—frigid scheming bitch—" He beckoned a pageboy violently, and I watched with hazy eyes as he emptied a packet of little crushed leaves into the wine flagon. "What'sat?" I giggled.

"Herbs—Indian, I think—" He downed an explosive mouthful. "Makes—makes colors—Paulinus, here—and Calpurnia—"

"I don't want any," she said distinctly.

"DRINK!" The Emperor thrust the goblet into her hand so half the wine slopped over her expensive gown, and she drank. I reached over to wrest the cup away, feeling Marcus's disgusted eyes as I drained the dregs. Old Falernian, with something bitter at the bottom.

"Good," the Emperor panted. Sweat crowned his forehead. "Feels, feels—good—hot in here—music—SOMEBODY FETCH ME ATHENA!" he shouted.

Warmer all of a sudden. Mosaics twisting and swirling like they were alive. My body grew hot and loose.

"Oh, gods, I feel sick." Calpurnia half fell off the couch and vomited by a rosy marble statue of a bathing Artemis.

I felt a quick rustle on the couch next to me as Marcus rose. "I think I'd better take Lady Calpurnia home, Caesar. She isn't well." He cupped a hand around her elbow, lifting her up. "Paulinus—"

But Paulinus sprawled panting and flaccid across the couch, his pupils swallowing up his eyes. "Y're beautiful," he mumbled to me. "Y're beautiful—"

"Good night," said Marcus, and he dragged out the reeling Calpurnia.

Paulinus's curls were moving. Twining around like snakes. I put out an interested finger, pulling back before I could be bitten. He rolled over and seized my wrist, attacking my shoulder and throat with his mouth.

"ATHENA!" the Emperor roared, and I looked up over Paulinus's shoulder to see Thea gliding through the door in apricot silk, at first pinprick-tiny like at the end of a tunnel, and then suddenly looming huge. The stone at her throat had grown into a vast black mouth. As Paulinus fumbled with stupid fingers at the clasp of my *stola*, the Emperor grabbed hold of Thea's arm, so hard his fingers left white marks on her flesh. "Drink," he whispered, forcing the goblet against her teeth. "Drink—we'll see what kind of goddess you are—" and as she choked on the wine he kissed her, eating her with his teeth and his hands.

My *stola* ripped, and Paulinus was a panting, sweating beast on top of me. I raked my nails, drawing blood that shifted colors in my eyes. Out of the corner of my eye I saw the Emperor doing something to Thea, Thea half-clothed and turning her head away on the cushions . . . Paulinus was hot hard invading flesh above me, diamond drops of sweat falling from his face, his eyes two dark pits, his mouth a square agonized hole. I rolled my eyes dizzily to look at Thea, crushed under a panting sweating beast of her own, and her eyes snapped open and met mine.

Eyes locked while our bodies writhed. The world cleared around Thea's face; Thea's white, hating face not two feet away. Blood on her lip, her hair a tangle of sweat and silver chains, her eyes dilated by the drug. Hated her—hated her—a leap of answering loathing in her eyes—speared down by hard male flesh, both of us, or we'd have leaped for each other's throats. Rocked and pinioned, we still reached out, clawing across the space. Her fingers crushed mine, trying to break bone, and I sank my nails deep into her knuckles and neither one of us would look away. Her eyes were the last thing I saw before the colors crashed in around my head.

* * *

"I'M going to be sick again," Calpurnia wailed, stumbling against Marcus's crooked shoulder.

"Then go ahead and be sick," he told his prospective daughter-in-law. She retched, lurching against the doorway, and Marcus steadied her. "Here, into the atrium. Fresh air will clear your head."

"I—I should get home—"

"Sit first."

She staggered into the atrium and collapsed onto the first bench, cradling her head. Marcus called a slave, sent for a flagon, and pushed a goblet into her hand. "Drink."

"No more wine, I can't—"

"It's water, not wine. Sip slowly."

She drank. Four hours ago, she had been a fresh-faced young girl in a new blue dress; now she was a wine-stained mess with her tangled hair descending down her back and an earring missing. She looked down at herself, flushing as she brushed at a vomit stain on her hem. "Oh, gods, I look like—"

"Never mind. How do you feel?"

She drank again. "My head feels like Vulcan's own anvil."

"That should pass. You threw up most of the drug."

"Thank you—for getting me out of there."

"You looked a trifle overwhelmed."

She shuddered, and Marcus thought of her shocked face as the Emperor's mouth bore down on hers, all wet sharp teeth. "Is he always like that?" she burst out.

"No." Marcus sat himself beside her on the marble bench. "Tonight was . . . exceptional."

"I can't go back there." Brushing uselessly at her gown. "Not ever."

"You saw the Emperor at his worst tonight. Tomorrow, when the effect of those Indian leaves wears off, he will have forgotten all about this evening and will treat you exactly as he treats all other women: he will ignore you."

"I still can't go back."

"As Paulinus's wife, you'll have to."

"Then I won't marry Paulinus." She looked up in desperate apology. "It—it isn't him. He seems perfectly pleasant when he's not—"

Gazing glaze-eyed at his stepmother?

"But surely he doesn't care much about marrying me, and I can't—can't deal with this life. Banquets and drinking and—and Indian leaves. Oh, maybe my family's been around since the Republic, but I'm a country girl." She leaned forward. "I grew up in Toscana, with vineyards and ponies and swimming holes. It's supposed to be a great thing for me, marrying the Praetorian Prefect, but I don't belong in palaces. Not palaces like *that*."

He thought she might burst into tears, but she looked away and controlled herself. Country-born, but patrician-bred.

Marcus considered his words. "Perhaps you won't believe me, considering what you've seen tonight, but this isn't Paulinus's world, either."

Calpurnia looked at him.

"My son is a simple sort: a soldier, an idealist, a good Roman. It's a great honor, his position as Prefect, but he's floundering. If someone were to help him find his feet, he'd be grateful."

"You want me to do that?"

"I think you could do that," Marcus said gravely. "You're a fine honorable girl, Calpurnia Sulpicia. I don't have to know you long to see that. My son needs a girl like you. He knows it."

"Maybe so." She pleated a fold of stained silk between her fingers. "But it's not what he wants. What he wants is—" She bit her lip just in time. She might not have known Lepida long but then again, one didn't have to.

Marcus looked at her baldly. *Yes. Your betrothed wants my wife.*

They both looked away.

"May I ask a favor of you?" Marcus spoke as formally as if he were quoting a point of law in the Senate. "Think long and hard before you end the betrothal. That's all I ask."

Calpurnia looked, twisting the ruby around her finger, and Marcus thought she would strip it off then and there. But she offered her hand instead. "All right, Senator."

"Marcus, please." He took her hand in both of his, and smiled. "And thank you."

Twenty-four

TIVOLI

Y OU'RE late," Arius greeted Vix.
"Had to rub down the horses."
"Run twice around the vineyard to warm up. Then start drill number five."

They sparred in the spring rains, slipping through liquid mud. Sparred under scorching midday sun as summer advanced, sweat slicking the hilts of the wooden practice swords. Sparred until the muscles screamed, until the bones creaked, until the palms of Vix's hands split and Arius staggered home wondering why he was doing this at all.

Maybe because his life behind the vineyard had gotten a little too quiet. Maybe swords and drills and practice bouts had gotten into his blood, like it or not.

"When do I get a real sword?" Vix complained.
"When you earn it," Arius growled, just as his brothers and endless gladiatorial trainers had growled at him.
"I have earned it!"
"Show me."
Vix launched an overhand attack. Arius clipped the wooden blade out of his hand and sent him sprawling.
Vix scowled. "Just because you're bigger."
"If you'd stepped inside and gone low, you'd have thrown me off balance. Keep pretending you're a big man when you fight,

and you'll die. Fight like a ten-year-old boy, you might be able to kill someone someday. Quit trying to impress me."

Vix swore. "Again?"

They circled briefly, then closed. Vix stepped under the swing of the sword, throwing his weight against Arius's side. The Barbarian staggered briefly; Vix brought the wooden sword up to clip his jaw.

"Better. Again."

"Yeah, and don't pull your blows this time."

Vix tried the same trick and came up against a solid wall of shoulder. He swung his wooden blade around in a hasty swing; Arius seized his arm, jerking him off balance, and the joint in his shoulder came apart with a pop. Vix yelled.

"Lie facedown and lift your arm straight back."

"What arm? You son of a bitch, I don't have any arm left—"

"Quit whining." Arius planted a foot on Vix's back, seized the misaligned arm, and tugged it briskly back into place. "Go ahead and throw up."

"I never puke." Vix reeled upright, flexing his elbow. "I'm good for another hour."

"Then go another hour with this." Arius tossed Vix his sword.

Vix caught the hilt in both hands, staggering. "Jeez, it's heavy."

"Too heavy for a boy, by rights. But it'll make you strong. Fight with that, you can fight with anything."

"Yessir." Vix turned the blade along the light, admiring the honed steel. "People said you fought with a lightning bolt for a sword and a thundercloud for a shield."

"People are idiots. Start drill number two, but twice as slow. Builds control."

"This how they taught you in gladiator school?" Groaning as he swung the heavy blade inch by slow, agonizing inch.

"No. This is how my brothers taught me. We'll start conditioning, next week, sprints and weights. You're fast, but you have no stamina. Again, five more times. Slower."

"Why didn't you like being a gladiator?" Lifting the blade in increments.

"It's a lousy profession."

"Sounds fun to me."

"You're young. Seen too many games."

"Only saw one, actually. M'mother says they're barbaric."

"Your mother's a sensible woman. Again. Slower."

"My arm's gonna drop off."

"Then you're doing it right."

"Bully."

"Whiner," said Arius, enjoying himself. "Ten more sets."

ROME

JUSTINA." Paulinus focused weary eyes on the disapproving Vestal. "I need to see Justina."

"Vestal Justina is occupied with her sacred duties."

"Get her. Prefect's orders."

He settled against the marble wall of the temple, ignoring the scandalized looks of the worshippers. He knew what he looked like: bloodshot, untidy, unshaven . . . It had been months since his betrothal banquet, but he still felt the need to get drunk at night so he could forget the things he'd done.

"Prefect?" Justina's voice. "Is there trouble? I haven't seen you in months."

Since his betrothal, he'd been too ashamed to visit, too embarrassed to look her in the eye. If he hadn't gotten half drunk this afternoon to get his courage up, he'd never be here now. "I'm sorry." He opened his eyes with an effort. "I just—I had to see you."

"I see." Her eyes ran over him, and he waited for a look of disgust. But—"It must be important. Sit down."

"Can—can we go someplace quiet?" He was aware of the other Vestals' disapproving eyes.

"I must be in public view whenever I speak to a man." She sat opposite him, white robes falling into place. "Just tell me."

He sat, cradling his aching head in his aching hands. "I—am—a—worm," he said carefully. Best to get that out of the way first.

". . . I see."

"Are you laughing at me?"

"Oh, no."

"I don't blame you." Morbidly. "I'm dirt. I'm scum—"

"All right, why don't we stop all the—"

"—and I'm in love with my father's wife."

"—name-calling." She blinked. "Well. That I didn't expect."

It was like shrugging off a great thorny weight. He hunched forward, locking his hands around his knees. "I—I don't know if it's love. Not love like I ever imagined it. I can't stop wanting her. She's more than beautiful; she's intoxicating. It's evil. *She's* evil. I swear she started it. I know that's what all men say, 'she led me on; it was her idea,' but she did. To get at my father."

"And does your father know?" Justina's voice was calm.

"Yes." He turned his eyes away from the memory. "He found us. I still can't—can't look him in the eye."

"Then she's won, hasn't she?" Justina shifted tack when he didn't answer. "Why the need to confess? Why now?"

"Because it hasn't stopped. It won't ever stop. She snaps her fingers, and I come like a dog. She knows it, my father knows it, gods, even my *betrothed* knows it now—" He ran his fingers through his hair. He had only seen Calpurnia a handful of times since their betrothal feast—and her eyes, regarding him, were always wary. "Oh, gods."

It all came spilling out: the banquet, the Emperor, the Indian drug, Lepida . . . "I *took* her, right there on the couch in the middle of the hall. Like an animal. The drug, that was part of it—I hardly knew what I was doing, but that's no excuse. I'm only glad my father wasn't there to see that part."

"And what did the Emperor say?" Justina sounded as if she were discussing the weather rather than a palatial orgy.

"He—didn't notice. He had his mistress there—we were all dizzy from the wine, whatever it was he put into it—"

"His mistress?" Justina's voice sharpened.

"Lady Athena. Thea. A singer. She's—she's a nice girl—and I remember—" He bit the words off. Babbling fool or not, there were some things one didn't say to a Vestal.

"What? Remember what?"

His head throbbed at her sharp tone. "I don't know what I remember. Don't know if it's right or if I dreamed it up. But—"

"What?"

"Thea. And the Emperor. He—I wasn't watching, but he—there were some things he . . . it was probably just the drug! Who knows what I saw? I saw snakes winding down from the ceiling and I saw the mosaics come to life and I saw Thea's blood turn green; who's to say what really happened?"

"Did you go to see her afterward? That would prove things."

He avoided Justina's eyes. "The Emperor would never hurt Thea. He loves her."

"Perhaps he does. Do you think that for all men love is kisses in the moonlight? For some men, love is pain."

"Justina"—very carefully—"I didn't come here to listen to you blacken my Emperor's name."

"What did you come here for, then?"

"I—I don't know. Confession? I need someone to know— what I am. The world looks at me and they see a hero. The Emperor's right arm. But it's all lies. I'm as stupid as my father is brilliant, I'm as fearful as my friend Trajan is brave, and I—am—a—*fake*."

"So you've confessed. What do you want now? Forgiveness?" He nodded slowly. "I'm sorry, Paulinus. No one can give you that but the gods."

It was the first time she had ever used his name.

"Comfort, then?" His tongue felt thick, and he looked at her humbly.

"Comfort I can give you."

Her hand was cool, calming his confused blood.

Twenty-five

❧❧

THEA
A.D. 95

"A NOTHER new year, Athena. We'll drink to that."
"As you please, Caesar." I sipped my wine, sitting where Domitian liked me to sit: at his feet, where he could stroke my head or strike it as the mood took him.

"To a new year." He drank, cheerful for now. "How long has it been for us?"

"Nearly four years." I felt I could hardly remember the whole last year—just a long continuous dream of pain.

"Four years. I hear the plebs call you the mistress of Rome . . ." A faint frown, and his hand stilled in my hair. "I suppose it's true enough, since I *am* Rome and you are my mistress, but I still dislike it. It's been four years, after all, and I know you no better than I did at the beginning." His hand began its stroking again. "You know what the new year heralds, Athena?"

"What?"

"The telling of secrets."

"I have no secrets."

"Oh, I think you have many. Tell me one."

"All right. Yes, all right. I'll tell you one. Just don't—all right!" Drawing in a sharp breath. "I was—I was taking a walk a month or so ago, past the Temple of Vesta, and a Vestal looked at me."

"And?"

". . . She pitied me."

"This is a secret?"

"It seemed important somehow." Her eyes had been enormous, all-knowing.

"The gaping of a dried-up old virgin? She was probably jealous. Tell me another secret."

"I have nothing to tell, Caesar."

"Shall I tell one for you, then? Shall I tell you about the gladiators you serviced at the age of fifteen? Oh yes, I know about that."

"I—I never—"

"You lie poorly, Athena. Lepida Pollia said you always did."

"You shouldn't believe Lepida Pollia, Caesar." I clutched for calm. "She hates me."

"Correct. Transparently. But she was such a font of information, what could I be but grateful? So, what was the Barbarian like in person?"

I opened my mouth but nothing came out—nothing. Inside I was freezing cold.

"Not your only catch, I understand, but certainly the prize. The gladiator they called the god of war—quite a prestigious achievement for a common slave girl. How much did he pay you?"

"No, I—he never—"

"Ah, so it was love, then. How touching, the Barbarian and his Jewess. Did you writhe and giggle for him, as you won't for me?"

"That—that hurts—"

"It hurt you more, watching him go to his death. Didn't it? Did it hurt as much as this?"

"I—"

"I don't suppose I have to be jealous of him anymore. But now I almost wish he were alive again. Just so I could look him in the eye and tell him that I have his woman. Twice a night, if I like. And she moans like the whore she is and wears my collar and takes my gold—"

I flung my goblet against the wall and it rebounded in a tinny clatter. *"Stop it!"*

"So the goddess of wisdom cracks at last? What a pretty little display. Please feel free to weep. I like tears in a woman.

You've been a good girl this evening, Athena. Good enough to deserve a reward. Would you like one?"

"No, Caesar." Fighting the tears back.

"No reward? Perhaps I'll just tell you one of my secrets, then. Yes, that seems fair." He settled back, stroking my head against his knee. "I've told you a good deal about my brother, haven't I? Titus the Golden, the darling of the people, cut off so tragically in the prime of his youth . . . well, I killed him. White arsenic in his wine. I killed my brother and then took his daughter. I think Julia suspected something. It may even have driven her mad. Will it drive you mad? I doubt it. You're too coarse-grained to go mad. The first person I've ever told . . . I imagine I'll have to keep you for good, now. Can't have you running away with a secret like that, can I?"

No. I suppose he couldn't.

"Drink up, Athena. Drink up." He sat back, jovial. "It's a whole new year."

J USTINA looked amused. "And why do you think me so cheated?"

"Not cheated," Paulinus amended. "I can see you're suited here. But that's just luck. If they took you when you were nine years old, you didn't know that it would all be worth giving up marriage and children and—and everything else. No one knows anything when they're nine years old."

"I did know it was a great honor to be chosen to serve Vesta. And in some ways, it's given me more power than you."

"How?" He rested his chin on his hand and looked at her.

"Whatever I say is believed wholly and absolutely, because as a priestess my word is sacred. Can you say as much?"

"No," he admitted. "No matter what I say, people assume I'm being devious."

"I am safe wherever I travel, because those who attack a priestess risk the wrath of her goddess. Can you say as much?"

"Certainly not. I've had two assassination attempts this year alone. I made a lot of enemies when the Emperor promoted me over so many other heads."

"If I meet a condemned prisoner on his way to execution, I can grant a divine pardon that not even the Emperor can revoke. Can you say as much?"

"Really?" said Paulinus, diverted. "You can pardon a criminal, just on whim?"

"Not on whim. On divine certainty. If Vesta whispers innocence in my ear."

"Does she whisper to you often?"

"On occasion." Justina folded her hands in goddesslike repose, but a little smile twitched her mouth.

"Well, I suppose you've got me beaten." Paulinus leaned back. "Unless . . . can you ride a horse at full gallop toward a herd of screaming blue-painted savages?"

"No." Gravely. "My veil would get dirty."

"Then let's call it even." Paulinus linked his hands behind his head.

"Paulinus."

"What?"

"You're bragging."

". . . Maybe I am."

"Why bother bragging to a woman who's taken a vow of chastity?"

"Because I want you to think well of me."

"I already do, Paulinus Norbanus. No need to brag."

"Good. Can I just ask one thing?"

"Of course."

"Are you impressed?"

She burst out laughing.

He grinned and looked at the floor, ruffling his hair. "Are you?" he insisted.

"Immeasurably."

"Really?" He felt like a boy again.

"I'm a Vestal, Paulinus." Another laugh. "My word is sacred."

TIVOLI

ARIUS'S sword sailed out of his hand, arcing gracefully to land in the spring mud.

For a moment Vix stared at it. Then he punched his own blade high in the air. "YES! I disarmed the Barbarian! Yes, I am a GOD!" He let out a war whoop that startled the crows in the vineyard. The three-legged dog, curled in the shade on her master's discarded cloak, looked up for a moment and then went back to sleep.

"Luck." Arius felt pleased, but knew better than to show it. "Try again."

Grinning, Vix stooped back into a fighting crouch, sword leaping to the ready. Arius launched a sideways swing. Vix blocked, ducked, and struck back, his well-trained muscles flowing from one blow to the next. He fought sensibly, refusing to lock body-to-body against Arius's greater strength, relying instead on speed. He was very fast now.

Only when the watery spring sunshine wavered away behind the vineyard did they stab their blades point-down into the earth and flop beside them. "We'll start shield work tomorrow." Arius passed a water jug. "Takes time, getting used to the weight."

"What kind of shield?" Shields marked a gladiator's class: a big shield for a *murmillo* with a long sword; a small round shield for a *thraex* with a little curved blade. No shield at all marked a *retiarius*, a net-and-trident man—as far as Vix was concerned, the lowest of the low.

"Big shield. You'll be a heavyweight." Arius sized up his pupil with a judicious eye. Vix had grown like a vine—his head topped Arius's shoulder, and at nearly twelve years old he was as compactly muscled as a pony. He'd be a big man someday.

Vix dunked his face in the water jug and mopped his forehead off with his arm, a gesture he'd picked up from Arius. He had also hacked his hair short, like Arius, and had started begging to drink unwatered wine as Arius did. Arius found himself oddly startled. He'd been many things in his life: a barbarian, a laborer, a gladiator, a slave, an entertainer, a monster. But he'd never been anyone's hero.

"Y'know my mother's coming to visit?" Vix was saying. "Lady Flavia got a letter."

"When's she coming?" Arius tilted the water jug so the dog could get a drink.

"Next month. End of May. You've never met my mother, have you?"

"No."

"She's awful," Vix said darkly. "She's *strict*. You'll like her. Hey, can we go one more before dark?"

"Why not?"

"I'll disarm you again."

"Don't get cocky." Arius hid a smile as he clouted Vix over the ear.

ROME

MARCUS had just paused below the steps of the Capitoline Library when Calpurnia Sulpicia called his name. "Marcus, is that you?"

"Calpurnia." Turning away from a hired litter where he had paused to have a word, Marcus smiled at his prospective daughter-in-law. A blue *palla* draped her shoulders, two slaves trotted at her back with fan and sunshade, and she had a basket on her arm like any Roman housewife. "How delightful."

"Was I interrupting?" Calpurnia gestured at the hired litter. A woman's pale emerald-studded hand had just twitched the gray curtains shut, and the litter-bearers were moving away at a trot.

"Not at all." Marcus did not elaborate. He shifted a load of scrolls to the other arm, balancing on his bad side as a harried-looking pleb woman brushed past in pursuit of her children. A bright spring morning, and every woman in Rome was pressing toward the forum. "What brings you out, Calpurnia Sulpicia? Shopping?"

"Yes, for earrings. I lost a stone out of my jade dangles."

"Buy topaz instead."

"Pardon?"

"Topaz," Marcus advised. "You have lovely hazel eyes. Wearing a yellow stone so close will make them look gold. Have you seen much of Paulinus lately?"

"No . . . he's been busy."

Marcus studied her. "He's been neglecting you, hasn't he?"

"Oh no." Fidgeting.

"Yes, he has. Has he even seen the augurs for a wedding date?"

"Of course. We thought perhaps last September, but my mother was so ill then that it seemed better to put everything off—"

"She's better?"

"Yes, now. So it isn't Paulinus's fault, you see." Smiling. "Just bad luck."

"He could try harder." Sternly. "Betrothed two years—bad

luck or no, your family would be within their rights to look elsewhere for you."

"Not when the Emperor himself wants the marriage. And besides—" A smile squeezed Calpurnia's hazel eyes. "My father said I could choose my second husband for myself. I want to marry Paulinus."

Marcus felt a surge of exasperation with his son. A fine girl like this waiting for him—pretty, well-bred, intelligent, understanding—and he couldn't take the jump. "I'll speak to him."

"No need for that, Marcus. I don't mind, truly." Calpurnia's slaves shifted behind her, adjusting the sunshade over her head, but she seemed in no hurry to move on. "Are you just coming back from the library? I was there myself not a week ago, reading your treatise. The one on the system of adoptive Emperors."

"Did you?" Marcus smiled. "What did you think?"

"I thought it was very well reasoned. Only I didn't really agree about the necessity of veto power in the Senate. If the Senate can overturn the Emperor's authority, then who will respect him?"

"And what if the Emperor's decisions are wrong?"

The discussion did not wind down for a half an hour. "I'd better get back," Calpurnia said at last. "My mother will worry."

"Come to dinner next Thursday?" He straightened his crooked shoulder a little, smiling. "I'll see if I can't track down that son of mine."

"I'd be delighted. And I'll buy those topaz earrings."

"Wear them when you next come to dinner."

CALPURNIA'S coming Thursday?" Sabina hopped into Marcus's lap almost before he had settled behind his desk. "Good. I like Calpurnia. Her clothes are all soft, not scratchy and fancy like Mother's. And she's nice. She has a nephew with epilepsia, and she showed me some breathing exercises to do when I get a headache."

"Did she?" Marcus stroked his daughter's hair.

"I'm glad she's marrying Paulinus. I wish she could move here."

"Why won't she?"

"Mother wouldn't let her. Mother isn't here, either, but she wouldn't let Calpurnia move in." Candidly. "She hates Calpurnia."

"What makes you say that?"

"Mother doesn't like other women if they're pretty. Like Aunt Diana—she *really* hates Aunt Diana because she's so beautiful and men like to look at her even more than Mother. But Calpurnia's pretty, too, so Mother would never let her move in here."

Marcus laughed. "What an imp you are."

"Though Mother may move out to Tivoli permanently, with the Emperor spending so much time there. Calpurnia can come visit us more after that."

"You see a good deal, don't you, Vibia Sabina?"

"Because no one ever notices me." A serene smile. "You'd be surprised how much I hear."

G OOD afternoon, Lady Athena." Paulinus bowed formally. "The Emperor desires me to tell you that he has been detained in the city. He will join you in two days' time." He looked away before he could see the naked relief spring into her eyes.

"Then will you take me to Lady Flavia's villa?" Thea whirled to grab up her *palla*. "Ganymede, get the litter! You'll come, too, Paulinus? If I have a Praetorian to clear the road I can be there in fifteen minutes."

"I shouldn't."

"But I haven't seen Vix in—"

"I don't like it. It's secretive."

"Paulinus, please!"

He looked at her. Lady Athena, the Imperial mistress, swathed in pearls and jade and cloudy green silk, her neck chafed by a welded silver collar. He thought of the girl who stretched herself woodenly under a panting madman at a drunken banquet, looking at the ceiling with drug-swollen eyes. He thought of the girl who had stood in a dusty road smiling at and scolding her son simultaneously.

"All right." Roughly. "I'll take you to Lady Flavia's."

Her face opened, and he couldn't bear to look at her.

All the way down the road she sat upright in her litter, foot drumming against the cushions, eyes stretching eagerly out over the blooming green hills. "Almost there?" she asked like an impatient child.

"Almost there," said Paulinus, and thought of the Emperor. The Emperor looking at him just that morning with trust and, yes, with love: "Whatever would I do without you, Paulinus?"

"You were born to serve," Nessus had told Paulinus, reading his horoscope. "Right arm of Emperors, never Emperor yourself."

He had never thought serving an Emperor would be easy. But he had not imagined it would be as hard as this.

Justina, he thought. *Justina, tell me what to do.*

"Thea!" Flavia laughed from the door of the villa, flanked by her boys and the usual clutter of slave children. "It's been too long. Yes, yes, Vix is well—he's off with Stephanus, of course; he's never anywhere else these days."

"Yes, this famous Stephanus I've heard about." Thea tumbled out of the litter before the slaves could lower it to the ground. "I'll have to meet him."

"Well, you won't have long to wait." Flavia pointed at the north end of the garden, where one tall figure and one shorter one had just rounded the edge of the wall. "Jupiter and Mars, in the flesh."

"Vix!" Athena gathered up her cloudy green gown and ran. The boy stopped, let out a shout, and bolted toward her. They collided halfway.

"Mother." With difficulty Vix pulled free long enough to speak. "I want you to meet somebody. My friend. Stephanus." Waving a hand at the gardener who stood leaning up against the wall. "It's a long story, actually—I'll tell you later. I let him teach me a few fighting tricks . . . Mother?"

Paulinus, turning to go, looked back and stopped. Thea had halted dead in the road, gazing before her as blindly as a statue.

He followed her eyes. The gardener. Just a gardener, in an earth-stained tunic and a short dark beard. Gazing back at the elegant woman in her silk and jade and pearls.

She swayed. Paulinus took a step forward. "Mother?" Vix blinked.

Slowly the gardener came forward, his big callused hand rising toward her face. His fingers brushed her cheek, dropped away.

She made a sound low in her throat.

"Mother?" Vix's voice was small.

"Thea," said the gardener. "Thea."

She took a step toward him, dropping her silk skirt in the dust.

The gardener reached out, his rough fingers just stirring the ends of her hair.

Paulinus couldn't say who moved first. But the gardener's arms were around her waist, and her face was pressed hard against his chest, her hands at his hair and his shoulders as if she were trying to convince herself that he was real. In the dust of the road they swayed, clutching each other and babbling incoherently.

Flavia moved first. "Oh, goodness." She clapped her hands. "All right, everyone. Boys, into the house. Paulinus, go home. Vix, go stab something. I imagine your mother and father want some time alone."

"Father?" The word broke simultaneously from Vix and Paulinus.

"Well, I assume that's what he is." She looked at Vix consideringly. "I knew you reminded me of somebody. And here he was, on my villa the whole time. I *am* dense."

Vix looked from his mother to the gardener and back again. He looked suddenly very young and uncertain.

"Into the house," Flavia said kindly.

He went in like a sleepwalker. The Emperor's niece turned to Paulinus. "Well? Haven't you got anything to do?"

"I'm supposed to be keeping an eye on her!" He pointed at Thea, murmuring what looked like rapid explanations against the gardener's mouth. "Who's he?"

"Vix's father, I think. Don't they look alike? Amazing none of us noticed before." She shooed at him. "Go away, Paulinus. Come back in a few hours."

"I can't do that."

"Why not?"

"I serve the Emperor. Always. I can't let his woman take up with some other—"

"Moving a little fast, aren't we? Five minutes of reunion and you're assuming a full-blown liaison?"

"What else am I supposed to make of it?" The gardener had his hands tangled deep into Thea's hair, his forehead leaned against hers.

"Oh, shut up, Paulinus," Flavia snapped. "Make anything out of it that you want. You were a prig when you were five, and now you're even worse." She marched into the house.

He looked irresolutely back and forth.

"Paulinus." Thea came toward him in short tremulous steps. "Paulinus, give me an hour."

"I won't help you betray the Emperor!"

"In the name of everything that's holy, I swear I'll betray no one. Just give me an hour to explain. For the love of God, give me an hour."

She looked open and joyful and young. The gardener, waiting behind her with folded arms and a smile splitting his face like the sun, could have been any lover of fifteen instead of a work-bowed man of nearly forty.

Something about his face . . . under the beard and the dark hair . . . ?

Oh, never mind. He was a slave. A common slave, who had loved the Emperor's mistress back in the days when she had been a common slave girl. Thea ran back as lightly as a girl, her hand slipping instantly into the gardener's, her head touching his shoulder.

In an hour she was ready, standing barefoot and alone in the doorway of the villa. There was no sign of either her son or his father, and she stepped back into the litter with perfect calm. Paulinus threw the reins of his horse to one of the Praetorians, and settled in opposite her.

"So?" he said.

"I told him I have a jealous lover."

"Did you say who?"

"No. I couldn't even say the name. They aren't two names that belong on the same breath." She fiddled with the litter's silk cushions. "I told him to ask anyone else on the villa if he wants to know."

"So what now?"

"That depends on you." She folded her hands, looking with absolute stillness out through the curtains.

"Me?"

"Will you tell the Emperor or not?"

Tell the Emperor. "He'll kill you," Paulinus said suddenly, and there was no excusing or apologizing or explaining away the bald words.

"Oh, yes." Calmly. "And he will kill the man you know as Stephanus . . . and our son. He might punish Flavia, too, for allowing us to meet. So the choice is yours."

"That isn't fair."

"You serve him." She turned her eyes back, away from the curtains. "I am owned by him, but you *serve* him. Nothing is fair."

He stared back at her. Another secret. Another secret between him and the man who held his oath.

Another secret.

"If I don't tell," he said, "what happens then?"

"I'll continue to see Vix," she said. "I'll see Vix's father, too, now and then. But nothing will happen. You have my word on that."

"Your word?"

"My solemn promise. Quite a selfish promise, really. If I took another man for a lover, then Domitian would know—he'd smell it on me—and that would be the end of both me and—and Stephanus. I don't want that."

She took a breath, stirring in her silks as if they were chains. "So, Paulinus. What's it to be?"

"We'll talk about it more in the morning," said Paulinus.

"Thank you." She leaned back against the cushions, closing her eyes. Tears glittered and ran down into her hair.

"One thing." Suddenly. "Your Stephanus—have I seen him before somewhere?"

"No." She opened her eyes. "Never."

For the rest of the ride back to the Villa Jovis, there was silence.

D ID she say who her jealous lover was?" Flavia's voice, at Arius's elbow.

"No." Wrenching his eyes away from the departing litter, he turned to the Emperor's niece. "You knew her—all this time you *knew* her—"

"Yes. Ironic, isn't it? The fates must have had a good laugh at our expense."

"Her lover—who is he?" He hadn't pressed Thea when she'd declined to say the name. Too glad to hear her voice, too glad to have her back. As long as she was close enough to hold, the lover didn't matter.

But now . . . "Who owns her?"

"Ask anyone." Flavia patted his arm and drifted out.

He collared the first slave he found. "The lady in that litter"—pointing to the cloud of dust that marked Thea's departure—"who is she?"

The slave looked at him as if he were half-witted. "I know you never come out of that hut, but don't you know anything? That's Lady Athena. The Emperor's mistress."

The Emperor.

Arius turned away blindly, latching his hands onto the wooden rail around the garden gate.

The demon, so long asleep in the bottom of his mind, stirred murderously.

Thea and the Emperor. *His* Thea, in the bed of a man who'd denied him his *rudius*, who'd shot arrows at him in the arena, who'd thought it funny to hack up his best friend.

Careful, big boy, Hercules rasped in his head. *Careful*.

The gate railing cracked in his hands.

"Arius?"

He whirled, hand leaping to his knife. But it was just Vix. Vix standing there looking unaccustomedly dazed and small.

"Born after I was sold," Thea had said sometime in that hour of recounted years. "I never told him—didn't think he'd ever see you."

He looked at Vix with new eyes. "Tell your son there to leave my horses alone," a drover had snapped to Arius two weeks ago, unloading barrels at Flavia's storeroom doors. "Not my son," Arius had said, amused. "Not that little devil."

He'd never dreamed of having a son. Never thought he'd live long enough.

Now he saw what the drover had seen. Vix's russet hair, his light eyes, his strong left hand. The reflexes, the strength, the vicious skill.

Even my own weaknesses. Why didn't I see it?

And Thea had named him Vercingetorix.

The world tilted. The woman he loved was alive, hope existed, and he had a son.

Vix took a step forward. "Who the hell are you?"

"Come here," Arius said thickly. "Come here."

He gripped Vix's shoulders between his hands, and began to talk.

Twenty-six

⊰≫ ≪⊱

LEPIDA

TWENTY-EIGHT. *Twenty-eight*. Gods, what an age. Almost old. Almost thirty!

I threw a scent bottle at my maid, ripped my rose-silk veil in half because it had a grease spot, and threw myself down in front of the polished steel mirror. At least I didn't look twenty-eight. My hair gleamed like ebony, my skin was white velvet, and I could show as much bosom as I liked without a qualm. Lady Lepida Pollia, although twenty-eight, had nothing to fear from the younger beauties of Rome's court. She still reigned supreme over all.

I scowled, dabbling among my rouge pots. The trouble was, I was bored with reigning supreme over all. I'd reigned supreme over all for years. I had only to walk into a room to have the men slavering and the women slit-eyed. I had only to give my slow smile to a man to have him at my feet. When I wore blue, everyone wore blue. When I laughed at a joke, everyone found it funny. I stood at the pinnacle of patrician society.

So what was the point of it all? If I couldn't go higher, then what was the point? And I *could* go higher, if it weren't for . . .

Unfair. Unfair! She always ruined everything, and now she was turning the Emperor into a recluse. He'd never shunned society before. He may have been a dour guest, but at least he'd *been* a guest. For this whole summer, though, he'd hardly gone anywhere except to the villa where his pet Jewess waited. He took other women to his bed, yes, but none lasted as she did.

"Surely she's put a spell on the Emperor," I wheedled Paulinus. "Jew magic—you could have her executed!"

"Don't be ridiculous," Paulinus said stiffly, and wouldn't be moved. He was taking her side now? Could he and she be . . . Paulinus and Thea . . . of course they'd been lovers before, back when she'd been just a common singer . . . I could tell Domitian that little piece of news! But no—it might rid me of Thea, but it might also rid me of Paulinus, and to have my stepson as the Emperor's best friend was very much to my taste. Anyway, I doubted there was anything between Thea and Paulinus. Even Paulinus wasn't so stupid as that.

There was something wrong with him though, even if it wasn't Thea. Oh, he still came despairingly to my bed whenever I called him, but . . . little things. Last time I'd twined my arms around his neck in the garden of some senator's dinner party, he'd tried to push me away for a moment before succumbing with a groan. His gaze held a sort of straight dislike that unsettled me. Of course he hated me. Naturally. But hatred had always been the other side of the coin that was desire. This look of flat distaste was something new. Something very like Marcus.

If it wasn't Thea, did he have another? Surely not the bovine Calpurnia: for all they'd been betrothed forever, no date was set and he'd hardly met with her all year. Well, no use worrying too much about Paulinus. No matter what kind of look I'd been seeing in his eyes lately, I'd always be able to bring him to heel. Thea—she was my little problem.

I gazed into the mirror a little longer, and then beckoned my cowed maid. "You must have friends among the Imperial slaves," I said, nailing her with a glance. "If you don't, make some. For any information they bring me about Lady Athena, there'll be a rich reward. For you, too. Now get out."

Let's see what comes of that.

"P**AULINUS.**" Flavia's voice was curt. "Don't you have anything better to do than spy on Thea?"

"I'm not spying." Paulinus felt mulish.

"You've been staring out that window at her for the past hour!"

"It is my duty as Prefect to extend my eye to all suspicious activity."

"'Suspicious activity?' She's just talking to her son's father! And it's the first time they've met at all since they found each other. Three weeks she waited to come back here—"

"I shouldn't allow it."

"Oh, for God's sake. Have they touched once in all the time you've watched?"

"They don't have to touch," Paulinus muttered. Athena and her gardener, sitting a decorous twelve inches apart on a marble atrium bench, generated enough heat between them to burn bread. But Flavia's face hardened.

"You sound like a jealous lover, Paulinus. I do hope you're not falling in love with Thea yourself. That would put a nice wrench in your loyalties, wouldn't it?"

He reddened. "I am not—"

"Then let her alone. She's given you her word that she won't betray the Emperor. Or is her word not worth anything because she's a Jew and a slave?"

"I'm sure she has every intention of keeping her word." Stiffly. "But my duty lies with the Emperor, and the Emperor would want to know about this."

"Tell my uncle, and you sign her death warrant."

". . . No . . ."

"You don't believe me?"

"He's a man of honor—"

"No, he's not!" she said witheringly.

"Lady Flavia, you don't know what you're saying."

"I know exactly what I'm saying!" Her voice rose. "Do you think you know him better than me?"

"I've served him for six years. In the thick of battle—"

"Battle!" Flavia spat. "Who cares about battle? I'm his niece! Do you know what I've seen? I've seen him stab flies out of the air on a pen and watch them writhe until they die. I've seen him shoot arrows at slaves until they look like sea urchins. I've seen him condemn men without trial for the pleasure of watching them beg. He's a hard man, my uncle; he's hard and he's cruel, and he's cruelest of all to his women."

Paulinus opened his mouth, but Flavia rushed on, her face flushed. "Did you know the Empress used to smile once? Even laugh? Then Domitian got hold of her and she turned into a marble statue covered in emeralds. You played with Julia when you were children, but you just dismissed her as mad when the rumors started to fly. You didn't get letters from her, letters getting thinner and thinner and more hopeless until when she finally died all you could do was be happy. And Thea—my God, you're not the only one who's served the Emperor for years! She's served him, too, filled his bed and made his music and *paid* for it. She hides her son and she hides her scars, but when she's alone she drains her blood into bowls and thinks about dying. Did you know that, Prefect? No, of course not. But I do, and not because she tells me. I know what to look for, because I've known Domitian all my life and I know what he thinks when he looks at people—*and because now he's looking at my sons!*"

She burst into tears. Paulinus stood blank and open-mouthed.

"So as far as I'm concerned, if Thea wants a lover then she's welcome to him!" Kohl ran down Flavia's cheeks, and she angrily smeared it away. "If all she wants is to sit in a garden and talk to a man who loves her—a man who's *normal*—then I'll cover for her. I couldn't do it for Julia, but I'll do it for Thea. She's earned it. And if you don't see that, Paulinus Norbanus, then for God's sake *open your eyes!*"

She rushed away, doubled over with sobs. Paulinus stared after her.

WHY didn't you come back sooner? Three weeks—"

"I'm watched, Arius. I didn't dare make it sooner."

"For twelve years I thought you were dead. Used to see you everywhere, like a ghost."

"I did see you everywhere. In Vix."

"I should have known—"

"I didn't know myself until after I was sold."

"I should have taken you away when I had the chance. Hauled you off over one shoulder like a proper barbarian."

"You're not a barbarian anymore." Lightly. "You're a gardener."

"Not a very good one. All the grapes have a blight since I started tending them. But I wasn't a very good barbarian, either, when I had you."

"Don't say things like that. You make it hard."

"You're beautiful. Silk, soft hands, no more calluses—"

"I'm not allowed to do anything anymore."

"Except wait on the Emperor?"

". . . Don't."

"Why can't I touch you?"

"He'd smell you on me."

"He's not a god."

"But I wear his eye . . . Arius, he'll never release me. Once he puts his mark on something, it's his forever."

Silence. He reached for her.

"Arius—Arius, don't."

"Don't what?"

"Don't touch me."

"What's wrong? You're shaking."

"No, I—I—just don't try to kiss me. Please."

"I need to know you're real. You look like a dream, and I'm old and ugly."

"Never that. Never that."

"Thea, we'll run. Take Vix, get out of Rome—"

"Arius, there's nowhere I could run where he couldn't find me."

Their hands touched diffidently on the bench between them. Tangled. Kneaded mutely.

ROME

I don't know what to think." Paulinus rested his elbows on his knees, interlocking his fingers. "But sometimes—sometimes I think she's right."

"Lady Flavia?" Justina's voice was a murmur around the marble walls.

"Yes." Over and over he kneaded his hands. "Because lots of things don't add up. Not quite. Things about the Emperor. That banquet the night of my betrothal. The Empress. Julia's death. The treason trials . . ."

"Do you believe Lady Flavia?"

"I don't know!" Raking his hands through his hair. "He's my friend! Gods, whatever Lady Flavia says about him, I can't see it. I just see him, pouring me wine and asking me questions about the army and—and joking about lazy legionnaires and incompetent governors. But as soon as I make up my mind to forget it, I think about the way Thea weaves when she comes out of his rooms, like she's drunk only she never drinks as much as that—and I start to wonder all over again."

"So what will you do?" The words were quiet drops of water into a pond, spreading ripples through the room.

"I don't know." He let out a ragged sigh. "I can't do nothing. Not now that Lady Flavia's waved it in front of me. But what proof do I have? Whose word stands up against the Emperor's? Thea's a slave. Julia's dead. Flavia's hated him since her sister's death; she already goes against him in her little child-rescuing business—"

Justina looked inquiring.

"Lady Flavia saves children from the Colosseum and the prisons," Paulinus explained tiredly. "Jews, Christians, other heretics; she's been doing it for years. She bribes the guards to let them out of the cells, brings them back to her villa as slaves, and finds them families among friends and tenants. The Emperor says let it be since it keeps her busy and who cares if a few children escape the lions?"

"He's the one who sentences them, isn't he?" Gently.

Silence.

Justina tilted her face toward him. "So if you doubt Lady Flavia's word, and if Julia isn't here to speak for herself, then whose word will you trust? Who has the best judgment of anyone you know?"

"My father." No hesitation.

"Why not ask him? This isn't about your stepmother, after all. It's about politics, and people. You can ask him what's right."

"When I can't even look him in the face?"

"Well, who else could you ask?"

"I could ask you." His eyes came up, locking hungrily on hers. "Do you—do you believe in the rumors?"

She folded her hands. "Yes."

He closed his eyes. "Then what should I do?"

"Are you asking me to be your conscience?"

"Yes, I—I am."

"I can't do that for you, Paulinus. No one can."

"Advise me, then. Help me."

"Tell me this. Of all the wrongs you've heard attributed to

Domitian, which would you right if you could? What would you undo?"

"I'd have gone to Lady Julia and seen for myself if she was truly mad." The words surprised him. "After a childhood of playing games in gardens, I owed her that."

"It's too late to help her. But it's not too late for Thea. Help her, in Julia's name."

". . . Don't tell the Emperor about her old lover?"

"It's a start."

"I watched them," Paulinus found himself saying. "All summer I watched them. Not that they met very often—two times, maybe three. They didn't touch each other; she kept her word about that. But they were like—like a team of matched horses."

"That's love for you."

"I'm not going to marry Calpurnia," he said suddenly. "She and I, we don't run in unison."

"Rather unfair to her, isn't it? You've been betrothed a long time."

"She doesn't want me. No more than I want her." Paulinus shook his head. "No wedding. Not until I find the one who—who runs in unison with me."

"Such things are rare."

He looked at Justina: the narrow three-cornered face between the white wings of veil, the deep grave gaze, the pale eyebrows hinting at pale hair he'd never seen.

"I'll wait."

THEA

I heard the voices dimly, outside my door.

"Gods, I don't know what to do with her." Nessus, agitated out of his usual ebullient cheer. "Hasn't even come out of her room since she came back from Tivoli. Came to see how she was faring, and found her like this—I couldn't even get the knife away from her!" Voice lowering. "Can you do something?"

A soft sound.

"Of course you can. No one's better than you at the whole soothing bit."

I looked up through half-closed eyes to see Ganymede drop

a kiss on his lover's head just at the spot where the hair was prematurely thinning and pad into my bedchamber. Such a nice bedchamber: all gray and white with its lavish silver-veiled sleeping couch and the statues of Minerva. The statues writhed when my blood-dreams were on me.

I fought him when he tried to take the knife, and the bowl upset. Blood everywhere, splashing the mosaics, from the bowl and from my arm, which I'd cut down to the blue gaping veins. But Ganymede paid no mind to the blood or my hazy cursing, just wrenched the billowing curtain off the sleeping couch and wadded the gauzy stuff around my wrist.

"No—no, don'—"

He picked me up easily, laying me on the couch. As soon as he pulled back I ripped the bandaging away from my wrist, clawing at the slit veins. He pinned my hand and wound my wrist in gauze again. The white was already checkered in scarlet.

"No—" I battered at his hands, weeping. "Let it go—let it go this time—'s the only way they'll leave; they'll never get out if I'm alive, just pull it *off*—" I gave a tremendous tug, and Ganymede pinioned me against his chest with both arms, crooning wordlessly.

"I can't stand it anymore—four years, four years, Julia stood eight and I don't know how—can't take another year, not one—toys and games—no more games—he'll see, Arius will see, he's not stupid; he'll see and that'll be the end of him, don't you see that? He'll come after the Emperor and he'll die, he'll die again and I—can't—take—it!"

I don't know if Ganymede could understand me through the sobs. He rocked me back and forth.

"And Vix, Vix will find out, too; it's a miracle I've fooled him this long; he'll find out and he'll be ashamed of me—and he should be, I'm a coward—oh, God, Arius will hate me when he finds out—"

The words went off into a howl, muffled against Ganymede's chest. He smoothed my hair; checked my wrist. I could already feel the blood drying.

"You know why he'll hate me?" Gasping. "Not because Domitian made me a whore; because he made me weak. Just four years and he's cut out my backbone. Four years of his toys and his games and his questions and his eye around my neck, and he's ruined me. Can't trust a man anymore, even Arius—when I would have put my life in his hands in a heartbeat once—can't bear to touch him, when I used to throw myself on him like a dog on a bone. Domitian's won, hasn't he? He's taken my lover away—didn't even know he was doing it; just a little bonus for him! All I'm good for anymore is closing my eyes and telling him I'm not afraid, and even that's a lie!"

Ganymede cradled me in the curve of his arm, humming low in his throat.

"Let me die. Oh God, let me die before Arius finds out what a worm I am. Let me die."

I shuddered in Ganymede's arms, strangling a little guttural sound in my throat, and he pulled me down into the cushions, tucking the coverlets up around us both. He shooed away my curious slaves and folded himself around me, holding me softly, and I knew he would be there all night. Dimly I hoped that Nessus would understand—but of course he would. He loved Ganymede, and what's more, he trusted him. I had no knowledge of love anymore, but I remembered something about trust.

LEPIDA

A man?"

"Yes, Domina. That's what she said." My maid fixed her eyes nervously on the tiles.

"So what is it this friend of yours saw, exactly? Tell me everything."

"My friend—she goes in at dawn to get the sheets off Lady Athena's bed, when Lady Athena's with the Emperor. But she's not this morning, she's sound asleep in her own bed and there's a man with her."

"Hmm." I tapped my lacquered scarlet nails against each other. "Who was he?"

"Just a slave, Domina. Ganymede, his name is. Her body slave. All folded up around Lady Athena. S'what my friend says, anyway."

"Well!" I made a note to find out more about this Ganymede. "You've done very nicely. Take this, and tell your friend there's another purse for her. Anything else she can tell me, of course—"

"Yes, Domina." My maid bowed out, already counting her coins. I sat down at my little desk, musing. A slave for a lover . . . not much to go on, really. I wished Thea had chosen someone a little more scandalworthy—say one of the Imperial cousins or even Paulinus. Bedding a slave wasn't much of a sin; even patrician ladies frequently amused themselves with handsome slaves. Lollia Cornelia, that famous patrician hostess who was mother to Lady Flavia Domitilla, was well known to have borne two children by her body servant. But Lady Lollia's husbands came and went, happy to let her do as she pleased . . . would the Emperor be so obliging? The Emperor who had once had some unassuming actor killed on the vaguest, most ridiculous rumor that the man was mounting his impeccable Empress?

I thought not.

Maybe Thea's indiscretion would give good value after all. Phrasing would be everything . . .

I began, delightedly, to compose a certain letter.

Twenty-seven

◦❦◦

"H EY!" Lady Flavia's son stumbled backward, looking down at the welt across his ribs. "Not so hard."

"And the crowds roar as first blood goes to Vercingetorix the Vicious!" Vix whooped, and he brought up his wooden sword again, circling in the practice ring of the gymnasium. Arius watched from the sidelines, chewing on a straw. Vix didn't often spar with the two princes—"They're too easy!" he scoffed—but the younger boy's tutor was laid up with a fever and he'd begged a workout from Vix. Arius wondered if he might be regretting it: The boy was Vix's age but a head smaller. A nice boy. He often sneaked meat scraps from his own plate for Arius's dog after dinner.

"The opponent begs for mercy," Vix chanted, swinging two-handed. *"The first games of October, and Vercingetorix the Vicious looks ready to take his first kill."*

The boy dodged, letting out a hiss of pain as the flat of Vix's blade cracked across his shoulder. "Vix, this isn't funny." Arius was starting to think it wasn't funny, either.

"Vercingetorix closes in—"

The young prince crumpled into the sand with a howl, leg streaming blood. "Vix, stop it! You've won, all right? You won!"

Arius spat out the straw in his mouth.

"The Colosseum erupts as Vercingetorix closes in for the

slow kill!" Vix flung himself on his opponent and laid the wooden blade across his throat, digging the dull edge slowly into the soft flesh.

"Vix—" Scrabbling.

"The thumbs signal for death across the stands—" Vix pressed his fingers against the beating jugular—

And slammed into the sand as Arius knocked him loose with the side of one fist.

"He's had enough," said the Barbarian.

Vix blinked, as if coming out of a dream. Flavia's son was on his knees, rasping for air. A wide shallow cut lay across his throat. "He was—he was going to kill me—"

"Go get patched up."

Lady Flavia's son didn't need to be told twice. He took one look and limped off.

Arius took a deep breath and kicked Vix over onto his back.

"Hey." Scrabbling upright. "I was just playing! I was in the Colosseum; they were all cheering me like they cheered you—"

The first blow knocked a tooth out of his head.

VIX puked twice on the way back to his father's hut. Both times Arius waited until he was finished, then picked him up again and hauled him onward.

"I'm bleeding," Vix said through puffy lips as Arius dumped him on the packed dirt floor of the vineyard hut.

"You'll live." Arius took stock of the injuries he'd inflicted on his son: one side tooth lost, jaw swollen, both eyes blacked, bloody nose, ribs marked by sandal prints. He winced inside, but clamped his teeth on it.

"You killed me," Vix rasped. "You son of a bitch, you've killed me."

"You deserved it," returned the Barbarian, tossing more wood on the fire. "Arrogant little bastard."

"Fuck you."

"Fuck *you*, boy."

Arius stripped off his sandals and settled down with his back against the wattled clay wall. He cored an apple with his dagger, eating off the point and wondering what the hell he was going to do next. He'd gotten a beating or two from his own father as a boy, but his dimly remembered mother had been the one to follow it up with the appropriate stern but kindly words. That was a mother's job, wasn't it? He didn't have the slightest idea what to say. *I wish Thea were here.*

"Don't I get any dinner?" Vix asked.

"No."

"How about a bandage?"

"You want to be a gladiator? Sit there and bleed, and hope you get better."

"Thanks."

Arius flicked the apple core at the dog.

Vix dragged himself up, resting his back against the wall by his father. "I wouldn't have hurt him."

Arius turned over a few responses to that, but decided on silence.

"I was just playing!"

"No more lessons," Arius said finally. "Not from me."

"That's not fair!"

"I won't have a bully for a son."

"You weren't even around the first ten years," Vix snarled.

"I'm around now, and I don't teach bullies how to fight."

Vix looked sullen.

"Just tell me something." Arius rotated the knife blade, looking at the fire. "Do you hear a voice in your head, when you fight? A little black voice?"

Vix looked startled. Arius looked at him, searching for words, but found none. He was no good with words. They both looked away, stretching their legs toward the fire, and Vix groaned as a joint popped. "I hate you."

"Likewise."

"I don't suppose Lady Flavia'll take me to Rome with her, now."

"I don't suppose she will."

"She's going to a dinner party at the palace, she said. Next month, when the Emperor announces the kids as heirs. Said she'd take me, so I could see Mother afterward." Vix shrugged. "Who cares about seeing the Emperor anyway."

"You ever seen the Emperor before?" Arius ripped a loaf of rough bread in half.

"Once."

"What'd you think?"

"I hated him," said Vix. "Pass the bread."

Arius guessed the stern lecture part of the night was done. He passed Vix the bread, wishing he could ask Thea if he'd done it right. They chewed; Vix painfully, Arius quietly.

"You heard from your mother?"

"Not much. She sends a word to Lady Flavia now and then. She says somebody probably reads her letters."

They leaned their heads back against the wall, closing their eyes. They linked identical sword-callused hands around identical scarred brown knees.

"Don't listen to that voice," Arius said, eyes still closed. "The one in your head. And you're still leaving yourself too wide on that underhand swing."

Maybe he wouldn't cut off Vix's lessons just yet.

THEA

"So, Athena." Domitian stroked my head as I sat at his feet. "Shall I tell you what I found out today?"

"Will I be able to stop you, Caesar?"

"Oh, Athena. Still so shrewish. I thought you would have learned better by now."

"All right. All right! I've learned."

"Then be quiet like a good girl, then, and listen. I have a certain spy out in Judaea. He must be quite industrious, because he's managed to find something that slipped past all my other spies."

"And what's that?"

"Your origins. My dear, you're looking pale. Some wine? It's an excellent vintage. Confiscated from the estate of Lucius Aesernia . . . who may have been a traitor, but he certainly knew his wines."

"What did he say?"

"Lucius Aesernia?"

"Your spy!"

"Oh, him. You know, I already uncovered most of your history—that Athenian merchant who taught you Greek and deflowered you, Quintus Pollio, your taste for gladiators. But the early years? A blank. Until a rather interesting report from a man of mine in Judaea. A cliff-top fortress, a hot night, a city full of dead Jews . . . and a few who survived. Need I go on?"

"No."

"Did you know that there were six other survivors besides you, Athena? Two old women and four other children, all of them boys. I had them traced, out of curiosity. Do you know where they are now, your brother and sister survivors?"

". . . Where?"

"Dead! Every one of them. Mostly killed for bringing bad luck to the families who bought them. The last Jews of Masada, spreading ill fortune to any they touched. You, it seems, are the only one left. And you've never brought me bad luck, have you?"

"Apparently not."

"I remember Masada, you know. Titus the Golden wept—he had a fondness for Jews—but I laughed."

"I'm sure you did."

Abruptly Domitian seized my head between his hands from behind.

"No—no that hurts, that hurts—"

"You said you were a goddess, Athena."

"I am—I am—"

"No, you're lying." He squeezed my head like a walnut in a vise. "You slipped out of some Jewess in a desert, screaming and covered in blood like any other mortal, and you aren't a goddess at all. I'm the god here, not you. Only one god in Rome. Got rid of Arius the Barbarian, got rid of you—"

"But you haven't gotten rid of me. Not yet. So stop babbling and do it."

"Oh yes, oh yes, but not until I hear it."

"Hear what?"

"You know what. Say it."

"That I'm afraid? You're afraid, Caesar, afraid of *me*, and I'm only a Jewess born wailing and screaming in a desert—"

"Stop laughing. Stop it!"

"I am Athena." Laughing with a crazy suicidal glee, despite the crushing pain in my skull. "Before that I was Thea, singer and slave and lover of gladiators. Before that I was Leah, daughter of Benjamin and Rachael of Masada. I am as mortal as you, you common little man." I raised my voice to a joyous shout for the slaves outside the chamber, for the Emperor's hangers-on, for the whole world. *"And I fear no one!"*

He stared down at me a moment. Then he laughed.

It was eight days before I could leave my bed.

I didn't think I'd see you so soon." Justina's eyes touched warmly on Paulinus. "But here you are, and in all your finery, too."

"I go to the Domus Flavia in an hour." Paulinus tucked his scarlet-crested helmet under his arm. "The Emperor is holding a formal banquet in honor of his niece and her sons."

They fell into step, perfectly synchronized as they walked along the pale marble corridor. Other priestesses hurried by in fluttering white veils, and Roman matrons come to whisper prayers in preparation for Saturnalia, the year-end festival where the household was turned upside-down and made ready for the new year. No one gave a second glance to the Vestal and the Prefect. The sight of their heads bent in consultation was a common one in the public rooms. In any case, those who might have been happy to speculate about a Vestal Virgin would not dare utter a word against the Emperor's best friend.

"I did something today." Paulinus clasped his hands at the small of his back, a gesture copied from Domitian. "Lepida—she sent me a note at the Praetorian barracks, the way she does sometimes. *'Tonight,'* that's what it said. I always tell my centurions to take over for the evening. But today—"

"What?"

"I started to call them in. And then—I don't know. I just turned the note over and wrote *'I'm busy'* on the other side, and sent it straight back." His eyes flicked up to Justina's. "I've never done that before."

"So why now?"

"I thought of what you'd say if you could see me. What you'd think."

"What did you think I'd think?"

"I thought you'd be—understanding. And I don't want you to be understanding. I want you to be proud."

"I *am* proud."

"Of me?"

"Of you."

He blew a long breath. "Can I ask you something?"

"Yes."

"How old are you?"

She blinked. "Twenty-nine."

"So you have ten more years of service to Vesta before you retire?"

"Yes."

"When your ten years are up," he said, "marry me."

Silence.

When he dared to look up, her eyes were huge. "Paulinus—"

"What?"

"I—" She looked away, fidgeting for the first time since he'd known her. "It's bad luck to wed a former Vestal."

"I'll take my chances with Fortuna."

"Paulinus, it's ten years from now. And I won't break my vows before that—"

"I know you won't. I'll wait."

"I'll be thirty-nine years old by then. Too old to give you children."

"I don't want children, I want you." He moved to seize her hand, thought of the stream of passing worshippers, and contented himself with lowering his voice. "I've known you forever, Justina. Long before I ever set eyes on you. I don't care how long I have to wait."

She pulled back. Her eyes touched his a moment, and then flitted away. She reached up to adjust her veil. "I can't—I don't know what to say."

"Say maybe. Think it over. You've got ten years to decide."

"But Calpurnia—"

"She doesn't want to marry me, either—we've traded one excuse after another these past years, any reason not to set a wedding date. Tonight I tell the Emperor I'm breaking off the betrothal. Calpurnia's an heiress; she won't have any trouble finding another husband. Say you'll think about it," he urged. "Just say that."

"All—all right." Faintly.

A mad rush of glory flooded his head. "Then I'll go. That's all I came to say—gods, it took me all day to work up the nerve! Even Saturninus and his Germans were better than this!" He laughed dizzily; wanting to shout, wanting to dance.

Her veil fluttered back as she looked up at him, and he caught sight of a loop of hair beside her ear. It must have slipped free when she adjusted her headdress . . . pale hair, just as he'd imagined. He reached out and touched it.

"It's like corn silk," he said. "Or Scythian gold."

She was still standing in the center of the marble room when he left her.

ROME

"WELL?" Marcus smiled. "Do I pass muster?"

Calpurnia adjusted the folds of his *palla* over his crooked shoulder. "You're perfect."

"You look lovely yourself. Yellow suits you."

She looked down, fidgeting with a gold bracelet. "I'd still rather stay here and read in the library than go to any Imperial dinner." Since the horror of the betrothal banquet she hadn't set foot in the palace. Marcus could imagine what she must be thinking.

He touched her chin, bringing her eyes up. "It won't be like that this time."

"But what if it is?"

He smiled. "Why, then I'll bring you home. I did before, didn't I?"

"You did." For a moment she stood still, cheek against his hand, before she turned away and picked up her amber-brown *palla*. "Well, I'm ready."

"Brave girl."

"Calpurnia!" Paulinus bounded through the door, a flash of gold and scarlet in his formal Praetorian's uniform, and kissed his betrothed's cheek. "Father! Are you well?" To Marcus's surprise, he offered a hug instead of the usual awkward handclasp.

"I'm very well." Marcus looked at his son. "So are you, I gather."

A cool voice came down from the stairs above. "Paulinus. How little we've seen of you these days." Lepida drifted down to join them, a bird of paradise in her gold-spangled scarlet silk, her hair caught in a net of rubies and pearls.

"Lady Lepida." He bowed. "You look nice."

" 'You look nice'? You ignore us all for a week and now you expect us to—" Lepida's icy words dropped off as Paulinus stepped around her and took the stairs two at a time to grab up his little sister as she poked her head around the door of her bedroom.

"Now here's the lady I've been ignoring!" He ruffled her feather-brown hair. "How are those headaches, 'Bina?"

"Better. And I've grown a whole inch."

"So I see." Paulinus set her down, and she giggled. "I'll have to take advantage of your company before I lose you to adoring suitors. Let's go riding tomorrow. Your crazy aunt Diana has a mare quiet enough for you—"

"I hate to break up this touching moment." Lepida's peacock feather fan twitched back and forth like a cat's tail. "But we're going to be late."

"Let me check Father first—"

"I checked him for you," said Calpurnia. "Do you think I'd let him go see the Emperor in rumpled linen?"

"Back to bed." Lepida took her daughter by the shoulder and spun her back toward her room. "It doesn't matter what your father wears to see the Emperor. Because whether his ancestors used to *be* Emperors or not, he's just a boring old cripple."

Sabina flinched. Disgust flickered across Paulinus's face.

Marcus shrugged. *Just wait*, he thought to his wife. *Just you wait.* "Go to bed, little one," he told his daughter.

"Well!" Lepida adjusted her gold silk veil over her hair as her daughter disappeared into her room. "Can we go now?"

Calpurnia looked down, aligning a bracelet precisely over her wrist. "Lepida," she said, "has anyone ever told you that you're a cruel, spiteful, selfish slut?"

Marcus blinked. Lepida's mouth dropped unattractively open.

"You're vicious. You're unprincipled. You mistreat your slaves and abuse your daughter—"

"Well." Lepida regrouped. "*You're* just a jealous—"

"And furthermore you're the worst, most neglectful, most *criminal* wife in Rome." Calpurnia looked at Marcus. "I think we can go now."

Paulinus stifled something that could have been a cough, and Marcus did more than smile. He found himself grinning, ear to ear, as he had not grinned in a long time. "Yes," he agreed. "I believe we're all ready."

The winter breeze outside had turned to a freezing rain, but the air inside the litter on the way to the palace was even colder.

P AULINUS saw one of the Praetorian soldiers flirting with a slave girl when he was supposed to be on duty. "Go on ahead," he told his father, and paused to give the man a brisk tongue-lashing. Hastening back toward the triclinium, he saw that Lady Flavia and her family had already arrived. The boys had gone ahead with their father, their exuberance awed by the magnificence around them, but Lady Flavia had paused in the adjoining anteroom, berating one of her slave boys. Thea's son, Vix, Paulinus saw, and he quickened his step.

"—you'll keep well back, you horrid child, until the banquet is over and then I'll drop a word in your mother's ear and you can see her—"

Vix wore an anonymous slave tunic with the badge of Flavia's family, but he had no slave's servility as he stared around the sumptuous mosaics and pillars of the new palace. "Whoa. This is some pile."

"Why did you bring him?" Paulinus lowered his voice.

"Thea hasn't seen him in months, I thought she might like—" Flavia hauled Vix back by the neck of his tunic and smacked him before he could prowl behind a column. "I'm beginning to think better of the idea."

"Keep him in the anteroom out of sight," Paulinus advised. Flavia's wail followed him toward the triclinium.

"Since when can anyone keep the little monster *any-where*?"

LEPIDA

A tedious evening, quite unlike that lovely banquet at the Domus Augustana that had celebrated Paulinus's betrothal. Everyone was being very formal tonight in the massive state banquet room of the new palace, subdued voices murmuring politely about inconsequentials, backed by the splashing of the massive oval fountain framed in the arched windows. Lady Flavia was engrossed with her husband, her two sons were pestering the fat little astrologer with questions, Marcus and Calpurnia were discussing some boring political theory or other, and Paulinus—Paulinus was ignoring me. Talking to the Emperor, his eyes a shade reserved. Had they quarreled? Well, who cared? He was ignoring me, and he'd even refused my last invitation. Something would have to be done about that.

My eyes fell on Thea. She'd worn carmine-colored silk, rich purple-red like old blood embroidered all around the hem with jet beads, a jet circlet dipping low on her forehead. Moping, hollow-eyed, ignored by the Emperor—

But she still sat on the same couch as the Emperor. In the place his wife would have occupied had she been there.

A big Greek in a white silk tunic bent to restock her plate, and my eyes sharpened. Her slave? He was a handsome one, whatever his name was. Tall, golden, muscular, beautiful. He leaned down, a lock of wheat-fair hair falling over his brow, and Thea gave him her first smile of the evening as he touched her hand.

"Athena."

She jumped, but the Emperor's voice was jovial. "You must sing for us."

"Of course, Caesar." She rose, taking up her lyre. Her royal lover watched her inscrutably. *Had he gotten my letter or not?*

"Beautiful." Marcus applauded as she finished. "I remember the first time I heard you sing, Lady Athena. Your voice has always given me great pleasure."

"I remember as well." She made a little bow. "I was still scrubbing out fountain tiles. You were very kind about my warbling."

"Then I owe you a great debt, Marcus Norbanus," the Emperor called from his couch. "Without her warbling, I would never have met Athena at all."

Happy thought.

"So what do you say, Athena?" The Imperial voice lashed out suddenly, freezing her in the act of swirling up her red-purple train. "Fortunate, isn't it, that you can sing like the goddess you aren't?"

". . . Yes, Caesar."

"I can see you now, scrubbing tiles and singing to frogs." His voice drawled out, jovial and hard. "No silks, no jewels, no soft feather beds . . . no lover."

A little nerve of excitement prickled along the back of my neck.

"No." Her voice was neutral. "I'd have none of that. I have been very fortunate."

"Yes, you have. All the luxury in the Empire at your disposal, an Emperor to dispense it to you . . . and behind his back, another man on which to shower it."

Quite slowly, her face turned the color of chalk.

"Really, Athena." Softly. "Did you think I wouldn't find out?"

A glorious golden shout erupted in my head.

Marcus and Calpurnia exchanged confused glances. Paulinus looked frozen. Flavia threw a quick glance from Domitian to Thea and back again. "Uncle, we shouldn't—not in front of the boys—"

"Oh, but why shouldn't they watch? Maybe they'll learn something. How to deal with traitors. With deceivers. With unfaithful women."

"Caesar—" Thea took a quick step forward. "Lord and God, I swear to you—"

"So I'm a god now, am I? How quickly you change your mind. Are you going to beg, Athena?"

I sat up eagerly. To see the so-called mistress of Rome on her knees—

"Sir." Paulinus came to absurd attention on the dining couch. "Sir, I should have told you. I know that. But she's done nothing wrong. I've watched her with him. There has been no betrayal—"

"Sshh, Paulinus." The Emperor's eyes never flickered from his concubine's.

"But sir, I swear it's the truth! Would I lie to you?"

"No, you wouldn't. But she would. You don't realize what liars women are. Athena—" The Imperial voice snapped out across the room again. "How easy was it to pull the wool over the eyes of an honest man like Paulinus?"

"I never—"

"*Shut up!*" he roared, and she recoiled.

"Sir!" Paulinus's eyes were frantic.

"I'll beg." In the middle of the room, Thea slipped to her knees. "Is that what you want? I'll beg. I'll do anything. If you'll just spare him."

"Too proud." He uncoiled from the couch, coming to her. "Still too proud."

"Please. Lord and God, please."

"Grovel."

She lowered her head to his feet, pressing her face against the lacings of his sandals, her hands caressing his ankles. "Domitian, I beg you—"

He leaned down to touch her bowed head, his eyes dreamy and distant, and my breath stopped. "Athena," he breathed. "Lovely Athena." Sinking his fingers into her piled hair. "No." He threw her away from him.

He whirled, snapping at the guards. "Kill the slave." Two Praetorians leaped forward with drawn swords.

Thea screamed.

Paulinus reared back.

I drew an anticipatory breath.

Ganymede let out a hoarse mute's cry as two Roman blades buried to the hilt in his stomach.

"NO!" The scream came from the fat little astrologer.

Ganymede staggered back, mouth a red square, beseeching with bloody hands. The Praetorian swords flashed again, shearing through his fingers on their way to his heart.

He fell, all his golden beauty a scarlet ruin. Such a waste.

"No, no, no—" The astrologer fell on the body. "No, no, Ganymede, no—"

Domitian dragged his eyes away from the corpse, breathing hard. His eyes turned toward me. "Thank you, Lady Lepida," he said formally. "For bringing this man to my attention."

"My pleasure, Lord and God." Dropping my lashes.

"You?" The astrologer looked at her with swimming eyes. "You said my Ganymede—gods, you bitch, I'll make you *pay*—" His voice choked off and he collapsed shuddering, clutching the bright golden head and rocking back and forth.

"Well, really," I said. "As if it was my fault that—"

"Get rid of that thing." Domitian brushed off his hands. "It stinks already."

"Caesar, he never touched me!" Thea leaped to her feet. "Ganymede never touched me, he was innocent—"

"Then who was guilty?" The Emperor stepped over the mute's outflung arm. "Name him, Athena. We'll have another execution, and you can watch that, too, because that's what every unfaithful woman deserves. To see her lover die before her eyes."

"I have no lover, you bastard!" she screamed.

With one sweep of his arm Domitian threw her against the wall. I leaned forward eagerly. No one was paying any attention to me, but for once I didn't mind. This was better than a play. Even the slaves clustered wide-eyed in the anteroom to watch.

"Stop."

Marcus slid off his dining couch and made his slow limping way across the triclinium, his eyes never leaving the Emperor's. In the voice of an Emperor he told the Emperor of all Rome, "Stop this."

Domitian stared into the eyes of Marcus Vibius Augustus Norbanus.

"Stop this," Marcus repeated quietly. "Now."

Domitian let out a breath like a gasp. "No." He sounded like a little boy whining at a difficult lesson, and when he put out both hands and shoved Marcus away it was the gesture of a little boy. But Marcus hit the floor on his bad shoulder, and when his face twisted with pain Domitian laughed, and the odd stillness broke. He drew back his foot to kick my husband, but Calpurnia flung herself over him, her yellow gown billowing, and the Emperor turned away with a shrug.

"Keep the senator from interfering again," he told the Praetorians, and moved toward Thea.

"No!" Paulinus stumbled forward, actually seizing the Emperor's arm. "You can't do this, sir—it's wrong, all of it—just let me explain—"

Domitian looked at Paulinus with a kind of crazy compassion. "You're too good for all this, Paulinus. You don't see the enemies around me, the snakes in the grass—you don't have the eye for evil." He flicked his fingers, and two more Praetorians seized my astonished stepson by the elbows. "It's for your own good," Domitian said earnestly. "Watch, now. This is how an Emperor deals with snakes."

He took two deliberate steps across the room and crashed his fist across Thea's face. She staggered, blood flying from her broken lips, and he hit her again, a blow across the back of the head that drove her to hands and knees. There was a dry crunch of snapping bones as he stepped on her fingers, then twisted her hair around his hand and pulled her up like a doll. Her breath coughed out in bloody bursts.

Domitian raised his hand for another blow, but it never landed. He staggered back instead, hit from behind by a soundless streak that darted from the crowd of slaves in the anteroom, and I was astonished to see a broad rip in the Emperor's toga.

"Vix—" I heard Thea shout. "Vix, *no!*"

The slave boy was tall, compactly muscled, hair shining nearly red under the lamplight, an ivory-hilted table knife growing from his fist like it belonged there. Perhaps twelve years old. So familiar—if I could just place him . . . He swept in toward the Emperor of Rome, blade scything down in a smooth lethal arc, and we were all frozen to our couches.

Domitian's body bent and blocked with the automatic speed of his years with the legions. The knife carved a path through his sleeve instead of his throat, and he captured the boy's wrist in his hand. The boy wrapped his arm around Domitian's throat and they stayed locked for a moment, swaying back and forth.

Then the Praetorians swept in, smashing the boy into the floor—"Don't kill him!" the Emperor rasped, and they wrestled the knife away. Even then he tried to fight, butting savagely with his head and nearly knocking himself out on a bronze breastplate.

Thea was screaming. Calpurnia had her arms around Marcus, still in the grip of his guards. Flavia's hands were over the eyes of her sons. Paulinus struggled uselessly in the grip of his own men.

"Lord and God, are you hurt?" One of the Praetorians stepped toward Domitian.

He gazed at the shredded folds of his tunic. "The blade tangled in the linen." Turning puzzled eyes on the boy, now forced bleeding to his knees between two guards. "Are the slaves going mad now?"

"Lord and God!" I looked rapidly from the boy to Thea and back again. "I think I can tell you who our little assassin is."

He turned his gaze on me. Thea stopped screaming, stared with huge eyes.

I smiled. No wonder the boy looked familiar. "He's Athena's son."

Thea moaned.

"Sir," said Paulinus rapidly. "Sir, if you'll just *stop*—stop and listen to me—"

The Emperor stood looking back and forth. "Her . . . son?"

The boy stopped struggling suddenly, frozen wide-eyed between the guards. Domitian didn't look at him. He looked at Thea; took one slow step toward her and then another. "Well, well." Softly. "You said you had a child. You didn't say you'd trained it to kill for you. You said, in fact, that you hadn't seen it since it was born."

"No—no, I don't know who he is; I don't know him—"

"She called him by name," I added helpfully. " 'Vix,' wasn't it?"

"Lepida!" Marcus's eyes drilled me. I poked my tongue out at him and giggled.

"So, Athena." Domitian drew a finger down her bruised cheek. "What shall I do with him? This precocious son of yours, who has just tried to kill me."

She stood, her bloody lips trembling, a bruise darkening the side of her face.

"Shall I kill him?"

"Go ahead," the boy snarled from his huddle of guards. "Just make it quick." He was shaking, but he bowed his head like a gladiator awaiting the death blow.

"How touching." The Emperor, turning away from Thea. "The little warrior bravely awaiting execution. How noble."

"Not that noble," the boy said, and moved like a snake. He got an arm free, just an arm, but it was all he needed to sweep a knife from a guard's belt. He lunged forward.

And staked the Emperor's foot to the floor.

Domitian howled, doubling over.

A shield smashed across Vix's head and he went down. He yelled in pain but grabbed the shield and pulled it across himself. A short blade stabbed where his neck should have been, and then Thea fell on the guard, wrenching at his arm.

A female voice cut through the din, halting the guards. "Wait!"

The cry came from Lady Flavia, who had crouched in the corner with her children and her husband through the madness. She stepped forward, a smile pasted over terror, and laid a placating hand on the Emperor's arm.

"Uncle—not in front of my boys." Cajoling. "Allow me to take them home—and my husband—it's no place for them. And the slave boy, he's nothing, he's certainly no son of Athena's. I'll take him home and see that he's punished harshly. Flogged. Let me take him—" She had her own sons halfway to the door, wide-eyed and terrified, as she gestured at Vix. "Uncle, please—he's not worthy of an Emperor's vengeance."

Domitian straightened, the bloody knife in his hand, blood welling under the arch of his foot. "But a child is needed, Flavia," he said reasonably. "A child is needed. So if not Thea's, yours."

He whirled, pointing at her eldest son. "Seize him. In fact"—consideringly, as Flavia cried out—"seize all. I'm tired of this whining woman and her brats."

They were dragged out, Flavia shrieking, her husband turning to all sides for the help that didn't come, the two princes white-faced. My thoughts leaped ahead like quicksilver. If Domitian had no heirs now, perhaps he'd want a wife who could give him one . . .

"Now for you!" The Emperor took a limping step toward Vix on his bleeding foot, smiling. "Goodness, what am I to do with you?"

"Fuck you." The boy bared his teeth like a cornered rat, but I saw fear flick across his eyes.

"Oh . . . I think not." Gently tugging a bloody flap of skin on his foot, the Emperor addressed the Praetorians again. "Take that Jewish whore out of the city and dump her."

"No!" Thea threw herself at his feet. "No, no, keep me, just let Vix go—"

The Emperor smiled. Bleeding, vicious, genial, he smiled. "Afraid now, Athena?"

She stared up at him.

He flicked his fingers at the Praetorians. "Take her. But first—" He bent over her with a knife, and in three sawing strokes sheared raggedly through the welded collar on her neck. Then he turned, the black eye shining in his hand, and with a grunt of effort he bent the silver band around the neck of Thea's son.

Thea moaned again as they dragged her out. "Excellent!" Domitian beamed, seeming not to feel his maimed foot. "Now take the boy to his mother's old quarters. Search them first for sharp objects. And will someone clear all this mess away?" His eyes swept the spilled wine and dishes, the bloody footprints that tracked the mosaics. "Paulinus, you should take your father home. He's too old for all this excitement."

Paulinus's face was white, glazed with shock. Slowly, never taking her eyes from Domitian, Calpurnia reached up and tugged at his sleeve. Moving like a puppet, he rose and put an arm under Marcus's shoulder. They huddled out in Vix's defiant wake.

Only one was left.

Me.

I arched subtly on my couch as the Emperor's eyes flicked toward me. Thank the gods no blood had splashed onto my dress.

"I think I owe you a reward." He came closer, an odd excitement flickering through his eyes. Being stabbed hadn't dimmed his ardor. "For bringing all this about. What shall it be, Lady Lepida?"

"Oh . . . I think you have an idea, Lord and God . . ." I slipped off my couch and sank to my knees before him, trailing a finger down his leg. "You're hurt. Let me tend you, Lord and God." I bound a napkin around his bleeding foot, then bent my head and kissed away the tendrils of blood about his ankle.

He yanked me up and kissed me with his teeth. I nailed my body against his, thrills of excitement racing up and down my spine.

"Yes," he said decisively, pulling back. "Yes, you'll do. Come here."

He took me in the middle of that bloody room.

Twenty-eight

❦ ❦

THEA

THE Praetorians left me in a muddy turnip field just outside
the city walls. Perhaps I was too bloody and battered for
their tastes, or perhaps they thought my bad fortune would
infect them, or perhaps the freezing rain quenched their ardor,
because they didn't try the Emperor's mistress for a ride of their
own before leaving her in the mud. They just pushed me off the
horse and galloped away. I huddled there, shivering in the waves
of rain.

All my nightmares were coming to pass. Every one.

Vix. My boy.

My fault. Should have gotten him away. Should have known
he wasn't safe.

Vix.

I pulled myself upright, stood swaying a moment. My stomach a mass of fire. Joints of my fingers grating like they'd been
filled with hot sand. Blood trickling in half a dozen places,
swiftly diluted by the rain.

I'd been worse after Domitian's bed-wrestling. At least my
feet would still carry me.

So I walked. Unsteadily, swaying across muddy fields. I
walked until the rain passed and a watery pale sun rose, walked
until it stood directly overhead in the restless clouds, walked until it fell again. Lay down in a ditch for a while. Picked myself

up when the cold became unbearable and stumbled on. People averted their eyes. Thought me a madwoman.

I didn't wonder where I was going until I saw the roof of Flavia's villa peaking against the orange sky just outside Tivoli.

"He's got a hut," Vix had told me. "On Lady Flavia's north vineyard."

I toiled across the vineyard, grape leaves brushing my face, thorns catching my ruined gown. Saw a hut on the hillside. Round, like the huts in Brigantia.

After sixteen miles of trudging, I couldn't walk the last sixteen feet. I crawled. Tapped on the bottom of the door.

"Vix," I said to the hard bare feet that answered my tap. "The Emperor's got Vix."

SHE sat like a doll before the fire while Arius sponged the crusts of dirt and blood from her face. "He just took him," she kept repeating. "Took him, and threw me out."

Arius could feel the rage banking but turned away from it. "Let's see your hands."

Three broken fingers. He bandaged and splinted them, as he had so often watched the barracks doctor bandage and splint his own, and heard the rest of the story in bursts. Lady Flavia. In the frozen agony over his son, Arius felt a sliver of grief for the woman who had delivered him from the Colosseum. She'd be dead soon, maybe. Dead and gone, never again to sit in her sunny atrium embroidering a shawl, or sweep through the bowels of the Colosseum stealing children from death's jaws. Lady Flavia, who had given him a hut of his own and teased him for mangling her grapes . . . Praetorians had already swept down on the villa, the morning before Thea had arrived, but they hadn't investigated the far vineyards, and Arius hadn't assigned any importance to the visit.

"Ssshh," he told Thea. "Sleep now."

"But Vix—"

"We'll get him back." In his mind's eye he saw Vix lunging at the Emperor, table knife in hand. Why had he ever taught the boy to fight?

"I can't sleep." But her eyes were half-closed already as he carried her to the bed. As he laid her down, a flicker of pain crossed her face.

"What?"

"Nothing—my ribs—"

He reached for the fastening of her gown.

"No!" Her hands pushed feebly at his. "No, I'm just bruised—"

He peeled away the crushed silk, feeling for breaks in the bones.

What he found was a bruise. Greenish, days old, not new. Under the curve of her breast. How would she get a bruise there . . . and one so oddly shaped?

His fingers found another. And another.

He pulled back the rest of her gown.

"Arius." Thea's voice was a whisper. "Don't."

In the flicker of firelight, the bruises and the scars and the burn marks were all but invisible. Not to his hands, though. By touch he found them all.

"Arius—"

He looked at her. He didn't know what expression was on his face, but she put her arm up as if to shield her eyes. The lines of the knife scars, he saw for the first time, now climbed nearly up to her elbow.

He reached out to touch her face but stopped. Every muscle in her body had pulled into a quivering knot.

He took his hand away. Tugged her gown around her again. "You're right," he said. "Just bruises."

She flinched as if he'd struck her. Her eyes were full of a sick self-loathing.

"Sleep." He rose, laid his cloak down along the opposite wall, and stretched himself out. "You keep the bed."

He saw the relief as she ducked her head away, huddling like a child. Although it was a long time before she slept.

Arius didn't sleep at all.

Careful, big boy, Hercules told him. *Don't stir up any graves better left alone.* But Hercules was the one rotting in a grave. Hercules was dead, and Stephanus the gardener would die with Lady Flavia.

Arius the Barbarian was still alive.

He unburied the demon, spade by patient spade of dark grave-earth. It unfolded itself, stretched, yawned from its long sleep. Then it settled down, and the two of them, Arius and his demon, planned with slow, burning pleasure exactly what they would do to the Emperor of Rome.

ROME

PAULINUS didn't have much time for a warning, but he tried his best.

"Look," he growled at the bristly head that topped his shoulder. "I'm fond of your mother, and for her sake I'll try to keep you alive. Keep your mouth shut, and give the Emperor whatever he wants."

"Yeah." The marble hall was cold, but sweat stood out along the boy's forehead.

"What possessed you?" Paulinus couldn't help asking. "Trying to stab the *Emperor*?"

"Dunno." Vix shrugged, chinking the chains between his wrists and ankles. "Seemed like a good idea at the time. I mean, maybe now it doesn't seem like such a great decision, but—"

The guards swept a door open before them and Paulinus pushed Vix into the black triclinium. The black-robed Emperor lounged on black velvet cushions on an ebony couch, his eyes as pitch-dark as the walls. The only splash of white was the bandage that swathed his foot. For once there were no servants, no slaves, no secretaries. "Stay," the Emperor said to Paulinus, eyes never moving from the boy, and Paulinus tried to melt against the wall.

"Sit, boy."

Vix sat, on a black silk cushion at the foot of the Emperor's couch.

"Your new room is comfortable, I hope."

Vix stared.

"Have you a tongue, boy? I haven't cut it out yet. Later, perhaps."

Stare.

"If you won't talk, then pass me the decanter. Don't bother searching the table for weapons; I had everything sharp removed."

After a pause, Vix shoved the wine over in its ebony decanter. The wine was a ruby stream of color in the blackness.

"Wine dulls the ache in this foot of mine." The Emperor regarded the bandaged limb with faint surprise. "The surgeon says it will heal quickly."

Vix shrugged. "Can I have some wine?"

Domitian passed his own goblet over, expressionless. Vix ostentatiously wiped the onyx rim with his sleeve, drank deep, passed it back.

"So." The Emperor settled back into the black cushions. "What shall I do with you?"

"You could let me walk out," Vix suggested.

"No . . . I don't think so."

"Worth a try."

"Correct."

They contemplated each other.

"All black, huh?" Vix looked around the black triclinium—chinking his wrist chains together, Paulinus noticed, to hide the fact his hands were trembling. "Scary."

"I haven't decided yet what to do with you, Vercingetorix," the Emperor mused. "I could throw you to the lions in the arena. Or perhaps I'll have you gelded. How would you like to sing as prettily as your mother?"

"I'm tone-deaf."

"A man of the sword, then. Like your father, perhaps. Who was he?"

"Dunno." *Clink clink clink.*

"Liar," Domitian said pleasantly. "We'll have to work on that."

"Oh boy. Can't wait." *Clink clink clink.*

"Stop that."

"Stop what?" *Clink clink clink.*

"That sound. It annoys me. A god's ears are acute."

"Well, we've all got problems." *Clink clink clink.*

"Stop that!"

"Okay."

Clink.

They stared at each other. Paulinus opened his mouth, then closed it. He'd stepped often enough between brawling men in the Praetorian barracks, but this was one duel he didn't dare interrupt.

"You're going to kill me," said Vix to the Emperor. "Aren't you."

"We'll see."

"We'll see, nothing. I've heard the stories. Gods squish mortals like ants."

"You believe me a god, then?"

"Well, I don't know." Another smile. "You sure bleed like a mortal, Caesar."

Domitian's eyes dropped to his bandaged foot again. "You stabbed me." There was something like wonder in his voice. "Fourteen years I've reigned on this throne, and not once have I been harmed. Until now."

"First time for everything."

"Not for me. I am Lord and God."

"Sure."

Silence.

"You know your mother is probably dead? I had my Praetorians dump her outside the city. If she hasn't been robbed or murdered by now, then she's no doubt sleeping in a ditch somewhere. Easy enough to find, if I so decide."

Vix looked at him.

"I could pick her up tomorrow, if I liked. Bring her back. You'd like that, wouldn't you?"

Vix leaned forward so suddenly that Paulinus's hand leaped to his dagger. "Leave her alone," the boy said to the Emperor.

"Why should I?" Avuncular.

"Let's make a deal. Leave her alone, keep me."

"Arrogant boy. Leave you alive to plant more knives in my back?"

"It'll sure make things interesting."

You crazy boy, Paulinus thought in distant, terrified admiration. *Maybe you're not as stupid as I thought.*

Domitian tilted his head at Thea's son, considering. "Are you afraid of me?"

Vix looked at him as if he were a moron. "One word from you and the pretty boy over there turns me into a twitching pile of blood and guts on the floor. Of course I'm afraid. I'm shitting myself."

Domitian looked at him.

"You're too proud to strike a bargain with a slave?" Vix taunted. Sweat beaded all along his forehead. "You balding freak?"

A long, barbed pause. Paulinus winced. No one teased the Emperor about his thinning hair. The last man who had . . .

"Why, no," the Emperor of Rome said, meditative. "I don't believe I'm too proud to strike a bargain with a slave, Vercingetorix."

Vix stuck his hand out. Incredibly, the Emperor took it. Palm against palm, flesh against flesh. Bones bending, knuckles whitening. Seeing who would flinch.

They looked into each other's eyes. Neither flinched.

"Well." Domitian smiled, genial. "I suspect I shall enjoy this. Your mother was a great challenge, but I think you're going to be an even greater one, Vercingetorix—or is it Vix?"

"Only Mother calls me Vix."

"I could very easily have been your father, you know. Were you a few years younger, I would wonder . . . but no."

"There's a God after all," Vix muttered, and finally Paulinus could drag him out.

"Are you crazy?" he hissed under his breath. "Talking to the Emperor like that—even worse than trying to stab him in the first place!"

"Mother said he plays games with people," Vix said. "I thought it might work."

He twitched away from Paulinus, fidgeting with his tunic, and Paulinus saw a wet patch on the white linen. The boy had pissed himself.

"You laughing at me?" Vix said fiercely. "You laugh at me, I'll beat your face in! Pretty boy palace soldier, you think you're tough—" His hands shook as he shoved Paulinus's chest.

"No," sighed Paulinus. "I'm not laughing at you." He led Vix back to his quarters.

THE Imperial court buzzed after that. Paulinus heard the whispers.

"I hear the boy has his own room right next to the Imperial suite—"

"The Emperor took him to the Senate hearings yesterday—"

"To the opening of the new aqueduct—in full public view—"

"You know what the people thought of that!"

"Really, though, they must be wrong. If it was Emperor Nero, now, or Galba, then they'd be right, but Domitian's never been a boy-fancier."

"Every man's entitled to a change in midlife. He did get rid of Athena—"

"Athena may be gone, but now he's mounting that pretty little Pollia weasel."

"Anyway, the child's a prisoner. Wears that bright red tunic so he'll be easily spotted if he tries to run away. Can't go a step without tripping over Praetorians. Though maybe it's the Emperor's protection they're looking after . . ."

"You mean the rumors about the boy trying to kill him at dinner? We all know the Emperor didn't get his foot broken by a horse, even if that's what the doctors say—"

"Nonsense. Domitian would have had the brat's head knocked off on the spot—"

"Not if he's the Emperor's bastard son."

"Can't be. You can always tell a Flavian: the high color, the nose. Big stocky lad like that; he's pure peasant stock—"

"Athena's?"

"No, then he'd have kept her, too. The boy's a by-blow on some other mistress, mark my words—some slave woman, probably—"

"Slave or no, he's the Emperor's new favorite. Time to start bowing to the boy in red, wouldn't you say?"

T HE Emperor's cousin Flavius Clemens and his elder son were executed on the Gemonian Stairs, sometimes known as the Stairs of Sighs. Two days later, it was Flavia Domitilla's turn to be escorted from her cell. The official charge was impiety.

Marcus watched her from the crowd, on foot with the rest of the plebs, fury surging impotently in his gut. He'd spoken as strongly in the Senate as he dared, and none would support him. All he could do now was watch Lady Flavia go to her death in the same gown she had donned for the banquet where her sons should have been confirmed heirs. One of those sons was dead now. No one knew whether the younger son lived or died. "The elder boy is old enough to be ambitious," Domitian had shrugged. "The younger—I haven't yet made up my mind." No one dared ask. The more lighthearted courtiers took bets on whether the boy had already been exiled, or whether he had

been strangled in his cell. Certainly the Emperor had not bothered, today, to watch his niece go to her execution.

The crowd was very silent as Lady Flavia made her last
procession. No one dared shout in protest, but she was popular.
She had done her duty by producing sons and heirs; she gave
generously to beggars and children; she might be a Christian
but she always bowed to the proper gods. Now she walked
blank-eyed and bloodstained down a few last moments of life.
Her son, if he was still alive, would surely not long survive her.
The last Flavian branches to be pruned from the tree.

"Halt."

Marcus turned his eyes sharply at the voice. A figure in
white, half-hidden by the red and gold solidarity of the Imperial
guards.

"Remove yourself," the Praetorian snapped. "We escort Flavia Domitilla to her execution."

"What is her charge?" The voice was female, low, unhurried.
Lady Flavia stood patiently, an ox waiting for the sacrificial ax.

"Impiety. Now remove yourself from the road, Lady."

"I am the Vestal Justina. In Vesta's name I pronounce her
innocent of the charge laid upon her. By my authority as a
priestess I lift the sentence of death levied upon her."

The crowd began to whisper.

Flavia opened her eyes.

"Oh, no," said Marcus quietly.

The Praetorian paused. Cleared his throat. "We—we
can't—"

"Do you disobey the laws of Vesta?" With every word the
Vestal's voice grew stronger, carried farther.

"No, but—but the Emperor—"

"In this matter the Emperor is powerless. My goddess has
extended the hand of mercy to this prisoner. Execute her and
you risk divine retribution."

The Praetorian groped. "We'll—we'll have to take you
before the Emperor, Lady. We can't—"

"Do so. I am sure that before all the people of Rome, he will
not fail to obey Rome's most ancient laws." The Vestal stepped
between a pair of guards, her veiled head dwarfed between their
armored shoulders. Lady Flavia was staring at her now, mud-
dled eyes clearing. Marcus heard her voice very clearly, as the

Praetorians reversed their path and bundled the two women back through the buzzing crowd toward the Domus Augustana.

"Why—what—why did you—?"

"Vesta told me to save you," the Vestal said calmly.

"But I don't believe in her—I'm a fish-painting Christian, I don't *believe* in her—"

"That doesn't matter. She still wants you alive."

· "But—" They passed out of Marcus's hearing, but he could still see the horror dawning in Flavia's eyes as she stared at her savior. The same horror rose in his own gut because he knew that voice—knew it very well. "Her death for yours," Marcus said aloud. "He'll have it no other way."

THEA

DOMITIAN'S tricky," I said. "But not trickier than Vix. Vix will do all right."

Arius, squatting by the fire, didn't answer. He'd hardly spoken ten words to me the past day.

"Really," I said as if he'd argued. "Vix will be fine. Domitian's weakness is games; he can't stop playing games with people. Vix will play him right back—"

Arius's dog growled in my lap. I stroked her over and over. "He'll be all right. He will."

Arius picked his head up. "Quiet." His nostrils flared, and for a moment he looked like nothing so much as a wolf catching the scent of the wind. In one fluid motion he was out the door. I sat clutching the dog, frozen.

He reappeared. "Praetorians," he said coolly. "Get your cloak."

After a day's rest I felt stronger again. I flung our cloaks over my arm and hastily bundled up the bread left over from dinner. Arius groped under his mattress, coming up with a long glimmer of metal it took me a moment to recognize.

"I didn't know you still had a sword," I said.

He hefted it a moment, carving a figure eight in the air, and a flash of light from the blade cut across his eyes. The Barbarian's eyes.

No, the sword wasn't gone. Neither was the blackness in his gaze.

"Ready?"

I scooped up the dog and ducked out of his hut. I risked a quick glance toward the villa, hearing the shatter of pottery even from a distance. Domitian's guards had already come once, no doubt to take anything valuable for their master, but now they were back to complete a more thorough destruction. The possessions of all traitors were forfeit to the Imperium, their fields no doubt sown with salt and their names never spoken again. For a man who hated Jews, Domitian certainly had a streak of Hebrew vengefulness.

Arius cut straight through the vineyards, holding back the branches for me not out of courtesy, but because I would slow him down if I had to fight my own way through. That was how he had been since he'd seen my strange bruises, since I'd flinched away from him. Silent. Cold. He hadn't tried to touch me again.

With the blackness reappearing in his eyes, I didn't want him to.

The dog yapped shrilly at the orange glow of flames licking toward the sky from the roof of the villa. I closed my hand around her muzzle and followed Arius's broad back straight toward Rome.

Toward our son.

Twenty-nine

⋘☞☜⋙

ROME

JUSTINA turned away from the little window of her dank cell. "Why, Paulinus. I believe that's the first time you've ever shouted at me."

"Shouted at you?" he shouted. "*Shouted* at you? The story's all over the city! The Vestal who stepped in front of the Praetorians and granted a goddess's mercy—"

She looked at him calmly. The frantic anger shriveled. "Justina—Justina, I don't know what he'll—"

"Sssshhh. It's in Vesta's hands, now." She smiled, a thin smile that quivered at the corners, and pulled her veil down over her face. "Take me to him."

He stared at her a moment, trying to find her eyes through the barrier of pale silk. Vestal Virgins, he remembered, veiled their faces at only one occasion.

At the time of sacrifice.

So," said Domitian. "This is the Vestal."

He was sitting at his desk with a pile of petitions and maps and letters, Thea's son cross-legged at his feet as he always was these days. The boy was nodding; Domitian himself looked sleepy, genial, barely interested in traitors after a long day's work at his desk. Paulinus felt an instant's flicker of hope.

Then Justina pulled off her veil. Pulled off her whole Vestal's headdress, shaking loose a head of fine pale hair. She smiled at the Emperor. "Hello, Uncle."

For an instant there was silence so absolute that Paulinus thought there would never be sound again.

Vix opened his eyes, turning a puzzled gaze on the Vestal. So did Paulinus, looking for the girl he loved—

Instead he found a stranger. Saw the bold Flavian nose shadowed against the lamplight; the curling Flavian hair he'd seen carved in marble, curling now over the collar of a Vestal's robe; the dark Flavian eyes filled with Domitian's enigma.

A buried memory surfaced: a tiny princess carrying the flags of childhood games.

"I've known you forever," he'd said to her once, "long before I ever set eyes on you."

"Julia?" he said to the daughter of Emperor Titus, the granddaughter of Emperor Vespasian, the niece and—according to some—mistress of Emperor Domitian: Lady Julia Flavia of the Imperial and divine Flavian dynasty.

I offered to marry her, he thought foolishly.

"Julia," echoed the Emperor. The look on his face was so strange, so complicated, that Paulinus knew he couldn't identify it in a thousand years.

But he was afraid of it.

"Sir," he said rapidly, "I apologize for allowing this impostor into your presence. I will remove and deal with her as she deserves to—"

"No," the Emperor said absently, eating his niece with his eyes. "No impostor. Tell me, Paulinus—did you know?"

His mouth was dry.

"No," said Justina—Julia. "He suspected nothing."

"Much becomes clear." Still in that musing tone. "Why, for instance, you chose to pardon that worthless Flavia. The pardon is invalid, of course. Since only Vestal Virgins can override an Imperial death sentence, and you—you are no virgin of any kind."

Incredibly, she smiled. Becoming Justina again, instead of some anonymous Flavian princess. "Ah, but if you were to override my so-very-public pardon, then the people would demand an explanation. What would you tell them?"

"An Emperor does not explain himself."

"You've been explaining your way out of my father's shadow all your life."

A restless movement. "And where have you been all this time, Julia?"

Paulinus opened his mouth—and found himself desperately wanting to hear the answer. He closed it again.

"In the Temple of Vesta. Where I always wanted to go. I had to die before I could go there."

"People said it was a child—"

"No child. I tried to stab myself, but—" A smile illuminated her face. "Vesta did not want me dead yet. So I went to her. She didn't seem to mind about the virgin part."

"Someone helped you to escape," Domitian snapped.

"The Chief Vestal—dead now. One or two others, whom I won't name."

A long pause. "I can still kill Flavia, you know." Abruptly. "I may have remanded execution to exile, but she goes tomorrow to Pandateria. Do you know what that is? A bare rock in the middle of the ocean, not even a mile square. A number of Imperial women have died there, one or two bearing your own name. Who's to know if one more royal prisoner falls off that rock and breaks her neck?"

"The people will know. They'll believe the worst because, Uncle, they don't much like you."

Vix, curled up on the floor like a dog, let out a faint snort. Domitian sent him a sharp glance before turning his eyes back to his niece. "So they dislike me. You think I torture myself over that?"

Her voice deepened in imitation of his. "Correct."

Before Paulinus could blink, Domitian had his hands around his niece's throat. It took Paulinus and two guards to pry him away. Vix took the opportunity to lunge back into the farthest corner, well out of the way.

"Tie her up," the Emperor snapped to the guards, breathing in fast snorts. "Tie her up. *Do it!*" he screamed as they hesitated, visibly, to lay hands on a princess—Vestal—whatever she was.

Paulinus turned away from the sight of Julia, red finger marks gleaming on her throat, passively surrendering her wrists. "Sir—" To Domitian. "Caesar, please—"

The Flavian voice overrode his own. "Guards. Restrain Prefect Norbanus."

The Praetorians grabbed his elbows. Paulinus got a hand free, grabbed for the Emperor's arm. "Caesar, have I ever asked you for anything?"

Domitian paused. The furious gaze lightened briefly and purely with love. "No," he said, covering Paulinus's hand with his own. "No. You haven't. Quiet, now."

He turned away, back to Julia, and touched her hair where the fine pale gold strands fell around her shoulders like a Vestal's veil. "I have a piece of this hair in my private chambers," he mused. "Resting alongside the urn containing your ashes. Although I suppose they aren't really your ashes, are they? Only the hair is real . . . You gave up your life for your half-sister, Julia. Was it worth it?"

"It was the will of my goddess."

"Would you do it again?"

"Of course."

"Then I'll give you the opportunity, shall I? Guards!"

Whispered orders. Paulinus turned his face away. He couldn't bear to see Lady Flavia. But it wasn't Lady Flavia the guards shoved into the room—it was her second son. Pale, chained, gaunt, trying desperately to keep a brave face. The last heir of the Flavian house. Exactly Vix's age. From the corner, Vix's eyes flickered.

"Flavia Domatilla's son," said Domitian, unnecessarily. "Bow to your aunt Julia, boy."

Trembling, the boy bowed.

"The last of his family," the Emperor continued. "His brother dead, his father dead, his mother all but dead. So what's to become of him? Will you save him, too?"

Her voice was low and even. "If I can."

"Ah, but can you? That's the question. What would you give to save this boy?"

"My life."

"But you've already given that, haven't you? For his mother. What can you possibly give for him?"

The boy looked from his uncle to his aunt and back, a moan deep in his throat. Vix sat frozen in his corner. Paulinus did not dare make a sound.

"What is it you want, Uncle?" Julia, very quiet. "*That* is the real question."

Domitian laughed, that open charming laugh he so rarely let

loose. "Of course it is," he said, amused. "It always is. For you, it always will be. Because that's what you were put on this earth to do, Julia. To please me. And if you please me again, now, and promise to go on pleasing me for the rest of your life, then I'll let the boy go."

"Oh, Uncle," Julia said rather sadly. "I don't think there is anything in this world that would truly please you."

Paulinus blinked. Flavia's son opened his mouth in a silent scream.

"You're quite right," Domitian admitted. "You always did understand me better than anyone, Julia."

Paulinus was still surprised. Even with his hackles prickling, he was still surprised when Domitian drew his dagger and gutted Flavia's son.

The boy's mouth opened soundlessly. He fell—slowly, it seemed to Paulinus. So slowly.

For a terrible moment all was frozen. Paulinus, his hands half out to stop the fatal blow. The boy clutching his torn belly on the floor, blood pooling over the mosaics. The Emperor, wiping his hands aimlessly down his tunic, leaving red smears. Vix, stopped midlunge from his corner. Julia, still as a statue of her goddess. Then the goddess turned from marble back to flesh and spoke.

"Paulinus," Julia said quite calmly. "Take the boy out. Vix, you will help him."

Prefect and slave boy found themselves moving as one.

"Yes," said Domitian to no one in particular. He dropped the dagger. "Yes, that's it—Julia—" He fell on his niece, wrenching the veil from her shoulders.

Paulinus half-turned, but Julia caught his eyes again over her uncle's shoulder, and her gaze was so stern that he turned back, hauling Flavia's moaning son out into the anteroom of the Emperor's bedchamber.

"She can take care of herself," Vix snapped. "Help me!" He had something wadded up in his hand, trying to close the gaping slash in the prince's belly. Julia's veil—he had Julia's veil.

From the bedroom Paulinus heard guttural sounds. Nothing from Julia—nothing. He rose, shoving back toward the bedchamber, but the guards pushed him away.

"You want to die, Prefect?" the *optio* snarled. "Let him at it!"

Somehow Paulinus found himself kneeling, looking for a

pulse in the dying prince. Blood pulsed thickly, almost black. Vix's fingers were gloved in it. "He's dying," Paulinus said numbly. "Surely he's dying—"

"You gonna help me, Prefect?" Vix was sweating, swearing, but he kept the wadded veil sunk over the wound.

Low anguished grunts from the bedroom, more like a rutting animal than an Emperor. Not a sound from Justina. Paulinus felt a sob catch like a splinter of ice in his throat. The thought came, small and terrible: *Maybe if he takes her, he'll spare her life.*

A moan sounded from Lady Flavia's son. Frantically Vix leaned his whole weight on the veil, his tunic and knees tacky with blood. A clammy eyelid flickered. Slaves were starting to gather, wide-eyed, and Paulinus spat curses at them. They scattered.

Flavia's son cried out, his hands coming up weakly to clutch at his belly. Vix leaned harder.

A pair of young Flavian eyes opened and stared into Vix's, alive with pain.

Kneeling in a puddle of blood, Paulinus found his skin crawling.

"Bitch," he heard indistinctly from the bedchamber. The Emperor's voice, thick and slurred. "You unmanning bitch—get out—"

The guards outside exchanged glances. "You heard him!" Paulinus snapped, scrambling to his feet and half-falling into the bedchamber. He took it all in, in one glance; the Emperor collapsed half off the couch, Julia quietly pulling her white robes around her.

"Take her," the Emperor said, and his whole body shook. "Oh, gods, just take her."

Paulinus raised Julia with trembling hands, but her own steps as she left the bedchamber were rock-steady. He led her through the blood, past Vix, who was now helping Flavia's son to sit up.

"The guards will take me," she said. "Help Vix with my nephew, Paulinus. He needs your help getting out of the palace."

"He won't live—he was gutted, ripped in half—"

"Was he?"

Vix was slinging an arm under his friend's shoulders and hauling him upright. He looked up, wary, and Julia gave him a cordial little nod. Her eyes, catching a glow from the lamps, didn't look quite . . . human.

"Give my regards to your mother, Vercingetorix," she said, and then the guards were hauling her away. They held her by the sleeve rather than her bare wrists, though, as if she might burn them. She left small bloody footprints behind her on the mosaics.

"We've gotta get him out." Vix had Flavia's son on his feet, moaning but unmistakably not dying. He still clutched Julia's veil against his stomach, now red rather than white.

"I imagined it," Paulinus muttered. "I didn't really see the Emperor gut him—couldn't have—"

"You're gonna faint," Vix said in disgust.

Paulinus felt laughter welling, huge hysterical bursts of laughter. He wanted to laugh until he died. But more guards were approaching at a trot, and curious courtiers, and gawking slaves. He took off his red Praetorian cloak, fingers moving stupidly, and dropped it around Flavia's son. Vix hauled a fold over his face.

"Tend to the Emperor," Paulinus ordered the guards. "Send for his physician. I'll see to the boy myself."

"Prefect, where are you taking him?"

"Emperor's orders," Paulinus said coldly. "*Private* orders." The guard's eyes dropped at once.

"How's it feel?" Vix whispered at the young prince as they hauled him away from the hall and its rapidly growing audience.

"It's—it's strange—it feels—I don't know." The boy was near tears.

Under the cloak, Paulinus peeled back Julia's veil. Underneath there was—a long shallow cut, oozing a little. Not the bloody wound Paulinus had expected.

"Guess the freak missed," Vix shrugged. "You're a lucky one."

Luck? Paulinus didn't want to think about that.

Vix was turned back at the outer gate, and Paulinus took Lady Flavia's son on himself. "What will you do with me?" the young prince gasped.

Tell the Emperor you died of your wound, thought Paulinus. *And that I disposed of your body quietly.* "Keep still," he snapped, and he kicked his horse forward with Flavia's son bent weakly over the saddle before him.

A quick canter to his father's house in the falling dark, marshaling desperate explanations, but his father required surprisingly few words. "Good lad," was all he said, and in half a moment he had the slaves dismissed and the fainting boy whisked inside.

"The Emperor—" Paulinus spoke around a leaden tongue. "The Emperor can't know you ever—"

"He won't." Coolly. "I'll have the boy out of the city before dawn."

"The Vestal," said Paulinus. "She was—she wasn't a Vestal—Julia, Lady Julia who was *dead*—"

"No time for that now." Marcus didn't seem surprised. Paulinus stared.

"You *knew*?"

"You think she faked her own death without help? Get back to the palace, boy, before you're missed."

Paulinus's feet took him past the circular Temple of Vesta first. Looking up, he saw the other Vestal Virgins watching; a silent white line. Their faces were all veiled.

He bunched Julia's bloody veil up and laid it on the first step. His knees gave out, and he sat there beside it until a pair of Praetorians came in search of him.

THE old year had died—and by the Emperor's decree, Rome would see the new year in with a death.

It was a strange, resentful crowd that gathered to watch Lady Flavia go into exile and the Vestal into death. The Emperor pronounced it a day of celebration, but the banners looked limp and the flowers fell like tears and the trumpets could have been dirges. Bad luck, people whispered, bad luck. A priestess and a princess both doomed before the year was a day old—the coming year would surely bring nothing good.

Paulinus, escorting the prisoners on his black horse, felt haggard.

A rustle greeted the two condemned women, walking in a cluster of Praetorians to their fates. Both small and fair-haired, one in stained coral-colored silk; the other in a pristine Vestal's robe. A ship awaited Lady Flavia, and then a small sea island;

but all that awaited the Vestal Justina was an airless bricked-up chamber.

Vestal Virgins who broke their vows were buried alive.

Arm in arm the two women passed through the street. "Why?" Paulinus heard Flavia say dully. "Leaving me alive on an island for the next forty years—why is that kinder than dying?"

"Who said the gods were kind?" Julia's voice was gentle.

"Oh, I know they aren't kind. Your goddess *or* my God. My boys are dead, Julia. My eldest with Flavius, my youngest—I won't even know when he's executed—"

"I wouldn't give up on him yet, Flavia."

"No. I know Domitian. He hates children because they remind him he's mortal—he beat his own children out of his wife before they were even born, and he'll kill mine, too—"

"Watch the horizon."

"W-what?"

"When you get to Pandateria. It's a silent place—sea grass waving in the wind, and quiet stretches of sand, and a little stone hut with a small shrine. You'll be alone, and the silence will be unbearable for a while, so listen to the sea birds cry and watch the horizon. You won't be alone for long."

Her voice was low and lulling. "One day soon you'll see a sail on the edge of the ocean. A faded red sail, I think, and a bank of oars flashing each side of it. You'll think of assassins and you'll want to run, but you'll stand proudly because you're a Flavian and you'll want to die like one. But the galley won't land. It will lower a tiny fishing boat, without oars, and the tide will carry it to shore, and long before it lands you'll see who sits in that boat waving his arms and calling for you. And you'll plunge into the ocean, and you'll reclaim your son."

"You can't know that." Flavia's voice was a whisper. "How can you know that?"

"I see things sometimes. And you have even more than that to live for, Flavia Domitilla."

Paulinus turned. Julia had stretched out a hand, placing it on Flavia's abdomen.

"What?"

"We'd better keep walking. I don't want to get Paulinus in trouble." Julia tugged her sister forward. "A daughter. You can't feel her yet, but she's there. She'll be born in the summer, on Pandateria, and I rather think you will name her after me."

Tears pricked Paulinus's eyes. He stared blindly ahead.

"But—but how do you—"

"Oh, I know. Let's leave it at that. I know, but I'm the only one. Domitian won't find out at all; once he's landed you on your quiet little island he'll forget all about you. But the Empress won't. She'll see you're fed, and I imagine she'll even smuggle you a midwife when your time comes. Maybe she'll even find a way to get you and the children off that island someday. She used to be brave—maybe she will be again."

"Julia—Julia, I—"

"It's time," said the guard at Paulinus's side.

"No!" Flavia's voice rose. "No, I can't—"

"Quiet, now," Julia said peaceably. "Safe journey, Flavia Domitilla. And if you don't mind—*do* name your daughter after me."

A breath, and Flavia was gone.

No Vestal could be killed within Rome's walls. A small chamber had been built near the Colline Gate, in the *campus sceleratus.* A place more often known as the Evil Fields. The Emperor had ordered a dais and stands erected, as if for a festival, but the crowd that gathered there was curiously hushed as they watched the Vestal Virgin pause before her burial chamber, gathering her snowy robes. Paulinus saw his father standing with Calpurnia, their hands unexpectedly linked tight. On the royal dais the Empress looked stiffer and more marble-carved than ever, the Emperor ruddy-faced and hard-eyed, Vix in his scarlet tunic frankly sick.

The Vestal put a bare foot over the lip of her grave and started down the rough steps.

"Halt!"

The tension snapped as Paulinus lunged off his horse. In half a second he was at her side, seizing her arm.

"Justina—Julia—"

"Justina. I like it better. It's what my father always called me. Because he said I looked as grave as a judge."

"You did—I remember." He could hardly see her for the tears in his eyes—she was just a white blur. "Justina, I can't let you—"

"So you'll make off with me over one shoulder? Slay the Emperor?"

"Justina—"

"Shhhh."

She put her hand over his mouth. He closed his eyes and leaned his mouth into her palm. For a moment it stayed there. Then it glided away under his hand like a ghost.

With his eyes still closed, he heard her bare feet against the makeshift steps. Imagined the Scythian-gold flash of her hair as she passed into the tomb. Saw in his mind's eye the door sealing her up. Heard the dreadful shoveling of earth, the clods of ground quickly clotting the entrance to the tomb.

He opened his eyes. Domitian looked down from the dais, watching with impassive black eyes as his niece was buried alive. He smiled. "Some dice later, Prefect?" he suggested, and went back to his portfolios.

L ET'S go," Arius said quietly, putting a hand on Thea's shoulder.

"Vix looked all right," Thea said in a thin, high voice. "He looked well. Didn't he look well?" She paused, then added very softly, "She *looked* at me."

"I saw."

Thea didn't say another word until Arius bolted the door of the tiny attic room in the slums that they'd managed to rent with the last of their money. Then she fell across the narrow fetid bed and lay shivering.

"Before she stepped down into that tomb—her eyes went over the crowd and she found me—like she knew I was there—"

"Thea—" Arius rested a tentative hand on her shoulder, and when she didn't flinch, he crawled into the cold bed beside her and stroked her hair. No tears, but her body racked itself now and then in a great shudder. Arius thought of the man she had shared with Julia.

Careful. Careful. He banished the demon, burying his face in Thea's hair. He touched her temple with his lips, meaning only to soothe her, but his mouth somehow strayed to the curve of her ear, then to the hollow behind her jaw.

She stirred and he pulled away, terrified of frightening her. But with a ragged sigh she nestled against his chest, settling her head in the hollow of his shoulder.

For a moment he lay still, holding her as if she were made of glass. Then he slid his fingers up into her hair, tipping her head back so he could kiss her. She had as cool and sweet a mouth as she'd had at fifteen.

He could feel the tension coiling back into her body, but when he pulled back she clutched him fiercely. So he kissed her again, soft as snow, then kissed the weals around her throat left by an Emperor's collar, and then the first of the white scars left under her breast by an Emperor's games. He pulled her tunic over her head and loved the abused, luxury-whitened body underneath; loved it and grieved over it, smoothing the scars away with his hands and his mouth, doing his rough and imprecise best to give her back the sun-browned, work-hardened, unscarred body she'd once given him.

She closed her eyes, back arching with a tentative pleasure, and he touched her with all the eloquence his voice could never find, fighting with all his strength to make her stubborn, clever brain understand how much he loved her . . . and maybe something worked, because she kissed him with half a sob as her arms closed like a vise around his neck, and through every bone in his body he felt a thrum of quiet, quiet joy. They fell asleep knotted like a tangle of warm rope, without saying a word.

THE Vestal Virgins gathered up the bloodied veil and laid it on their altar.

PART FIVE

JULIA

In the Last Temple

It is a small tomb, this place beneath the earth. Small enough to touch all four walls without stirring from my stool. There is a candle, guttering low because candles need air to breathe as much as people, and the air in this earth chamber is growing short.

I sit in the flickering dark, and smile.

Vesta, I thank you. For so many things, I thank you. I thank you for allowing me to serve you. I thank you for the man who loved me. I thank you for the courage to save my sister. I thank you for the gift you gave her son.

I thank you for a life that has not been wasted.

I stretch forward, and blow out the candle.

Vesta, goddess of hearth and home . . .

Is that You?

I did not know You would be so beautiful.

Thirty

❦

LEPIDA

"MARVELOUS," I said lazily. "What is it?"

"The juice from some flower or other," said my Imperial lover. He took the goblet from my limp hand, excitement coming in blank flickers across his eyes.

Who would have thought that a flower crushed into old Falernian could produce this delightful torpor? I closed my eyes, letting the Emperor labor over my passive body. He had rather peculiar tastes, but nothing one couldn't get used to. Nothing one couldn't even grow to be excited by.

To be the mistress of the Emperor . . . that was exciting enough!

Oh, these last three months were everything I had ever dreamed of. The applause. The power. People bowing when I paraded past. People begging me to drop just one word in the Emperor's ear. Power a thousand times magnified. *I* was the mistress of Rome now!

As for Domitian himself . . . well, I didn't see what all the dark rumors were about. He was a man. Odd-tempered, mercurial, but still a man. I'd known how to handle men since I was fourteen. Emperor or no, I never let him be too sure of me. Sometimes when the Imperial freedman knocked on my door I told him I was "out." Sometimes I hinted at rendezvous with unnamed men. Sometimes I threw myself adoringly at his feet, sometimes I just smiled remotely. Just to keep him interested.

"Cover yourself." Finishing, he pulled away. "You look like a whore."

He was already reaching for his folders, his tablets and slates. I lifted a languid arm and draped my body with a fold of silk. "By the way"—casually—"you really must do something about that astrologer of yours. He's abominably rude. Three times I've asked him to draw up my horoscope, and he ignores me."

"He sees the future as clearly as the rest of us see the past." My Imperial lover never looked up from his work. "Eyes like that are worth all the gold in Egypt."

"Very rude eyes. He's always glaring at me."

"Then look the other way."

"You're in a temper tonight, Lord and God." I rolled over, propping my chin on my hand and letting my hair fall in a wave over my eye. "So you keep the astrologer for his precious eyes. Why do you keep Athena's beastly brat of a son?"

That, of course, was what I really wanted to know.

"Do you really want a reminder of her underfoot everywhere you go?" I persisted when an Imperial silence answered me.

He turned a slate over, working rapid figures on the back.

"Lord and God?" I dandled my fingers along his wrist.

He jerked his wrist away. "Go home. And send in my secretaries."

Crossly I slid off the bed, tugging my gown over my head with fingers still sluggish from the drug. I stalked out with my most enticing sway of hips, but he never called me back. Well, he was prone to odd little moods. More of them than usual, since the rebellious Vestal's execution . . . but never mind that. Next time I'd make him forget all about it.

"Watch where you're stepping," said a voice at my feet.

I jumped. In the marble corridor outside the Emperor's apartments, Thea's son sat cross-legged on the mosaics. He rolled a pair of grubby dice in one hard palm, and he cocked his head back up at me. "Roll?" he suggested.

From the corner of my eye I saw the usual hovering freedmen and courtiers, pricking their ears at the sight of the Emperor's two favorites. "Why not?" I said sweetly, taking the dice and dropping them as fast as possible. No doubt they were crawling with street-urchin diseases.

He whistled, looking at the dice. "Bad luck, Lady Lepida."

"What would you know about luck?"

"I've got my mother's luck," he shrugged. "All Jews are born lucky, or we wouldn't any of us still be alive."

"But what about your father? Didn't you inherit half your luck from him?" I smiled. "Perhaps gladiators aren't so lucky as Jews."

We regarded each other. For the benefit of the audience—an Emperor's favorites always have an audience—I patted his head. He snapped at my fingers like a dog, and I took a step back. It wouldn't do to be careless. Not with a boy who had been fathered by a man called Barbarian.

I took a quick look back over my shoulder, and Thea's son put two fingers in his mouth and let out a piercing whistle that made every slave, freedman, and courtier within fifty yards spin around. "Better hope your luck changes, Lady Lepida," he shouted. "Or you're *screwed*, *screwed*, *screwed*."

One or two titters reached my ears.

"MARCUS?" Calpurnia slipped through the door of his library, smiling. "Why are you sitting in the dark?"

"Enjoying a pretty sunset on a spring night." He smiled. "Enjoy it with me?"

"Of course." She took a stool. "Though the sunset's that way, and you're turned away from it."

"I'm arranging a journey." Marcus rolled some papers out of sight.

"For yourself?"

"No, not for me." For Flavia's son, recuperating quietly at the house in Brundisium. From Brundisium it was a short sea voyage to Pandateria, where his mother had already been delivered. The Empress had assured Marcus of secrecy.

"I'll see Flavia and her son cared for," the Empress had said impassively. "It was Julia's last wish. Marcus—she could not have falsified her own death and escaped to the House of the Vestal Virgins without help. Did you . . ."

"I did." Marcus had shrugged. "She wrote to me in Cremona, after the madness had gone. After she tried to open her stomach. I hadn't believed her before, but I believed her then. I helped."

Something had gleamed in the Empress's usually impassive eyes. "Marcus," she'd begun—

"Keep your secrets." Calpurnia's voice broke his thoughts. She pulled a chair beside his, turning her face toward the orange sunset. "I'll not pry."

"You never do. You realize, Calpurnia Sulpicia, how unusual that makes you?"

She smiled. "I sent a slave to Paulinus's apartments at the palace—they say he hasn't come out of his bedchamber yet, except for his work."

"How long has he been in there?"

"Since the Vestal's execution."

They were silent a moment.

"Sabina has a request." Calpurnia leaned forward to refill Marcus's wine goblet. "She asked me to make it for her, since she thinks I can persuade you to anything. She wants to go to the games with you tomorrow."

"The games?" Marcus blinked. "She's too young to go to the games."

"She said she's been before."

"I didn't allow her to *watch*. She was seven years old. She sat with her back to the carnage, playing with the slaves. That is, until the Emperor began tossing people into the arena."

"Well, it must have made an impression on her because she wants to go back. She says it will be interesting. She also says Paulinus will be there, and she never gets to see Paulinus anymore." Calpurnia smiled. "She means it. She looked just like you at the last Senate debate when you were determined to get the tenements in the south quarter shored up before they collapsed, and Publius's claque was objecting."

"I didn't know you came to watch the Senate debates," Marcus said mildly.

Calpurnia flushed. "I sit at the back."

"I see." He smiled, rotating a pen between his fingers. "You think I should take Sabina to the games, then?"

"You're asking for my opinion?"

"I've come to value it."

Calpurnia looked down, fussing with the folds of her dress, but Marcus saw her smile. "Take her long enough to visit with Paulinus—perhaps she can get a smile out of him. Then we can take her home before the blood starts to flow."

"No. If she goes, she stays for it all. A Norbanus doesn't cover his eyes at the unpleasant. Or her eyes."

"Heavens, how grim. I suppose I'll have to stay for it all, too."

"You'll go?"

"I'll go, and you owe me for it. I hate the games."

"What would I do without you, Calpurnia?"

She smoothed a tendril of hair behind her ear. "Dinner will be ready in a quarter of an hour. Pheasant and onions, in sweet pepper sauce."

"Have you been browbeating the cook again?"

"She's terrible. I'm going to buy you a new cook."

"Shouldn't I be the one to buy you a wedding present?"

"I'm not married yet, Marcus Norbanus."

THEA

IT'S his birthday today." I propped my chin on my hand. "The ides of June. He's thirteen."

"I was going to give him a sword." Arius's voice muffled briefly as he pulled his tunic over his head.

"Encouraging the dreams of gladiatorial glory, Barbarian?" I teased.

Arius's head emerged. "Thea, our son *wants* to be a gladiator. He's an idiot."

"Yes," I agreed, scratching the ears of the dog curled on my knee. "He is an idiot. Must come from his father's side of the family."

Arius grabbed me around the waist, pulling me onto his lap. As I pummeled his chest, the dog slid to the floor, yapping shrilly. Arius dragged my head down to his, kissing me firmly, and my bones dissolved.

"There," he murmured against my mouth.

I smiled, my lashes brushing his cheek. On days like this, blue and gold mornings when our bare little attic room warmed in the sun and Arius's gaze made my whole body sing, the world brightened. It was possible to believe, not just hope, that everything might turn out all right.

"Your hair's getting long." I ran my hand slowly up the nape of his neck, feeling the flesh shiver under my touch. "Shall I give you a haircut?"

"Better leave it long. I look less like the Barbarian."

"You don't look anything like the Barbarian in that ridiculous disguise." Whenever we set foot outside he insisted on donning a heavy cloak, a hat, and an eye patch.

"If I go out undisguised, someone will recognize me. I'm supposed to be dead."

"Darling." I touched a finger to his chin, drawing his eyes to mine. "No one has recognized you. No one's even taken a second glance at you, except to think, 'Who's that bizarre man in a hat, an eye patch, and a heavy cloak in the middle of summer?'"

"I had the most famous face in Rome for eight years." A little huffily.

"But it's been five years since you died. The mob only remembers you as a dim legend. It's Thurius the Murmillo they all rave about now." I held out my hand. "Your knife, please. You prickle in bed."

He lowered his face into my neck and I sawed contentedly, watching the dark-dyed locks fall on the splintery floor.

"Thurius the Murmillo?" he said eventually.

"Or there's a Thracian who's popular. I saw the graffiti on the wall of the bathhouse on Pomegranate Street—'*Brebix the Thracian makes all the women sigh.*'"

"Brebix," Arius muttered. "My name was on that bathhouse for years."

I laughed. Arius turned his cheek against the back of my hand, and his short beard scratched my knuckles. "Someday we'll shave that off, too," I said. "You don't just prickle, you scrape."

"I don't—oh," he said as I tugged the tunic off my shoulder to show a red patch left by his mouth. "Did I do that?"

"Never mind." I pushed him straight, cutting around the nape of his neck. "He loves me hard," I said in Greek, smiling. My Arius. Someday he wouldn't need a beard anymore, or silly eye patches and hats. We'd live on a mountain where no one had ever heard of the Barbarian, and no one would care if they did know. And our son would never, ever get near an arena.

I stepped back, brushing the last stray bits of hair from Arius's shoulder. He pulled me down onto his lap again, and I laid my head on his shoulder. Sliding my hand along his chest under the tunic, I felt the heat of his hard flesh, the heart pounding underneath. "Will it be all right? Going to the Colosseum?"

"Yes." He kissed my eyebrow. "We'll be watching Vix, not the games."

"We won't be allowed to watch together—women have their own section."

Arius scowled. "They'll let you sit with me."

For two weeks we'd tried to keep an eye on our son, merging with the crowds that followed the Emperor on his daily tours of the city and watching the figure in the red tunic that always sat at the Imperial feet. "The Emperor's pet," the citizens of Rome called him, and they speculated that he was the Emperor's bastard son. Never more than an arm's length away from the Emperor. Never a chance to snatch him and run for it. And no way to get into the palace grounds; not two ragged runaway slaves who could bribe no one.

Even if we somehow got Vix away, where could we all run where Domitian couldn't find us?

The bright morning dimmed a little.

Arius's hand enfolded mine. "Let's go."

For the first time since we'd come back to Rome, we headed for the Colosseum.

LEPIDA

IT was perfectly sickening, the roar that went up from the crowd when Thea's brat came into the Imperial box and waved. "Behind me," I hissed, swatting at him.

"Lay off, cow," he said bluntly, and flopped down at Domitian's feet. I settled fuming on the other side. Not only was he a brat and a boor, his red tunic clashed horridly with my rose-colored *stola* and pink sapphires. I beckoned a pair of slaves forward with their ostrich fans. The Matralia games were always hideously hot.

Domitian was busying himself with a load of scrolls and his hovering secretaries, but Vix sat drinking everything in. "Whoa," he whistled at the vast expanse of sand stretching before the Imperial box. Usually he was tensed statue-hard in the Emperor's presence, but now he gaped as eagerly as any pleb brat in the stands. "This being-the-Emperor's-shadow thing has its benefits. The *view* here—"

"Do you suppose your mother's out there?" Domitian made a check on one of his lists, then shuffled to another.

"Dunno," Vix shrugged. "How about some dice, Caesar? The opening parade's always pretty pointless." Vix fleeced the Imperial chamberlain, a tribune, two languid Gracchi noblemen, and the Emperor himself, until I bumped his shoulder at just the right moment and his hands slipped.

"Cheating." The Emperor snatched up the pair of dice that fell out of Vix's sleeve. "What else could one expect from a gutter rat?" Courtiers exchanged glances.

"What do Emperors do to cheats?" I said in my most velvety voice.

"Cheats are traditionally thrown to the lions, Lepida. Even young cheats. How's that for a birthday present, Vercingetorix?" The Emperor's face was inscrutable. "A dance with a lion on the sands of the great arena?"

"I'll pass, Caesar, thanks." Uneasily.

"Cheat." Caressing the word. *"Cheat."*

"And here's how to cheat like a champion!" Vix produced a cajoling smile from somewhere. "Palm the crooked dice like this . . ." Demonstrating with a rapid hand. "See?"

The Emperor regarded him another silent moment, then grinned. "Show me again."

"Like this." Correcting the Imperial grip. "No, no, Caesar. Like this. God, you're slow."

They diced through the morning's wild beast hunts and the midday executions. I frowned. "The gladiators now, Lord and God—your favorite."

Domitian shoved the dice aside and leaned forward. On the sand, an African and a Thracian were pairing for the first duel.

"The African," said Domitian. "He'll win."

"The Lord and God has such a discerning eye," I murmured, and a ripple of agreement ran around the box.

"Nope," said Vix. "That African's clumsy. Tripped on his net just walking through the gate. I'd go with the Thracian."

"Really?"

"What do you know?" I snapped. But they both sank chins into hands and bent their eyes on the arena, ignoring me. Not enemies for the time being, or even prisoner and captor. Just two lovers of the games.

The Thracian took the African, and then a pair of Numidians came out, and after that two Gauls. Several good fights, not that I enjoyed them. Normally I quite liked a good brisk slaughter, but with the Emperor ignoring me for a vulgar gutter brat—

"You do have an eye, young Vercingetorix," Domitian was saying. "How did you know that Macedonian would lose?"

"Hung over. See the way he avoided looking at the light?" Vix popped a handful of fresh figs, chewing vigorously. The victorious fighters had trooped wearily through the Gate of Life, the losers raked away by arena slaves. "Look for fighters like that Gaul who cut the Greek's arm off, Caesar. The lean mean ones."

"Really," I murmured, seeing a chance. "Who taught you that?"

"My father." Falling into the trap. "He was the best. Rules didn't apply to him, he used to go in as hung over as all hell and he still—" Suddenly breaking off.

"So your father was a gladiator." Domitian sat back. "How interesting. I suppose your mother told you it was the noble Barbarian. How romantic, the great gladiator leaving a long-lost son behind him—"

"Hey," Vix flung at him. "The Barbarian *was* my father."

The lounging courtiers tittered. "Likely story!" someone whispered. "That brat's a lying little toad—!" I tittered, too.

"Perhaps not such a lie." The Emperor set down his wine goblet. "There is a certain coarse resemblance. I met the Barbarian once or twice, and I never forget a face. What I wonder is, how did *you* ever meet him?"

"After I ran away from Brundisium." I could feel Vix shift on the marble step, uneasy. "He taught me a bit."

"Hence your facility with knives." The Emperor contemplated the knot of healed scar tissue on his foot. "Do you want to be a gladiator, Vercingetorix?"

". . . No."

"Liar," said Domitian pleasantly.

"Liar as well as cheat," I interjected.

"Keep out of this, you cow," glared the Barbarian's son, and he squared his shoulders as he looked the Emperor in the eye.

"Yeah, I want to be a gladiator. Just like my father. Only my father hated the games. Hated them like poison, and look how good he was. So I'll be better, 'cause I love it. Your fault, Caesar. My father's your fault because you put him in the arena in the first place. And I'm your fault because you're the first blood I ever drew."

Sweat was pouring down his face, and I could feel him trembling against the arm of my chair. But that mad crazy grin appeared, spreading until it nearly hooked behind his ears. I wondered if Domitian would kill him personally. I hoped so—a dagger in the gut would serve the little bastard right, although if he bled all over my new pink *stola*—

Domitian moved so quickly when he wanted to. In one movement he lunged, grabbed the front of Vix's tunic, and threw him out over the railing like a doll.

He landed on burning sand. I heard the air whoosh from his lungs, and he sat up gasping for air. The arena buzzed like a beehive.

"Bring back the Gaul," the Emperor was saying coolly to the arena guards. "The lean mean one who cut the Greek's arm off."

Vix scrambled up, looking around him wildly. I leaned forward. Oh, this was something different—!

The Emperor tossed his own dagger into the sand at Vix's feet. "Time to prove yourself, young Arius."

"A sword." Vix dragged his paralyzed gaze up to the box. "At least give me a sword!"

Domitian considered. "Lord and God," I murmured, "a dagger will be *much* more amusing."

"Correct." He settled back.

The crowd's buzzing had mounted to uproar now. The games announcer looked from Vix to the Emperor and back again, rifling the schedule to see what this unexpected event might be called. "An, ah, extra bout for our Emperor's pleasure," he announced at last, voice ringing through the packed tiers. "The Gaul versus, ah, the boy."

With a crisp crunch of sand the Gaul stepped up beside Vix. He cast an incredulous look sideways, and I giggled at the paralyzed look on Vix's face. "Not so cocky now, are you?" I called down.

"Hail, Emperor." The Gaul saluted a rock-hard arm up at the Imperial box.

The Emperor looked at Vix. "Have you anything to say, Gladiator?"

Vix launched himself forward and sank the knife deep into the Gaul's knee.

The Gaul screamed. Vix tugged the blade free and took off running.

A RIUS'S belly crawled up the back of his throat. Freezing sweat trickled down his spine and the smells of the arena hit him like a slap: fear, sweat, iron, fresh-raked sand, the rotted flesh on the breath of the lions, the stains of old blood. Any minute now he'd wake up—he'd wake up and it would be him out on the arena sand, waiting for an enemy to strike.

But it wasn't him.

It was Vix.

The Gaul's first angry sweep whistled through Vix's hair. He stumbled away from the next feint, reeled back from a vicious thrust. The Gaul's curved blade ripped through his tunic. Thea moaned, and Arius's hand tightened around hers until the bones ground together.

Remember the drills, Vix. Arius felt terror clench somewhere inside his chest, a tight frozen ball, but he didn't dare let it thaw. He willed his thoughts out to the impossibly small red spot in the arena, calm as if this were just another training exercise behind the vineyard. *Remember what I taught you. Because there's no mercy here for beginners, Vix, no start-over for mistakes.*

Vix fell to one knee in the sand. The hand with the knife supported his trembling weight. The Gaul stepped forward, dragging a ruined leg and raising a shining sword.

Thea moaned again.

Kill him. Arius sent the thought out to his son. Not what he wanted, making his son a killer at thirteen, but this was the Colosseum and here the rules were different. *Kill him, Vix. Find a way.*

Vix flung a handful of sand into the Gaul's eyes. The Gaul yelled and stepped back blindly. Vix ducked under his shield and stabbed.

Arius froze. The Colosseum waited.

When Vix crawled out from under the still body of the Gaul,

they clapped. When he dragged himself to his feet, they cheered. When he retrieved his knife and scrubbed the blood off his face with an unsteady hand, they howled. Howled for twenty minutes, raining rose petals and silver coins down on his head. As they had once done for Arius.

Praetorians hauled Vix out of the arena and hoisted him on their shoulders, dousing his bristly hair with wine and thumping him on the back. Vix hardly seemed to notice. He stared around him with blank dazed eyes as they trooped him up to the Imperial box, and Arius remembered his own first arena kill in the middle of that deafening crash of applause.

Not like you imagined, is it, boy?

"I give you Vercingetorix!" The Emperor took Vix's arm and raised it high, spurring another wave of cheers. Domitian's voice carried over the screaming, the stamping, the clapping, all the way to the last tier of spectators at the top of the arena. "Vercingetorix, son of the Barbarian!"

Bᴀᴄᴋ in their rented tenement room, Thea lay rigid in Arius's arms. He clung gratefully to her tense body, closing his eyes in her hair. He couldn't get away from the images, images that left the ash-taste of horror in his mouth: Vix stumbling and stalling, Vix straightening and lunging, Vix taking his first kill . . .

Behind the horror, the demon was quietly taking the Emperor apart limb by limb.

"We'll have to kill him." The sudden harsh voice made him start, so unlike Thea it took him a moment to recognize it.

"The Emperor?" Of course the Emperor. The demon purred agreement.

"He did it to get at me." Thea stared ahead, unseeing. "He knew I'd be watching. He'll throw Vix back into that arena until he dies. And he *will* die. Maybe you trained him, but he's still just a child."

"Yes."

"And even if we could get Vix away, Domitian would find us. Wherever we ran."

"Yes."

"So he's got to die. That's all there is to it."

"I'll kill him," said Arius quite calmly. "You and Vix flee Rome." He wanted to live, but if it was the only way—

"No." For the first time her body trembled. "No."

"But—"

"I said no!" She turned in his arms, taking his face hard between her hands. "There's a man I know—we'll go to him. He'll manage something."

"Thea—"

She crushed her body fiercely against his, and for a while there was no more talk.

W̅HAT'S on your mind, Paulinus?" Marcus asked as soon as the library door closed behind his son. Sabina had been very poised through her first games, not crying or wincing at the bloodshed, but she'd unexpectedly had a seizure in the litter on the way back, and Calpurnia was tending her now. Marcus would be tending her himself, if his son hadn't stridden unexpectedly into the atrium.

"Paulinus?" Marcus paused. "I'd have thought you would be at the palace."

"The Emperor already had me take Vix back." Paulinus's hands bunched at his sides.

"The boy?" Marcus grimaced. "Children fighting in the Colosseum now. Barbaric."

"Oh, the boy's all right." Paulinus jerked. "Shaking, doing his best not to cry. Said he'd kill me if I laughed at him. Never felt less like laughing in my life."

Paulinus's eyes skittered over the pool in the atrium floor, the columns about the roof. Marcus regarded him a moment. "Perhaps you'd better come into my study, Paulinus."

"Yes," Paulinus said in a rush. "I must talk to you. I need your advice."

"What is it?"

Paulinus came to parade rest. "Sir." He fixed his eyes on the wall over Marcus's shoulder, and recited in the tones of a reporting legionnaire. "I have come to the conclusion that Emperor Domitian is unfit for the office he holds."

Marcus blinked. He lowered himself into the nearest chair. "Go on."

"He exiled his niece Lady Flavia Domitilla and executed her husband and children, all without just cause." Eyes still fixed stonily on the wall. "I have reason to believe him guilty of torturing his mistress Athena, and his niece Lady Julia. Julia he—he also murdered without cause. I believe he is a monster."

"Perhaps," Marcus said mildly. "But he is a good Emperor, is he not?"

"A monster can't—"

"Of course a monster can be a good Emperor, Paulinus. Domitian's personal habits may leave much to be desired, but there is no doubt he is a good administrator, a fine jurist, and a capable general. We have enjoyed stability under his reign. Stability, and boring peaceful things like a balanced economy and historically low corruption levels." Marcus rotated a pen between his hands. "You may be too young to remember the Year of Four Emperors, Paulinus, but many who do may be willing to balance a little monstrosity against stability."

"I'm not one of them." Paulinus looked him square in the eye. "I believe Domitian must be removed."

Marcus wondered how much blood those words had wrenched out of his son's heart. "Why ask my advice, then?" Quietly.

"Because you're a man of principles. Maybe the only one left. If you tell me Domitian is not worth his office, that's good enough for me."

Another pint of heart's blood, Marcus judged. *Fortunate that he has so great a heart to spare it.*

He opened his mouth—and the door crashed inward.

"Marcus," said Calpurnia. "Paulinus. There's someone here to—um. Here's Lady Athena. And this is—?"

"Arius," the big man said. "You'll know me."

"Who?" Marcus said politely.

"Never mind." Thea crossed the room, her eyes burning Paulinus.

Marcus looked at Calpurnia. "If you don't mind, my dear—"

"Oh, I'm leaving." She raised a hasty hand. "Whatever it is, I don't want to know." As she shut the door—"I'll just go keep the slaves quiet."

"Good girl."

"Paulinus." Thea stopped before Marcus's son. "We need you."

Paulinus looked at her, and his gaze didn't slide away. "You want your son back."

"I want my son back," said Thea. "And I want the Emperor dead."

Marcus spoke. "We all do."

Thirty-one

❦

"DIVORCE?" Lepida perched on the edge of Marcus's desk, raising her penciled brows. "Really, Marcus, why should I do that?"

"The Emperor is besotted with you, from all accounts. Six months now, isn't it?" Marcus shrugged. "I thought you might wish to make yourself . . . available."

"Oh, a man doesn't want his mistress to be available unless he suggests it." But Lepida preened a little. "You heard he's besotted with me?"

Marcus hid a smile. "He must have a stronger nose than I, if he can stand that vulgar perfume."

"Claws in, darling. I'm not getting rid of you yet. Though if he *does* decide to make me his Empress . . ."

"If."

She bristled. "Why not? He divorced his wife once; he can do it again. Aren't I worthy of a crown?"

Marcus looked at his wife: slim and luscious in saffron silk with a collar of Indian gold covering her throat and ropes of scented black hair coiled around her elegant head. "Every inch the Empress," he agreed. "Let's hope he lives to crown you."

"You've been listening to gossip."

"It's been kept quiet, Lepida, but I caught a whisper—I do

keep my ear to the ground, you know. The Emperor asked his astrologer to predict the date of his death, and he got a much nearer date than he liked."

"Nessus is unreliable now," Lepida snapped. "Nothing will kill Domitian."

"Of course. Though the thought must make you nervous."

"Don't try me, Marcus. If I ever do become Empress"—a swirl of saffron silk and a jangle of gold bracelets—"I'll have your head on a spike."

Marcus smiled as she clicked out of his tablinum in her gold-trimmed sandals. *Nicely planted*, he thought. If Lepida pushed to be Empress she'd be out in a fortnight—out from Domitian's charmed circle of protection. And if Marcus's suspicions were right and Paulinus was shaking off her malign influence as well . . .

"Father?" Sabina's feather-brown head poked around the door.

"Are you listening at keyholes again, Vibia Sabina?"

"How else am I supposed to learn anything?" She slipped in, shutting the door behind her. "Father . . . why did you suggest a divorce? You didn't think she'd take it."

"Didn't I?"

"I know your voice."

He looked at her. "No." After a pause. "I didn't think she'd take a divorce."

Sabina took a step closer. "So divorce *her.*"

"Should I?"

"She's my mother. I know I should honor her." Sabina paused. "But . . ."

"But?"

"She's beautiful. She's even sort of interesting, like the way poisonous snakes are interesting. But she's *awful*. Why didn't you divorce her years ago?"

"That's not for you to question, Vibia Sabina."

"Yes, it is. What happened? Did she threaten you?"

You, Marcus wanted to say. Paulinus was a Praetorian Prefect, the Emperor's best friend; no slander of Lepida's would stick long to his name. But Sabina had no such protection.

"Did she threaten me instead?" Sabina's question didn't surprise Marcus. His daughter's thoughts and his had always run close together. "That shouldn't have stopped you, Father."

"No." He smiled. "But I had thought to see you married first." Married, grown, out of reach of Lepida's malice.

"I don't think I want to get married. I'd rather see the world." Sabina's mouth firmed. "Divorce her."

He looked up at his child, and didn't see her. He saw a girl grown almost to his own height, her hair coiled on her neck like a woman's and a woman's steady eyes gazing into his.

"Gods," he said. "You grew up behind my back."

"Think about it?" she pleaded.

He smiled, smoothing her hair. "Yes, I'll think about it. Now, are you too big to give me a hug?"

She leaned her sleek brown head on his crooked shoulder. "Never."

THEA

FOR a moment my mouth hung open like a bumpkin's.

"Athena." The Empress of Rome glided across Marcus's tablinum and pressed my hand as if we were old friends. "Lovely to see you, my dear. I haven't heard a note of good music since you left the palace. And this is the famous Arius? I've watched you a good many times, with great pleasure. Paulinus, you don't look well. Have you been ill? My husband has been worried. Marcus, are we all here?"

It was the most I'd ever heard her say in all the years I'd observed her.

"We should get down to business." She arranged herself briskly on a padded stool. "Officially I'm dining with my sister Cornelia and her husband, which gives me only a few hours. Domitian still tracks my comings and goings."

I closed my mouth with a snap. She was a conspirator, too? Domitian's marble-perfect wife with her emeralds and her good works? The *Empress*?

Paulinus looked as if someone had just whacked him right between the eyes. Arius's gaze flicked back and forth between her and me as if drawing comparisons. And Marcus kissed her cheek with the ease of an old friend.

"The usual precautions?" she asked him.

"The usual. I'm supposed to be dining with Lady Diana; we've been friends for years, so no one will question it."

"Yes, Diana will cover for you." The Empress cast a glance at all of us. "Are they trustworthy, Marcus?"

"What about you?" I stepped forward. "Are you trustworthy, Domina?"

Marcus spoke as formally as if addressing the Senate. "The Empress and I have been working together since Lady Julia's death, Thea."

"Then why isn't the Emperor dead yet?" Arius folded his arms across his chest. "I decide I want a man dead, I don't wait around six months to do it."

"See here," Paulinus began.

"No, he's right to ask." Marcus looked at my lover. "The Empress and I took some time feeling each other out—neither of us being terribly trusting."

"Normally I would prefer to work alone." The Empress's fine patrician voice was matter-of-fact. "But I realized it would take more than me to bring down Domitian." She looked at me, speculative. "I did consider recruiting you, my dear, but I wasn't sure if Domitian had cut all your nerve out or not. He has a tendency to do that with his women."

He hadn't done it to her.

She looked around our little circle. "Is everyone satisfied now?"

Paulinus rubbed a hand through his hair. "Before we go any further," he said unhappily, "I want to make one thing clear. I won't do it myself. I'll smooth the way for you, but I won't do it. Not if it's poison, not if it's a knife." Looking away. "I owe him that much."

"We don't expect it of you," the Empress assured him.

Arius looked disgusted, and I nudged him. He wasn't disposed to like Paulinus, probably because he knew I'd once shared Paulinus's bed. "In another lifetime," I'd assured him. "I hardly remember it."

"Don't think much of your taste," Arius had grumped.

"And your bed was empty all those years you mourned for me?" I said tartly. He'd at once found something else to talk about.

We sat down, awkwardly, to plan the death of an Emperor. That is, Arius and Paulinus and I were awkward. Marcus and the Empress were quite at ease—and at once, they turned to Arius.

"As an assassin, you are the logical choice," said Marcus. "Are you willing?"

"Just get me a knife." Arius's voice was level, but my stomach jumped.

"He's a common thug!" Paulinus burst out.

Arius grinned. The Empress looked at him, speculative. "You were the best fighter in Rome once, but you aren't young anymore. Are you still the best?"

Arius gave her a long contemptuous blink.

"He is," I said. "It may have been years since he fought in any arena, but he's as good now as he was then." *Maybe better*, I added to myself. *Because then he didn't have anything to love.*

"It won't be easy," the Empress went on. "My husband may look lazy, but he can still fight with the best of them."

"He sleeps with a dagger under his pillow," I added.

Arius looked at me.

"Well, he does."

"Really?" said the Empress, diverted. "A new development, since my day. Out of curiosity, my dear, why didn't you ever stab him with it when he slept?"

"Because I wanted to live," I shot back. "Why didn't *you* ever stab him while he slept? You had as many chances as I did." I looked around the little circle. "Anyone can kill an Emperor. It's living to tell the tale that's the hard part. So if Arius kills Domitian for you, there had better be a plan to get him out alive afterward."

"He'll get out alive." The Empress produced a neat list and in a cool voice outlined the plan she and Marcus had constructed between them. "Paulinus, I trust you can take care of the guards?"

"Yes, but—" Paulinus looked at his father. "I don't like it. You're entrusting the fate of Rome to this—this *criminal*—"

Arius just shrugged, but I stiffened. "He's not a criminal."

"But neither is he exactly a model citizen," the Empress murmured, a gleam of amusement in her eye. If there was one thing I'd never suspected her of possessing, it was a sense of humor.

Marcus was addressing his son in low tones. "Paulinus, assassination is not a pretty business. You knew that when you agreed to join us. You can't quibble about means and methods. There is *no* honorable way to do this."

"But he—"

"He has talents we need. So do you. Are you going to contribute them?"

A long pause. Then—"Yes."

"Good," said Marcus. "Then we have a chain of two."

Arius and Paulinus eyed each other unenthusiastically. I looked down at my lap. I didn't want to sit at home, waiting to see if my lover came back alive. I was tired of that. I wanted—I wanted to be a link in the chain for once.

Arius spoke over Paulinus's head, to Marcus. "One more thing," he said. "How do we know we can trust you?"

Paulinus blinked. Marcus and the Empress looked impassive.

"You patricians are used to sacrificing people for your politics," Arius rumbled. "What's a worn-out old gladiator's life worth to you? What's a Jewish singer's life? Who says you won't throw us to the lions once we do your dirty work?"

"Listen—" Paulinus bristled. Marcus quelled him with a finger.

"How do you know you can trust us?" he asked Arius. "You don't. But you won't get your son back any other way."

A brief silence. I looked at the Empress, and the Empress looked at me. Arius looked at Marcus, and Marcus looked at him. Paulinus scowled between them.

The Empress rustled her green silk gown as she set down her wine cup. "It looks like we'll just have to trust each other, Athena," she said. "No, it's Thea, isn't it?"

"That's right," I said. "So how soon can you smuggle Arius into the palace?"

"Not soon," said the Empress. "We wait until September."

"September?" Arius and I broke out in unison. Months away—and Vix was scheduled to fight again in the Colosseum next month. Sketches of him armed and helmeted like his father were already plastered all over the city. I'd even seen the words chalked on a schoolroom door: *'Vercingetorix the Young Barbarian makes all the little girls' hearts beat faster.'* "I want Domitian dead now!"

"It's only been whispered so far," said the Empress, "but my husband has recently received from Nessus the date of his death. According to Nessus and the stars, Domitian will die on the eighteenth of this September, in the fifth hour of the evening. Until that day and that hour is past, he'll be impossible to catch off-guard. We strike the next day, when he is rejoicing at his survival. Just when he is feeling invincible."

"You're saying we have to wait nearly three *months*?" I cried out. "My son may die within weeks!"

"Vix will get through," said the Empress. "That little hooligan of yours is a horror, but he keeps Domitian entertained. As long as my husband is entertained, he won't kill anyone."

"Understand one thing." Arius's hands locked around each other like carved wood. "We'll wait. But if my son dies in the arena, then Domitian dies, too. Same day. Same hour. Hell with your plans."

The Empress looked at him, considering. "Did you train your son, Barbarian?"

"I did."

"Then I'm confident he will survive the arena in style."

I turned my face away. Arius's hand found mine and swallowed it.

"I believe we've covered everything now." The Empress reached for her *palla*. "And I believe it's time I got back to the Domus Augustana. If I'm even a minute late, Domitian will send the guards out to question my sister. She'd lie for me, though she dislikes me heartily, but that stalwart husband of hers couldn't tell a lie to save his life."

We broke apart without speaking. Paulinus stood turning his Praetorian's helmet over in his hands and looking awkward. The Empress nodded a general farewell and climbed into a hired litter. Marcus tidied up the wine cups, the cushions, and circle of chairs with the calm of one long used to covering his tracks. Arius and I slipped out the slave entrance into the dark street without a word.

"Congratulations," I said. "From gladiator to assassin. I hope it's worth giving up our son."

"He'll survive." Gripping my hand. "Thea. Trust me."

Thirty-two

~~~☙ ❧~~~

LEPIDA

WHAT do you mean, he won't see me?" I stared down my nose at the Imperial chamberlain, but he stared right back.

"The Emperor is engaged at the moment, Domina."

"But he'll see *me*." I arched subtly inside my jade silk drapes, a reminder of exactly what I was to the Lord and God of Rome.

"He commands you to wait with the others, Domina."

Fuming, I waited. Outside his door in the marble hall like a loitering slave with all the rest of the petitioners and servants and courtiers who hovered in hopes of any brief moment of Imperial favor. Suffering the curiosity, the glances, the whispers of those who both fawned on me and prayed for my downfall.

At last the doors swung wide—but it was not my Imperial lover who sallied forth. It was a girl with golden hair and a simper; a Lady Aurelia Rufina, senator's wife and much-gossiped-about beauty. A seventeen-year-old girl fanning herself prettily as she slouched out of Domitian's private chambers. A seventeen-year-old girl who bestowed on me, as she strolled past, an unmistakable smirk.

Stretching my lips into a smile, I boldly struck open the door of the Imperial tablinum before the steward could object.

"Lepida Pollia." Domitian barely glanced up, scribbling

away at a postscript for a letter while one secretary hovered at
his elbow with a slate, another brought a pile of fresh pens, two
couriers hurried in with more scrolls and out with freshly sealed
Imperial screeds, and a centurion shifted from foot to foot waiting to make a report. "I thought I might see you."

"How could I possibly stay away from you any longer, Lord
and God?" I held my smile with an effort. No doubt he was testing my loyalty, seeing if I'd fuss over a little indiscretion. "Why
don't you send the secretaries away? Don't you think you've
worked enough for now?"

"I'm busy." He sealed a packet of letters and tossed it over to
a slave.

I trailed my fingers over Domitian's arm. "Then I'll see you
at the games tomorrow morning?" I was to sit in the Imperial
box for the Ludi Saeculares, the biggest games of the year. I had
a new flame-colored *stola*, specially made to set off the collar
of fire opals Domitian had given me last month—

"I shan't need you during the games tomorrow." He flicked
his fingers, and I found an unctuous freedman at my elbow,
murmuring me out the door. A few petitioners flew to my side at
once, bowing and gushing; a few courtiers with honey tongues
and envying eyes—but even more were clustered around that
simpering blond child, Aurelia Rufina.

"Too bad, Lady Lepida." The loathsome voice of Thea's brat
piped up at my elbow. "The Emperor get tired of you already?
Toldja you had lousy luck."

"Shut up," I hissed. "Shut up; you'll be dead anyway; killed
in the arena just like your father, so what do you know about
luck?" I slapped the grinning face as hard as I could.

"Sure. Maybe I'll be dead." He danced out of reach, rubbing
his face comically. "But nobody forgets a dead gladiator—they
go out heroes. How do old whores like you go out?"

"You're not a gladiator, you little runt!" I lunged for him, but
he slipped, grinning, out of my hands. "You only won last time
because you threw sand in the Gaul's face! Your father might
have been a man, but you're just a cowardly slave brat!"

He made an obscene gesture and sauntered away. Little monster. I smoothed a lock of hair off my forehead and the frown off
my face, putting the brat's words behind me. I certainly had not
lost the Emperor. He was just having a little indulgence, and

he'd come back to me when it was sated. He'd done that in the past, after all. The trick was not to look worried.

I sallied out to the Saeculares games the following morning, bestowing a lavish smile on every speculative glance that came my way, my flame-colored gown and fire opals wasted on Marcus. I entered the Norbanus box on my husband's arm, displacing the plain Calpurnia in her brown silk—really, why was she still such a regular guest? Shortly after the Vestal had been executed, Paulinus had asked Domitian rather halfheartedly if he could break the betrothal. "No," snapped Domitian, and that had been that. Still, she had to know she wasn't wanted. I bumped her off Marcus's arm and outdid her laughing at Marcus's mild jests. No one would catch *me* looking worried.

"Overdoing it a bit, aren't you?" my husband murmured.

"Just smile and kiss me, darling," I ordered under cover of my peacock fan as we settled into our seats. "If you know what's good for you. Look, there's the parade." I directed a serene gaze out over the arena; ignoring my husband's slow dry smile, ignoring my daughter drawing away from me—and especially ignoring the stares that slipped my way as the Emperor appeared in the Imperial box. What did I have to worry about? I was the most beautiful, the most alluring and seductive woman in Rome. No yellow-haired chit of seventeen could compete. Domitian would be calling me back to his bed by the end of the week.

I watched the opening wild beast duels, the comic acts, the white bulls plodding past in their garlands of flowers. I reached to refill my wine goblet, and my eyes fell on Paulinus. He looked rather well these days—fit and brown, even smiling now and then. Perhaps he'd gotten over his touching little crush on the dead Vestal. Paulinus and a *Vestal*—how utterly, utterly typical.

His friend—Majan or Trajan or something, a regular guest in our box since Marcus had learned he was some kind of distant cousin—leaned over to give Paulinus a nudge, looking exasperated, and Paulinus turned rather dutifully to his betrothed.

"I trust you are enjoying the parade, Calpurnia?"

"It's very splendid."

"I've seen very little of you lately. My duties have been

pressing. Perhaps you would like to accompany me to an Imperial banquet next week?"

"The first time I went to an Imperial banquet I saw an orgy," Calpurnia said bluntly. "And the second time I went I saw an assassination attempt, an arrest, and a murder. I don't really think I want to try a third time."

Paulinus could not stifle a smile, teeth gleaming in his sun-darkened face. "I suppose I can't blame you."

"I've been to see the augurs, Paulinus," Calpurnia said. "About a date for our wedding."

"Oh?" said Paulinus cautiously.

"It seems there is nothing auspicious enough," said Calpurnia. "Not for months."

"Oh," said Paulinus.

They exchanged a certain glance, and restored their attention to Trajan and Marcus respectively. I sent Paulinus the slow smile that always turned his knees to water. He nodded back curtly, and looked away. Playing cool in front of his friend and fiancée, of course. We'd see how cool he was once I got him alone. Really, if Domitian could amuse himself, why shouldn't I?

The midday executions dragged past, and then the gladiators marched through the Gate of Life in their purple cloaks, pairing off for the preliminary fights. My daughter leaned forward, her eyes bending on the muscled armored figures. I looked at her irritably. "Since when is Little Lady Squeamish a gladiator fan?"

"I'm not," she said, eyes still fixed on the arena. "I went for the first time at Matralia, and it was all fairly awful. But it is interesting."

I brushed a fly away from my wine cup. "You've got a crush on a trident fighter, I suppose."

"No . . . it's just that the gladiators are supposed to care about dying well, and all they care about is not dying at all." Her eyes traveled from the arena to the packed tiers of the Colosseum, the laughing cheering crowds of plebs and patricians alike. "People don't seem to see that."

"Perhaps it's the young Barbarian who makes your heart pound?" I smiled. "Such low tastes, Sabina. Even an ugly little girl with foaming fits can do better than a gladiator."

"Trade seats with me, Sabina," Marcus intervened smoothly. "My view is better."

They traded seats, a move that placed her on Marcus's other side next to Calpurnia. Sabina leaned forward toward the arena again, and my husband immediately engaged his almost-daughter-in-law in some boring discussion. Paulinus was busy listening to Trajan outline a proposed method of revamping the legions, and around us the crowd was shouting encouragement to the gladiators as they warmed up with wooden weapons. "Marcus," I said, "fill my cup, will you?"

"Of course, my dear." He leaned over to fill my goblet, and I leaned toward the arena, at last starting to enjoy myself as the Emperor gave the signal and the gladiators fell on each other with hoarse shouts. Nothing like a good slaughter to clear the head.

"By the way," Marcus said casually, handing me my goblet. "I'm divorcing you."

"Mmm?" I blinked, looking up from a pair of Egyptians tussling over a trident.

His voice was clear, carrying over the shouts around the box. "I'm divorcing you." Calpurnia glanced over.

"What?"

Sabina glanced up at me. Behind her a Numidian shrieked as a little Gaul chopped his knee out from under him.

"You shouldn't joke, Marcus." I tossed my head. "You know what the Emperor will do to you if I whisper in his ear."

"It looks like someone else is whispering in his ear now." Marcus indicated the Imperial box. The Empress had retired for the afternoon, and a figure in a pink silk *stola* had just slouched in to perch on the arm of Domitian's chair. A yellow-haired figure.

"Aurelia Rufina? She's temporary, just a whim—it's me Domitian wants—"

"I think he's done with you, Lepida. And so am I." Marcus looked at me the way he looked at opposing senators in debates about water rights. "I am hereby divorcing you—legally, of course, I can do that with a word. I'll give you until the end of the day to remove what possessions you have from my house."

I thrust the question of the Emperor aside. What did Marcus know about Domitian? Nothing, that's what, but the other attack had come so suddenly and I unsheathed my claws. "Emperor or no Emperor, Marcus, you know what I'll do to you if you divorce me. Your precious Paulinus will—"

"In addition," Marcus overrode me, "I will be charging you

with adultery. Within the sixty days prescribed by law I will present the courts with my extensively gathered evidence." He smiled at me, quite gently. "Yes, Lepida. I'm putting my foot down."

I stared at him a full minute. *Marcus?*

Calpurnia's eyes sparkled. Sabina looked from her father's face to mine and back. The arena slaves darted swiftly over the bloody sand, dodging the battling gladiators, raking away the dead ones.

"Calpurnia, darling," I said in a loud voice. "Would you like to know something about Paulinus? He raped me as a young bride, and your future father-in-law let him. Sabina is Paulinus's child, not Marcus's, and I'm going to charge Paulinus in the courts with rape. What do you think of that?"

"I think you're lying," Calpurnia said equably.

Marcus laid his hand over her square peasant fingers in brief thanks. "Good try, Lepida," he said. "That story might have worked eight years ago. But bring it out now, and everyone will wonder why you didn't come forward sooner. And of course there's the matter of your own reputation, which has hardly remained spotless in eight years. Do you want all the skeletons to come out of your closet into the light of day?"

"You—you wouldn't dare—"

"The affair with my son when you were—Calpurnia, kindly cover my daughter's ears—a bride of twenty-one. The affairs with, at my last count, twenty-two senators, nine praetors, three judges, and five provincial governors."

"It's—it's not true, I never—"

"At least they were men of your own class," Marcus rode over me. "What about the affairs with the charioteers, and the masseurs at the public bathhouses, and the legionnaires— especially the two brothers from Gaul who took you at the same time, front and back?" Marcus raised his eyebrows, and behind him a trident fighter died with a sword through his gullet. "Governors and senators are one thing, Lepida, but trash from the gutters . . ."

My lips parted, dry as parchment. "You can't possibly—you never look up from your stupid *scrolls*—"

"Oh, I see a great deal over my scrolls. In fact, I've been amassing evidence for years. I have documents, witnesses, slaves who will talk—eagerly, I might add, and without threat of torture. You were never a kind mistress, Lepida. I also have a few of your former lovers as witnesses. Junius Clodius, for example, once I offered to pay his debts."

"And what will their evidence do to you?" I rallied. "You'll be the senator whose wife took on every man in Rome—"

"Oh, I think my reputation will survive." A smile. "Will yours?"

Sabina brushed Calpurnia's hands away from her ears, giggling.

"You!" I rounded on her. "If you think any man will want a cuckold's daughter—once I've done there won't be a man in the Empire who will touch you—"

"By law," Marcus intoned the words as he did in the Senate, "a man is entitled to retain his former wife's dowry if her adultery is sufficiently proved. Every aureus of your dowry will go to Sabina. Sufficient gold, I think, to catch her any husband she likes—even if she were not already a prize for any man."

"I've still got a chance," I hissed at him. "Courts are made up of men, remember? I can make any man believe me!"

"I'll risk it."

He sat there, Sabina and Calpurnia at his back; a triumvirate of judges with an ocean of slaughter behind them. The gladiators were done, the victors raising their arms winded and triumphant, the losers raked away to feed the lions. The gladiators were done and so was I.

It couldn't have gotten this far; it couldn't. I'd be an outcast, looking for any man to marry me—I cast around for a weapon, any weapon, and heard Paulinus laugh with Trajan behind me. "What about your son, Marcus? Who do you think he'll side with? He loves me, in case you've forgotten. He'll roll over and beg like a dog if I want, and if you think he'll stand for this—"

"Then why don't we ask him? Paulinus!" Before I could stop him, Marcus called politely over my shoulder to his son, who was tossing coins down from the box to a triumphant German in a wolf skin. "Paulinus, I am divorcing your stepmother. Have you any objection?"

Paulinus paused, his eyes flicking over my bare arms and enticing shoulders; the body he had once slavered over. "None," he said, and his voice was so cold it hit me like a slap of wind from the north.

"Paulinus—" I leaned forward to offer him a glimpse of my breasts. "Paulinus, he's vindictive, he'll shame me—I'm counting on you—"

He turned his back. Simply turned his back on me and began speaking again to a puzzled Trajan. "I think you're right about the legionnaire training. Too focused on conformity—"

This couldn't be happening. Couldn't be happening.

"Lepida." Marcus's voice again.

No. No. NO.

"Lepida, I will not strip you of everything. Keep your slanders away from Paulinus and Sabina, and I'll withhold my charge of adultery and leave you your dowry."

My dowry? What good was money if I had no husband? A Roman woman without a husband is nothing. Even if Marcus didn't blacken my reputation in court, what man of patrician stature would marry me after Marcus so unceremoniously divorced me . . . if Domitian really had abandoned me?

I began to shake.

Marcus had already turned back to Calpurnia, discussing Senate debates as if nothing had happened at all. Sabina leaned on the marble railing over the arena, watching as slaves darted out to rake fresh sand over the bloody patches. Paulinus outlined training tactics with Trajan. Up in the Imperial box, Aurelia Rufina had slipped from the arm of Domitian's chair into his lap.

Divorced. I had been divorced. Just Lepida Pollia, instead of Lady Lepida Pollia the senator's wife and the Emperor's mistress.

Dimly I heard a roar from the crowd and looked up at the Imperial box. Domitian had just given his signal for the next act, a trident fighter against an armored Gaul.

He could not have tired of me already. He could *not*. Thea had lasted nearly five years. I had reigned supreme for barely seven months.

The trident fighter died quickly. The crowd roared for the next duel, the young Barbarian against a famous Syrian, and I had time for a fleeting hope that Thea's horrid son would die slowly with a sword in his gut. Then I began planning exactly how I would oust the pretty little Aurelia from the Imperial box in the next interlude . . .

And how I would make Marcus and Paulinus *pay*.

THEA

THEY'D given Vix his father's old armor, resized to fit. The mail sleeve, the blue-plumed helmet, the shin plates. His face, in the shadow of his helmet, was set like stone. They set him against an enormous Syrian, and my heart crawled into my throat. I'd always thought him big for his age, but I was wrong. He looked so terribly small beside the Syrian's hulking shoulder as they bowed before the Emperor.

It took a moment to realize, through my fog of terror, that Vix was holding his own.

The Syrian launched an overhand swing, the clean ring of steel on steel vibrating through the arena as the blades met. He took a compensating step as Vix disengaged and ducked back, then parried as my son's sword flashed out with a slow looping ease.

"That Syrian's never fought a left-hander before." Arius looked gray and lined, scared as he had never looked during his own bouts, but he spoke calmly. "Vix'll keep turning him to his weak side."

Close, duck, disengage. Close, duck, disengage. *Sensible*, I thought, trying to breathe. *Don't close with a stronger opponent; wait it out.* My son seemed to hear me, crouching and circling as if he had all the time in the world. His chest was pink with sunburn, and the helmet turned his eyes to dark slits.

Close, duck, disengage. The Syrian lost patience, lashing forward. Vix parried the first two strokes, ducked the third, and then ran, his feet skimming the sand. Laughter rippled over the Colosseum. The Syrian stopped, crouching again, and Vix fell back into the pattern of his own making. Close, duck, disengage.

"Good," Arius murmured. "Good."

The Syrian's foot wobbled in the sand; he cursed as if he had twisted the joint, and retreated limping. "Get him!" I whispered, but Arius gave a sharp shake. Vix stood back, head cocked to one side, and ducked easily when the Syrian made a leap for him. God, but my son was fast.

The Syrian slashed again, letting Vix dance back. Lunged. Feinted.

"Don't let him herd you," Arius said, but Vix took two more hasty steps back and then froze with the marble of the arena wall against his back.

"*Vix!*" I screamed along with all the other screaming fans, as the Syrian raised his sword.

Vix charged. The Syrian barely had time to correct the blade's angle before it punched through the strap of Vix's mail sleeve and bit smoothly through the flesh, through the shoulder and out again.

"Too high," Arius murmured, whitely.

One more blow through the lung for the slow kill. The Syrian tugged his sword.

Then Vix grabbed it.

He wrapped his hand around the blade piercing his shoulder. Held it there, blood dripping from his hand, and I saw the muscles bunch in his arm. His teeth bared, he held the blade steady while he drove his shoulder farther up toward the hilt.

Not far. Just within arm's reach.

Just close enough to strike.

Arius nodded professional approval as Vix's sword flashed up, and the Syrian's blood jetted out to stain the sand. "Pretty work," he said as if Vix had just finished a training bout.

I turned and vomited over the ground.

LEPIDA

Strategy! In the arena, no less." Trajan pounded his fist against the railing. "If that isn't the prettiest piece of blindsiding—There's a place in my legion for that boy if he ever earns his freedom—"

"If he lives," I said sourly, but nobody was listening to me.

"I'll beat you out for him and offer a place in the Praetorians." Paulinus tossed a coin down at the Young Barbarian, who had reached around with his good arm and tugged the Syrian's blade out of his shoulder. He stood looking at it for a moment, and then very quietly crumpled up on the sand.

"Oh dear," I heard Sabina say. Her little rat-narrow face was all pink. "The poor boy." She folded up into a seizure.

I had no desire to be seen with a jerking, writhing brat. As Calpurnia and Marcus bent over her, I slipped out of the box. In the arena they were rigging a hasty stretcher for the unconscious Vix, and the audience was still screaming approval. Domitian had leaned forward to clap, but Aurelia Rufina looked half-asleep at his side. She never had understood what the games were all about. Surely he'd want my company now.

The chamberlain blocked my way as I slipped up to the back entrance of the royal box. "The Emperor has observed the disturbance in your box," he informed me in bored tones. "Your child appears to be ill. Your place is with her."

"But she's in good hands. Her father—"

"Children are women's work. You are Imperially commanded to take your child home." Just a hint of a smirk hovered around the chamberlain's rouged lips. "The Emperor instructs me to give you this, Lady Lepida." He pressed a rather inferior string of pearls into my hand. "He will no longer be requiring your services."

A soundless explosion rocked my vision, made up of Marcus's dry warning and Thea's mocking face and the tittering of the courtiers. *Not even a year,* I thought numbly, my fingers clenching around the puny string of pearls. *Thea lasted nearly five*—"Who's taken my place?" I demanded. "That stupid little Aurelia Rufina? Why is she better than me? Does she serve the Emperor more eagerly?"

"Not at all, Lady Lepida." The chamberlain smirked again, openly. "She is, however, *newer.*"

My stomach twisted as though he'd kicked me. Dear gods, how could I have lost the Emperor? Just a week and a half ago I'd been dropping hints about leaving Marcus, dreaming of being crowned Empress—

The chamberlain shooed at me. "The guards will show you out, Lady Lepida."

A T the last minute Paulinus was detained—"the Emperor desires your company"—so Trajan offered his services in taking Sabina home.

"I'll carry her." He cheerfully took the limp form from

Paulinus's arms. "She's no heavier than a feather, and anyway, according to my mother she's some kind of great-niece four times removed or something. Where's that litter?" He muscled his way through the crowds, down the marble steps, out one of the rear archways. Marcus followed gratefully with Calpurnia, Lepida sulking behind. She'd returned white-faced from the Imperial box, and Marcus refrained from baiting her. Vipers, even with their poison drawn, could still bite. But he had to restrain himself from smiling. *Serious things*, he thought sternly. *Funerals. Budget meetings. The last third of the Iliad.*

"You're not fooling me, Marcus Norbanus," Calpurnia whispered at his side. "Your eyes are dancing."

"They are not." *Raised taxes. Bad poetry. The declining birth rate . . .*

Lepida climbed up into the Norbanus litter, her small chin jutting as if she dared anyone to toss her out. Trajan shrugged and merely swung her small gold-shod feet out of the way, making room for Sabina. "You next, Lady Calpurnia. Put the little one's head in your lap." He waited courteously for Marcus to settle himself, hopped in, and the overcrowded litter swayed down the street. Lepida shot Trajan a poisonous look. Marcus couldn't hide a smile then.

Sabina was pale and sweating, but her eyelids flickered. "She'll be out of it soon," said Trajan.

"You know a great deal about epilepsia, Commander." Marcus watched Trajan lift Sabina's head.

"The disease every soldier prays for, Senator. Alexander the Great had it, and Julius Caesar, too."

Lepida wrinkled her pretty nose. "She's an embarrassment. Falling down in front of my friends like some drooling idiot—"

"Will you *shut up*?" said Calpurnia ferociously before Marcus could speak.

Trajan grinned. "No shame in epilepsia. No hardship to cure it, either. In fact—" He poked his head through the curtains and shouted down at the bearers. "Turn right up ahead."

"What's all that shouting?" Calpurnia wondered. Sabina moaned, head turning back and forth. There certainly was a great deal of shouting. The sort heard from only two kinds of crowds: triumphal processions and games fans. Or in this case, both.

The path back to the Domus Augustana was mobbed with

screaming plebs, all shoving and stretching their hands out toward the cluster of red-and-gold Praetorians in the middle. Praetorians bearing on their shoulders the Young Barbarian on a makeshift stretcher.

Trajan hopped down nimbly, applying his armored shoulder to the crush. "Commander Trajan here; official business. Out of the way, please, out of the way—look, will you move? Yes, thank you, out of the way—A moment, tribune," he said to the Praetorian, and swung up beside the stretcher. Marcus heard his battle-trained voice clearly, even over the din. "Just want to congratulate this young man here on his fight."

"Who the hell are you?" Marcus half-glimpsed the Young Barbarian hoisted high on his stretcher, scattered with flowers like a bier, blood streaming down his arm. Hands darted at him, pulling bits of his hair or threads of his tunic for souvenirs.

"Commander Trajan. Just wanted to tell you that was a fine bout." He clapped the boy's wounded shoulder, hard. "If you'd ever like a job in the legions—"

"Bugger off!" Vix howled, clutching his shoulder.

"Excellent, excellent. Carry on, tribune." His hand covered in blood, Trajan leaped back toward the waiting litter.

"What—" Marcus exclaimed as he climbed back in.

"Fresh gladiator blood." Trajan painted Sabina's lips with one scarlet finger. "Bound to cure epilepsia every time; any soldier knows that."

"I will not have my daughter drinking blood!"

"I know, I know. Barbaric." Trajan smeared the rest of the blood on her temples and forehead. "But it works."

Lepida shivered. "If anyone gets blood on my skirts—"

Sabina's eyes fluttered open. "Ow," she said.

"How do you feel?" Calpurnia felt her forehead.

"My head hurts." Pushing herself upright. "Did he die?"

"Did who die, sweetheart?" Marcus took her hand.

"The boy."

"No, he's swearing like a soldier," Trajan said cheerfully. He looked at Marcus. "See?"

"He'll get better, won't he?" Sabina pressed.

"Rest your head, little one, he won't die."

"My word," Lepida yawned, drawing her skirt aside. "So much passion for a gutter rat."

"You know," said Trajan. "I think this litter's a little crowded after all." He leaned forward, seized Lepida around the waist, and dropped her briskly on the road outside. He yanked the curtains shut on a shrill yelp and a flood of cursing. "Carry on," he shouted down to the bearers. "She's no longer your mistress!" The bearers grinned and trotted away double-time. Marcus heard Lepida's shriek after them and laughed aloud, regarding Trajan thoughtfully.

"Young man," he said, "I like your style."

"So do I," giggled Sabina. When the litter reached the Norbanus house, she all but skipped up the steps.

"Leave the blood the rest of the day," Trajan advised. "Use her to scare a few visitors while she looks like a demon."

Calpurnia looked after Sabina. "Do you think she'll ever have another seizure?"

"Of course she will," said Marcus. "Gladiator blood isn't medicine; it's rank superstition. She'll have another seizure next week."

But she didn't.

I wonder who will be Emperor next?" Thea asked the question idly as they tidied away their stools and wine goblets. "When Domitian is gone."

"Some proper senatorial graybeard," Paulinus shrugged. "Senator Nerva, maybe—good lineage, distinguished record of service, no vices. One or two others might put themselves forward—"

"Hardly a matter to discuss before slaves," the Empress broke in, casting a glance at Arius and Thea.

"That's right," Arius agreed. "Those of us who hope Rome and everyone in it falls into hell."

"As long as we get Vix . . ." Thea rubbed her forehead, and Arius caressed the back of her neck with a comforting hand. She turned her cheek against his palm, and Paulinus looked away, fumbling a handful of black grapes from a silver bowl on the table. The trusting angle of her head reminded him of Julia.

The conspirators broke apart through the doors, leaving Marcus to extinguish the lamps. The Empress reached for her *palla*, Arius and Thea slipped out arm in arm like wraiths, and Paulinus set about helping his father clear away the evidence that anyone had been here but themselves. The day was almost upon them, come nightmare-slow but still too fast: the day when they would try to kill an Emperor. The matter had loomed so huge and hideous Paulinus had not even stopped to think what came after.

"Who *will* be Emperor next?" he wondered aloud, putting away the wine decanter. "Whoever gets the most legions, I suppose. Although . . . Father, didn't you write a treatise about how an Emperor should be childless so he can adopt a talented successor rather than rely on blood?"

"I've written a great many treatises," Marcus said vaguely, but a fast look flashed between him and the Empress. Paulinus looked at them both, quizzical, but the Empress broke in smoothly.

"I'm sure an appropriate candidate will present himself." She drew her *palla* up over her hair. "No doubt by killing all his rivals. Good night, Paulinus, Marcus." She gave her curved smile and passed into the darkness.

Paulinus shrugged as the door clicked shut, still musing. His Praetorians would be a factor in the succession, too, as much as any of the legions. As commander of the Imperium's own personal army, Paulinus's support would be invaluable to whoever claimed the throne. Frightening thought . . .

"Sabina, is that you?" Marcus straightened toward the door with a smile of welcome, but Paulinus saw how speedily his father whisked the extra wine cups out of sight. "What are you doing awake?"

"I heard voices downstairs." Small and neat in her white night robe, Sabina traced the curve of a mosaic serpent with one bare toe.

"'Linus was arguing with me about Cicero's *Commentaries*," Marcus said calmly. "He should know better, but he is a soldier and he does learn slowly."

"I heard voices besides yours." Still tracing the serpent. "And saw a hired litter out the window. You have some very *interesting* guests, Father."

Paulinus opened his mouth, but Sabina put out a hand in a remarkably adult gesture. "Don't tell me," she said, and she turned with a hint of a smile back toward her bedchamber. "I don't want to know."

Thirty-three

❦❦

"YOU'RE cheating again." The Imperial voice was a snarl.

"Just lucky, Caesar." Vix shook his empty sleeves; no loaded dice.

"Not luck. Cheat."

"I will remove the boy if he displeases you, Caesar," Paulinus said quickly.

"All Jews are cheats." The Emperor flung the dice across the room. He had paneled the walls in moonstone in preparation for this day, so he could see anyone who might be lurking behind him. "Like Athena. Not even her real name. Should have killed her. Should have killed you all." The Emperor's eyes had a wild uneasy flicker, and he scratched distractedly at his forehead. "Are you the one who will try to kill me today, Vercingetorix? At the fifth hour?"

Vix looked weary.

"According to Nessus, today brings my death. Are you the one to bring it?"

Paulinus cleared his throat. "He's only a boy, Caesar—"

"Boys can kill," Domitian snapped. His eyes prowled the dull silver reflections of the room, wary, and he still scratched at his forehead. Paulinus saw he had drawn blood, and despite everything could not help a leap of pity.

"Caesar," he said gently.

Domitian dropped his hand, seeing the blood under his nails. "Gods," he muttered, "I hope this is all the blood required today."

"I'm hoping for more, myself," Vix muttered.

"Oh, get him out," Domitian snarled.

Vix darted out before Paulinus could take hold of his arm. The boy's shoulder had half-healed after his last bout in the Colosseum, and he rubbed it absently as he looked out into the green wetness of the gardens. Paulinus spoke briefly to a pair of guards and then joined him. They were the only loiterers. The Emperor, on the day of his supposed death, had ordered the Domus Augustana cleared of everyone but Praetorians, slaves, and a few selected Imperial pets. Where normally the marble halls thronged with togas and buzzed with whispers, today there was only the slap of sandals as slaves hurried about their tasks, the nervous exchange of passwords as the guards changed, and the lonely *plash* of the massive fountain. "Quiet today," Vix observed.

"It'd be quieter if you quit baiting the Emperor," said Paulinus. "The mood he's in, he might lop your head off."

"He's always in a mood." Vix pried up a pebble from an urn of flowers and lobbed it into the massive oval fountain with a splash. "Doubt he'll kill me, though. He's looking forward to my next bout too much."

"Aren't you? Your mother said you always wanted to be a gladiator."

"Wasn't exactly what I thought it would be." Vix hesitated. "People—they die hard."

Vix's head drooped wearily, and it trembled on Paulinus's tongue to tell the boy he wouldn't be fighting in any more arenas if Fortuna favored their plan that night. But they'd kept the secret too well to spread it now.

"Cheer up, young Vix." Nessus wandered past in old scuffed sandals, dull-eyed and vague-faced, fingering a little gold chain about his neck that had once belonged to Ganymede. "The stars all say the Emperor will be dead by tonight's moonrise, and then all your troubles are over."

"Not him. He won't die today." Vix lobbed another stone, viciously. "He'll die old, in a nice soft feather bed with a cup of wine in his hand. Bastard."

"You'll die old, too," said Nessus, indifferent. "Driving a

chariot too fast because even when you're an old general with a
devoted legion that calls you Vercingetorix the Red, you'll still
like fast horses and fast fights. You'll die fast, too, though you'll
hang on long enough for your officers to crowd around you and
weep. There's a woman who will weep for you, too, though she
won't be able to show it. An arch will be built in your honor, and
afterward your men will toast your memory on enough wine to
float your funeral barge down to Pluto, and swear there was
never a man like you. How's that for a death, young Vercingetorix? Not that you believe me anyway, because you don't believe
in the stars."

"You're nuts," Vix muttered.

"Do I get a prediction, too?" Paulinus called after Nessus,
but the astrologer had already drifted away: a fading ghost
down the silent, echoing hallways.

LEPIDA

I came to Marcus's house for a last attempt to persuade him
to remarry me—I hadn't slept with him for years, but it was
worth a try. But he wasn't there. "Gone to the Capitoline
Library, Domina. He left orders we were not to allow you—"

"Allow?" Five minutes of my tongue brought the slaves into
a more submissive mood; they'd obeyed me too long as mistress
to be shed of the habit yet. I wandered inside, flopping moodily
on a blue-cushioned couch in the atrium. Poky quiet house. No
one had ever made assignations in the corners here, or giggled
over risqué jokes, or even drunk too much wine. And I was no
longer mistress of this poky little house. No longer Lady Lepida
Pollia, the senator's wife. Oh, I laughed it off as best I could—
"Really, I was so tired of dreary old Marcus, you can't
imagine!"—but people whispered about the speed with which
Marcus had disposed of me after thirteen years of marriage . . .
and so soon after Domitian had disposed of me as well. Marcus
hadn't charged me with adultery—I'd kept my mouth shut about
Paulinus, and so far Marcus had kept his word—but all those
fat Roman matrons jealous of my success took any chance they
could to whisper. And one or two of my lovers had found themselves inexplicably busy these past weeks, wary that I was looking for a new husband.

Everyone who was anyone wanted Lady Lepida Pollia for a mistress. No one who was anyone wanted me for a wife.

"Mother?" Sabina came into the room, reading a scroll, and curtsied hastily as she saw me. "Father's not here. An Imperial messenger came, and he had to go out. I'll tell him you called." She turned away.

"Wait," I said. "I thought he went to the library."

"Oh—" Sabina dropped her scroll, leaned down to pick it up again. "Well, maybe he did. Excuse me, Mother, my tutor is expecting me."

"Stop." I uncoiled off the couch. "Did you say an *Imperial* messenger?"

Her eyes slid to one side. "I thought—"

"The Domus Augustana has been locked up like a fortress for weeks. The Emperor's orders. Who would be sending Marcus messages?"

"The Empress." Sabina drew herself up. "She has great respect for my father. Some people do, you know."

"Well, what a rude little queen you are." My daughter turned hastily to go, and my hand shot out and fastened on her wrist. "I think we need to have a little chat, darling. After all, now that I've been divorced I have so much more time to spend with you."

"I don't have anything to say to you." Edging back.

"Oh, I think you do." Something clicked in my head, the reason why Domitian had locked his palace up like a fortress. "Today is the day Domitian is supposed to die. On a day like that, the Empress should be locked up tight with her guards. So why is she sending your father messages?"

THEY met in the Gardens of Lucullus: two curtained litters pausing briefly beside each other.

"Thank you," said the Empress behind her half-drawn curtain. "I know it's short notice."

"Paulinus?" Marcus said sharply.

"No, no, he's at the palace soothing Domitian. He's the only one who can. We've a different problem. I've sent my page to summon Arius and Thea—your house is empty?"

"Yes, Sabina is busy with her tutor in the afternoons and I've ordered the slaves to turn away all visitors. What's wrong?"

"We may have to put the plan forward."

LEPIDA

Dᴀʀʟɪɴɢ, I don't like it when you lie to me." I stroked Sabina's arm. "The slaves say Marcus went to the library. You say
he got a message from the Empress. So who is lying?" My nails
were freshly lacquered, and they left little red marks in her arm.

"I was wrong, he's at the library."

"Oh, I don't think so." Stroking my daughter's hair. "You
saw him get a message from the palace, and away he went.
Probably to meet the Empress. What can they possibly want to
talk about on a day like today?" I wound my fingers into her
hair. Just a little tug, to encourage her.

"I don't know, I—*ouch*—"

Irritation surged. I gave her hair a sharp yank. "You're lying."

"I'm not lying, I'm not—"

A knock sounded at the door. "Domina?" A slave's timid
voice.

"My daughter is having one of her fits," I said. "Go away."
As soon as the footsteps retreated, I jerked Sabina's head back
nearly between her shoulder blades. "Marcus and the Empress
meet often, do they?"

"Why shouldn't they?" She was sniveling now, tears swimming in her eyes.

"They're not humping each other, that's for certain. So why
else would they meet?" Another little jerk. "Does anyone else
meet with them?"

"Let me go!"

I hauled her upright. "Oh dear," I sighed. "Am I hurting
you?" I stroked Sabina's cheek, and then slapped her. She cried
out, and rage surged up suddenly—rage I'd felt stewing in my
middle since Marcus divorced me. *Who? Who do they meet?*
Sabina was on the floor, shielding herself from my slaps.

"I don't know! I never saw them!"

"You do know! You filthy little rabbit-faced liar, how dare
you lie to me!" I seized her hair, wrenching her head around
and bringing it against the corner of the table. I could hardly
see my daughter through the red fog. "Where—did—you—
see—them?"

"Here," said Sabina, and began to sob.

* * *

Read it, Marcus." A folded piece of parchment passed between the litters. "One of my slaves brought it to me an hour ago."

Marcus read swiftly. "I see." His voice was neutral. "Will he deliver it soon?"

"Domitian is not slow to send out death warrants."

"It lists only 'treason' as cause of arrest. Does he know something?"

"No, I wasn't followed to any of our meetings. But he's wanted me dead for a decade, and whatever his reasons he's decided now is the time. I will probably"—calmly—"be dead very soon. Unless tonight—"

"Tonight? No. He'll be too wary—Paulinus would have to press him, and then he'd suspect Paulinus—"

"Domitian will certainly torture me for the names of my fellow traitors," the Empress said crisply. "As Domitian's wife I have acquired a certain endurance against pain, but I doubt you'll wager Paulinus's life on that. Will you?"

LEPIDA

It—it was weeks ago—after I went to bed, I heard voices—looked out my window—"

"Who did you see?" My hands stung, but I gave her another slap.

"The Empress. And—and a woman with dark hair—"

"What woman?"

"Just a slave woman! She had dark hair and a low voice. And there was a man with her, a legionnaire or something—he, he had lots of scars—"

Ice crawled down my spine. I took Sabina's ear between my lacquered nails, pinching as hard as I could. "A slave woman with a low voice? Tall? Scars on her arms?"

". . . Yes."

"Thea," I said aloud. Of course. She was always turning up in my path. "And a soldier, you say?" No doubt her latest protector, after she'd dried her tears over the Barbarian. Some aging thug she'd wiled into helping her get her ghastly son back. "Is that all, Sabina? If you're holding anything back—"

"I'm not, I'm not, I swear!"

I released Sabina's ear, and she fell forward onto the tiles, tears running down out of her eyes to mix with the blood on her mouth. I really felt quite benevolent toward her. Who would have thought such a stupid little thing could be so observant? She might not know anything more, but I could figure out the rest on my own. Put a cast-off wife, a jealous old senator, and a discarded mistress into the same picture . . . well, what did they all have in common? Who did they all hate?

Besides me, of course.

I bent and kissed Sabina's forehead, brushing the tears away with a finger. "Thank you ever so much, darling. Goodness, I'm sorry about the bruises, but you really did make me very angry. I'll buy you something pretty tomorrow to make up for it." Now, of course, I had to leave for the Domus Augustana—perhaps a quick pause by my Palatine villa to change into my new blue silk with sapphires? No, no time to waste; the red silk and pearls I'd worn today would do well enough. I already had my good litter pulled up at the house's back entrance, and the two big slaves I'd brought for guards—

"Sabina, if anyone comes to the house, don't tell them I was here—"

My daughter stumbled to her feet and shoved me away. Her lip was bleeding, and I noticed with surprise that she was almost as tall as I was. *Get away from me!* she shrieked, and she fled the room.

Well, really. What a whining little weasel.

THEA

THE steward's scandalized glance told me that he was not accustomed to admitting wild-eyed women and scarred thugs to the Norbanus house.

"Is Senator Norbanus at home?" I asked.

"No one. May I ask what—"

"No." I swept ahead with my chin in the air as if I were still Lady Athena, and he moved out of my way. Perhaps Arius's scowl over my shoulder helped. "Where is the senator?"

"I really can't let you—"

"Shut up," Arius growled.

We crowded down the narrow entrance passage: the steward wringing his hands, Arius fingering his knife, me turning back to hush them all—and when I rounded the corner I bumped into a small soft figure backed by two huge slaves. A figure in red silk, smelling strongly of musk.

For one wild second, Lepida Pollia and I gazed at each other.

She was faster. "Grab them," she said to her slaves, and then she stepped out of the way.

Arius lunged, blade whipping out. But in that narrow passage his shoulder slammed into mine, knocking me sprawling, and before I could take a breath one of Lepida's slaves grabbed me by the hair and thrust me up against the wall with a knife against my throat.

I froze, the blade pricking the flesh under my jaw. The steward froze, his mouth a round O of surprise. Arius froze, knife paused halfway through its arc to the second guard's belly.

Only Lepida moved.

"Drop that knife," she said to Arius. "Or watch her die."

The knife clattered on the floor.

"Still the same Barbarian," she trilled. Her eyes were glowing. "My, I was certain you were dead—but I'd know you anywhere. Even with that dreadful beard. Walk," she told the slave at my back. "Take her to—oh, Marcus's library will do. Arius, follow slowly. One sudden move, and she dies."

The big slave walked me into the library. My mind was numb. *Marcus, Marcus, did you betray us?*

"Tie them up." Lepida pointed; an imperious child. "Use lots of rope on him."

Arius stood quite still in the middle of the room, his eyes flicking from Lepida to me and back again. The slaves roped him roughly, and his eyes blazed.

"Better tie him to a pillar, too," Lepida decided. "Just to be safe. As for her, you can just put her on that chair and tie her hands. She's too stupid to be dangerous."

The slave took the knife away from my throat, and Arius lunged. The rope caught his feet around the ankles and he fell, taking half a dozen slaves with him. He got an arm free, and one of the guards howled as his nose exploded in a spray of blood.

But the other closed in, swinging a club, and I heard the familiar sound of my lover's bones snapping.

No. No. No.

They roped him to a pillar, cracking his head against the marble, and I saw a trickle of blood slide from his hair into his dizzied eyes.

"I hope they didn't break anything too important." Lepida peered at Arius from a good distance. "Leave some for the Imperial executioners."

Arius spat a mouthful of blood at her.

"Your temper hasn't sweetened with age, has it?" She looked back and forth between us. "Excellent. Now, as for you"—to the slaves—"back to your quarters, all of you. If any of you make a sound, I'll find out and I'll feed you to the eels. You two"—pointing to her own hulking guards—"lock the slaves in their quarters. Search the house; I want them *all* confined in case anyone decides to run a message to Marcus. Then wait outside with my litter."

She might not be mistress here anymore, but the slaves had lost none of their fear of her. They filed meekly through the door, throwing wide-eyed looks behind them, prodded along by Lepida's two thugs. Lepida waited until the door closed, then whirled on us, color shining high in her cheeks. "Oh, how lovely," she breathed. "What am I going to do with you two?"

Over her shoulder through the half-open door, I saw a flicker. A pair of blue eyes in a narrow bruised little face. Marcus's daughter? Lepida's daughter? I expected a scream, but the blue eyes took everything in silently, and she was gone as fast as she'd come.

"Well," said Lepida, oblivious. "I can't be too long, because I've got an appointment at the Domus Augustana. And you two have an appointment here—with my husband, I assume. Some plot against the Emperor? How like Marcus."

I couldn't breathe. Couldn't swallow. Couldn't even blink. *No. No.*

"I can't imagine the details of your little plot, but I'm sure the Emperor's torturers will get it out of Marcus." Lepida smiled. "The Emperor will be very grateful to me, I imagine. What should I ask for? I won't have to ask him to knock the head off your beloved Arius here, or your son. He'll do that any-way. I could ask him to leave you alive, though—you could be my maid again! Polish my nails, scrub my back, do my hair. You were always very good at hair."

I had nothing to say to her. I could only hope her daughter had her father's character instead of her mother's and had gone to warn him.

Lepida whirled, showing off the flash of her white arms and ankles against the crimson silk, and then suddenly bent low. "So what's your secret?"

"Secret?"

"You held Domitian for years. How?"

Her pointed tongue flickered over her rouged lips, and I saw just how badly she wanted to know. From despair I dredged a smile. "I didn't give him what he wanted."

"What did he want?"

"Everything. So I didn't give it, and it kept him interested. I imagine you gave him everything? You've always been obvious. No wonder he got tired of you so soon."

Her smile slipped.

"Not only are you obvious," I added for good measure. "You're a crashing bore."

She slapped me across the face. "You gave *him* everything!" She pointed a scarlet-lacquered fingernail at Arius: roped, slit-eyed, and silent against his pillar. "You'd have spread your legs for him in the middle of the forum if he wanted! How did you keep him for so long, if you didn't hold anything back?"

"Because Arius isn't insane," I explained patiently. "Domitian, in case you haven't noticed, is."

"You don't know anything about men."

"Of course," I agreed, feeling light-headed. "And that's why they all like me better than you."

She slapped me again. This time I was ready for it, and I got her little finger with my teeth. She had to pull at my hair to get free.

"You get everything!" She glared at me, shaking her fingers. "You got Domitian; you got him—" Lepida whirled on Arius. "Why her? She's a gawky Jewish slave; there are a thousand girls like her. There's only one of me!"

At any other time I would have thought it funny; a decade-old insult still biting at her pride. Beautiful women are so easily crushed.

"Why?" She drew back her silk skirts and kicked Arius in

his injured ankle; he drew a breath through his teeth. "Why her? Why not me?"

He regarded her briefly. "Because you look like a ferret."

She hissed, drawing back to slap him. His eyes gleamed. For a moment her hand hovered.

Then she straightened. Smoothed her hair and her face. Turned her elegant head back toward me, pearls swinging in her ears. "Well, Thea. It's been lovely, but I really must be going. I could take you with me, but Arius is so unpredictable in close quarters . . . no, I'd better leave you here. There aren't any slaves to free you, after all, and Marcus is off whispering with the Empress. He won't get to you before I get to the Domus Augustana, if that's what you're hoping. Yes, I'll just leave you here. The Emperor awaits."

She whirled back suddenly and gave Arius a brief, savage kiss. Pulling away before he could move, she strolled to the polished steel mirror on the wall and patted her lip rouge. "He has a sweet mouth, Thea," she said. "The next to kiss it will be the ravens flying around the Gemonian Stairs. When they eat his head off a spear."

P REFECT." One of the guards snapped a salute, catching Paulinus as he restlessly paced the atrium wondering if the sun had actually come to a halt in the sky. "Someone to see you, sir."

"No visitors today, you know the orders."

"She was most insistent, Prefect. She claims to be your sister."

"My sister?" For gods' sake. "Tell her I'll visit her tomorrow."

"She says it's vital, Prefect."

Paulinus hesitated. When had Sabina ever imposed on him here? And how had she *gotten* here . . . or was their father with her? "Where is she?"

"The Tiber Gate."

She wasn't alone by the time he reached her. "It's important," he heard the small figure in blue say in exasperation to someone behind the gateway pillar. "I have to get a message to Prefect Norbanus, and if they won't let me in to see him—"

"C'mon, it can't be that serious. Why don't you give me a kiss instead?" Paulinus quickened his pace to the gate, seeing a rough brown tunic and a familiar blunt head bent far too close to his little sister. "I'm the Young Barbarian, maybe you've heard of me. Seen me in the arena, even? I've killed two men, I'm the next great gladiator—"

Paulinus clubbed the back of Vix's head. "That's my sister you're pressing up against the wall, boy." He usually felt more sorry for Thea's son than anything, but Vix looked so much like his thug of a father as he loomed over Sabina that all sympathy vanished. Paulinus aimed another swat, and Vix ducked with easy speed. The Colosseum had certainly honed the brat's reflexes. "Go away," Paulinus ordered. "Find something to kill."

"Who's gonna make me?"

"About two cohorts of Praetorian guards if I give the order, so—"

"Boys." Sabina's voice cut across them both. She stood glaring at them with the Tiber sparkling behind her, small and pretty with her blue veil pulled up over her head—and bruised, Paulinus saw for the first time. Disheveled, too, as though she had run gasping all the way from his father's house.

Dread prickled him.

Sabina grabbed Paulinus's fingers in one hand and Vix's rough paw in the other, tugging them both back into the shadow of the gate beyond the earshot of the guards. "He can stay," she said as Paulinus glanced at Vix. "It's his business, too."

"It is?" Vix blinked.

"Hush." She lowered her voice and began to speak rapidly.

MARCUS was late back to the house—a cart had overturned on Quirinal Hill, blocking the flow of litters and wagons for three blocks. He'd finally abandoned his litter and walked, worry snapping at him sharper than the ache of the limp he'd acquired in the Year of Four Emperors. Putting the plan forward, it was mad—

"Quintus?" Marcus called for his steward as he limped painfully into his blue-tiled atrium. A muffled voice called back. Not his steward's.

"Up here!"

Marcus mounted the stairs, trepidation rising, and struck open the door of his tablinum.

"No questions," Thea said wearily. "Just untie us."

He set to work on the knots binding her wrists. "What happened?"

"Lepida." Thea stood up, rubbing her chafed hands. "She's on the way to the Domus Augustana now. To tell the Emperor."

Marcus swore. "How did she—"

"Does it matter?" Arius shrugged against his pillar. "She knows. Tied us up here and took off for the palace."

"We were going to put the plan forward anyway. Tonight—"

"Not tonight. Now."

Marcus looked at the sun outside the window, just starting to slant over the Tiber. "He won't believe he's safe for another two hours. Until then he'll be on his guard—"

"Too bad." Thea worked at the knots on Arius's ankles. "Can you hold a sword?"

He nodded impatiently. But when he rose his foot gave way and he staggered.

"What happened?" Every curse Marcus had ever heard poured through his head in six separate languages.

"Your wife's thugs. But"—taking a series of hopping steps across the room—"if the bones aren't poking out of the skin, they'll hold."

Marcus stared at him. "You're mad."

Arius bent into a series of stretches.

"Even if you can hold yourself together, we can't get you into the Emperor's suite. Even Paulinus can't persuade Domitian to receive visitors, not until the hour of his supposed death is past."

Thea unraveled her hair from its plait, letting it fall over her shoulders. "There's someone he'll receive."

Marcus looked at her. Arius looked at her. "No," said Arius.

"Can you distract him long enough?" said Marcus.

"She's not distracting anyone. She's not going."

"I *am* going." She headed for the door. Arius reached her in two strides—strides without even a trace of a limp, Marcus noticed—and seized her arm. He grabbed her elbows, lifting her off her feet when she tried to jerk away.

"You can't go. He'll kill you."

"He'll kill you, too."

"The danger's less. He doesn't know me, hasn't even seen me for years. You he'll take apart."

"He's tried to take me apart many times before. I can get

through it once more when my son's life is at stake." Her voice hardened. "I'm not just going to sit in the stands and pray this time. *I want my share.*"

Arius swung on Marcus. "You know what he is. What he'll do."

Marcus shrugged. "Her choice."

"Exactly." Thea's eyes slitted.

"Thea." Arius gripped her shoulders. "You'll be killed. I can't stand—"

"Oh, you can stand it." Her voice was brutal. "I've stood it often, watching you in the arena. *Let me go.*"

They stood swaying, breast to breast, eye to eye.

Arius's fingers uncurled, one at a time. His eyes burned black.

"Damn you," he whispered. "God damn you."

She turned her back on him, sweeping through the door. Arius stared after her for a moment, then turned to look at Marcus. There was something blank and savage and impersonal in his gaze now that made Marcus want to retreat.

"Time to lie low, Senator," said the Barbarian. "Nothing more for you to do."

Thea was already descending the stairs, every inch the Imperial mistress: head high, hair loose, eyes empty.

SABINA spoke rapidly. "'Linus, my mother found out what you're plotting—"

Paulinus blinked shock. "I'm not plotting anyth—"

"Oh, don't be stupid! There isn't time." Giving his hand a little shake. "She found out, and she's coming here, and—"

"Huh?" said Vix.

"'Linus and my father are plotting with your father—"

"Hey, my father's dead." Vix suddenly looked wary.

"No, he's not." Exasperated. "Somebody Father called the Barbarian came to our house a few nights ago. And you're the Young Barbarian, aren't you? It wasn't hard to figure out. So they're all plotting, and my mother—"

"Who's your mother?" Vix interrupted before Paulinus could grab hold of this strange streaming conversation.

"Lady Lepida Pollia."

"That bitch?" He pulled back, wary again.

"That bitch," Sabina agreed, making Paulinus blink again.

Vix shrugged sagely. "You can't let a mother get in your way."

"No, you can't," Sabina agreed, much struck, and turned back to Paulinus. She outlined what had happened—her mother, Arius and Thea, all of it—in a few cool words. They all stood regarding each other. The Praetorian guard shouted something toward Paulinus. For the first time he saw the nervous crowds streaming past them toward the Forum, the guards edgy and restless at the gate, the sun slanting down toward the river. "I'll take care of everything," he said, then bent down to kiss Sabina on her bruised forehead. When this was all over, he'd take Lepida apart for daring to hurt his sister. "You were very brave to come here, Vibia Sabina."

"Yeah." Vix reached out and tipped her face up, admiring her bruises. "That bitch really went to work on you, didn't she? You know, a kiss from a gladiator will clear those marks right up—"

Paulinus swatted him.

"You've already cured me once, Vercingetorix." Sabina's eyes rested on Vix a moment, thoughtful. "We've met before, you know."

"We have?"

"At the games, when I was seven years old. You stole my pearl haircomb."

"Did not," Vix said automatically.

"Did too. But it's not important." Sabina smiled. "I had epilepsia back then. Someone got me some of your blood. Gladiator's blood cures fits, they say."

Vix grinned. "Did it work?"

"I ran all the way here from my house, and I kept thinking I'd have a seizure and not get here in time. But I didn't. In fact, I've never felt better." She stood on tiptoe, putting a small hand on the back of Vix's sunburned neck, and brushed her lips against his. "Worth a kiss, I'd say."

Vix's arms came instantly around her waist, but she disengaged herself, eyes going back to Paulinus before he could bristle. "Head off my mother, 'Linus," Sabina warned. "Or she'll ruin everything."

Paulinus gave a reluctant little salute in response and turned back toward the gate, propelling Vix before him. Easy enough to give a word to the guards, forbid Lepida entrance—although a large enough bribe might get her inside even so . . . He looked back at his sister, a small straight blue figure receding into the crowds. Thank all the gods there were for Sabina.

Vix swaggered, grinning. "She loves me."

"She's *twelve years old*," Paulinus growled, shoving Vix ahead of him. "Keep your grubby hands off!"

Thirty-four

❧❧

"THE wolves are gathering."

"Caesar?"

"They think they go unnoticed." Domitian prowled from one corner of the bedchamber to the other. His shape followed him in the dim reflections of the moonstone-paneled wall. "But a god hears all."

Paulinus shifted from foot to foot. He opened his mouth; closed it again.

"The Moon will be bloodied as she enters Aquarius." Domitian's voice was barely more than a whisper. "And a deed will be done that will be the talk of the entire world."

Paulinus's heart thudded sickly in his chest. *Now—now—now*—the time was now, and suddenly he could not speak. He heard the dull whine of a fly, and at the same moment Domitian's hand flashed. The whine muffled as tiny wings buzzed against the Imperial palm, and Domitian gave a wintry smile. "Flies don't interest me anymore," he told Paulinus. "People give so many more varied and interesting reactions."

"Caesar?" Paulinus ventured.

"Yes?" Crushing the fly idly.

"There's someone I think you should see." The words came out steady.

"Not before the fifth hour. You know my orders."

"She says—she says . . . I think you should see her."

"Who?"

"Athena, Caesar."

The silence spread out in ripples around the name.

"Athena." A tremor in the voice? The Emperor still stood with his face toward the corner, rich purple robe falling in grand lines from his shoulders, lamplight shining through the thin spot in his hair. "Did you have her stripped, checked for weapons?"

"I did, sir."

"Did she hide her face in shame?" Domitian raised a hand before Paulinus could answer. "No, she wouldn't. She stared straight ahead, didn't she, as the guards groped her. As if she didn't care. Like Julia when she stopped eating. May the gods rot her."

"Rot . . . who, Caesar?"

Domitian turned. "Show her in."

He took a seat on his sleeping couch, one hand sliding under the pillow to the dagger Paulinus knew he kept there. "Careful," Paulinus breathed to Thea as he marched her in, barely a breath of a warning, but she never blinked. She just stood, framed by the door, hair mantling her shoulders, her face blank—but her eyes watchful.

"Athena." The Emperor sounded jovial. "You look well. Hardy, even. A fit mother for a gladiator's brats. Come to beg for your son?"

"Yes, Caesar."

"Why today? You thought you'd ask for my mercy now, just in case I die in an hour as my astrologer predicts?"

"Yes."

"A practical people, you Jews."

"So we are."

Domitian's clenched fist struck his own knee, and Paulinus flinched. The Emperor had been relaxed and joking when he faced mutinous legions and blue-painted Chatti savages, but today he faced only fate . . . and Thea.

"You never say anything," Domitian said, staring at her. "Not really. I'd have the head ripped off your body, just so I could tear it open and see what was inside at last." Beckoning her closer. "But I know what I'd find."

"What would you find, Caesar?" Coming forward from the doorway.

"Nothing." He ran his fingers through the ends of her loose hair. "Smoke and a song."

"Caesar." She took a step forward, pressing her cheek against his hand. "Please."

"Please spare your son? Why should I?"

"Because he's a child."

"Don't you Jews have a saying—'the sins of the father shall be visited upon the children?' "

Paulinus opened his mouth, but found no words. Nothing, nothing could break the terrible duel before him.

Thea held out her hands. "Mercy. Mercy, Domitian."

Domitian tilted his head. "Did it hurt you, when I made him fight in the Colosseum?"

"You know it did." Pressing her face against his hand again. "Please—let Vix go. Take me instead."

"You're a common singing Jew. What makes you think I want you?"

"Because you do."

"Damn you." Domitian released her face abruptly and turned away. "Damn you. A common singing Jew, and you're the only one who plays back. The only one—"

His voice trembled a moment, and Paulinus saw Thea's eyes flare. She took a step forward, running a hand along the end of the sleeping couch.

"What do you want with Vix, anyway?" she cajoled. "What use is he to you? You don't like children—and as children go, he's appalling."

"True." Domitian turned. "Is he mine?"

She blinked. "You know he isn't. He's too old to be yours."

"I know." Domitian looked up at the ceiling, reflective. "I suppose it's just as well. A God cannot have sons—Jupiter himself murdered his child by Metis when he discovered that it would grow to be greater than he. But Vix . . ."

"What?"

Domitian shrugged. "He amuses me."

"I used to amuse you." Thea took another step forward. "Didn't I?"

He reached up toward her cheek again. But this time he wound her hair around his hand and forced her to her knees.

"Fear me?" he said, and for the first time Paulinus saw terror in his face. "You fear me, Athena? Say it. Please say it. Please—"

Then she said it.

"Yes."

LEPIDA

A short ride to the palace took me nearly an hour. A cart had turned over on some street or other; the wagons and litters were jammed for blocks. I had another time of it persuading the Praetorian to let me in. Only the assurance that I had information about a conspiracy—plus a good number of sesterces—bought me entry. Quite a changed place, with no messengers or courtiers or hangers-on scurrying about the lavish halls in their finest silks and perfumes. Only bunches of nervous-looking slaves, and absolutely hordes of guards.

"Lady Lepida!" Vix, the young darling of the Colosseum, caught my elbow impudently. "I've been looking for you—me and Prefect Paulinus."

"You were expecting me?"

"We had a warning you'd come. I'll take you to the Emperor. He's gone mad; only you can calm him down."

I smiled, letting him take my arm as I imagined his head stuck on a spear right beside his father's. It was such a pretty picture that I didn't notice when he led me down the wrong corridor. An empty slave's passageway, not an Imperial hall.

"This isn't—"

He caught my elbows behind me and popped my knees out with an expert jerk. Even before I hit the mosaics, he had his foot planted firmly between my shoulder blades.

"What are you doing?"

He doubled my arms up behind my back and began looping them with coils of cord pulled out of his sleeve.

I twisted and writhed underneath him, scratching at his hands. He shifted out of reach, his knee sinking into my back like lead. Impossible. Absurd. I was a grown woman; he was a boy of thirteen. Ridiculous that he should—get—the upper hand—this way—impossible—

I drew breath to scream, and he slapped a rag into my mouth. This couldn't be happening. He was a *child*.

He was tying up my ankles.

I kicked and struggled. I screamed curses through the gag. He took me by the feet and dragged me along the hall like a sack of potatoes. Dragged me to a little door in the wall that looked like a closet. It couldn't be a closet.

It was a closet.

He calmly put me in it. I doubled my feet up to kick him, but he jumped to one side and stuffed my knees through.

No. No. Lepida Pollia, soon to be Empress and Augusta of all Rome—stuffed into a broom closet by a thug of a child?

The door clicked shut. He stood on the other side, breathing a trifle heavily, and I waited for mockery. But like his father, he wasted no words. Just turned away and left me there, doubled up in the dark. Dimly I heard his voice farther down the hall.

"That you, Nessus? Look, do something for me—"

"The Emperor wants you." The astrologer's vague tones. "Now."

Vix cursed. "Look, find Prefect Norbanus for me and tell him Lady Lepida's been taken care of. All right?"

"What do you mean?" The astrologer's voice held a faint question.

"None of your business. Just tell him she's out of the way. And, um. Don't go looking in any closets."

Retreating footsteps—and then I was alone.

THEA

THE look in my son's eyes appalled me as the guards shoved him through the door, but for a moment all I could do was drink in the sight of him. Taller, almost as tall as me, with new muscle in his right arm where he'd practiced with a shield. Oh, Vix—

"Spring for my throat, Young Barbarian," said the Emperor, "and she dies."

I could feel Domitian grinning over my head. His eyes sparkled, color rose high in his cheeks, and his mouth parted in that Flavian smile that could charm the gods. His hand rested casually on the stem of my neck, and my hair coiled over his feet where I crouched on the floor.

"Say hello to your son, Athena," said the Emperor, stroking my throat.

"Hello, Vix." Through the curtain of my hair I saw the shock jagging away from his face, swiftly replaced by terror.

"Say hello, Vercingetorix. Like a good boy."

"You—" Vix sounded as if he'd eaten arena sand. "You said you'd let her alone."

"Oh, but she came to me. To beg for your life, of course. Which must have taken a great deal of courage because—tell him why, Athena."

I pitched my voice low and unsteady. The best performance I'd ever have to give, and there wasn't even any music. "Because I fear you."

Domitian set his foot against my shoulder and shoved me sprawling. "Make your son believe it. Make him see."

"All right!" I reared up on my knees, biting down hard on my tongue to bring the tears springing to my eyes. "All right, I'm terrified! Is that what you want to hear? Every time you touch me, every time you look at me—I can't think, can't breathe—and I hate you! Hate you—*hate you*—" I collapsed into sobs, rocking back and forth on my knees. But my eyes burned dryly against my hands.

Domitian threw his head back and laughed as if he'd just heard a good joke. I heard Vix lunge, but the Emperor just snapped his fingers, still chuckling, and two Praetorians grabbed my son at the elbows. "Aren't you the dutiful son, Vercingetorix."

Vix wrenched at the grip on his arms, muscles bunching like snakes under the skin—and stopped. Because I shot him a look between my splayed fingers, a look of pure iron. *Vix, you never obeyed me in your life*, I prayed. *Obey me now.*

"You fear me." Domitian petted my hair as he would have petted a dog.

"Yes, Lord and God." Dropping my face instantly back into my hands.

"Take your hands off her!" Vix howled.

Domitian frowned. Dropping my hair, he crossed the room and belted Vix twice across the face. His fists fell like Vulcan's hammers. "Quiet now," he said. "I'll get to you later—what?"

The Emperor whipped around, following the flick of Vix's eyes, but only saw me shivering beside the sleeping couch. It had taken just a bare instant while Domitian's back was turned and the guards struggled to hold Vix: a bare instant to flash my hand under his pillows and draw out his dagger. Another instant to flick it spinning below the couch, and then I was rocking and weeping again: a threat to no one.

Domitian crossed back to my side. "So. Where were we, Athena?"

The guards hammered at Vix to still him, and I longed to leap for the dagger. Not yet. So I crouched and cried as my son sagged bloody-nosed between two Praetorians, and the Emperor pulled me onto his lap on the bed.

"Crying," he said. "You've never cried easily."

I found it quite easy now.

"Perhaps I'll take you again, one more time—for old times' sake, shall we say. Your son here can watch. But afterward, my dear, I don't think I'll bother watching you die. One dead Jewess is very much like another, after all."

"Sir." A double knock at the door; Paulinus's voice. I'd never heard anything so welcome in my life. "A moment?"

"Enter."

Paulinus gave a smart salute, meticulously keeping his eyes from me. Domitian pushed me aside and saluted back, smiling. I wondered with a mad calmness if he had orders for Paulinus's death, too, once his own finally struck. The best friend of a god would surely not be allowed to outlast the god himself . . .

"A slave has arrived, sir," Paulinus was saying. "He claims to have information about a conspiracy."

"Conspiracy." Domitian started upright. "Dear gods, what time is it?"

I spoke, muffling my voice in the corner of the couch. "A little past the sixth hour." I raised my eyes, red-rimmed with surreptitious rubbing. "You managed to cheat death after all, Caesar. May God damn you."

"The sixth hour?" Domitian's eyes swung toward the vast window, where the sun still showed over the Tiber.

"The sixth." Paulinus sounded puzzled. "I thought you'd be keeping track."

"I was . . . distracted." Domitian's smile grew and broadened. "Nessus caught in a mistake at last! Him and his stars." The Lord and God of Rome rose from the sleeping couch. "I feel young again—like I could conquer Persia. Perhaps I will. My cloak, Paulinus. I'll dine well tonight."

"The slave, sir?" Paulinus asked. "He says he has important information."

Domitian hesitated, then shrugged. "Show him in."

Paulinus dismissed the guards, and Domitian settled himself on the edge of his sleeping couch. "Enter, slave. You are—?"

"Stephanus, Lord and God." The voice rumbled in my ears. "Former gardener to Lady Flavia Domitilla." I trained my eyes on the carved silver arm of the sleeping couch, still weeping softly, every nerve in my body humming like a harp string. The only thing I saw of Arius was the white sling that muffled his arm.

Domitian frowned. "You have information?"

"Found papers. Didn't look right to me." The knotted brown hand I loved so well passed over a scroll: lists of closely written names.

"Senator Nerva?" said Domitian, reading. "Who would have thought?" He unrolled the parchment, and as I risked a glance up, I saw his eyes fell on Vix. My son, crouched forgotten in the corner where the guards had dropped him—but his head was up, and his blazing eyes fixed directly on the slave supposedly named Stephanus. The slave behind whose head the sun slanted much too high over the Tiber for twilight.

DOMITIAN'S eyes flicked back and forth, panic settling in just as Arius pulled a dagger from the sling around his arm.

The Emperor screamed as the dagger plunged into his groin.

The demon howled its pleasure. Arius howled back.

He flung himself forward, shaking the false bandage off his arm, and struck again. The Emperor got an arm up and the blade sheared along the length of the bone. Blood leaped up, spraying Arius's face. He breathed it in like Indian perfume.

In the dull reflection of the moonstone, he saw Thea grope under the bed in the tangle of silk sheets, snatching up the Emperor's fallen dagger, half-running and half-falling across the room to throw herself over Vix. That first blow in the groin had been for her. For the weeping he'd heard as he waited outside the door. For the Emperor's laughter.

Domitian clawed screaming for his eyes. Arius twitched his head to one side, feeling the bloody fingers skate off his cheek, and drove his fist into Domitian's throat. The blow flung the

Emperor against the silk cushions of the couch, where he scuttled backward like a spider, scrabbling for the dagger that never left its place under his pillow. Arius waited until his groping fingers had found nothing—until his eyes flew to Thea in panicked accusation.

Then he gutted Domitian like a fish.

"GUARDS!" the Emperor screamed, doubling over. "GUARDS!"

No guards. Paulinus had assigned them to the other end of the palace grounds, sent them on pointless errands, bluntly bribed them with Marcus's gold. Arius could see Paulinus from the corner of his other eye, pressed rigid against the wall.

Pretty boy, the demon whispered. *Forget him.*

The mad black fury roared up so fast his vision slipped. Just like the early days of the Colosseum, the days when the world had been a sword and a stretch of sand and someone to kill, nightmares afterward and no Thea to sing them away. He struck again, crushing Domitian down into a bed full of blood and silk, and it wasn't enough.

"Paulinus!" Domitian shouted. The pretty boy's hand went to his *gladius* as if he were about to fall on Arius, and Arius tensed to fight two men at once, but Paulinus never moved. Only stood against the wall, rock still, his eyes huge.

"*Paulinus!*" Domitian looked at his closest friend with eyes swimming in blood, and Arius let him look until betrayal swam to the top and Paulinus looked away.

The Emperor howled, scrabbling, and Arius straddled Domitian without haste, dropping a knee between the Emperor's shoulder blades. He plunged his blade into the broad back, shearing the spine through like a silk rope. The Emperor gave a quiet gasp.

He's dying, thought Arius remotely. *I'm killing the Emperor of Rome.*

"No!" The shout broke from Paulinus as he lunged away from the wall. The blow caught Arius sideways, knocking him off the Emperor. He came up rolling, but Paulinus had dropped to one knee over the Emperor's body, holding Arius off at dagger point. "It's enough, for gods' sake, let him die like a man—"

"*He's not a man!*" Arius snarled.

But Paulinus never heard him. He lifted Domitian up in frantic, loving hands. Blood poured everywhere. Paulinus was weeping.

"Caesar—Caesar, I'm sorry—*get away from him*," he snarled at Arius, slashing out with the dagger. The blade missed Arius by an inch.

Domitian tugged the hard brown arm.

"Caesar—" Paulinus bent closer. "Sir—"

Domitian tore the dagger from Paulinus's hand, and ripped his throat out.

Thea screamed.

Arius lunged. Too late.

"Justina," Paulinus whispered in surprise, and died.

THEA

I struggled stiffly away from my son, falling across Paulinus, toward Domitian where he lay faceup on the mosaics, strangling on his pulped lungs. I crawled over him, nailing his body with my body, his gaze with my gaze.

I never feared you, I told him. *I never feared you.*

I looked into his black eyes until they glazed over.

FOR a long time there was no talk. I lay across Domitian, covered in his blood. Vix sat frozen in his corner. Arius half-knelt beside Paulinus's body, gazing blindly ahead. No one stirred. No one spoke.

Then Arius threw the dagger away from him. It bounced off the opposite wall, and at the clatter Vix gave a violent tremor.

"God," he said in a cracked voice. "God."

Arius stretched out a tired arm, and Vix turned into the hard shoulder. Arius reached around the back of his weeping son's neck, took the welded silver collar between his hands, and snapped it in two. He flung it against the wall where it fell with a soft rattle, the black eye just a lump of jet. Arius's eyes squeezed shut a moment, and when they opened again the demon had gone out of them.

I crawled over Domitian's body and collapsed on my lover's other shoulder. He turned his lips into my hair, and I felt the tremors deep in his body.

We were still sitting like that, three locked in one, when the world crashed in.

LEPIDA

HOURS in the dark—hours and hours. I screamed through the gag, pounding at the door of the closet with my sandaled feet, but no one came. Domitian had ordered most of the slaves away, on the day he was supposed to die.

He wasn't dead yet. He couldn't be dead yet. He'd live to hear me speak, and then he'd kiss my feet and crown me Lady and Goddess, because thanks to *me* he was alive.

Scuffling sounds outside. I shrieked through the gag, drumming my heels. A scraping sound, and then light blinded my eyes as the door dragged open. I blinked furiously, and saw the blank round face of the astrologer. Nessus.

"There are a great many closets in this palace," he said, expressionless. "I must have looked through a hundred."

"Untie me at once," I spat as he pulled the gag from my mouth. "Where is the Emperor? I have information about a conspiracy. The Empress is involved, and his precious pet Vix—"

"Ganymede," said the astrologer.

"What?" Loosening cords from my wrists. If I could just get to Domitian, I could have Thea and Arius and Vix and Marcus and Paulinus in chains by night's end, every enemy I had—

"Ganymede. Do you remember him?"

"Remember who?"

His hands locked about my throat before I knew what he was doing. "Nessus—" I choked out, and then his fingers took my breath away.

"Ganymede." He crushed me back against the wall, squeezing. "Ganymede."

I gasped, scrabbling at his wrists. Two of my nails broke—he'd pay for that—!

"Ganymede." His face was blank as marble as his hands sank deeper and deeper into my throat, like a ring of red-hot iron. "Ganymede."

I left great claw marks on the skin of his arms, thrashing from side to side as a choking blindness filled my head. Guards would come, they would kill Nessus, they would take me to the Emperor—my hair came down in tangled snakes; I'd be a mess when Domitian saw me—

"Ganymede." Squeezing. "Ganymede."

My throat was a mass of flames, and numb little flickers of pain trickled down my limbs. No. This could not happen. I was Lepida Pollia, Lady and Goddess of Rome—I was beautiful, and Fortuna loved me—

"Ganymede."

I feel the blood pump through my neck between his hands.

"Ganymede," he says. Blood runs down his arms from my scratches. I bat weakly at his hands, and the red of my lacquered nails mixes with the blood on his arms.

I summon all my strength and scream. Nothing comes out—nothing but a single strangled gasp as my eyes darken and my limbs go numb.

"Ganymede," he whispers.

I sag against the wall, feeling my tongue protruding. The astrologer's contorted face comes to me dimly through the black flowers blooming across my eyes. *Who*, I try to say, *who, who*—but I have no breath left.

Who is Ganymede?

Thirty-five

～❦❦～

MARCUS walked home, and with every uneven step the thought repeated itself.

My son is dead.

He'd been unable to go home and wait when Arius and Thea left for the Domus Augustana. He'd found some pretext for loitering outside the palace gates . . . so he'd been one of the first on the scene when the blood was done flowing and the panic set in. One of the first to see Paulinus's gaping throat, the loose-tangled limbs, the outflung hand.

"Leave him, Marcus," the Empress had said. "We'll prepare him for a hero's funeral. The Emperor's friend who died trying to defend him."

Paulinus is dead.

Marcus stared at his own gate a moment before recognizing it. Slowly he struck the latch, limped through the garden, stepped into the dark empty hall.

Paulinus is dead.

He turned his head away from the thought, and his eyes fell on the atrium. A shadowy figure stood there in the moonlight, leaning against a pillar. "Calpurnia?"

She started, whirling around. Her eyes were huge holes in a white face. "Marcus," she whispered. "Oh gods, Marcus." She took three running steps across the atrium and flung her arms around him.

He opened his mouth to tell her, and drew in a confused breath of her scents: herbs, crushed mint, bread rising sweet in the oven; and then the pain kicked sharply, swelling through him until he thought he would die. He turned his face into her shoulder, dimly hearing her dismiss the curious slaves.

"You're all right." Her arms closed tight around his neck, her cheek pressed against his hair. "I can't believe it—waited for hours—didn't know where you were—and I don't want to know, but you're all right; you're all right and that's all I want. Oh gods, Marcus, don't leave me." She kissed his mouth and his eyes and his hands, over and over. "Don't leave me again, I can't bear it." She couldn't stop kissing him, and her mouth tasted like all good things on earth.

He reached up, slowly, and cupped her face in his hands.

"You're crying." She drew back, tasting the salt on his cheeks. "What is it?"

"Paulinus—Paulinus is—" He said the words while he could still force them out. "He's dead."

"Dead?" He felt a jerk go through her. "What do you mean, how—"

"Killed. And the Emperor," Marcus added leadenly.

"But Paulinus—" Her hand went to her mouth. "Oh, gods. Oh, Marcus, I'm sorry." She stepped close, leaning her forehead against his. "I'm so sorry."

"I've been offered—" He stopped, looking at his son's betrothed: pressed against him, her arms about his neck. His for the asking. When had that happened?

He drew a finger along her wide clear brow. "How would you like to be an Empress?"

"What?"

They've offered me the Empire, Calpurnia. The Empress offered it to me before, but because of Paulinus I refused. Because an Emperor should put the Empire above his family; he should adopt an heir to follow him, to be sure of getting the best man for Rome. And such a system will never work unless the Emperor has no jealous sons of his own blood who would expect to inherit. "You have no son now, Marcus Norbanus," the Empress had said over Paulinus's body. "Adopt the man we spoke of as your heir. Adopt him, and take the purple."

"Marcus?" Calpurnia kissed him again. "Marcus, what is it?"

"Nothing." He shook his head. "Calpurnia—I need to be alone. Will you—?"

She retreated at once, without question. Not so far he couldn't call her back with a single word, if he wanted.

He lowered himself onto the atrium's marble bench. *You have an hour*, the Empress had said. *In an hour, we must have an Emperor. You or another.* Half that time was gone. He folded his hands.

Emperor Marcus Vibius Augustus Norbanus.

Even with the grief howling inside him, he'd live for years yet. Enough years to get an Empire in order for a gifted and vigorous young successor. Enough years to soften the treason laws, repair relations with the Senate, commission enough monuments and temples to make Rome beautiful. Work—hard work, and years of it to undo the bad times—but he might as well use up his last years in the Empire's service.

Emperor Marcus Augustus. Living his days out in the palace surrounded by guards, addressing the Senate from the center of the floor instead of the back, raising his arm to acknowledge the cheers of the populace, presiding over triumphs and games in a purple cloak. Working his nights away to strengthen coinage and expand borders and build aqueducts. A man with no Empress—foolish of him to have mentioned it, because a young healthy wife would have children, sons who would expect to inherit the Empire themselves. A man with a princess for a daughter, a princess who would have to marry his adopted heir—a man three times her age—in order to strengthen the alliance. Marcus Augustus Caesar, twelfth Emperor of the Roman Empire, a face to be feared in life, worshipped in death, sculpted in marble for posterity.

You should be Emperor, Marcus, he remembered a woman saying to him once, long ago. Well, now he had his chance. The minutes ticked away, and he sat as still as the statue he could commission of himself by tomorrow morning, if he liked.

He fished for a scrap of parchment. For a pen. For ink. He wrote a single word. A yawning slave, roused from bed, ambled off with it toward the Domus Augustana.

Marcus turned his head into the shadows. He held out his

hand and waited with a slow, reluctant flutter of hope for the touch of Calpurnia's warm fingers.

THEA

T HE Empress brought the silence with her into her private tablinum. Outside, slaves screamed, guards rushed back and forth, the marble halls echoed with uproar, but she closed the door firmly behind me and locked it all out.

"The noise," she grimaced. "It's going to be a very noisy few days, I'm afraid. As soon as the Empire is staggering along under its own power again, I'm going to retire to a quiet little villa in Baiae where you can't hear anything but birds." The woman who had just murdered her husband settled down behind her desk with a businesslike air. "Perhaps I shall write my memoirs."

I blinked. A dozen slave women could testify that the Empress had been sitting innocently at her loom weaving household cloth when her husband was hacked apart, but she had certainly arrived speedily on the scene as soon as everything was done. Before the rush of slaves and guards flooded into the bloody Imperial bedchamber in her wake, Arius and Vix and I had all been efficiently whirled in separate directions. "For anonymity's sake," the Empress had explained as Vix disappeared down one hall, Arius down another, and she had grasped my elbow and escorted me personally from the moonstone-sheathed, blood-soaked bedchamber to her own private tablinum. I had no guarantee that she wouldn't . . . well, do anything. How well did I really know the Empress? How well did *anyone* know her?

"So where are Arius and my son?" I said, feeling the words float up from a long distance. "Some quiet little cell where you'll soon take me, where we'll all be strangled and disposed of? Is that part of your mopping up?"

"Twenty years ago, yes." The Empress frowned absently at one of her many lists. "But I've grown a trifle wiser with age. You and I, Thea, have the merit of being the only two women in the world to survive Domitian's affection. Surely a sign of divine favor, and I am not one to tamper with the gods' chosen."

"Then where is Arius?"

"Arius." The Empress checked off a point on one list. "Being privately patched up by my personal physician, who says he'll be good as new far sooner than any man of his age and habits has a right to expect. Although we'll put out an official announcement that he's dead," she added. " 'The slave Stephanus, chief assassin of our beloved Emperor, was mortally wounded himself during the epic struggle' etc. At least one villain must be publicly accounted for. We'll find a criminal's body to display on the Gemonian Stairs."

"Vix," I said. "What about him?"

"Your horrid son? Do you know, that child has destroyed an entire wing of the new palace? Gladiated it to smithereens! And there's been more than one coin purse missing ever since he— well, never mind. He ran off after being splinted."

"What? Where? You let him *go*?"

"Of course I didn't let him go. I would have known better than to turn my back on that beastly child for an instant. The physician did not. Oh, don't worry. The horrid boy—oh, he makes me so glad I never had children—will be back in no time. Probably going to fetch that little three-legged dog of yours. Arius was asking for it rather forcibly."

"Do you know everything, Domina?"

"Nearly," she said tranquilly. "I have the best spy network in the Empire."

She pulled out a wax tablet and began to write. I let out a shaky sigh and sank down onto the stool by the desk. My head hurt. I was still splashed in Domitian's blood. My son had disappeared; my lover was off getting patched up for the thousandth time. The last time? Surely that was too much to hope for.

"What are you writing?" I asked Domitian's widow.

"A nice new list." She vigorously underscored the heading with her stylus. " 'Things to Do.' Prepare a formal announcement for the public, summon the Senate to approve the new Emperor, arrange a quick coronation, do something about Flavia—"

"Lady Flavia? She's all right, then?"

"Oh, yes. I made sure of that. She's got her boy with her, the one your son and Paulinus saved, and was safely delivered of a little girl a few months ago. They're doing nicely, Flavia and the children, but it's high time someone got them off that dreary rock."

"You can't bring her back to Rome, surely."

"No. Better, I think, that the Flavian dynasty be pronounced extinct. But a country estate in Spain or Syria for a respectable widow and her two children—that should do very well. Yes, Spain would be nice. Perhaps I'll send her Nessus, too. He's looking rather lost, these days." A knock sounded at the door. "Enter."

A silent slave handed over a folded scrap of paper. "From Senator Marcus Norbanus, Domina."

Her eyes flicked across the single word on the scrap. "I thought so." She laid the parchment aside, picked up two sealed letters, and handed them to the slave. "Please deliver these to the appropriate addresses."

"Senator Norbanus won't take the purple?" I guessed as soon as the door clicked shut.

"What makes you think—"

"I'm not stupid, Domina."

"Well . . ." A shrug. "Marcus won't be Emperor. He'll probably try to retire from the Senate, too, but I won't have any of that. He's got years of service left in him, and anyway that rather sweet little Calpurnia Sulpicia should revive him."

I propped my chin on my hand. "He'd have made quite a Caesar."

The Empress raised an eyebrow as if surprised to hear a slave's opinion on such a subject. But I wasn't really much of a slave anymore, and the eyebrow went down again. "Well, we'll make do with Senator Nerva. Marcus and I settled on him originally—good lineage, distinguished career, utterly boring. I'd have preferred Marcus, but Nerva will do."

"Oh, he's not bad," I said. "I used to sing for him in Brundisium. Very generous with tips."

"Let us hope he is as generous with his taxes." The Empress leaned back in her chair, relaxing for the first time in all the years I'd observed her. "So," she said.

"So," I said.

We looked at each other.

"What will you do now, Domina?" I asked.

"Well—" she looked thoughtful. "I have a sister and two

cousins who haven't spoken to me in twenty years. This isn't the first time I've meddled with the doings of Emperors, you see, and they have always disapproved. Time to mend fences. Afterward, I think I shall retire to that quiet little villa in Baiae and live to an extremely virtuous old age." The Empress tilted her head. "And you, my dear?"

I shrugged. "Arius wants a mountain. He says he's going to be a gardener."

"How pastoral. Can he garden?"

"Lady Flavia said he killed most of the grapes in her north vineyard."

"Perhaps he'll get better. What about you—what do you want?"

"I just want Arius. Gardener or gladiator."

"What about your horrid son? Will he be happy with a mountain?"

"Maybe he'll have a few brothers and sisters he can drill into a legion."

"You're already carrying a child, aren't you?"

I smiled.

"Excellent. Raise it in good health. As for young Vercingeto-rix—" The Empress looked thoughtful. "He may command a real legion someday, if Nessus's horoscope is correct. That dreadful son of yours has talent, Thea. If he wants a job when he's a little older, he will be welcome in Rome. Under a different name, perhaps. I think we may have seen the last of the Young Barbarian. Though not, perhaps, of Vercingetorix." She shuddered.

Perhaps I should defend my son. Oh, perhaps not. I shrugged.

She produced a bundle of impressively stamped and sealed letters, counting them out one by one. "Papers of freedom for you, Arius, and that appalling child. Board of passage on a ship to Gibraltar, and then to Britannia. A purse with a sum for beginning a new life. An annual stipend to be paid anonymously on the first of every year, forwarded in trust to the governor at Londinium who will ask no questions of whoever comes to collect it." She pushed them all across the table. "Your reward."

I picked up the packet holding my future. "We earned it."

"So you did." She rose and proceeded to strip each and every emerald from her fingers and throat. "I'm done with green," she announced. "I think I'll give all my emeralds away to my sister and cousins. Choose something for yourself first, my dear." I chose a broad collar of glittering emeralds that would easily buy a house in Brigantia, or perhaps an entire mountain.

"You'll need some new gowns before you leave," the Empress continued, coming around the edge of the desk. "Blood is no longer so fashionable as it once was. I'll send you some of my own clothes. We are the same size, I believe."

In fact, we were the same in many ways. The same size, the same height, the same brown hair. Domitian had loved her and then hated her; moved on to Julia who was as unlike her as possible; moved on to me because I was as unlike Julia as possible . . . which meant I was more like the Empress than Julia. But was there ever anyone like Julia?

"Why are you helping me, Domina?" I asked. "Is it because of Lady Julia?"

"Not that it's any of your business." Calmly. "But yes. I was relieved when Domitian's eye moved from me to someone else—you can understand why. So very much relieved that I rather threw Julia to the wolves."

"Wolves would have been kinder than Domitian."

"Yes." Unruffled. "But I was probably a little mad by then. So were you, at one point, and so was Julia. At least we all managed to fight back, in our ways."

"Some more than others," I said.

The Empress laughed. In that silent room I imagined I could hear Lady Julia laughing, too.

"Now, a question for you." The Empress looked at me. "Did you really tell Domitian he was a common little man?"

"Yes."

"Oh, dear, I wish I could have seen his face." The Empress stepped forward and pressed her cheek briefly to mine in farewell. I smiled, but I shivered a little as well at her touch. They had called me the mistress of Rome, as they had called Julia, but they had been wrong about us both. *Here* was the mistress of Rome: power made flesh in one cool-voiced woman who looked a little like me.

"Good luck, Thea," said the Empress.

Good luck, Thea, Julia echoed. And the three of us parted company.

In the hall outside, I saw two men surrounded by Praetorian

guards. Senator Marcus Cocceius Nerva, cross and fussy and still in his sleeping robe, complaining about the night air. And the man who would be adopted as his heir, the great soldier and calm leader undoubtedly suggested to the Empress by Senator Norbanus: Commander Marcus Ulpius Trajan, yawning hugely but still alert in full armor.

"Hail, Caesar," I said, and passed by before either of them could look puzzled.

ROSE petals. Trumpets. Chariots. Cheering. Rome, laughing and happy in her festival colors, was ready to celebrate. Marcus could feel it.

Emperor Nerva, in a gold circlet and purple cloak, was borne along in a gilded litter by eight Nubians. Old and fussy, Marcus thought, and he'd be sure to rub the legions the wrong way—but he bowed with appropriate humility before the statues of the gods, and he had been more than generous with the largesse thrown into the crowd. Trajan got a bigger swell of cheers as he rode behind on a gray horse, a laurel crown tipped back on his head at a cheerful angle. Marcus wondered if he should ever tell Trajan that he'd earned his Emperor's crown by throwing Lepida Pollia out of a litter and making Marcus laugh . . . Perhaps not.

Emperor Nerva took his throne.

Priests came forward, leading rose-garlanded sacrificial bulls. Vestal Virgins in a silent white line. Senators in their formal purple-banded togas. Marcus claimed his place among them, bowing very deeply. He stepped back, joined by Sabina, who looked so tall and pretty in her first woman's gown that he realized she'd soon be grown up. He'd have her for a few years though, before she married. Marcus wondered if he should ever tell his daughter how close he had come to being Emperor, to making her an Empress by marrying her to the cheerful Trajan . . . Perhaps not.

Calpurnia joined them, glowing like a spring daffodil in a yellow gown. Marcus brought her hand up, pressing it against his cheek, and knew people were murmuring. He had not married Calpurnia yet, not until the end of September when the augurs had declared the date most auspicious, but she had already moved quite openly into the Norbanus household with all her slaves and belongings. Her family wailed and Rome whispered, but his betrothed was impervious. "I adore you, Marcus," she said frankly. "I'm not wasting one more day away from you." Marcus found it rather entertaining, at his age, to be scandalous. Only one person's opinion mattered, and she had given her consent immediately.

"I like to see you happy," Sabina had said, looking up from a map she had spread out on his library table. "Not that you're exactly happy right now, but you will be. Calpurnia will see to it. And she'll have lots more children, which is good because I plan on seeing the world, not marrying a senator and being a dull Roman matron. So there should be someone besides me to carry on the family name."

She saw his face then and tucked her narrow brown head against his shoulder. "'Linus wouldn't grudge it," she said gently. "He'd want you to be happy, too."

"And your mother?" Marcus managed to speak around the terrible block in his throat that rose whenever Paulinus came to his thoughts. He couldn't talk about Paulinus, not yet—even to Sabina.

"Well, Mother wouldn't have wanted you to be happy," Sabina admitted. "But that doesn't matter now." Lady Lepida Pollia had been found dead in the Domus Augustana, stuffed ignominiously into a closet . . . another victim, all assumed, of the assassin who had claimed the Emperor's life. Marcus, who knew better, did not inquire into the death of his former wife. In the pain of losing Paulinus, he did not even care.

Rome's former Empress made her solitary way up to Emperor Nerva and sank into a magnificent curtsy. She'd been true to her word, seeing that Paulinus was given a hero's funeral as the man who had died trying to protect his Emperor and friend. An arch was to be constructed in Paulinus's honor, his name known forever. The Empress had already bullied it through the Senate in her last act as Empress before she announced her retirement to Baiae and her own family. She curtsied now before the new Emperor in her white silk, a woman for Roman matrons everywhere to hold before their daughters as a model of virtue and decency. Marcus remembered the Empress back when she had been a brown-haired girl named

Marcella, a girl with a talent for scheming whom he had not
liked. He liked her well enough now, but would he hold her up
as a role model for Sabina? Perhaps not . . .

Nessus the astrologer delivered a ringing prophecy, his
round face plump and beaming. Marcus felt Calpurnia's fingers
squeeze his as he heard that eighty years of glory lay ahead for
the Roman Empire. The golden age of Rome, Nessus promised,
had dawned.

Marcus—and Rome—felt collectively that they had earned it.

W E should go." Arius felt Thea tap his shoulder. "The boat's
waiting. Oh!" she exclaimed as he turned around. "You're
you again!"

He ran a hand over his hair, scrubbed clean of walnut juice
to its original russet. The beard was gone, too. "Like it?"

"I love it." She twined her arms around his neck, pressing
her cheek against his clean jaw. He turned her hand over and
kissed the inside of her wrist. She had a sunburned flush across
her nose, her hair hung in a rope down her back, and when he
looked at her he didn't know if the world was up or down.

"Hey," said Vix, appearing with the dog panting happily
under his arm. "Save it for the boat." Arius walloped him and
Vix swung back, grinning. He'd shot up another three inches
during his months at the palace, and his bouts in the Colosseum
had added more muscle to his arms, but he looked like a boy
again. The drawn, wary look had gone from his face, and he
was bounding up the street with his old cocky swagger.

They slipped through the empty side streets, Thea's hand
locked in Arius's and Vix jogging ahead throwing a stick for the
dog. No need to worry about being stopped; with the Empress's
seal on their documents, not a soldier in Rome would do anything but salute and let them pass. Anyway, all the soldiers were
busy watching their new Emperor. No one knew or cared that
a family of three was bound for a boat on the Tiber.

Brigantia. Arius hadn't seen it since he was Vix's age. But
when he drew in a breath, he could still smell the mountain
mist.

He bumped into Vix, who had stopped in the middle of the
street. "What—" His eyes followed his son's.

Gladiators.

A stream of big, scarred men in purple cloaks trooped out of an unbarred gate into a waiting wagon. Armored men, their faces distant and strained under their helmets. Casting sour looks at the perfumed, powdered *lanista* leaning out of his gilded litter to scold them along.

"Games," said Thea. "To celebrate the coronation. Trajan loves the games . . ."

Arius shivered. Looking down at Vix, he saw a sickly expression on his son's face.

"Let's go," Arius said.

They walked on in silence. Behind them, the wagon rumbled heavily on its way.

Arius looked back over his shoulder. The Colosseum loomed, a round marble shadow holding a stretch of empty sand and all his nightmares.

Thea's hand squeezed his. "Don't look back," she said. "Remember what happened to Lot's wife."

He blinked. "Who?"

"A Jewish story. Take my word for it: You don't want to look back."

He tore his eyes from the Colosseum. Reached out tentatively in his mind, listening for the demon's voice.

It's dead, said Hercules. *That demon's as dead as the Emperor. You big dummy.*

A clean, empty silence.

"Arius?"

He squeezed Thea's hand, the Colosseum dropping off his back and disappearing into limbo, and set his eyes forward.

THEA

IT was just a small fast boat, made for ferrying up and down the Tiber, but it would carry us to the sea. Arius was already sniffing the wind and prowling the deck with the new lightened step that made my heart glad. He also threw a sailor overboard before we'd quite cleared the city, but the sailor had aimed a kick at the dog, and anyway Arius fished him out again quite amiably. Another sailor had kicked Vix for climbing into the rigging, but Arius didn't throw him overboard. He advised the sailor to kick our son as often as he liked since Vix was a slow learner. Nice to see Arius so calm and cheerful. Nice to have Vix out of my hair, too.

"Good thing he outgrew the arena," Arius commented in the sunny afternoon that followed, leaning beside me on the rail as we watched Vix try to talk the captain into letting him plot a course on the maps. "He may be an idiot, but even an idiot's too smart for the arena."

"How long do you think we'll keep him?" I watched Vix ruffle his russet hair in a gesture exactly copied from his father. He'd been talking about coming back to Rome someday, becoming an officer in the legions, leading armies and slaying dragons . . .

"A few years."

"Can we stop him?"

"The Emperor of the known world couldn't stop him." Arius hugged my waist, resting his chin on top of my head. "Didn't that astrologer say Vix would lead an army one day?"

"He'll lead an army of thugs, that's what he'll lead! Our son is headed for a life of crime." Still . . . my child, son of a singer and a gladiator, growing up to command legions . . . how Lepida Pollia would have hated that! But Lepida wasn't around to hate anything anymore. I didn't care much about that, one way or another. When I'd helped bring down an Emperor, other things looked smaller—even Lepida. I'd hardly bothered to wonder who killed her. It could have been anyone. How many enemies had her years of scheming earned her?

Nessus had been looking more and more like his old self. He'd come up to me just yesterday, pressed my hand, and told me my baby was going to be a girl. "The first of a whole mess of them," he said. "Red-haired and horrible; won't you have fun? Good luck, m'dear." Kissing my cheek.

A girl. I'd like a girl. A daughter born in Brigantia.

"What?" Arius caught my smile.

"Later." No use telling him until the journey was over—he'd fret terribly. "Can I borrow your knife?"

"Why?"

I plucked it out of its sheath at his waist, and pricked my wrist in one smooth motion. He whipped it out of my hand. "Thea—"

"No, that's all." Smiling, I held my hand over the rail and shook a single drop of blood into the Tiber before pressing the cut closed. "Last time."

He looked at me.

"I swear." Holding up my hand in pledge.

He took my wrist, blocking the trickle of blood with his hard thumb. He wound his free hand deep into my hair and kissed me.

I lifted my head, dizzy and laughing, and saw the sea. I hadn't even noticed that we'd left Rome behind.

Historical Note

Emperor Titus Flavius Domitianus died at five in the evening on September 18, A.D. 96. He was a man of many contradictions: a soldier idolized by his legions, an administrator admired for his attention to detail, a paranoid given to random executions. Many of the peculiarities described in this book are true, and were described by Suetonis in his gossipy first-century memoir *The Twelve Caesars*: Domitian's popularity among common soldiers, his jealousy of his elder brother Titus, his dislike of Jews, his love of the gladiatorial games, his black dinner parties, his treatise on hair care, and his peculiar habit of killing flies on the point of a pen.

   Thea is a fictional character, but her background at Masada is real enough. An entire city of Jewish rebels committed suicide there rather than submit to Roman rule, and only a handful survived. I wondered what kind of survivor's guilt would manifest from surviving such a horrific experience, and so Thea was born. Lepida Pollia and Marcus Norbanus are also fictional creations, but many of the others are based upon fact. Emperor Domitian did take his niece Julia as a mistress until she supposedly died of a botched abortion; her continued existence as a Vestal Virgin is my own creation, though such an escape would have been far more difficult than I have implied here, given that the Vestals were chosen as children with much pomp and public ceremony. However, Domitian did execute several Vestals during his reign in the manner described, for the crime of breaking their vows. His second niece Flavia (in reality Julia's cousin and not her half-sister) was eventually exiled to Pandateria as a convicted Christian, her husband executed, and the fate of their two young sons unknown. Domitian was often attended at the games by a young boy garbed in a red tunic, leading to the character of Vix. There was a Praetorian Prefect Norbanus whose role in Domitian's assassination is prominent but unclear, and his death unknown. The Empress was also a conspirator; she did discover a death warrant with her name upon it, which prompted her to put the assassination forward, and she did manage to live to a virtuous old age after her husband's death. Domitian's principal assassin was a slave of Lady Flavia's, a man named Stephanus who smuggled a knife into the Imperial presence in a sling. History proclaims that he died after a bloody struggle with the Emperor; in my imagination he became the gladiator Arius instead, and escaped to a happier life. I have taken some liberties with the games as depicted in *Mistress of Rome*: The Roman gladiatorial games were every bit as violent as described, but there were strict rules that would have prevented Arius from fighting one against six, or unarmored against wild beasts, or against women. Fik Meijer's excellent book *The Gladiators: History's Most Deadly Sport* proved invaluable in providing details about the games, as A. J. Boyle's *Flavian Rome*, Michael Grant's *The Twelve Caesars*, Brian Jones's *Emperor Domitian*, and Matthew Bunson's *Encyclopedia of the Roman Empire* proved invaluable for their descriptions of Domitian and the empire he ruled.

Domitian is remembered poorly as the last of the Flavian dynasty, an ill successor to his great brother and father. But his reign led smoothly into Rome's golden age, eighty years of prosperity beginning with the fussy Senator Nerva and the glorious soldier Trajan. Thea and Arius will find their mountain and raise their family in peace, so their story is done. But Sabina has an interesting life ahead of her, and Rome is not done with Vix, either.

Characters

ROYALTY
Titus Flavius Domitianus, Emperor of the Roman Empire
Empress Domitia Longina, his wife
Julia Flavia, daughter of Domitian's brother Titus from his second marriage
Flavia Domitilla, daughter of Domitian's brother Titus from his first marriage; Julia's half-sister
Flavius Clemens, her husband
*Their two sons
Gaius Titus Flavius, Domitian's cousin, Julia's husband

SENATORS AND THEIR FAMILIES
Marcus Vibius Augustus Norbanus, Roman senator, grandson of Emperor Augustus
Lepida Pollia, his second wife
Vibia Sabina, their daughter
Paulinus Vibius Augustus Norbanus, Praetorian, Marcus's son from first marriage
Lappius Maximus Norbanus, governor of Lower Germania, Marcus's cousin
Lady Diana, Marcus's cousin
Senator Marcus Cocceius Nerva

SLAVES AND SERVANTS
Thea, a Jewish slave belonging to Lepida Pollia
Vercingetorix, slave boy

Stephanus, gardener to Lady Flavia Domitilla
Penelope, freedwoman to Praetor Larcius
Nessus, Imperial astrologer
Ganymede, Imperial body slave
Quintus, steward to Marcus Norbanus
Iris, Lepida's maid
Laelia, Roman courtesan
Chloe, slave woman of Praetor Larcius

GLADIATORS
Arius, gladiator and slave
Gallus, lanista, Arius's master and owner of a gladiator school, and his gladiators
Belleraphon, star gladiator
Hercules, dwarf and comic gladiator

SOLDIERS
Centurion Densus, Paulinus's commander in Brundisium
Verus, Praetorian, Paulinus's friend
Marcus Ulpius Trajan, legion commander

ROMANS
Quintus Pollio, games organizer, father of Lepida Pollia
Larcius, praetor and music aficionado of Brundisium
Saturninus, governor of Upper Germania
Justina, Vestal Virgin
Calpurnia Helena Sulpicia, patrician heiress

*denotes actual historical figure

"She is a rebel, a rule-breaker,
and above all, a romantic."
—Lisa Kleypas

FROM

SHERRY THOMAS
Author of *Private Arrangements*

Beguiling the Beauty

When the Duke of Lexington meets the mysterious Baroness von Seidlitz-Hardenberg on a transatlantic liner, he is fascinated. She's exactly what he's been searching for—a beautiful woman who interests and entices him. He falls hard and fast—and soon proposes marriage.

And then she disappears without a trace . . .

For in reality, the "baroness" is Venetia Easterbrook—a proper young widow who had her own vengeful reasons for instigating an affair with the duke. But the plan has backfired. Venetia has fallen in love with the man she despised—and there's no telling what might happen when she is finally unmasked . . .

M1056T0212

From the award-winning author of **Open Country** *and* **Pieces of Sky**

KAKI WARNER

Heartbreak Creek

A RUNAWAY BRIDES NOVEL

From Kaki Warner comes an exciting new series about four unlikely brides who make their way west— and find love where they least expect it . . .

Edwina Ladoux hoped becoming a mail-order bride would be her way out of the war-torn South and into a better life, but as soon as she arrives in Heartbreak Creek, Colorado, and meets her hulking, taciturn groom, she realizes she's made a terrible mistake.

Declan Brodie already had one flighty wife who ran off with a gambler before being killed by Indians. He's hoping this new one will be a practical, sturdy farm woman who can help with chores and corral his four rambunctious children. Instead, he gets a skinny Southern princess who doesn't even know how to cook.

Luckily, Edwina and Declan agreed on a three-month courtship period, which should give them time to get the proxy marriage annulled. Except that as the weeks pass, thoughts of annulment turn into hopes for a real marriage—until Declan's first wife returns after being held captive for the last four years. Now an honorable man must choose between duty and desire, and a woman who's never had to fight for anything must do battle for the family she's grown to love . . .

Praise for the novels of Kaki Warner

"Emotionally compelling."
—*Chicago Tribune*

"Thoroughly enjoyable."
—*Night Owl Reviews* (Top Pick)

M909T0611

Enter the rich world of
historical romance
with Berkley Books . . .

Madeline Hunter

Jennifer Ashley

Joanna Bourne

Lynn Kurland

Jodi Thomas

Anne Gracie

Love is timeless.

berkleyjoveauthors.com

M9G0610

LOVE
ROMANCE
NOVELS?

For news on all your favorite romance authors, sneak peeks into the newest releases, book giveaways, and much more—

"Like" Love Always on Facebook!
 LoveAlwaysBooks

M1063G0212